HOME TEAM 2

Dave Pratt is a master story teller making this well-crafted book fun to read and hard to put down. It grabs you from the beginning and holds you till the end. It is full of life, surprises, twists, and turns. He takes us along with the Home Team as they confront the very present scourge of human trafficking and smuggling. Dave's life experiences as a martial arts master and military officer brings an authenticity to the action scenes that put you right there in the middle with the team. Each move they make is written from personal experience and knowledge, which really brings it to life. Dave takes you to real places that you can see and feel. Dave's deep Christian faith is evident as he shows us how believers live their faith in this broken world in the midst of challenging circumstances. Can God really change lives in the real world? If He can, whose life will he change? This book is a fitting and fascinating sequel to the first book in the *Home Team* series. What a joy to be able to read a timely, well written, action book written from a Christian perspective. It is a fun book to read that everyone in the family can enjoy. It could also be a springboard to family discussion of serious questions.

Robert Samuelson
Retired Pastor and Dave's brother in Christ

WHAT OTHERS SAY ABOUT DAVE PRATT AND *THE HOME TEAM*

Written from Dave's deep knowledge of tactical operations and martial arts, and with a Northwest flair mixed in, *The Home Team* grabs you from the start and surprises you at the end. As Dave's former pastor, it was thrilling to read a story of authentic faith lived out in gripping circumstances. A great read that is both tightly written and timely.

Rev. Brian Wiele
www.bluespigot.org

The Home Team is a wonderful story that weaves Dave Pratt's life experience as a Tae Kwan Do master, Christian, and retired army officer. It is a reminder that God's will, love, and guidance are everywhere. Dave brings together his military experience, lifelong journey in martial arts, and his commitment to God and blends it into an action-packed, compelling story of human nature, conflict, faith, and self-discovery. It has the power to touch the heart and to awaken consciousness. It is a story well-worth reading and contains a message we can all relate to.

Grand Master Richard Na

Master Na's Black Belt Academy

HOME TEAM 2

DAVE PRATT

Ambassador International
GREENVILLE, SOUTH CAROLINA & BELFAST, NORTHERN IRELAND

www.ambassador-international.com

HOME TEAM 2

©2023 by Dave Pratt
All rights reserved

ISBN: 978-1-64960-409-5
eISBN: 978-1-64960-457-6
Library of Congress Control Number: 2023939934

Cover Design by Hannah Linder Designs
Interior Typesetting by Dentelle Design
Edited by Martin Wiles

AMBASSADOR INTERNATIONAL
Emerald House
411 University Ridge, Suite B14
Greenville, SC 29601
United States
www.ambassador-international.com

AMBASSADOR BOOKS
The Mount
2 Woodstock Link
Belfast, BT6 8DD
Northern Ireland, United Kingdom
www.ambassadormedia.co.uk

The colophon is a trademark of Ambassador, a Christian publishing company.

This book is for my wife, Rafaela.

Without her support and understanding of my pleasant addiction to writing, this story could not have come to life.

ACKNOWLEDGMENTS

A special thanks goes to the Washington State Patrol's Investigative Assistance Division for their insight into human trafficking and their efforts to combat it and bring survivors home.

I would also like to thank my readers, Rob A., Marianne B., and Jan M. for their valuable insight, attention to detail, and thoughtful suggestions, without which this story would be much less than it is.

Further, I offer my undying gratitude to the Ambassador International team for their belief in the story and their efforts to bring it to you, the reader, with such faith and commitment.

And of course, I need to thank Martin Wiles, a key member of the AI team. His mastery of words, flow, candor, and willingness to collaborate make a huge difference with every story I write.

Finally, I thank Jesus Christ for His inspiration and amazing grace and for how He lifts those engaged in the daily battle against evil.

CHAPTER 1

Ellen Evander felt her consciousness slipping away, but she had to hang on. Forty other people depended on her to get them out of this mess.

The heat inside the shipping container had been unbearable—hardly survivable. Her stomach roiled at the stench from the captives who had been with her for three weeks in the forty-by-eight-by-eight rusted green steel container. Tiny fans mounted on the front and back walls whined feebly, pushing a barely perceptible flow of air up from cleverly positioned rust holes along the bottom of the container's walls.

A hand pressed down on her shoulder and drew her attention as she squatted on her heels, six feet from the container's steel doors. Rosa, the twenty-two-year-old mother of two who had befriended her when she'd awakened inside the container three weeks ago, leaned close to her ear and whispered, "The ship no longer rocks. We are docked. They will be here to take us soon. We are ready when you are, senorita."

Ell nodded, covering Rosa's hand with her own. "Tell everyone to stay back until I make my move. Then come out in a rush. It's our only chance. Anyone who doesn't want to do it should stay out of the way."

Rosa squeezed Ell's shoulder, then left to tell the others.

After three weeks with insufficient food and a small barrel of tepid water replenished infrequently, Ell wondered how her posse, as they called themselves, would do against whoever showed up to take them away. The other option was to be sold as sex slaves or slave laborers—not much of a choice as she saw it. She stopped before thoughts of how things could go wrong crept into her mind.

Ell ran a hand through her short, brown hair—usually silky and fine but now matted like a skull cap. The tan she'd worked on so hard before being taken was gone. Instead, her skin was now pocked and dirty from weeks with nothing but a bucket in the corner as a toilet and no way to wash. Typically, a slender, conditioned, 125 pounds on a five-five frame, she wondered how much weight she'd lost. Even with the exercising she'd done—and that she'd gotten the other prisoners to do—she wondered if they could overtake their captors.

Through the dim light, Ell glanced around at the others huddled in the space behind her—some sat, and some lay prone on the shipping container's dirty plywood floor. She wondered how many could stand, let alone help with what they needed to do when the doors opened. But they had to try. She had to try. She had dedicated her life to serving and protecting others and now was the time.

Ell knew she had messed up, getting taken as she had. She was paying the price. Until now, it seemed as if everything had gone her way. She had completed four years of duty as a military police sergeant with two tours in Iraq and had returned with awards she'd rather forget for all they cost her. After her last enlistment, she had applied to and graduated from the Washington State Patrol's academy. Upon graduation, the patrol selected her for membership on its SWAT team and sent her to sniper school. Then the pandemic had hit, and everything was delayed, including her assignment to SWAT. So instead, she had been assigned to the patrol's Bellingham district, where she'd served for four years.

Because of her youthful appearance—she'd been told she looked like a tall pixie with bright blue eyes; a button nose; and a round, freckled face—she had been recruited to help with the state patrol's human trafficking joint task force. Naturally, she'd jumped at the chance.

Human traffickers had kidnapped Ell's niece five years before. Maria was only eight then, and the loss had nearly destroyed Ell's sister and her family. The kidnapping had lit an unquenchable flame of anger in Ell's gut that drove her to battle anyone engaged in human trafficking, perhaps to find and free her niece.

Then she'd gone too far. A month ago, after a day working on the Human Trafficking Task Force, she had overheard several agents from the Federal Bureau of Investigation and Homeland Security Investigations (HSI) discussing a lead they'd received. A shipment of human trafficking victims might be headed out of Boston, but the FBI and HSI didn't have the manpower to follow up. The same was true of the agencies' New England offices. And the Washington State Patrol had no jurisdiction in that area. Everyone was too stretched.

Ell had sneaked back into the task force's office after everyone left for the day and located the lead documentation on an FBI agent's desk. She had snapped pictures of it and accessed the state patrol's network in her tiny Bellingham apartment to check the Port of Boston's files. She had found only one container ship scheduled for departure on the date identified in the lead. Ell had recorded the ship's name and called up its manifest. The ship's owner had only one container scheduled for loading. The rest belonged to various import and export companies and government agencies. It made sense that they would try to hide the container among hundreds of others belonging to legitimate business interests. If the FBI and HSI couldn't do it, she would take some vacation and check out the lead herself.

The next day, Ell had loaded her 9.0mm Beretta pistol and a 30-30 lever-action Winchester rifle in the trunk of her car and headed for Boston. Entering the Port of Boston was easy enough. She had flashed her state patrol badge at the port's administrative building and told them she was on a fact-finding mission. Thirty minutes later, she located the alleged shipping container by its unique identification number. She had waited until sundown before approaching the container, easing her way to it through the shadows as the sun faded behind the Boston skyline. Her two-hour surveillance beforehand had only revealed two men with pistols at the front of the container. As she watched, one had received a call on his cellphone, then pocketed the phone and led the other man away. Perfect timing.

With the coast clear, Ell had eased her way along the side of the shipping container, putting her ear to its warm steel siding. Just as she thought she had heard something inside, pain flared on the back of her head, and the lights went out. She had awakened the next day inside the container with a splitting headache and her head in Rosa's lap.

That seemed so long ago now. What had she been thinking? How could a woman like her, a simple state patrol trooper, expect to tackle a human trafficking gang by herself?

Sure, she'd undergone a lifetime of martial arts and weapons training. Her federal agent parents had seen to that almost as soon as she could walk. They'd lived and worked with the underbelly of humanity, knew the capability of the bad elements of society, and determined their daughter would never be a victim of those kinds of people. Ell wondered what they would think of her now—trapped in a shipping container with forty other human trafficking victims.

A lever on the outside of the container's doors clunked, then squealed as someone pulled it open. Ell reached out a hand and gripped Rosa's arm.

"Ready, Rosa?"

"Listo, Hermana," Rosa replied, using the Spanish term for sister. Ell smiled. After all they'd been through together for the past three weeks, sisters were who they were, for sure.

Rosa glanced over her shoulder to indicate the rest of the people in the container. "We are all ready. Todos!" All of us.

In the container's dim light, Ell saw the two fourteen-year-old boys creep up next to her and Rosa.

"Now we go, senorita?" one of the boys asked in heavily accented English. They were both gangly, with dark hair and eyes.

"First, we wait," Ell said. "Follow Rosa's lead. When you see me take down the group's leader, Rosa will lead the way. Run out of the container as fast as you can and stay together. Hit them like a herd of bulls charging a crowd. Grab their weapons if you can and point them to the sky. Wrap yourselves around their legs. Kick them. Bite them. Doing that for even a moment might make the difference for all of us."

Rosa and the boys nodded, the fire in their eyes evident, even in the pale light.

Ell jerked her head toward the sound of the container's screeching hinges as the locking mechanism was pulled away and the left door swung open. A fleshy-faced man peered in the narrow opening. She felt the stirring of forty frightened souls in the container behind her.

"Wait for Rosa," she said again.

Rosa repeated Ell's words softly in Spanish. One of the boys did the same in a language Ell guessed was Chinese, perhaps Mandarin. The rest of the captives spoke English. Rosa spread the message to them as well.

Ell smiled at the thought of forty people rushing their captors. Finally, the doors opened wide enough for a person to fit through. Ell closed her eyes against the sunlight glaring in.

"Get these doors open," a gruff, heavily accented voice bellowed.

He sounded Greek, although it was not one of the languages Ell spoke. It didn't matter. The only thing that mattered was escaping.

"I want this cargo moved quickly," the voice continued. "The trucks are on the dock, and we only have a few minutes to get them all photographed and loaded before the authorities arrive. We've got three more containers after this one, so get moving."

A heavy-set man in white linen pants and a floral shirt stepped into the container. He held a flashlight in one hand and a long-barreled pistol in the other. He shoved the flashlight ahead of him and waved it around inside the container. Ell squinted to avoid the blinding glare.

"Good. They are all alive," he said.

Ell sprang forward, clawed hands reaching for the man's pistol.

"Attack the weapon first," her father had always said—words that now echoed through her mind as she charged into the light. "Take the offensive. Attack, always attack."

CHAPTER 2

U.S. Army Ranger Captain Alexander Anthem lay prone on the top shipping container. The containers were stacked five high on the cargo ship he'd followed online for the past two weeks. He'd tracked the ship using an international website that ensured someone knew where ships were should they have trouble. He then waited until it docked at Turkey's largest privately owned port a few hours ago. He boarded it by swimming under the port's oil-sheened waters and then using a maintenance ladder built on the side of the ship's hull.

The Turkish sun beat down through a crystalline blue sky, superheating the metal roof of the container. Sweat soaked through his gray tactical coveralls and hood, dripped into his eyes, and pooled beneath him on the hot metal. He carried a twenty-inch expandable baton, Beretta .40 caliber pistol, and a Ka-Bar tactical knife on his army surplus flack vest and nylon, web tactical harness. Purchased on the cheap, it felt like the gear had burned its outline into his back and hips.

His position was not usual for a ranger, but that was the point. It wasn't a mission sanctioned by any legitimate authority but himself. On his own time and dime, he stalked the ship to free any human trafficking victims who might be aboard. The word he'd received indirectly through the informal ranger network was that the container on the deck below him held human trafficking victims. The arrival of a gang of Turkish thugs a few minutes before suggested his intel was correct. Alex himself had been kidnapped when he was ten. He'd eventually escaped but didn't want anyone else to go through that grinder.

As captain and commander of a company of elite U.S. Army Rangers stationed at Joint Base Lewis-McChord in Washington State, Alex possessed the necessary skills. When he wasn't leading one of his unit's frequent deployments, he used his annual leave and savings to help those in need.

Occasionally, he'd uncover a lead about human trafficking victims about to be taken or moved. If he were available, he'd take a shot at intervening. Sometimes, he'd work through the local police or contacts in the FBI and Homeland Security. Rarely, as in this case, he'd take direct action when those agencies could not help. Most of his leads came up dry, but this one seemed to have hit paydirt.

Alex used a monocular scope to watch four men in jeans and t-shirts armed with AK-47 rifles approach the container. A heavyset man in white linen pants and a brightly colored shirt led them. He carried a large flashlight and pistol. It seemed as if the leader of the group and his men carried their weapons carelessly as they pulled open the container's locking lever and cracked the door.

As Alex watched, the leader leaned into the container and shouted, "Get these doors open. We need to get this cargo moved now."

Alex reached for the thick rope coiled at his side that he had attached to the container's corner casting. He levered his body around and lay parallel with the edge of his perch—ready to drop the line down and fast-rope to the ship's deck.

But a sudden movement made him pause. A blur of action exploded from the container. A small, slender woman with a skullcap of brownish-gold hair flew out the container's doors. She charged the man with the flashlight, ducked under his arm and grabbed at the man's pistol. In the next instant, she leaned left and lashed out with her right foot, connecting with the heavyset man's ribs. The man yelled as she connected a second kick to his groin. He staggered and dropped the flashlight. Alex heard the snap of bone as the woman twisted the man's gun away, breaking his trigger finger in the process.

Entranced, Alex watched as the slender, bedraggled woman rose from her crouched position, the man's gun in hand, and followed the man as he lurched back. She grabbed the man by his shoulder and pistol-whipped him in the side of his head. The man crumpled to the ground. Straddling him, she then faced the remaining four men armed with assault rifles. By their expressions, Alex could see they were shocked at seeing their boss go down.

Alex clenched the rope, ready to drop into the action. But what the woman did next stilled his hand. Amazed and impressed by the small, ragged but strangely attractive ball of fury, he watched intently as she side-stepped to her right and shot a powerful side kick that crashed into the stomach of the armed man to her right. He folded and crumpled. Throwing the first man's pistol aside, she ripped the second man's AK from his grip. The sound of her racking a round into the rifle's chamber told Alex the woman knew her weapons and might not need his help after all.

At the same instant, Alex heard a roar inside the container as the container's doors were flung wide and forty men, women, and boys burst through the doors. The captives quickly overran the three remaining thugs—clutching at rifles, wrapping themselves around their legs, and dragging the men to the deck. He smiled grimly as a young Hispanic woman in the lead tore an AK out of a man's hands and butt-stroked him. The gunman crumpled to the ship's deck.

No shots were fired as the remaining men were tackled, kicked, punched, scratched, and clawed by the captives, who relieved them of their weapons.

The action stopped suddenly as another voice, loud like gravel churned under heavy tires, barked from several containers away. "Stop this at once."

Alex saw another large man wearing gray slacks and a dark polo shirt with the Ambarli Turkish Port Authority logo on the front striding up the space between tall stacks of shipping containers. He waved a sawed-off shotgun as he approached the victims. Four other men trailed him; shotguns held at chest level.

These are bad guys of a different order, Alex thought.

The man triggered a shotgun blast that sounded like cannon fire into the air. Alex drew back as buckshot pinged off the containers' metal siding, narrowly missing his head. Once it was safe, he inched forward to see below.

"You will cease and desist!" the man growled, approaching the tiny, brown-haired woman. "You will drop your weapon now and return to the container with the rest of these people until I call for you. Fail to do so, and I will kill every one of you, one at a time, until you comply."

Alex's blood ran cold. She'd fought so hard. He couldn't let her lose now.

"You are the troublemaker, I think," the man said, shoving the barrel of the shotgun under the tiny spitfire's chin. "I think I will make an example of you and kill you now. It will be a valuable lesson for the rest."

Alex took a short breath and whispered, "Not on my watch. Guide me, Lord. Please don't let me fail."

Alex grabbed the thick rope, dropped it over the edge of the container, and followed it down quickly, the thick hemp smoking against his leather gloves. He touched down on crepe-soled boots and drew the ten-inch tube of steel from the side of his tactical vest, snapping down hard the expandable baton and extending it to its full twenty-two-inch length.

At the sound of the steel baton clicking into place, two port authority men spun to face him—but not quickly enough. Alex twisted left, sweeping the baton around and slashing it against the arm of the shotgun-wielding man on his left. Continuing in a smooth, circular, rising motion, Alex shifted right, reversed direction, and smashed his baton against the man's temple.

Spinning further right, Alex then brought the baton around in a high arc to smash the exposed trigger hand of another man on his right who carried a shotgun. The man gasped as bone crunched. Alex finished the job by snapping the baton away, then back again to connect with the side of the man's head. The man dropped, unconscious.

Alex shifted his weight left, flowing like water as he swung the baton wide again and crashed it against the side of the neck of the first gunman, who was dazed but still upright. The strike compressed the artery carrying blood to the man's brain. The man grunted before dropping to the ground to lay beside his partner in crime.

In seconds, two men were down. Inhaling deeply, heart rate elevated, Alex stepped back and shifted the baton to his left hand. With his right, he drew his Sig Sauer .40 caliber pistol.

He glanced toward where the woman stood, the port authority leader at her feet, the man's shotgun in her hands. The two remaining port authority men had their cold, dark eyes fixed on her, heavy shotgun barrels targeting her chest from only a few yards away. Alex met her gaze as she met his glance and seemed to freeze in place. The shotgun wavered in her hands, weakened, no doubt, from her time in the container.

As she stared back at Alex, the exhaustion and desperation in her eyes seemed to say, "Do something. Help us!"

CHAPTER 3

Ell stood still as her eyes shifted from the two remaining port authority men, their shotguns pointed at her chest, to the man with the baton who had materialized from nowhere. If she shot the two gunmen, they might shoot back. The shotgun blast would surely injure or kill the people behind her if they did.

Do something, please, she cried out in her thoughts as her eyes met those of the man with the baton. With the mask he wore, his eyes were all she could see.

She growled deeply as one of the men stepped toward her, placed the barrel of his shotgun against her chest, and snatched her shotgun. She let it go without a fight. She didn't want anyone else to get hurt.

Suddenly, the man wielding the baton crouched, lifted a large semiautomatic pistol to eye level. Flame blossomed from the barrel of the pistol. The bullet connected with the shoulder of the port authority man closest to her, spinning him around and away.

It was all Ell needed to make her move. She lunged, closed on the remaining gunman, knocked his shotgun aside, and snapped a high front kick. The heel of her foot connected with the man's face, staggered him and weakening his grip on his shotgun. She ripped it from his hands. Then, she reversed the weapon's barrel, thrust it into his sternum like a sword, and heard bones and cartilage crack.

When the man stepped back farther, Ell snapped her right foot up and around, delivering a roundhouse kick that smashed into the side of his head.

With all their attackers down, Ell examined the man who'd come out of nowhere to rescue her. A black mask covered the lower half of his face—like those used during the pandemic. A hood covered the rest of his head, except for his intense hazel eyes. His tactical vest looked old—pre-Gulf War or even Vietnam era—but he carried it like someone accustomed to the extra load. There was something about those eyes . . . an expression that stirred and seemed to draw her in.

She shook off the thought. Now was not the time. She lifted her shotgun and aimed it at his chest.

"If you're thinking of taking advantage of this situation . . ."

The man shook his head, aimed his baton tip toward the deck, and pushed it down, hard, collapsing the baton. Then he holstered his pistol and held his arms to his sides. "A second ago, you were about to have your chest opened by a shotgun blast. Now, you're asking me my intentions?"

"Right," Ell said, lowering the shotgun. "I suppose I should be thanking you. Everything happened quickly, and it's been a long stretch of weeks."

"No thanks required," the man replied. "You have it from here?"

Ell nodded.

"Then I'll be leaving."

"Not so quick," a female voice called.

Two men and two women in black tactical overalls and facemasks stepped into view. They all carried the M4 automatic carbines favored by the SWAT team back home. Black face masks covered everything but their eyes, just like the man with the baton. The web harnesses across their chests dripped with grenades, magazine pouches, and other tactical necessities. They appeared to wear bullet-proof vests so thin, they seemed like cloth. She'd heard about the new antiballistic material but had never seen the vest.

"This sort of feels like a ninja convention," Ell said.

The smaller of the two women chuckled. "Not likely."

The taller female operator, apparently the leader of the team, towered over the woman standing next to her. A thick, ebony braid draped over her left shoulder and extended from the back of a black baseball hat. The dark eyes above her facemask appeared calculating and cool.

"We're no ninjas, but we are the good guys. You can relax."

Something about the shorter female operator seemed familiar, although it was hard to tell with her body covered from head to toe. Arm muscles bulged beneath her thin, tactical shirtsleeves as she pointed her M4 carbine at the port authority manager lying at Ell's feet. Elbowing her taller counterpart, she whispered, "It's her. I told you so."

"Not now," the taller woman replied, then turned to Ell. "Feel free to lower your weapon. We are here to help."

Ell lowered her shotgun and glanced at two male operators silently approaching from the other direction. They were similarly equipped and moved with the same deliberate confidence as the two women. They held their weapons loosely but looked as though they could bring them to bear before a person could blink. These were all top-tier operators, but where did they come from?

The tall woman raised her hand, palm down—the universal sign for quiet—then turned to the baton-wielding man.

"How about you pull that baton and pistol and drop them to the deck? Do that, and you may live to explain yourself to the authorities when they arrive."

The port authority man lying behind Ell suddenly sat up and pointed an empty hand at the tall female operator.

"You have no authority here," he said.

The female operator drew a small pistol and shot the man in the neck. Ell expected the man's head to disintegrate, but saw a bright red dart instead. The man gave a small whimper and crumpled over. The other three operators drew similar pistols and darted the remaining port authority men.

"That should do it," the tall woman said as she holstered her dart gun. "Now, about the guy with the baton . . ."

One of the male operators cleared his throat softly. "He's gone. He escaped while we were darting the tangos."

"Well, well," the tall woman replied. "Slippery guy." She turned to the other female operator and asked, "Did you get him?"

The smaller woman shrugged. "You doubt me?"

The tall woman's smile showed in her eyes. "Never that, Romeo."

The tall woman faced Ell more directly. "I take it you're Washington State Trooper Ellen Marie Evander."

Ell nodded. "I am. And you are?"

The woman ignored Ell's question.

"Do you know who he was? The guy in gray with the baton?" the tall woman continued.

"No idea," Ell said, her thoughts returning to the impact of the baton-man's gaze, how it made something twist in her gut. She shook off the thought. She had felt like that once before, and it had not worked out well. "He literally dropped out of nowhere."

"Doesn't really matter, I suppose. He was obviously acting on your behalf."

Ell nodded. "Until you got here, he was all I had."

The tall woman glanced around at the other people who'd been in the container with Ell, many guarding a downed trafficker.

"I'd say you had forty or more people helping you." She paused, as if listening to something Ell couldn't hear, then continued. "I have been informed there's a Homeland Security Investigations team inbound as we speak. They were supposed to be here earlier, but Turkish bureaucracy delayed them."

"So, they followed up on the lead after all," Ell said.

"If you're talking about this shipping container of human trafficking victims, it seems so," the operator replied. "That said, someone in authority at the port wanted your rescuers delayed. That sounds suspicious to me. You might consider that when you get back to your home base. It may have been a ploy to get all of you off the ship and on your way to the flesh markets before anyone got here to intervene. We were a few minutes away by chopper when we got a call to assist."

"Well, I'm glad you showed up," Ell said. "You saved my bacon."

The tall operative laid a black-gloved hand on Ell's shoulder. "Interestingly, we didn't know you'd be in the shipping container when it opened. Your chief of the Washington State Patrol has a long-standing relationship with the person we work for. He believed your disappearance three weeks ago might be related to human trafficking and sent out an all-points bulletin."

"Even so, your timing was perfect," Ell said, bending down to set the shotgun she still held on the deck. "Who'd you say you work for?"

"I didn't," the tall woman replied, then raised a hand to fend off further questions. She raised her tactical watch to her lips. "Overwatch, this is Charlie Papa. Confirmed that the HSI tactical team is ten minutes out. The tangos are sleeping peacefully. Did you get a fix on the people we tagged?"

She paused, then said, "Good news. Exfil in five minutes. Rendezvous point one."

The tall woman extended a hand to Ell, then said, "Never doubt it was you who led the rescue today, Trooper Evander. You organized the people and led the first charge. It was a nice job. We could use someone like you on our team."

Without another word, the tall woman and her team jogged down the long corridor separating the tall stacks of rusty shipping containers.

CHAPTER 4

The Homeland Security Investigations tactical team arrived ten minutes later, just as Ell heard a helicopter lifting off in the background. Six men and two women clad in black jumpsuits, Kevlar face masks, skull helmets, and weapons approached Ell, the captives, and the downed human traffickers. A tall man, who led the team, raised a closed fist and pointed toward Ell. Two members of his team closed on her with the barrels of their MP5 machine guns raised.

Ell ignored the threatening weapons, approached the team leader, and glared into his eyes. "A little late, aren't you? And you point your weapons at me and the people who spent three weeks in that shipping container? All that's left is to cuff and tag the bad guys, so I suggest you lower your weapons and focus on getting us back home."

The team leader locked eyes with Ell, then called over his shoulder, "Stand down."

The man stepped back, removed his facemask, and revealed a narrow face with a hook nose and a week of grey beard stubble. "Trooper Ellen Evander, no doubt. My name is Special Agent-in-Charge Williams. A lot of people have been looking for you. The Washington State Patrol alerted us about your disappearance through the human trafficking joint task force."

The man paused as he glanced at the men lying unconsciously on the deck.

"Seems as if you have the situation under control."

Ell gestured toward the rest of the people gathered in front of the shipping container. "I had help—these people, a solo operator, and a team of four who left just before you arrived."

The team leader's eyes crinkled. "We got an encrypted message from an anonymous source an hour ago that identified your container and the locations of the three other shipping containers with human trafficking victims. I've got two other teams working those containers now. But about the solo operator you mentioned—we've heard about some vigilante. Can you tell me anything about him?"

Something in Ell's gut told her to keep what she'd seen to herself. She wasn't sure why. Maybe it was those eyes of his. Then again, her instincts had paid off more than once in her military and civilian law enforcement career.

She shook her head. "Sorry."

Agent Williams cast her a curious look, as though trying to read her thoughts, then nodded. "What about the other team you mentioned?"

Ell stepped over to the man she'd faced coming out of the shipping container. She bent down and turned the man's head to the side.

"There were four of them. Moved like pros. They darted this guy first and then the rest. Once the dart hit, you couldn't count to two before they were out."

She pointed at the site where she'd seen the tiny red dart strike the man's neck. All that was left was a small, red speck on the skin.

"There was a dart here; I swear it."

Williams examined the side of the man's neck, placing a gloved finger next to the small, red burn mark below the man's ear.

"I've heard about something like this. Very new tech. Darts made with an extremely durable wood that trigger a small grain of magnesium once the dart injects the knock-out drug. The dart goes up in a tiny puff of smoke. No muss, no fuss, and no residual to be tracked by curious people like us."

"Somehow, I'm not surprised," Ell replied. "That team gave the impression they were something special."

Ell felt a hot ball of anger grow inside her as she squatted next to the unconscious leader of the port authority's gang. She balled her fists into tight, strong hammers.

"Now, how about you process the captives and the rest of the perps while I wake this one up and talk with him."

Williams stood. "I appreciate your enthusiasm, Trooper Evander. I've read your file. I know your military police background, what you did in Afghanistan, and how your niece was kidnapped. But as much as I understand your position, you know I can't let you do that."

Ell glared at Williams again. "I was inside that metal box with these people for three weeks," she said in whispered, clipped words. "If he has any information, I guarantee I can get it from him. And I deserve the chance."

Agent Williams placed a hand on Ell's shoulder and shifted her back a step. "You're a state trooper and a war veteran. I respect you for your career choices and experience, but this is not your turf."

About to speak again, Ell felt a gentle hand grip her arm. She spun to meet Rosa's kind expression. "Yours is not the way. Throughout our experience, you held us together, kept our hopes alive, and assured us the bad people who did this to us would pay. You told us justice would be served, and we would be freed. Now we are free, just as you said. You have done your job. Let these agents do theirs."

Ell felt the anger flow from her body, like a balloon released of its air. She turned to face Rosa as the woman continued.

"You worked with us to exercise our bodies and keep our spirits alive," Rosa continued. "You joined in our prayers, even though I know you do not yet strongly believe in God. You risked your life when you attacked those men for us. You are an angel from God sent to inspire and free us, whether you believe or not. You must not soil our faith in you by taking justice into your own hands."

"She's right," Williams added. "Wait! You took on these men alone before anyone arrived to help you?"

Ell felt her shoulders drop. "I did. We did. It was foolhardy, I know, but I also knew what lay in store for us if they'd gotten us off the ships before help arrived."

"We will talk more about that later," Williams said, then turned to face Rosa more directly. "You, ma'am, are an uncommonly wise woman."

Rosa blushed and turned away to join the other captives.

Agent Williams clapped his gloved hands together to get everyone's attention. "It's time we get you home."

The captives raised a tired cheer in response.

Williams turned back to Ell. "You did a good job here, Trooper Evander, but that bit about tackling the traffickers on your own concerns me. I do not doubt your courage or commitment, but I can't help but think you let your passion overrule your senses. One wrong move and you could have gotten any number of these people hurt or killed."

Ell started to protest, but Williams turned away, cutting her off. Over his shoulder, he said, "There's a car waiting on the dock to take you to a place where you can clean up and get a change of clothes before you catch your plane home. I'll join you at that location before you go for a debrief."

Ell nodded, then asked, "Would you have any idea who that group was who arrived ahead of you and darted all the traffickers?"

Williams paused. "Describe them again."

"Two men. Two women. They moved more like cats than humans—fluid, confident, and efficient. They wore a dark tactical getup, much like yours, and carried suppressed M4s, although the carbines looked modified—not like the ones we used in the military."

Williams flashed a quick smile and nodded. "If I were to guess, they were carrying M4A7 carbines—experimental models not generally available to us more common crime-fighters. If so, I ran into the same group during an operation in Central America some time ago. I heard them refer to themselves as the Home Team. I expect they're an off-the-books group of some kind."

"Whoever they were, I'm glad they were on my side."

"No doubt," Williams replied. "There's a lot of myth surrounding the group, but if the stories are half true, they're amazing operators."

"They were real. I can attest to that," Ell replied.

And the man with the baton, too, she added, although only in her thoughts.

CHAPTER 5

From the second-story window of his luxury office, Lee Chao looked out over Old Shanghai's damp, cobbled streets. Pairs of tourists cruised the lanes between quaint shops and restaurants that were decorated in traditional Chinese styles. He frowned as he recalled days past when crowds choked those streets. With the pandemic only a few years removed, he wondered how long it would be before the tourist trade picked up and Shanghai returned to the bustling metropolis it once was.

Lee Chao typically found viewing the ancient architecture of Old Shanghai calming. The sweeping rooflines and brightly colored murals on the buildings' walls lifted his spirits, like stepping back to a quieter era. Today, not so much.

The son of a Chinese diplomat and a British heiress, his Chinese peers looked down on him for his half-blood heritage. British people considered him Asian because of his appearance and never fully allowed him into their circles. As a result, Lee Chao became obsessed with proving himself a true-blooded, if not full-blooded, Chinese man in every way.

On the desk before him, under a protective glass dome, sat a millenniums-old Chinese ceramic jar secured surreptitiously from an American museum several years ago. The jar stood as a testament to all he saw in himself—more Chinese than anyone around him ever could be and attained through uncommon means.

A tap sounded on the thick teak doors leading into his darkly paneled office. "Enter," he called, spinning his office chair around to face his visitors.

Two men and a woman approached, their soft-soled shoes padding silently across the thick Turkish carpets that blanketed the office's floor. The two men stopped a respectable two paces from his desk. Both were in their twenties and athletic. They donned close-cropped, dark hair and dressed in custom-tailored Italian suits. The woman was tall and slender. Thick, ebony hair cascaded over suggestive curves accentuated by a form-fitting blood-red qipao dress with gold embroidery.

All three bowed in unison. Then, the man on the left stepped forward and placed a sixteen-ounce coffee cup on the edge of Lee's desk.

"Your coffee mocha, Master Lee."

Lee Chao sipped at the mocha, then said in a low, gravelly voice, "The western world's single great accomplishment." He sighed, took another sip, and continued, "Have you confirmed the shipment was compromised?"

The man nodded. "We received word a few minutes ago, Master Lee."

"And the cargo?" Lee Chao asked.

The young woman standing behind the two men stepped forward, nudging the man on the left aside.

Lee Fan, Lee Chao's adopted daughter, stood in contrast with the men flanking her. Where they presented by design an apparent threat to anyone they approached, Fan came across as a traditional beauty, full of calm and grace. Yet as much as she looked less imposing and softer than her male counterparts, she was perhaps the most dangerous of the three.

As Lee Chao's second-in-command in his global shipping empire, Fan possessed a keen analytical mind, extensive business acumen, and exceptional fighting skills with and without any number of weapons. If the two men were Lee's strong arm, she was his sharp razor's edge when solving complex problems.

Fan bowed to her father again. "I regret all 160 people were freed from the four containers on that ship. Considering a potential profit of twenty-one thousand dollars per person, that represents a loss of more than three million dollars."

Lee Chao waved off her words. "What of the other cargo? The loss of our human trafficking profits is nothing compared to that."

The man standing to Lee's right cleared his throat. He was leaner than his compatriot, with the athletic lines of a runner. "We have learned the additional cargo has not yet been discovered. However, we believe the raw heroin and prototype chip technology hidden in the back wall of the container remains secure."

"We must retrieve that cargo immediately," Lee Chao said in a soft voice that nevertheless projected a do-not-fail-me tone. "That cargo is worth five times what we lost in human cargo."

"It will be done, Father," Fan replied. "We have the jet prepared for departure in the morning. The assistant manager of the port authority is on our payroll. His manager was taken captive by the Turkish government and will not be freed from jail for another two days. So, the assistant manager will ensure no one approaches the shipping container before we can arrive and take possession."

Lee Chao nodded, confident in his daughter's assessment. He knew Fan to be loyal to a fault, literally owing him her life.

"Recover that cargo at all costs," Lee Chao said. "Do not fail. The heroin will provide funding for a specific plan I have in mind. Our peers need the technology in our nation's industrial complex. Should you succeed, there will be a substantial bonus for each of you."

The man who'd brought the coffee to Lee Chao smiled and bowed again. "Understood, Master Lee. We will not fail you."

Fan cocked her head, as though already thinking through the mission ahead. "What about the people who the authorities freed? Do you want us to take some action on that part, perhaps against those in Istanbul who failed you?"

Lee Chao snorted, then took another swallow of the warm coffee. "Not at all. We can always get more human cargo to fill our customers' needs, and we need those people in place at the ports to support us. Human trafficking captives flow out of the US, Canada, and Mexico from an endless tap. Even more so from our neighboring Asian countries. No one in power cares. Hold back the regular payments for the people in Turkey who've let us down but let them know they can make it up to us in the future."

"Of course," Fan replied.

"Be on your way. Do what you must to retrieve the heroin and the technology."

CHAPTER 6

Captain Alex Anthem stepped from behind a large clump of volcanic rock onto a yellow-sand beach, north of the Turkish port where he'd help free the human trafficking victims. The polarized windows of a resort's two-story building stretched the length of the long, sandy beach and gleamed in the afternoon sun. The warm air smelled clear and clean compared to the stench of diesel fuel and rusting metal at the port.

He'd replaced his tactical uniform with baggy blue shorts and a brightly flowered t-shirt. He slung a white canvas duffle over his shoulder with his sea water-soaked tactical gear stowed inside. The scuba tanks and aqua sled he left stashed in the water below the rocks for pickup by his source in the area.

As much as the air around him tasted fresh and clean, he knew he smelled of diesel fuel and dead fish and hoped he could skirt the other visitors at the resort before managing a quick shower. It felt good to be on dry land again, and he sucked in deep breaths of the clean air as he passed dozens of tall beach umbrellas that shaded the well-oiled tourists from the morning sun.

Alex walked with an easy stride, even though his lean, toned body groaned with each step. He'd barely made it off the ship, and the sixty-foot drop into the ocean had not gone as planned. He'd landed at an angle, pulling muscles in his right thigh, ribs, and shoulder. The swim against a strong current and the outgoing tide—even with a battery-operated aqua-scooter—strained his muscles even more. As much as he relished the physical challenges of being a ranger, he knew he would be feeling the aftereffects of this unofficial adventure for some time.

A man with close-cropped, sandy hair; a deep tan; similar shorts; and no shirt approached as Alex made his way up the beach. Mark Simpson—a bodybuilder, as well as a ranger from Alex's unit back at Joint Base Lewis-McChord—liked to show off his muscular torso.

"Really?" Alex said as they met. "You're trolling for girls this early in the morning?"

Mark waved off the comment. "How'd things go?"

"Definitely an interesting morning," Alex replied, tossing the heavy duffle to the man. Mark caught it with one hand and slung it over a shoulder.

"Did not expect the crowd that showed up," Alex continued. "The place was swarming with tangos and operators. I barely got off the ship before the good guys started asking questions I did not want to answer."

"And the captives? We both know how bad the intel you get can be. Your trip to Brazil last month came up with nothing."

Alex grinned. "We definitely hit paydirt this time. I'm guessing there were fifty or so captives in the one shipping container I knew about. For all I know, there may have been additional containers of people on that boat. I expect they're all free by now."

"After all you've been through, that must have felt good," Mark said.

Alex nodded. "A good day, for sure. But there was the strangest thing . . .

"You led the way, Ranger," Mark replied, paraphrasing the US Army Ranger motto: "Rangers lead the way!" Mark paused, then said, "What strange thing?"

"There was this woman," Alex started.

Mark stopped in his tracks, spun Alex around by the shoulder. "Explain."

"Okay," Alex replied. "This tiny slip of a woman sort of exploded from the shipping container, taking on the traffickers single-handedly. Well, not exactly single-handedly. She seemed to have mustered her fellow captives to charge their captors. It was amazing. She was . . . magnificent."

"Whoa," Mark replied. "I see that look in your eyes. That woman managed to catch your interest in a single morning, after I've tried to set you up with dates for the past year?"

"She didn't capture my interest," Alex replied, his tone droll. "Besides, she looked like a street urchin, all sweaty, filthy, hair matted. But she was fearless, and the way she moved . . . Fluid, like she had been battling bad guys her whole life. And those eyes . . ."

"Wow, man," Mark replied. "The woman had an effect on you."

"It's strange, but maybe so," Alex admitted. "Then again, what's the odds I'll ever see her again?"

"Pretty low, man." Mark clapped a hand on Alex's shoulder. "But more about the woman later. Let's head to the resort and grab some lunch. I got a call from Fort Lewis. Company A has been put on alert. The Russians are planning to move on the Balkans."

"Then I'd better get packed," Alex said.

"Only A Company's been alerted. Not Company B. Your unit remains on standdown from that last mission on Poland's border.

One of us should stick around and enjoy all this sun. Our op-tempo has been a killer for the past year. 2nd Ranger Battalion has had a dozen different missions, not counting the times we went out in ones and twos."

Alex glanced at the sun gleaming off the resort's windows, then out to the crystalline sea. "It would be a shame to waste all the money we spent getting here. Maybe I will stick around for a bit."

"Now you're talking. You've given those human traffickers a little payback for what they did to you as a kid. Enjoy the victory. Soak it up a little."

The two men bumped fists. "Right on," Alex muttered. "Now, let's get some grub."

Mark wrinkled his nose. "Not until you get a shower. You stink, Ranger."

CHAPTER 7

Ell walked into the small living room of the safe house, operated by Homeland Security Investigations. The apartment reeked of stale spice and cigarette smoke, and the paint on the walls was stained and peeling. The room's only window looked out over Istanbul's Grand Bazar, with its long rows of colorful tents and awnings crowded with early-morning marketgoers. Heat waves rose from the asphalt and gravel walkways, and dust motes littered the air in swirls above the mass of humanity in motion.

"Good evening," Agent Williams said as he entered the room.

He had replaced his tactical uniform with faded jeans and a long-sleeve polo shirt. With his lean, angular physique; dark features; and wavy, black hair, Williams looked more like a local resident than a U.S. operator.

"Can I go now?" she asked.

Williams ignored the question and dropped onto a thread-worn sofa, crossing his legs at the heels as he cradled a steaming mug of coffee. He waved a hand toward another mug of coffee on the cracked laminate counter of the apartment's tiny kitchenette.

Ell's stomach growled at the pleasant aroma. "Thanks," she said, although her response sounded more like a grunt.

"Why don't you take a seat?" Williams asked.

Ell lowered herself onto a cracked Naugahyde recliner and gave Williams what she hoped was her best stink-eye glare.

Williams sipped at his coffee, then shifted his gaze from her to the window. "I'll get to the point."

"Please do. I'd like to get home."

Williams' eyes jerked back to hers. "That's your problem, isn't it?"

"Come again? I have no problem, except being here with you right now instead of catching a flight home."

Ell did not attempt to hide her annoyance.

Williams slammed his coffee cup on the small table beside the couch and stood. "That's enough, Trooper Evander. We've pieced together your story. You went rogue and followed up on the Boston human trafficking lead without any backup. No one else put you into the shipping container but you. Many people went to a lot of trouble searching for you when you disappeared."

Ell sucked in a long breath. "Fine. I followed up on a lead that your organization, the FBI, and the Washington State Patrol chose to ignore. I was on vacation when I did that. From where I stand, I didn't go rogue. I acted on my own time and dime."

"You knew the agencies on the task force in Washington didn't have the resources to follow that lead. So, you went on your own, just another hot-headed do-gooder too righteous to think through the ramifications of her actions," Williams growled.

Ell glared at him briefly before gazing at the light shimmering through the apartment's dusty window. When she replied, her voice was a whisper. "That was not just a lead. There were plenty of real people in that shipping container with me. You and your agency choose to ignore that potential. You could have done something other than let those people be sold into a who-knows-what sort of nightmare. I acted."

"And you failed," Williams replied. "Stop with the self-righteous attitude, Evander. We know about your niece. That's horrible for any family to bear, but it doesn't mean you should take the law into your own hands. When all is said and done, you may have helped those people today; but you might have compromised a dozen other leads, informants, and operations in planning."

Ell gazed at her lap. "A lot of human trafficking victims were freed today, including me. Saving one person is a good outcome on any day, let alone that many. Don't look to me to pity you and your people. You aren't the victims in this."

She met his gaze directly. "And it just keeps happening. There's no end to the flow of people kidnapped by greedy and immoral people around the globe. Have you seen the figures lately? The FBI has over eighty-nine thousand active missing persons cases, and that's only from a U.S. perspective. You'd think the COVID-19 pandemic would have slowed things down, but the flow out of Asia into the U.S. and Europe is staggering and keeps growing overseas. When that man and the mystery team showed up to free me and the people with me in that container . . . The people we saved this morning aren't even near the tip of the iceberg."

Williams sighed. "You're right—to the extent you understand things. The FBI fights this battle every day but has nowhere close to the number of agents needed to make a dent. Homeland Security Investigations and your Washington State Patrol are in the same boat. But we keep trying, even though we fall behind five steps for every step we take forward."

Williams rose and paced to the window, his glance drifting outside. Over his shoulder, he whispered, "As much as today turned out well for you and the people on that ship, you cannot do this again. You've reached a dangerous point in your personal and professional life. Those who fight human trafficking are good at what we do and care about what we do. Unfortunately, people like you create a real problem for us. We were there today for you and those people, but we missed out on several stronger leads we could have been following."

Ell stood, clenching her fists as she spit out her next words. "You have got to be kidding. You think you're good at this? We might not be talking right now if it hadn't been for the four mystery operators who showed up out of nowhere. Instead, I might be dead, and those people in the containers would be on trucks headed who-knows-where."

Williams waved her back into her chair. Ell ran a hand through her damp, shoulder-length hair, surprised at its slick, smooth texture after three weeks of sweat and grime, making the anger she felt in her gut that much hotter.

"There's some truth in what you say, although I'll never agree with you," Williams said. "But as a trooper and a past member of the military police with a combat infantry badge to your credit, you should understand the need to let the professionals do the job. You need to work within the system you've been hired to support and not go off alone. You could have hurt more than you helped."

Ell shook her head, brushing her golden-brown hair from her eyes. "I don't see it, and you won't convince me."

Williams turned away from the window to face her. "No matter. I called your district commander at the Washington State Patrol. He informed me that a letter of reprimand will be placed in your file for acting out of line with state patrol policy."

"That's not right . . ."

"You've been AWOL from the state patrol for three weeks. You abandoned your beat."

"That's not fair. I was taken."

Williams smiled, but his expression held no warmth. "The good news for you is your employment with the state patrol hasn't been terminated—although that's not what I would have done."

Williams stepped over to where Ell sat and dropped a printed text message into her lap. She unfolded it and read its simple words before lifting her eyes.

"I've been suspended for three months?"

"You have," Williams replied. "Believe me. It would have been much worse if you had worked for me. There's no denying your bravery, Trooper Evander. Few people would have put themselves on the line as you did to free the captives. But your reckless behavior could have just as easily put those same people at risk."

Ell tried to speak but felt as if she'd been gut-punched and couldn't find the wind to force out the words. They were taking her work away from her. The one thing she had—her hope of finding her niece.

Williams squatted on his heels, eye-to-eye with her, and tossed another sheet of paper into her lap. "At this moment, you are at a critical juncture in your career and life. Your frustration with the progress others are making in the fight against human trafficking has escalated beyond reason. Whether you like it or not, you need a break. I have a letter for you, sent this morning by the chief of the Washington State Patrol. He has requested you spend your suspension with a special unit not far from your home. He seems to feel the unit can train the recklessness out of you. The letter says if you agree to those terms, your suspension will include full pay and benefits. If you don't, you're alone for three months without pay and benefits. This is much more than you deserve."

Ell glared at Williams.

Williams laughed. "I suggest you accept his offer."

"Wonderful," she mumbled. "I'll be counting recycled bottles in some remote corner of the Olympic Peninsula."

"Your boss has offered you a chance to learn and redeem yourself simultaneously. I don't care which way you go on this, but I will state without reservation that if I encounter you again for any reason, anywhere near one of my operations, I will put you in chains and lock you away somewhere no one will ever find you. You may have come out okay today, but you have intruded on more than you can possibly fathom. People won't forget that. I won't forget that. If something happens to you again, you may not have the support you need next time."

"Is that a threat?"

Williams smiled, turned, and headed for the apartment's front door. "Your car's waiting downstairs. Your airline tickets are waiting for you at the airline's ticket counter, courtesy of Uncle Sam."

CHAPTER 8

A day later, Captain Alexander Anthem pulled into the parking lot in front of the B Company, 2nd Battalion, 75th Ranger Regiment headquarters building at Fort Lewis. The sun had just crested the eastern horizon behind Mount Rainier. The red-stained dawn rose clearly, and the humid air promised afternoon rain.

Alex caught the first flight home the following morning, despite his friend's suggestion. Alex loved his job as the commander of a ranger company. A driven man, he had enlisted in the army as soon as he'd graduated high school.

The recruiter was surprised and pleased when the young man with a thin body and dark hazel eyes told him he wanted to be an infantryman. Most kids he talked to at the recruiting office wanted to fly drones or work with computers. Alex wanted to hump a rifle, which was just fine with the recruiter who never seemed to satisfy his quota for infantry soldiers. What Alex didn't reveal to the recruiter was that he planned to use the skills he'd learned in the infantry to track down the people who'd taken him from his family so long ago. He planned to shut their operations down.

Alex saluted the battalion logo on the glass doors to his company's headquarters building and removed his burgundy beret as he stepped inside. He made it only a few feet before the massive form of his battalion commander intercepted him. Easily the largest man Alex had ever met, Lieutenant Colonel Joel Anderson stood six feet four and was 240 pounds of sheer muscle and cold-fighting fury. With a keen mind and experience beyond what most people could imagine, Anderson was the man Alex would have chosen to serve as a subordinate company commander if the colonel hadn't chosen him first.

Alex snapped to attention. "Rangers lead the way, sir!"

Anderson smiled and returned the salute. "At ease, Captain. I have orders for you directly from the joint chiefs of staff."

Alex felt one eyebrow shoot up. Anderson smiled at his mannerism.

"Thought that might get your attention. Surprised me, too! We get a lot of important documents around here, but that's the first I've ever received directly from the joint chiefs."

Alex paused, the confusion evident on his face as Anderson handed him a sealed envelope.

"Open it and read it already. I want to see what it says, too."

Alex ripped open the envelope and scanned the brief note, including the signature of the U.S. Army Chief of Staff.

"It says I'm assigned temporary duty to some unit here at Joint Base Lewis-McChord," Alex said. "It doesn't say which unit. Only provides a building number on North Fort Lewis."

"Let me see that."

Alex handed the document to his commander. Anderson shook his head. "And you're to report today."

"I'm relieved of command?" Alex said.

He attempted to control his voice. The men in his company were like family. They'd deployed too many times to too many dangerous places, saw too much combat, and held each other up through so much.

He felt a profound responsibility for every person in his company. To be relieved before his two-year command tour was unthinkable.

Anderson shook his head. "You've not been relieved, Alex. You're headed there on temporary duty but without an end date. This letter says you are to remain the commander of B Company during that time until specifically directed by the chief of staff. We'll assume you'll be returning once the assignment is over. In the meantime, I'll assign your executive officer to act in your stead. He's a good man. He'll hold down the fort until you return."

Anderson reached out a huge paw and clapped it hard on Alex's shoulder. "I have a feeling about this assignment, Captain. There aren't many rangers with two silver stars and a bronze star with 'V' devices for valor on each one. I think someone's noticed you. I suggest you roll with it. This could turn out to be an incredible opportunity."

"Yes, sir," Alex replied, although he didn't feel good about the opportunity in his gut or heart.

"Just roll with it, Captain," Anderson repeated. "Just roll with it."

CHAPTER 9

Sam Anthem, Alex's cousin and an operator assigned to the Home Team, stepped onto the front porch of the familiar two-story suburban home just as his cell phone vibrated. Average height, lean, and broad-shouldered, Sam retrieved the encrypted phone from the front pocket of his jeans. He glanced at the number for the incoming call and raised a fist to halt the four people trailing him onto the porch. He held the phone, so they could all see the screen. It was Director Paul Samuelson, the director of the Extreme Operations Group. Sam pressed the onscreen button to accept the call.

The response was immediate. "Can you talk?" Paul asked in a hushed, gravelly voice.

"I have you on speaker with Cap, Romeo, Fox, and Pastor Carson. We're at Consuelo's front door. No one else is within hearing distance."

Paul chuckled, although it came out like the soft growl of a bear. Sam raised an eyebrow in surprise. The man never laughed, ever.

"Today is the day, then?" Paul asked.

Sam noticed Jessica Falcone blush. Her call sign was Charlie Papa, or CAP. She was a tall, elegant thirty-year-old with thick, black hair; bronze skin; and the piercing brown eyes of her first-generation Mexican heritage. She possessed the brain of Einstein, the frame of an Olympic athlete, and the fighting skills of a mixed martial arts champion—which she was.

Jess served as the Home Team's political and technological expert when they encountered the need for the missions their employer, the Extreme Operations Group, assigned the team. Jess was usually trustworthy with many of the nation's greatest secrets, but Sam knew she'd spilled the beans when he met her eyes.

Jess tugged at the loose, aqua designer blouse that hung over her stylish blue jeans and concealed the Smith and Wesson 9mm pistol holstered at her side. She tucked a long strand of ebony hair behind one ear and shifted her dark brown eyes away to scan the ground at her feet.

"It may have slipped out during a call the other day."

Standing next to her, Leah McCarthy—call sign Romeo Alpha, or Romeo for short—chuckled. "Wow, Jess. Our team's intelligence officer can't keep one simple secret?"

Twenty-eight years old and five feet one with thick, sunset bronze hair and startling blue eyes, Leah was often mistaken for the diminutive soft woman she appeared to be. It was a judgment people only made once about the strong, driven woman with whipcord muscles and a keen mind.

Her hair hung loose around her shoulders and danced in the warm afternoon breeze. She wore a loose-fitting University of Washington sweatshirt low over her hips, hiding the Glock 19, 9mm pistol holstered at the small of her back. Leah's startling blue eyes sparkled from within her heavily freckled pixie face. The team's sniper and armorer, she hated the "Romeo" moniker, insisting it was more appropriate for a male team member. But her protests only encouraged her teammates to use it more.

Allen Farrell stood behind the two women. Call sign Fox Tango—or Fox, for short—Allen chuckled and rolled his eyes at Jess's discomfort. Always the quiet one of the group, Allen matched Sam for size and physique—a surfer-blond, blue-eyed wizard with anything that blows up. Fox and Sam could have been brothers. They both stood at five eleven and weighed 185 pounds; but Sam had gray-speckled black hair, brown eyes, and a darker complexion. Allen wore a thin leather jacket over a dark blue t-shirt and jeans. Sam felt confident Allen had his ever-present Beretta on his left hip, grip facing forward, covered by his jacket.

Pastor Jim Carson pulled up the rear. He was the unofficial chaplain for the Extreme Operations Group and the Home Team. He was also a past member of the Central Intelligence Agency's top-tier tactical team and was a gentle bear of a man and a legend in the special operations world.

As one of the agency's first and most successful career African American operatives, Pastor Carson served in the CIA with Paul before he retired to follow the Lord. At about that same time, Paul left to lead the Extreme Operations Group. They had remained close friends ever since.

Carson pastored a local church where three Home Team members attended services when they weren't on a mission. The man wore a perpetual smile, and today was no exception.

Sam glared at Jess, then said to Paul, "Yes, sir. Today's the day."

"I hope it goes well for you." Paul laughed again. "It's a dangerous thing you're doing."

"He's struggling more than when he found Consuelo in the hut in Mexico and rescued her from the cartel," Allen said loud enough for Paul and the rest to hear.

That got a laugh from Pastor Carson and the team.

Paul paused, seemingly collecting his thoughts. "Knowing what you're about to do, I apologize for the interruption, but I have important news."

"Sir?" Sam prodded.

"You're getting an addition to the Home Team tomorrow. It's the woman you saw in action in Turkey. She's a capable law enforcement officer, who's worked for the past five years with the Washington State Patrol and on a human trafficking task force with Homeland Security Investigations, ICE, and the FBI. As you know, the chief of the Washington State Patrol is a good friend.

"It seems this trooper went rogue a month ago, going after some human traffickers alone. The chief asked if we could give her a home for three months to cool her heels and expose her to another side of tactical operations. He feels she's talented, a skilled sniper, and a good cop. Additionally, she's trained far beyond the requirements of her current job. Her parents are retired intelligence officers and saw to her training from an early age. Since you're currently recruiting new operators for a second Home Team, I agreed to have her join you for her suspension period. She's in Olympia now; and I've sent her your location, so she can meet up with you."

Sam grimaced, noticing the same reaction from his three teammates. Six months ago, they'd relocated from Florida to Joint Base Lewis-McChord near Tacoma, Washington. They'd established the Extreme Operations Group's western headquarters and training facility during that time. It had been a challenging job, given the facilities available on north Fort Lewis; but less than a month ago, they had finally finished refurbishing and outfitting an old maintenance building near the edge of the base.

As part of the Home Team's relocation, several potential new operators had been invited to test for membership over the past month. But none were acceptable. Another cohort of candidates was scheduled to arrive in the next few days. Babysitting a rogue cop, even one as good as they'd observed in Turkey, was not something they had time for right now.

Leah groaned. As though reading her thoughts, Paul said, "I agree this is the last thing you need right now. However, give her a home for a few months. Train her and help her vent some of the steam built up inside. I hope you'll either return her to the state patrol in good shape once her time is up or see her as a viable candidate for H.T. Two."

"No guarantees, but will do, sir," Sam said.

The words erupted as more of a groan than an agreement. But then, as with so many of Paul's communications, the call disconnected before Sam voiced the last word.

Jessica laid a hand on Sam's shoulder and turned him around to the house's front door. "Back on task, Casanova," she said.

Sam tucked the cell phone back into his pocket and reached for the doorbell beside the house's soft yellow front door.

He paused before pushing it, then heard Leah laugh softly. "It's nice to see our empty-hand fighting expert finally face something that has him afraid."

"Funny," Sam replied.

Leah reached around him and pressed the doorbell. Sam cringed as it rang loudly from inside the house.

"I'm glad you guys are having so much fun with this," he whispered. "Just wait till you need me to have your back."

Sam turned pleading eyes to Allen, who'd gone through a similar experience a few months earlier. His teammate shrugged. "You're on your own on this one, buddy."

A second later, the door burst open, and a gangly teenage boy with a mop of dark, unruly hair and a broad smile appeared.

"Empty!" he cheered, calling Sam by his team name, a contraction of his call sign, Mike Tango.

The boy wrapped Sam in an enthusiastic, bone-crunching hug. Sam returned the embrace, then pushed the young boy back.

"I've only been gone a few weeks, and you're at least an inch taller. And quit getting so strong. You just re-broke the ribs I cracked on our last mission."

Tony flexed a small bump on his still-bony bicep. "I'm doing all the exercises you told me about, and it's paying off."

"Anthony, let our guests into the house," a soft voice called from behind the boy.

The musical Spanish accent always stirred something inside Sam. As Tony stepped away, his adopted mother stepped around him, drawing Sam into a warm, lingering embrace. Then, after a long, quiet moment, Consuelo Zamora stepped back, keeping one of Sam's hands in hers as she waved the rest of the Home Team into the house.

Standing somewhere between Leah's tiny frame and Jessica's taller height, Consuelo was trim and had the glossy black hair for which models paid fortunes. Her natural mocha complexion and expressive brown eyes, set above a small but classically shaped Aztec nose, marked her unique Mexican heritage. Her wide smile spoke to her kind heart and love for Sam and his friends from the Home Team.

Sam thought he saw her wink as Jessica entered the house. "Such an unexpected surprise. So nice to see you all here on such a pleasant Sunday afternoon."

When Connie emphasized "surprise," Sam knew the secret was out.

"Great to see you, too, Connie," Leah replied as everyone gathered in a half-circle around Sam and Consuelo in the great room.

The great room's cathedral ceiling and wall of west-facing windows gave it an airy, bright feel Sam thought perfect for the occasion. The far end of the great room blended seamlessly into an eating area and kitchen. Sam inhaled the aroma of something wonderful.

Unlike Sam's one-room Olympia cottage overlooking the expansive waters of Puget Sound, Connie's house was large enough to spread out in and breathe in the comfort Consuelo brought to the place. A large island with tall bar stools separated the great room from the kitchen. Plates, glasses, a chilled pitcher of something red, and various foods covered the island.

Sam lifted a hand toward the island of food and glared at Jessica. "You really cannot keep a secret."

Leah and Jessica both shrugged. Allen glanced around the room, avoiding Sam's eyes.

"You've decorated since I was here," Allen said to deflect Sam's attention.

Sam wanted to frown but found it impossible. So instead, he laughed and said, "I know that look, Fox. You're just as guilty as the rest of them."

"I have no idea what you mean," Allen replied.

Sam picked up Consuelo's other hand, holding both as he faced her. She blushed brightly as one of Sam's teammates let out a soft "Here it comes . . . "

"I guess you know why I'm here," Sam said, meeting Consuelo's wide, soft eyes with his own.

Consuelo rolled her eyes toward the ceiling, making no attempt to stifle her wide smile. "I might have a clue, but please do proceed."

Sam dropped one of Connie's hands and retrieved a blue velvet box from the back pocket of his jeans. He opened the box's lid and held it out to her.

"Consuelo Zamora, if you know why I'm here, I'd like your answer. Will you marry me?"

Consuelo's mouth drew into a thin line that twitched slightly at the corners.

"Of course not," she said. "Not like this!" She let go of his hand and folded her arms across her chest. "You think I'm so easy . . . "

Her response struck Sam like a punch to the gut. He dropped his eyes to his feet. What had gone wrong? He'd rehearsed this again and again. She loved him. He loved her. They had talked about getting married many times.

Sam heard three whoops of laughter from his teammates, then heard Tony's agonized question. "Mommmm! Why didn't you say yes?"

Jessica laid a comforting hand on Tony's shoulder. "Hush," she said. "Give it a moment."

Sam felt confused, stripped of the confidence he'd walked in with. "I've loved you since the day we met. We've been through so much, and I thought you loved me. I thought you wanted this." Sam's voice was barely a whisper.

Consuelo feigned indignation, confusing Sam even more with the bright smile in her eyes and the conflicting frown on her face. She tapped the toe of her foot on the soft carpet at her feet.

"Just because you rescue a girl from the cartel and protect her reputation against those who'd do her harm doesn't mean she should just throw herself at your feet without the proper ceremony."

Sam felt his face turn crimson. "But I thought . . . "

"Of course, she loves you, you idiot," Leah said from behind him. "She just wants you to—"

"Quiet," Jessica interrupted. "If you want her to marry you, you must do it right."

Pastor Carson gently kicked the back of Sam's left knee, causing Sam to stagger and drop to one knee.

Pastor Carson chuckled. "I've had to do this more than once."

"Nicely done!" Leah said.

"It's the down-on-one-knee thing, right?" Sam asked.

"A little slow, but you're catching on," Allen said.

"A girl gets only one proposal in her life. So, it should be done right," Jessica added.

Sam met Consuelo's eyes. "How about it, Consuelo? Will you be my wife and partner and spend the rest of your life with me?"

Consuelo laughed softly. To Sam, it sounded like the ringing of tiny heavenly bells.

"Of course, I will."

Consuelo held out her left hand so Sam could slip on the engagement ring.

Then, Sam pulled Connie into a long embrace. The two kissed for a long moment as everyone clapped their approval.

"It's about time," Tony said. "First, Sam rescued Mom and me from the cartel. Then Mom brought me to the US and adopted me. Now, I'm going to have a dad. After my parents died in Mexico, I never thought anything like this would ever happen."

Allen and Jessica wrapped their arms around Tony's shoulders. "You've got a family again, Anthony," Allen said. "And that includes all of us."

The front doorbell broke the moment. All stood in silence as the four operators instinctively reached for their pistols. Then, heedless of the team's suspicious vigilance, Tony jogged to the door and opened it.

Leah growled when she saw who was there. The woman was slender with an angular face, brilliant green eyes, and a tangled mop of light brown hair streaked with gold. Her complexion was pale, as if she'd been too long without the sun.

"Hello, Leah," Ell said.

"I'd hoped never to see your ugly face again," Leah replied.

"Pleased to see you, too. But same here, I'm sure," Ell replied.

Tony stepped aside to let Ell into the room.

Jessica shoved at Leah's shoulder. "Explain. This is the woman you tagged from the shipping container. She's the one Paul said would be contacting us. So, what's the issue?"

Leah's tone was flat. "Let me introduce Ellen Maria Evander, a.k.a. Ell. We attended sniper school together some years back. She's an entitled, spoiled brat who would cheat her mother out of her last morsel of food."

Ell shrugged, inadvertently raising the hem of her worn, gray t-shirt, and revealing a small 9mm pistol holstered at her hip. "You only say that because you love me so much—that and because I beat you on the sniper school challenge by a full point."

"It wouldn't have been a big deal if you hadn't cheated," Leah replied. "Her father's a retired spy with connections to a weapons manufacturer. He snuck a fancy high-tech sniper scope to her for the final test. That scope calculated distance, windage, drop—everything. It also used lasers. All she had to do was point and shoot while the rest of us completed the final exam the old-fashioned way with our assigned weapons—taking measurements manually, crunching numbers, and adjusting our scopes by hand. If you'd used the standard equipment, you never would have beaten me."

Ell smiled, although it came off more as a smirk. "At sniper school, they taught us to use whatever resources we could find. So, that's what I did. Besides, that was five years ago. Don't you think it's time to let it go?"

Leah's narrowed eyes met Ell's gaze. "So, you're our babysitting assignment."

"That's enough," Sam said, stepping between the two women. "You're the state trooper assigned to work with us for the next three months? The one we met in Turkey?"

"Ah, I get it," Ell paused. "The four of you—you were the team that showed up at the port."

Sam nodded. "We are those people."

Ell handed Sam a paper she produced from the back pocket of her jeans. "That's my direction to work with you for the next three months, co-signed by your director and my chief at the state patrol. I just got into town from Bellingham after the long flight home from Turkey. I contacted your director per my directions in that letter.

Director Paul Samuelson suggested I catch up with you here before arriving at your headquarters tomorrow."

Sam faced the rest of the team. "We'll dig into this tomorrow, but for now, I think we should do our best to welcome Trooper Ellen."

"It's just Ell," she said, cutting off Sam.

Sam scanned the document, frowned, and then continued. "Once we've verified her credentials, she will be treated as a fully qualified team member." He directed his last words at Leah.

"Fine," Leah muttered. "But I don't have to trust her, not for a minute."

Sam's cell phone vibrated again. Jessica, Allen, and Leah's all did the same. "Mission Alert" showed in bold letters across his cellphone's screen.

"Time to go, folks." Sam turned to Consuelo. "Duty calls. I'd hoped we'd spend more time celebrating our engagement."

Consuelo gave Sam one of the smiles he remembered from the first time he had met her, a look that accelerated his heartbeat every time.

"I knew whom I was falling in love with when it happened," she replied, then pulled him into a long, warm embrace. "Go do your job. Save the world or whatever you need to do. I can freeze all the food, so we can enjoy it later. Anthony and I will be here when you're done."

Consuelo stepped up to Ell. "And welcome. You're working with an amazing group of people. When you get done with whatever awaits you today, come see me. I'd love to get to know you better. I pray God blesses you with His protection and provides you with strength and courage."

Ell felt her cheeks warm, not sure she'd ever met anyone so direct and yet so . . . sincere.

"Thank you. And I'll do that," she said.

Consuelo placed a small but firm hand on Ell's arm. "I'll consider that a promise. We'll meet at one of my favorite coffee shops."

Sam cleared his throat softly to draw everyone's attention. "We'll meet at the headquarters in two hours."

Consuelo held up a hand. "I'd like to pray before you go."

"Of course," Jessica replied.

"Bring it in, folks," Pastor Carson said.

They gathered in a small circle, Consuelo bringing Ell to her side. "This is something we like to do, when possible," Connie whispered. "If it bothers you . . ."

"Not at all," Ell said. "My mom was religious. So, we were always doing this sort of thing."

"Lord, be with these brave people. I pray You hold them close and protect them as they venture into the unknown to carry out Your good work. Please grant them Your grace and guide them home to those who love them once their mission is complete. We pray this in the name of our Lord Jesus Christ, amen."

"Amen," the rest intoned. Ell even joined in, surprising herself once again.

Sam and Consuelo hugged once more. He ruffled Tony's thick mop of hair as he passed the boy. Tony punched Sam in the shoulder in return, a sad smile on his face.

Still standing at the door, Ell snagged Leah's arm as she stepped through the door.

"I gather you're all federal agents of some kind. Doesn't praying on the job break just about every federal employment law there is?"

Leah stopped, not bothering to force a smile. "As a matter of fact, it doesn't. No one is required to pray when we do, and we do it often.

It's important to us as individuals; and, in our case, as a team, it is something we share. There are no laws against praying on the job when you're a government employee, only laws against making faith a condition of employment."

Pastor Carson added, "I spent twenty years as a tier-one operator. Some of the best operators I worked with were spiritual people. But don't worry. There will be no pressure for you to join in unless you want to, and it will not get in the way of the team's ops."

"Right," Ell mumbled, following the group out the door and across the yard to her car. "This just gets better and better."

CHAPTER 10

Ell followed Leah up Interstate 5 to Joint Base Lewis-McChord, a combined army and air force military base twenty miles north of Olympia. After passing through security, they drove to a nondescript warehouse on the northern fringe of the base. She had little time to examine the facility as she pulled into the building's small parking area; but it appeared to be a massive structure, spanning the equivalent of many football fields. She saw no lights on the inside as she stepped out of her Subaru Forrester and locked it behind her.

Leah parked next to her and led the way inside without a word. *The girl can hold a grudge*, Ell thought, as she pushed her way in through swinging thick, steel doors.

Lights flicked on as they walked across the expansive building, illuminating a massive structure with thirty-foot-high beams. To her right was a long row of offices. Next to the offices and extending to the center of the building was an open expanse of red and blue checkerboard exercise mats and an assortment of exercise equipment. Opposite where she entered the building was a long wall of doors leading to what she guessed were locker rooms.

Ell followed as Leah made a beeline to the building's conference room on the right wall. As they entered the room, Ell found Sam, Jessica, and Allen already in place. The craggy face of the man she assumed was Director Paul Samuelson dominated the middle of three large monitors covering the conference room's far wall.

The air smelled of popcorn, the universal food for soldiers forced to cool their heels before yet another briefing. Allen tossed Ell a closed paper bag stained with cooking oil. Ell's stomach rumbled in response.

Paul raised an eyebrow as Ell and Leah took seats at a conference table big enough for twenty people.

"Welcome, Trooper Evander," he said. "I'm happy you found the team. When your chief called and expressed confidence in your skills, I was happy to bring you to our team, even briefly."

Not sure what to say, Ell nodded.

"I have a mission we need to act on immediately. Intel from the Drug Enforcement Agency and Alcohol, Tobacco, Firearms and Explosives suggests the shipping container Ell lived in for three weeks may have contained more than human trafficking victims. It may also contain highly classified, pirated technology and pure, raw heroin. What we originally thought was a human trafficking crime, which does not fall under our organization's charter, is now a multi-department mutual concern well within our purview. The DEA, HSI, CIA, and ATF have requested the State Department take point in the investigation. To clarify this for Trooper Evander—"

"It's just Ell, sir," Ell said.

"Thank you. Ell, it is. As I said, the Extreme Operations Group (EOG) reports to the United States Secretary of State. We carry out operations within and outside the continental United States. That is often problematic for the federal agencies."

Ell nodded, her heart rate increasing at his words. With that sort of charter, the EOG might have the resources and clout to make a dent in human trafficking if she could convince them to do so.

Before Ell could frame her thoughts, Paul continued. "I need people in Turkey to check out the shipping container. The National Security Agency has positioned a satellite over the port since Trooper Evander and the other human trafficking victims have been removed. Our intel suggests no one's been near the shipping container since Trooper Evander—I mean, Ell—and the other human trafficking victims were removed. The same intel connects ownership of the vessel and the container to the same company: New Asian Imports and Exports, Incorporated of Shanghai. It's a top-five shipping conglomerate owned by Lee Chao. Homeland Security suspects the company may be involved in human trafficking and smuggling everything from drugs to technology to weapons."

Paul gazed directly at Ell. "I want Allen and Ell in Istanbul for another look at the shipping container. I know you've only been with us a day, Ell, but you're familiar with the shipping container and understand how the drugs and technology might have been hidden in it. I want your eyes on that box before anyone else gets there, or it gets sent back to sea."

"What about the rest of us?" Sam asked. "How can we help?"

"I'd like you and Leah to talk with the owner of New Asian Imports and Exports. See what you can find out. The U.S. has a delegation in Shanghai right now, negotiating a trade deal with the Chinese government. It's a coincidence we can leverage to get you into Lee's office. From what we know of Lee, he'll be more than happy to receive you if he thinks there's a lucrative shipping deal in the offing."

The director then looked at Jessica. "I'd like you to provide overwatch from the headquarters at JBLM. Dig into New Asian Imports and Exports and see what you can find."

"Yes, sir," Jessica replied, making a note on a yellow legal tablet.

"The EOG's two jets are standing by at McChord Air Force Base to take you to your respective destinations. Departure is two hours—or sooner, if you can swing it. Please be careful."

"The candidates for H.T. Two arrive tomorrow," Sam said.

Paul smiled and nodded. "I've talked to Pastor Carson. He'll stay close to the building while you're gone. Jessica can help him receive the candidates when she has time. He'll work with my folks here in Florida to process and settle them as they arrive. Good hunting."

CHAPTER 11

F an strolled along a winding pathway through the broad expanses of Shanghai's riverside Binjiang Park. The winding concrete walkway was flanked by manicured grass and ornate flower gardens, fading after a long, hot summer. The wide Huangpu River flowed serenely beyond the gardens to her right. A blue sky tinged with Shanghai's traditional brown haze promised a warm, humid day.

With two hours before their jet was to depart, Fan took a few moments to settle her thoughts in her favorite place, the Binjiang Park. The large park skirted the Huangpu River's winding route between the two major sections of the city. Across the river, towering skyscrapers dotted the skyline. Today, those buildings stood empty. Sunday was a day for rest for those who could afford not to work and for family gatherings and celebrations.

Family gatherings . . . The thought brought unwelcome musings, as it did often of late. As she did so many times, her thoughts were cluttered by questions about her biological parents—where did they live, and were they even alive? She also wondered if she had siblings.

She was grateful for all Lee Chao had done for her. Master Lee or Lee Chao, not father. Not Dad, like other kids referred to their fathers. Instead, he preferred the honorific of "master," as though it imparted a special power. And lately, he treated her more like a lieutenant than a daughter, which left her feeling empty and cold, despite the trust she knew he placed in her judgment and actions.

In truth, he'd spared no expense over the past twenty years in raising her. But family was not a concept close to his heart. For him, life was about striving, working, climbing the ladder of power and success, and being recognized in China's political and economic machine.

The thought of having a family somewhere tugged at the corners of her mouth, bringing a soft smile that brightened her small, oval face with its expressive, almond eyes. She ran a finger down her dark brown, waist-length braid, then flipped it over one shoulder. Power, he possessed without a doubt. His legitimate shipping ventures spanned the globe—so significant to the world economy that a minuscule change in the company's strategic focus could impact whole governments and economies.

A handful of shipping companies dominated the world's ability to import, export, and transport goods worldwide. Her father's company was one of them. New Asian Imports and Exports, Incorporated—with its expansive fleet of ships, trains, and trucks on every continent—was one of those companies, the fifth largest in the world in terms of volume of business. And that figure did not count the business kept off the books.

Even though she knew this latest assignment was essential to her father, the challenge of it didn't captivate her at all, leaving her cold. On the contrary, the prospect of involving herself in another of her father's criminal activities left her nauseous.

If Fan could, she'd shut it all down—the drugs and the human trafficking. As vice president of operations, she ran New Asian Imports and Exports' legitimate ocean-going operations. The work stimulated her, introducing her to interesting people and places around the globe. She loved the work but led those operations knowing the company carried out other, illegal activities off the books using the same land and sea carriers she managed. That made her an accessory, and the idea scared her.

Fan took in a cleansing breath. Master Lee was her father, and she owed him too much to have such thoughts. Her country's culture dictated a daughter capitulate regarding decisions made by the family's eldest male. She loved her country and her father for all he'd done for her. She would do as he asked and quit letting these disturbing thoughts enter her mind.

Fan rounded a bend in the trail and saw a popular coffee shop nestled against the backdrop of the park's manicured lawns, tall trees, and gardens. From a distance, the modernistic, single-story wood and metal building appeared packed with people. Not a surprise. While tea remained the go-to drink across China, coffee had displaced the more traditional drink for many people.

She glanced at her watch—almost noon. From her many visits here in the past, she knew most of the luxuriously padded chairs lining the coffee shop's broad windows overlooking the river would be occupied. Her only chance for a seat was on the patio.

Fan entered the smoked-glass swinging doors. The contrast between the humid atmosphere outside and the air-conditioned inside felt good. She got lucky at the checkout counter and held a steaming mocha in less than two minutes as she headed back into the heat.

She saw no vacant chairs on the patio and propped a hip against the low stone wall that framed the area. She smiled at the soft tone of conversation flowing around her. People gathered at small tables, old and young, some in family groups with three or more generations. Younger groups occupied other tables, perhaps college students who talked in hushed tones and solved the world's problems. She remembered those days at Oxford when no problem seemed out of reach.

Fan glanced across the park at the river, tracking a passenger ferry crossing from the nearby side, headed for the opposite side of the city. As she did, she unconsciously registered the number of tables on the patio, the number of people at each table, and the potential threats any of them might present. She shook her head at the unbidden thoughts, feeling the perpetual tension she carried on her shoulders ease a little.

A light touch on her arm distracted her. She turned sharply, then relaxed to find a woman with sad eyes that drooped at the corners facing her.

"We have an extra chair at our table," the woman said, "if you want to join us."

The demands of Fan's daily routine of training, conditioning, studying, and administering her father's company meant she had no friends. Her two minders, whom she'd nicknamed Archie and Devon and who accompanied her to her father's office and had been with her as long as she could remember, served more as bodyguards than friends. At twenty-seven, she couldn't remember a single day she'd been without either of them. Even today, as she walked alone through the park, she felt their unseen presence in the distance.

This woman and her invitation presented an unexpected opportunity. With a few hours before heading out for Turkey, she could finish the coffee alone and continue her walk in solitude as she typically did or join the woman and her friends at their table. She felt no alarms going off in her finely trained mind, so she opted for the latter. She nodded and followed the woman to a small table with half a dozen people around it. Fan lowered herself into a vacant metal chair as the woman began introductions.

"I am Zhang Wei," the woman said.

She then pointed around the table, naming each person in turn. First was a college female student named Wang Fang, perhaps a few years younger than Fan. Next to her sat a woman in her late forties named Li Jing and her teenage daughter, Li Wei. Next, three men in the group sat in a semi-circle as though presenting a united front. Each wore a broad smile as they were introduced: two college students named Zhi Peng and Zu Guan and a man in his late fifties named Feng.

Fan nodded politely as each name was spoken, then said, "My name is Fan. I am pleased to meet you."

"You are the daughter of Lee Chao, the famous shipment magnet," one of the male college students proclaimed. "I recognize you from your picture online."

Fan had already forgotten the young man's name but replied with a nod she hoped reflected an appropriate degree of humility.

"I am. And I thank you for inviting me to sit with you. In my line of business, I have little time for socialization. So being invited to your table and meeting each of you is quite special."

Her hostess, Zhang Wei, cocked her head slightly to one side, then said, "We are a small group who share a faith that encourages us to welcome strangers to our table. So, when I saw you standing at the patio's edge, it seemed like you could use a friend."

Fan dropped her eyes to her paper cup, sitting on the table before her. "Your observation was astute, although I don't often seek the companionship of strangers."

"We believe we should love our neighbors as ourselves. You are our neighbor, so we welcome you," teenage Li Jing offered.

Fan smiled. "Sound advice from someone so young, although often a challenging thing to do. You mentioned you are gathered together because of your shared faith."

"We gather together for fellowship, to share each other's joys and sorrows, to laugh and to cry with each other, and to look into the Bible to see what Christ says about what we should do in our lives," the elder male Feng replied.

His bluntness surprised Fan. China had outlawed Christianity. She spent a moment assessing the man before responding. With thick, gray hair swept back from a high forehead and a wrinkled face, the man appeared much older and perhaps wiser than Fan guessed his years to be.

Feng looked at his lap, then back to Fan. His smile was gentle and a little lopsided as he spoke. "Our government espouses atheism, as you undoubtedly know. However, we have observed a growing Christian population in every region of China. Of late, as long as we practice our faith in private and do not bring it to the attention of the authorities, we are generally left alone. Of course, we still worry about persecution by the government, but we accept persecution from others because of what our Savior Jesus Christ went through to free us from our sins."

Fan sipped her drink, considering his words, then replied, "I travel to many countries as part of my work. I have encountered people claiming the Christian faith, so I studied it a bit. I understand you are directed to love God with all your heart, mind, soul, and strength and to love your neighbor as yourself.[1] But I often find it

---

1   Mark 12:30-31

difficult to reconcile the actions of some of those I meet who claim to be Christian with their actions in the boardroom. I also find people in my business, especially my company's competitors, would see loving their neighbors' weaknesses as something to be leveraged rather than loved."

Young Zhang Wei reached a hand across the space between their chairs and laid it gently on Fan's arm. "In our faith, we recognize the inherent sin in all of us and how we all stray from our faith occasionally. We know everyone, except God and Jesus Christ, are imperfect in that and many other ways. Our Lord tells us even though we sin, our Savior died on the cross so we can be forgiven those sins. All we have to do is invite Him into our lives and ask for His forgiveness. When we do that and give up our sinful ways, we can be saved and find peace, joy, and eternal life."

"That's a lot to count on when you live and work in a society that does not tolerate failure well at all," Fan replied.

"True," the elder Feng said as he ran a hand through his long hair, brushing it back into place after a breeze tossed it awry. "But may I ask you a personal question?"

Fan nodded. As her British colleagues always said, "In for a penny and in for a pound." Then she said, "Although I reserve the right not to answer."

"Fair enough," Feng replied. "Have you ever hoped for anything?"

Fan glanced at Zhang Wei, wondering if it was a trick question. The woman only smiled and nodded, encouraging her to answer.

Fan recalled her childhood and the persistent wonderings about her biological parents. "I grew up hoping for certain things, as most children do. Perhaps I even hope for some of those same things today."

"As a child, I bet you whispered your hopes to yourself. When you did, you expressed your hopes to someone you couldn't yet see, but you did it anyway. That's the nature of our living God. We can't see Him, but we believe in Him, feel Him all around us, and talk to Him about our hopes and dreams. What's amazing is He always answers those prayers."

Fan felt an unfamiliar and odd feeling rising inside her. On the one hand, she knew intellectually what this man and these people believed was too unbelievable. But on the other hand, she felt the hairs on her arms rise and an odd chill streak through her, a sensation too seldom experienced that she'd come to recognize as a sense of total truth. The experience was always accompanied by a dead, empty feeling when someone lied to her, whether business or personal. But when someone expressed a profound, sincere truth, the chill she felt now often accompanied their words.

She swallowed another sip of coffee, then said, "I'm not sure I can wrap my mind around an absolute, generous Someone I can't see when competitors who I *can* see would like to harm my father or me."

"Understandable," Feng replied. "Whether anyone accepts or rejects God and His Son is a personal choice. You asked about our faith, and we have described the truth of it to you. We will be here for you if you have any questions about it. If you would like to learn more, we can help you with that, too."

"At some risk to ourselves, I might add," one of the male college students said. "If we are caught pushing Christianity in a public place like this, we could be arrested."

"We call ourselves Closet Christians for that reason," Zhang said. "We practice our faith in private and come into the daylight infrequently. But it's such a glorious day, none of us could stay inside, so here we are talking with you."

Fan downed the rest of her mocha and glanced at her watch. "I have a plane to catch."

Zhang Wei gave Fan the same sad smile as when she had invited Fan to join her Closet Christians at their table. "Thank you for sitting with us. I hope we did not make you uncomfortable sharing our faith."

Fan met the woman's gaze, once more impressed by the depth of the sincerity she saw. Despite her usual reluctance to make physical contact with other people, she reached out and squeezed Zhang's hand lightly. "I do not believe there is any way I could be offended by your words or your friends' words."

"Give us a little more time," one of the male college students said with a wide grin. "We can work on that." The other two male students laughed.

Fan chuckled. "While I may not share your faith, I have enjoyed your company. You have been a wonderful distraction from what will likely become an intense and long day. I hope we meet again."

The elder Feng reached into his pocket and retrieved a business card, handing it to Fan. "The cell phone numbers for Zhang Wei and me are on this card. Call anytime, even if you want to share another cup of coffee."

"Or tea," Zhang Wei added. "Unlike these other people, I still like a nice cup of tea."

Fan chuckled, relishing the relaxed feel of the group. She stood, placed the card in her pocket, and bowed to the group. "I like tea, as well. I look forward to the opportunity."

As Fan stepped off the patio, her eyes scanned the grassy fields of the park surrounding the coffee shop. Against a backdrop of tall flowering plants, she spied two familiar forms. She lifted a hand, waved to Archie and Devon, and walked over to meet them.

"You met some new friends," Devon said. At six feet two, Devon stood out in any crowd in China, where the average height was much less. His light blue, open-collared shirt strained against his broad chest and shoulder muscles. He smiled, showing his eyes' dark slits, covered by a thick skull of dark hair cut close to the scalp.

"Friends, indeed," Fan replied. "It was the only chair available in the place. I did enjoy their company, however."

"Odd behavior for someone who won't share tea with two of your oldest friends," Archie said.

Archie was small and lean with a broad face and a quick smile. Shoulder-length, sandy brown hair flopped around his face as he moved. From years of training with both men, Fan knew that as much as they differed in outward appearance, both were highly trained, intelligent, and loyal operators who would give their lives to protect her. Over the years, under their tutelage, she had learned to fight, think, and function in business and the field. They might be her father's employees, but having them nearby always comforted her.

"We have a car waiting at the park's number six gate," Devon said as they turned and walked three abreast down the park's long, concrete pathway. "We packed a bag for you. The jet will be warmed up and ready for our trip to Turkey when we reach the airport."

"Efficient as always," Fan said, making Devon smile. "What would I do without the two of you?"

Archie laughed. "You'd get fat drinking that horrible American coffee, that's what."

"Probably true," Fan replied.

Her thoughts had already drifted back to the conversation with the Closet Christians. What would it be like to find peace and joy as they'd found, to know Someone was watching out for her, sincerely interested in more than her business and operator skills?

She shook her head once, then raised her eyes to the path's end and the waiting car. For now, she had a job for the only person who'd ever given her anything, who'd ever looked out for her welfare. She might not agree with all her father did, but she owed him her life and would see his directions through.

CHAPTER 12

Ell and Allen strode into the administrative office at the Ambarli port dressed as officials from the Australian Department of Foreign Affairs and Trade and flashed authentic, if hastily made, identification badges. Both wore creased gray slacks; starched, open-collar, white shirts; and blue blazers with the Australian flag on the left breast pocket. They planned to leverage the deference Turkey paid to Australian businesses, which constituted a significant portion of their international market.

The trip to Turkey passed quickly enough for Ell, even with the graveyard silence emanating from Allen. In an unexpected act of kindness and concern, Leah told Ell that Allen was an introvert and even shy with anyone outside the team. This had been particularly true since he'd gotten engaged just over ten months ago. But even for an introvert, his silence disarmed Ell.

In the extended silence, Ell found herself wondering, once again, about the mysterious stranger who had come to her rescue not far from where they stood today. She was not used to being rescued, not since she had been on that mission in Afghanistan when she'd been the one rescuing her team. And she had failed then, when the one guy she'd let herself become emotionally involved with hadn't made it. Ell shook off the thought. That was then. This was now, and she'd never fail another person as long as she lived. She'd worked long hours over the last bunch of years, hardening her body and mind. She had no time for such things, and she certainly did not need a man or anyone else rescuing her. Intent to follow Allen's lead on their mission, Ell felt out of her element. Would he finally open up and take charge as the senior operator, or would she have to step forward?

Their Australian credentials and cover stories placed them at the port to research solutions to lingering post-COVID pandemic supply chain issues. Ell breathed an inward sigh of relief as Allen stepped forward and greeted the port authority's new director. After some carefully scripted banter and a subtly delivered envelope full of Australian currency, he presented their credentials and requested an unescorted tour of the port's loading and unloading facilities. Since this was not an unusual request, the authorities didn't give it a second thought.

Twenty minutes later, Allen and Ell strode through the gate to the port's expansive shipping container staging yard. Following what would appear to an observer as a wandering path, they went through a sea of forty-feet-long, eight-feet-tall steel boxes in a rainbow of rusted reds, blues, greens, and yellows that were stacked three and four high.

As they searched for their target container, the sun beat down on them with a vengeance. The air felt heavy, and the smell of rusting metal and diesel-tainted saltwater permeated the air. Their blazers and slacks were soaked in a matter of minutes.

Ell pulled out her cell phone, holding it to her ear as if receiving a call, then punched in the code that activated the shipping container tracking application. Security cameras covered every corner of the container yard, so she made it appear as if she were in a conversation on her phone as they walked.

"Every shipping container has a transponder that identifies it by its container number and owner," Ell said as they paused at the junction of narrow paths between the tall stacks. "Jessica installed the app for detecting it and directing us to the container. I should pick up the signal once we get close."

"We'll just have to walk until you pick up the signal," Allen replied, sounding less sullen now that they were on the job.

Ell smiled. *He speaks.* But the words echoed only in her thoughts.

Thirty minutes later, they rounded the corner of a three-tall stack of shipping containers and spotted a small cluster of containers set against the back fence of the staging area.

Ell nodded toward the cluster of shipping containers. "I've got the signal."

She led the way to one container sitting alone. She nodded and stuffed her cell phone into the pocket of her sweat-soaked blazer.

"That's the one," she said.

"Notice the fence to the container's right," Allen said. "A padlocked gate's been added."

Allen pulled out his cell phone, snapped a photo of the container and gate, and then spoke into his tactical watch.

"Overwatch, this is Team Two. We have located the shipping container. We are status two."

Status two was code for being positioned and ready to continue their mission once Overwatch gave the word.

Jessica's response was immediate and clear over Ell's earbuds. "Roger, Team Two. Satellite images show you are alone in the container yard. When you enter the shipping container, we'll lose communications. You are status three. Next contact is due in five minutes, or I call out the cavalry."

Status three gave Allen and Ell clearance to move forward with their mission.

"Status three confirmed. Five minutes, roger," Allen replied.

Allen took position at one corner of the shipping container to scan the open space between their container while Ell inspected the container's door locking mechanism. A shiny, new padlock secured the doors.

Ell waved Allen over, and he pulled a package of paper matches from his pocket. He tore off three matches, then rolled them between his fingers until they formed a single thread of a soft claylike substance about the length of his little finger. He wrapped the string of putty around the padlock's hasp and poked a primer the size of a toothpick into the putty. Then, he twisted the end of the primer stick and backed up two steps as the putty flared and cut cleanly through the padlock's hasp. The lock dropped open, hanging limply on the door's handle.

"I like your toys," Ell whispered.

"We get all the good ones," Allen replied with a rare smile. "I never leave home without my handy matchbook."

Allen lifted the steel door's locking lever and rotated it to the right, pulling open the righthand door. He waved Ell inside and followed, pulling the door closed behind them. They each donned a powerful headlamp that illuminated the container's interior with a soft white light.

"Empty," Ell said, scanning the container's walls. "It's been cleaned, probably disinfected. The wooden floor looks brand new."

"They worked fast," Allen added. "I expected it to be empty, but it looks like it's never been used."

Ell moved to the far-right back corner and pointed at the floor. "This is where they kept the latrine bucket. There should be stains all over this area."

Allen joined her, touching fresh splinters at the bottom of the container's steel wall. "They gutted it and replaced the floor wood."

They stood silently for a few minutes, casting their headlamps around the container's dark interior. It was Allen who finally broke the silence.

"Something feels off. How big are these things?"

"Forty feet long, eight feet wide, eight-and-a-half feet tall."

"That's what I thought," Allen said. "Do you have the laser measure Jess gave you?"

Ell pulled a pack of cigarettes from her pocket, tore off the plastic wrapper and foil top, and handed it to him. Allen wedged the bottom of the pack against the container' back wall and squeezed both sides of the cigarette pack. A tiny, red dot appeared on the unopened left door of the container. He glanced at his tactical watch and punched a button on its side to sync the watch's microcomputer with the laser ruler. A green light blinked once, and the numbers three and eight illuminated on the face of his watch. He showed it to Ell, clicked off the laser ruler, and tossed it back to her.

"That's what bugged me. The inside of this container measures two feet short."

Ell pumped a fist. "A secret compartment, concealed behind the back wall."

They each took a side of the back wall and ran their fingers and headlamp beams over every inch. It wasn't long before Ell located a tiny button shaped like a standard metal bolt in the bottom right corner of the wall. She called Allen over.

"It's positioned directly behind where the latrine bucket was. They knew no one would want to look here for anything out of sorts."

"Stinking clever," Allen replied.

Ell made a show of gasping. "A joke from the stony, silent operator? Well, I never."

Allen smiled sheepishly, then pushed the bolt's head to the left. The bottom of the container wall slid up an inch. They both grabbed the edge of the sliding panel and pulled it up to waist-high, where it locked into place. Their headlamps revealed an empty hidden compartment.

"If anything was in here, it's gone now," Allen said.

"No doubt," Ell said, not taking her eyes off the compartment floor. "But this is one area they should have cleaned more thoroughly. Look at this."

She squatted and ran a finger along the compartment floor near the edge where the sliding door closed to meet the floor. Her finger came up coated with a sticky, brown substance. She sniffed the residue on her finger and held it out for Allen to inspect.

"Raw heroin is my bet," she said. "I saw it once during a bust back in Washington."

"I wouldn't bet against you on that," Allen said.

Allen leaned deeper into the secret compartment, then said, "Eureka." He leaned back, holding a small piece of brown paper. "I found it jammed into the corner of the opposite side of the hidden compartment. It has the word 'Comtel' printed on it. Other words were destroyed when the label was torn from the original packaging."

Ell raised an eyebrow. "Comtel makes cutting-edge technology. This confirms the rumors of stolen tech. A hidden compartment this size can store a lot of raw heroin and tech."

Allen nodded. "I'll snap pictures for our report. Then, you scrape up as much of the heroin residue as possible and bag it."

Allen took the Comtel label and slid it into a small plastic bag. Ell retrieved a thumbnail full of the brown paste from the floor and placed it in another evidence bag just as the shipping container's heavy metal door clanged shut. She jumped to her feet and heard the unmistakable sound of the door's heavy steel locking lever slamming into place.

"We're trapped. Someone knows we're here."

The container shifted as four metal-on-metal clanks sounded from the top corners.

"They're connecting the container to a crane," Allen said. "I'm thinking we've been made."

"I have no desire to take another long trip in this container," Ell said, pulling her Beretta from its holster at her back.

"Not to worry," Allen replied.

Allen pulled off his belt and stretched it between his hands. A split appeared down the inside of the belt's leather lining. He reached into the opening and coaxed out a long, thin string of putty.

"Another one of your never-leave-home-without-it things?" Ell asked.

Allen smiled. "You bet."

The container lifted into the air and swung wildly to the right. Ell staggered. Allen stepped back, braced himself against the container wall, and returned his belt around his waist. He wadded the string and rubbed it briskly between his palms. They staggered again as the container spun ninety degrees to the right and the door end tilted upward.

"Whatever you've got dreamed up needs to happen soon," Ell said. "This container is on the move."

"Not to worry," Allen replied, crouching next to the steel wall of the container. He stretched the string between the thumb and index fingers of both hands and spread them wide. The clay string stretched to a fine line like the modeling clay Ell had played with as a young girl. Allen pressed the clay against the metal side of the shipping container near the floor, then shaped it into a three-foot circle. He retrieved another toothpick-sized primer, inserted it into the putty string, and twisted the tiny primer's end.

"Close your eyes," he said.

Ell stepped back and complied. The putty flared, and the entire circle ignited almost at once. Allen jumped forward as soon as the flare subsided and kicked at the metal circle cut from the container's wall. It fell away and clattered to the ground. Ell never thought muggy air could smell so good.

"After you," Allen said, waving a hand toward the hole in the container wall.

"Gladly," Ell replied.

She holstered her pistol, swung her legs through the hole, and dropped to the ground. Then, she drew her pistol and checked for the opposition. Allen followed behind her, absorbing the eight-foot drop and drawing his pistol as he landed. Then, with no one in view, they sprinted away just as a bullet pinged off a nearby container's steel wall.

Ell dropped and peered around the container's corner she hid behind. The long arm of a massive crane hung above the shipping container they'd been in. The container now swung gently from side to side beneath from the crane's long arm and steel cables. Allen touched her shoulder and pointed to a security camera not far off.

"They've got those everywhere. Let's holster our weapons and sprint for it. If anyone sees us, we can say we were ambushed by someone raiding the container yard and ran for our lives."

"That's the best plan we have," Ell said, replacing her pistol in its holster.

Ell scanned the area again and saw three figures standing at the far side of the container yard near the main gate. A woman and two men watched as the container she and Allen had been in swung out of the yard and toward another staging area next to a ship being loaded. One of the men held a long-barreled rifle and lowered it to his side.

"You see those three people? The one with the rifle put that shot over here. The woman with them appears to be in charge," Ell said as she watched the woman shove the barrel of the man's rifle downward and yell at the man in what sounded like Chinese, maybe Mandarin.

"We need to move," Allen said. "Thankfully, we got out of the shipping container when we did."

"I'm thanking you and your magic belt."

They trotted away as Ell heard Allen speak into his tactical watch's microphone. "We found drugs and evidence of tech, but we've been compromised. So, we're on the run. Expedite exfil."

The response was immediate. "Your ride is outside the port authority main gate. Gray Peugeot sedan."

Running in a crouch, Allen led the way through the tall stacks of containers toward the gate leading from the container yard. No more shots were fired as they moved, so they slowed to a walk as they neared the guards at the port facility's entry gate. The Peugeot arrived as they stepped through the gate.

As a resident FBI agent sped through the winding streets of Istanbul, Ell caught her breath and turned to Allen. "Do all your missions go like that?"

Allen stared at the passing buildings as their driver laid down a complex route of turns through back streets and thoroughfares to avoid being followed.

"Pretty much," he replied. "They are seldom dull."

After a long pause, he said, "You did all right back there."

This was the most action Ell had seen since her time in Iraq, and she had done all right. She smiled at the thought—and liked it.

CHAPTER 13

Sam and Leah paused on the street in the Old Shanghai section of the city, across from the building housing the offices of New Asian Imports and Exports. The chill air smelled of impending rain and car exhaust. The humidity hung thickly in the air, casting a sheen on the ancient street's cobblestones.

"Elegant architecture," Sam said as they took in the two-story building's brick façade with its elaborate wooden trim carved in intricate designs depicting China's history. "Too bad we don't have time to appreciate it."

The building's broad, polarized windows reflected the gold, orange, and green sculpted architecture of the stores and shops across the street. A steady stream of customers flowed in and out of a first-floor restaurant with doors adjacent to the import-export company's entrance.

"Convenient. Work on the second floor and eat on the first," Leah said. "I wonder if the food's any good."

"Having a location in Old Shanghai is a real measure of a business's status," Sam said. "Space here rents for exorbitant rates, although I bet Lee Chao owns the building. Either way, that restaurant must be a money-maker to survive the cost of being in a location like this."

"A demonstration of his position and power," Leah added. "He's compensating for his lack of full-blooded status in Chinese culture. That's good to know about the man."

"It might be or simply be a good investment. The man's worth hundreds of millions," Sam replied.

Sam tugged at the bottom of his pinstriped gray suit jacket, smoothing it over his starched, white business shirt. Leah straightened his red-striped necktie.

"Poor Consuelo," she muttered. "She'll have to dress you herself to get things right."

He reached to the small of his back, ensuring his Sig Sauer .40 caliber pistol sat snugly in its holster. "I figure I'm dressed just right," he said.

"Showtime," Sam continued. "You look great, by the way. Business-like, yet . . ."

Leah made a show of smoothing her trim, charcoal gray pantsuit and white blouse with wide frills at the neckline. Her long, red-bronze hair hung loosely in a wavy cascade over her shoulders. It was a look contrived to come across as both professional and to put any man she met off-guard.

"We work with what we have," she said.

Her .9mm Beretta sat in a thigh holster tucked beneath the hem of her knee-length skirt.

Sam led the way to the double-glass doors with the words "New Asian Imports and Exports, Inc." engraved across the top in Chinese characters and English script. Once inside, they discovered thickly carpeted stairs leading to another set of doors. The walls were cloaked in dark mahogany paneling. Leah took lead as they mounted the stairs.

A trim woman dressed in a form-fitting qipao dress in brilliant turquoise with a peacock design embroidered across the breast met them at the top of the stairs. Bowing deeply with eyes riveted on Sam, her ebony hair was pinned up in a complex pattern of waves and curls, with a thick braid across her hairline like a tiara. Gold pins and small fans held the complicated coiffeur in place.

"Ms. Arthur. Mr. Feldman," the receptionist said in clipped British English. "Welcome to New Asian Imports and Exports. Master Lee looks forward to meeting with you."

"Thank you," Leah said. "As the senior United States representative for agricultural exports, I hope for a mutually productive visit."

The receptionist diverted her gaze from Sam to Leah. In China, a woman leading such a team was a rare occurrence.

"Would you care for a refreshment?"

Sam started to reply, but Leah raised a hand to cut off his words. "We are on a tight schedule. I would appreciate meeting with Company President Lee Chao as soon as possible."

The woman bowed again. "Of course. Please follow me."

The receptionist led them to an imposing set of polished teak doors at least ten feet tall and four feet across. Both doors swung open silently to reveal an expansive office littered with mixed Chinese and French heritage antiques. Expensive-looking art covered dark paneled walls, each piece illuminated by recessed lights. A massive crystal chandelier hung in the center of the room's arched ceiling. The place looked like a museum, obviously staged to impress visitors.

Lee Chao sat behind an antique mahogany desk and stood as they approached. Sam was surprised by his short stature, slightly protruding belly, and narrow shoulders. His hair was cut short, and his expensive white shirt lay open-collared. From all Sam had read about the man, he anticipated someone more physically substantial.

The receptionist stopped several paces in front of his desk and bowed deeply. "Master Lee, may I present the United States Trade Mission representatives."

Lee Chao stepped around his desk to greet the duo, his eyes lingering on Leah's trim form. He bowed only slightly, as befitted a person of high status, then held out a hand. Leah hesitated only a second before grasping Lee's hand in as soft a grip as she could manage. She then nodded in Sam's direction.

"My assistant, Marty Feldman."

Sam bowed at the waist. Lee Chao made no effort to shake his hand or return the bow. Instead, he gestured toward a leather loveseat and pair of matching chairs to one side of the office.

"Please join me where we can be more comfortable."

Leah followed him to the loveseat, modestly holding her knee-length skirt as she lowered herself onto its deep cushions. She crossed her feet at the ankles, her posture perfectly erect. Sam dropped into one of the wingback chairs, as did Lee.

"Now, what can I do for you?" Lee Chao asked, folding his hands in his lap as his dark eyes searched Leah's face.

"We represent an agricultural cooperative that supplies China with everything from rice to lumber," Leah replied. "Previously, we have relied on various shippers to deliver our goods. Like so many things with the supply chain following the pandemic, the cost of transporting those goods has risen beyond expectations. We want to consolidate our shipping partnership, perhaps with your company, and gain significant economies of scale. My question is whether your company would be interested in such a venture."

Sam said a silent prayer of thanks for Leah's keen memory and ability to draw upon the research she'd done about Lee's company and the shipping industry.

"If we are to work together, please call me Chao, Miss Arthur," Lee Chao said.

"Rebecca," Leah replied.

"You honor me, Rebecca." Chao cocked his head to one side, his glance speculative. "If I understand your proposal, I believe we can come to common ground and reach such an agreement. I have been studying the potential of partnering with your cooperative for some time. I solely own this company, so I can expedite such an agreement if it is mutually beneficial."

"Your encouraging words are appreciated," Leah replied, giving Lee Chao one of her brightest smiles. "Your company ranks as the second-largest shipping firm in China and fifth in the world."

Lee Chao bowed his head slightly in her direction. "You honor me again with your knowledge of my organization."

Leah returned his gesture. "Should we choose to do business with you, our venture would place your company at the top of the Chinese list and in the top three largest shipping firms in the world," Leah said.

"I cannot deny the potential excites me," Lee Chao replied.

"I do have one concern before we agree. Marty will frame it for you since he is an expert in such matters."

Lee Chao shifted his gaze to Sam, who withdrew a single folded piece of paper from his suit jacket pocket. He handed the paper to Lee Chao, who unfolded it and scanned its contents.

"You appear well-informed about my business, indeed," Lee said as he refolded the paper and dropped it beside his chair.

"It is our business to know such things," Sam replied. "While your fleet of ships is extensive and plies the waters of all the major oceans and inland seas, we are concerned those numbers may not be sufficient to support our cooperative's needs."

As Lee Chao framed his words, Sam noticed a slight crinkle forming at the edge of the man's lips, as though he were holding back something. "I can access any additional vessels through my organization's subsidiary firms and others who owe me allegiance. I assure you, my company will be up to the task, should we reach an agreement."

Leah cleared her throat softly to draw Lee's attention. "It is not our intention to offend you, Chao. We must confirm your ability to commit sufficient resources to meet our needs."

"I am aware of the volume of business your cooperative carries around the globe," Lee Chao replied. "I can assure you we are well positioned to support your shipments. I am prepared to commit to that in writing if you like."

"In due time," Leah said, then softly clapped her hands and stood. "I believe we have the information we need. I will relay your information to the other leaders of our trade mission. I am sure you will hear from us shortly."

Lee Chao bowed more deeply than before. "I am glad we have reached an agreement in principle. I look forward to hearing from you again," he said, glancing again from her head to her toes in a deliberate assessment. "Perhaps I could interest you in joining me for dinner this evening once you have concluded your business for the day."

Leah smiled. Sam noticed the light of her usually bright smile did not reach her eyes. Instead, she bowed her head ever so slightly, almost dismissively.

"Unfortunately, we are returning to the United States this evening. There are timber issues in Washington State that need our attention."

"Perhaps another time," Lee Chao said.

He snapped his fingers, and the receptionist appeared at the doorway to his office. Lee Chao walked between the duo as they headed for the office's exit. He stopped at the office's wide double doors and turned to Sam.

"I have the feeling we have met before."

Sam gave Lee Chao a deliberately quizzical look. "I am certain our paths have not crossed previously."

Lee Chao shook his head. "I must be mistaken." He bowed deeply, first to Sam and then Leah. "Until we meet again . . ."

Leah bowed only slightly, as before. "Until then."

After they left, Sam and Leah strolled through Old Shanghai's rapidly darkening, cobbled streets. As they did, Sam kept an eye on their back trail, finally breaking the silence as he spoke into his tactical watch.

"This is Team One. We are status one and ready for exfil. No one's sniffing our trail at this point."

"This is Overwatch. Roger, team one," Jessica replied. "Your exfil is now at the private airstrip, gassed and ready. Time for takeoff is twenty minutes plus or minus, allowing for traffic. Your ground transportation is approaching your position now."

A nondescript black sedan pulled up beside them with the logo of the hotel where the actual US Trade Mission met. Sam opened the back right-side door, and Leah slid into the car. Sam walked around the car to the front passenger door, using the moment to scan their surroundings one last time before he climbed in and motioned for the resident CIA agent to drive on.

Sam faced Leah. "Marty Feldman? As in the comedian? Really?"

Leah gave Sam an impish smile. "You were only listed as Mr. M. Feldman in our cover story, and I loved Marty Feldman. He could make his eyes bug out at the right time, just like you do sometimes. Haven't you seen the movie *Young Frankenstein*?"

"Yes, I have," Sam replied, keeping his eyes on the street ahead. "But my eyes don't bug out nearly that much."

They both laughed. Even the CIA driver smiled.

"But seriously, what's your impression of the CEO of one of the world's largest shipping companies?" Sam asked.

"The man's a pig." Leah's words came out like ice. "Did you see how he sized me up? Totally sexist."

"Understood. What other impressions did you gather?" Sam asked.

Leah smiled. "The most important one is that Lee Chao has access to any number of container ships to smuggle people and things, some of which may not be directly linked to his company. So, he's well-positioned to carry out any illegal operation and remain shielded from discovery."

Sam felt his cell phone vibrate and glanced at the text that appeared.

"Jessica's traced ownership of the shipping container through a series of shell companies back to Lee. I guess he's not as shielded as he thought."

Sam toggled the phone's screen and moved to a second text. "Allen and Ell found evidence of a hidden storage compartment in the back wall of the shipping container Ell traveled in, including evidence of raw heroin and some sort of technology."

"We can definitely add smuggling to the human trafficking charges against Lee," Leah said.

"You bet. I believe our time with Mr. Lee Chao and his compatriots is just beginning," Sam replied.

CHAPTER 14

From her room in a dank, out-of-the-way hotel in Istanbul, Fan punched her father's number into her satellite phone. Andy and Devon stood at a respectful distance. She felt the muscles of her lower abdomen tighten involuntarily as her father answered on the first ring.

"Report," he said in a voice that was at once soft, stern, and demanding.

"We located the container at the port, Master Lee," she said. "Two people were inside the container when we arrived."

"And?" her father prompted.

"It appears they located the concealed storage area. We came upon them unexpectedly and attempted to capture them, but they escaped. They used a cutting device to cut a hole in the container's steel wall. I have not seen anything like it."

"That suggests we face a sophisticated opponent. Where are those two people now? Did you follow them?" Lee Chao's voice climbed in pitch as he spoke the words.

"We lost them," she replied.

Fan imagined the frustration and anger on her father's face in the silence that followed.

"Did you recover anything from the situation that might help us find those people and who they work for?" he asked after a long pause.

"We did," she replied, knowing what she was about to say might mean the difference between life and death for her and her companions—adopted daughter or not. "We recovered security footage showing their faces. We sent the footage to our technology office for facial recognition."

Her father sighed, a signal Fan recognized as his wrath diminished. After twenty-five years of living with her adopted father, she knew his shifts in moods well.

"Good. Once you have their identities, I expect you to track them down and eliminate them and anyone working with them before they become a further nuisance."

"It will be done, Father," Fan started to say, but the line was already dead.

———————

Lee Chao summoned his diminutive administrative assistant. "What have you discovered about our two visitors?"

"They appear to be who they say they are. Their background checks and credentials appear legitimate."

She said the words, but her tone left Lee Chao wondering.

"What's bothering you?" he asked.

"Their credentials appear to be almost too clean," she replied. "It's as if they both led model lives without dark marks or family connections. The man had a telling bulge in the center of his back, as though he was carrying a weapon. I believe his suit was carefully tailored to hide it."

"They were more than they appeared to be, then," Lee Chao said.

"I believe so."

He considered his next move. Like any good chess player or business strategist, he prided himself on remaining one step ahead of his opponents.

"Call our agents in the United States and have them do a deep dive into Ms. Arthur and her assistant. Call in favors where you need to. Lean on those American agents we've paid so much money to this past year."

"And if they are not who they said they were?" she replied.

Lee Chao steepled his hands on the top of his desk. "Then we will deal with them as we deal with others who get in our way."

"It will be done," his assistant replied before quietly leaving.

CHAPTER 15

Alex climbed from his Countryman Mini Cooper near the entrance for the headquarters, B Company, 2nd Ranger Battalion on Fort Lewis at Joint Base Lewis-McChord. The trip back from Turkey proved long, and he had only managed a few hours of sleep. At 5:30 Monday morning, he looked forward to a cup of his first sergeant's thick, dark coffee before the day began and he joined his unit for its morning fitness training.

Alex locked the Mini and made his way to the front door, grateful that as the unit commander, he warranted a reserved parking space near the door. But unfortunately, he only made it partway through the front door before Lieutenant Colonel Parks, his battalion commander, pulled open the door and waved him inside.

"Welcome back, Alex," the tall, Mexican American ranger said.

As usual, the man's battle dress uniform was creased and sharp—an example of how a ranger should look in garrison. The man's appearance made Alex acutely conscious he had not given his own beige, green, and black uniform even a light pressing before heading for the office. However, the wide smile on his boss' face meant something was up.

Colonel Parks gestured toward Alex's office, which was adjacent to the building's entrance. "After you," he said.

Alex swallowed hard and led the way into the small office, furnished with its Vietnam-era gunmetal gray desk; creaky, gray desk chair; and two gray chairs with cracked vinyl seats.

"Don't bother taking a seat," Colonel Parks said. "You're not staying."

With his chest forward, Alex came to rigid attention and braced for bad news. Had his trip to Turkey been reported back to the colonel? He had technically been on leave and used his own gear, so that should not be the problem.

"At ease, Captain. Relax." The colonel cupped a hand to his mouth. "Sam, can you please come in here?"

Colonel Parks lifted a hand. "Alex, I believe you know Major Sam Anthem. He was one of the operators who came to your aid on the container ship in Turkey."

Major Sam Anthem looked fit and stood taller than Alex. The man's close-cropped dark hair looked familiar in a way Alex couldn't place.

"Hello, Cousin," he said, approaching Alex with a smile and outstretched hand.

"Come again?"

"I'm your cousin. Your father was my father's brother. We haven't seen each other since you survived the human traffickers when you were little—until Turkey, that is—but I remember you. You look a lot like my younger brother."

Alex took Sam's hand, then did an abbreviated version of the man-hug/back slap. Alex felt a warm sensation infuse him. This was a cousin he'd forgotten he had.

Not knowing what to say, Alex turned back to the colonel.

"The family resemblance is striking, I must say," said the colonel. "But getting back to the matter at hand, you can't possibly think I don't know how you've spent your time off. You're not in trouble, Captain. We're all proud of your efforts to fight human trafficking, and it appears others have taken notice."

So, the old man knew about his time in Turkey and his other personal missions. Alex let out a long sigh. It felt good to get that off his chest. Major Anthem stepped forward and extended a hand. Alex hesitated, then gripped his hand.

"Major Anthem explained how he encountered you this past weekend at a port in Turkey. I found his story informative. You did a credible superhero imitation, took on a gang of human traffickers, and helped save many potential victims."

Alex dropped his eyes, uncertain of what to say, then lifted his eyes to meet his cousin's gaze. "That was you with the team at the port?"

Sam nodded. "And before you made your escape, we hit you with a nanotag pellet, a chemical allowing us to track you when you left."

Alex sighed. "You must have access to some impressive tools."

"You have no idea," Sam replied. "I cannot tell you more than that now, but we were impressed with your actions in Turkey. We want to introduce you to our unit and gauge your interest in working with us."

Sam handed Alex a small piece of paper.

"This note provides you with an address on North Fort Lewis where our unit is located. I would like you to be there early tomorrow so that I can tell you more."

Alex glanced over to his battalion commander for help.

"He is making it sound like a request, Alex. It's not. The Special Operations Command has cut orders for this. You are to report there in the morning, as the major suggests. Spend the time between now and then bringing your company's executive officer up to speed."

"But my command . . . " Alex protested. "I worked years to qualify for a ranger command."

The colonel stepped around the desk and clamped two massive hands on Alex's shoulders. "I know just a little bit about what Major Anthem does for a living, and I can tell you, it is impressive. You need to give this thing a chance. You have always said you became a ranger to make a difference. I think this may be an amazing opportunity to do just that. Your executive officer will fill in for you while you're gone. Your company will be in good hands under his guidance."

"Rangers led the way, sir," Alex said, calling on his unit's unique slogan.

Alex said the words, but in his heart, he felt dubious.

"Make us proud, Captain," the colonel said as he turned to leave the office.

"Then I'll see you in the morning," Sam said, following the colonel out.

The office felt quiet and empty after they left. It felt as if he was losing all he had worked for over the past seven years. Alex moved around the desk and dropped onto the stiff cushions of his uncomfortable desk chair. It creaked under his weight as he leaned back and said a short prayer for God to brace him for what came next.

CHAPTER 16

Pulling up to the Home Team's headquarters building at Joint Base Lewis-McChord the next day, Alex was not impressed. The building appeared old and rundown, with rusted gray metal siding and a faded gray roof. It covered a space the size of several football fields. The steel front doors appeared typical of any of the warehouses in the area.

Another car pulled up next to his, and his cousin stepped out to greet him. Soon, another car pulled up. A man who could be Sam's brother stepped out and joined them.

"Allen Farrell," the man said as he shook Alex's hand. "I remember you from Turkey."

"You both were part of the group who helped the woman and the human trafficking victims, right?" Alex asked.

Sam and Allen both nodded. "Follow me."

Alex followed Sam and Allen through a card reader and retinal scan as they entered the building. This special operations world was smaller than he thought. Sam pointed out the automated metal detectors and facial recognition technology built into the doors as they stepped inside.

"If we don't know you, the building will lock you out. If you get inside and we don't know who you are, the building will lock you in. These doors will take a .50 caliber hit and not show the wear."

As they went deeper inside, Sam waved a hand to include the whole building.

"The exterior walls are two feet of steel-reinforced cinder block infused with a Kevlar-plexiglass foam. The place can take a strike from a small missile and not flinch."

Alex noticed a suite of offices to the right of the entryway. Immediately adjacent to that area was the massive training space, complete with the latest in circuit training, free-weight equipment, and a mat area he estimated at least three-thousand-feet square. On the far side of the building was a bank of six doors Sam identified as locker rooms and barracks for visitors—and for times when the team needed a place to rest between missions without time for a trip home. Finally, to his left and halfway down the length of the building, Sam saw a wall bisecting the building and reaching up to the rafters.

From where he stood, Alex noticed two doors. The one on the extreme left of the wall had a sign that read, "Confidence Course." The other door was positioned on the extreme right side with a sign indicating it led to a sniper simulator and firing range.

"The confidence course is pretty high-tech and challenging," Sam said. "We can configure it for just about any climate or condition you'd encounter anywhere in the world: temp, humidity, air quality, rain, and so on. And we have some of the most demanding obstacles you've ever seen. It's my favorite space in the building."

"Sounds fun," Alex said.

When Alex had been ordered to leave his command to meet these people, he hated the idea. Now, seeing some of the resources they possessed, he found his respect for them growing.

Alex followed Sam and Allen into the conference room. The image of an older man with a craggy face and ruffled hair illuminated the center of three monitors at the room's far end. Two female operators sat on the table's far side. A third woman sat with them—the one from the container ship. He felt an unusual sensation down low in his gut as their eyes met. Those same, crystal clear, fearless eyes; the confident expression; the freshly scrubbed face full of determination framed by light brown hair that seemed more like a halo around her face than anything natural.

Alex sucked in a quick breath, calming his heart and his breathing as he made his way over to where she sat. *What is happening to me? I don't know the woman at all. I have no time in my life for this, even if she turned out to be the most amazing woman on earth. God, please grant me calm,* he thought as he dropped into a chair across the table.

Alex extended his hand as she stood from her chair to meet him. "Captain Alex Anthem. I was impressed by your actions in Turkey."

A wide smile lit up her face, her cheeks colored with the lightest shade of pink. Cleaned up as she was, Alex had to admit she was very attractive. Although she wore little makeup and did not don fancy hair, he noticed a brightness, honesty, and eagerness in her expression that he had not seen in a long time.

He found himself reconsidering his earlier thoughts. *If I had time for anyone in my life, this might well be her. The thought came instantly to his mind, and he found himself thinking yet another prayer. God, weren't You listening to my earlier prayer? I don't have time . . .*

Ell took his hand firmly in hers. "You're the baton man in the ragged tactical gear who came to my rescue."

Alex felt his face warm. "Guess so. That tactical outfit was all I could come up with on short notice."

"Alex is a U.S. Army Ranger," the man on the screen announced. "He's also the commander of one of the local ranger companies."

"I'm impressed," Ell replied, her eyes clear and dancing.

"I'd advise you to wait before being too impressed. I can mess things up with the best of them," Alex replied.

Ell laughed as she dropped back into her chair. "We'll have to see about that."

Alex moved back around the table and into a chair next to Allen. Sam seated himself at the head of the table.

"For your benefit, Captain Anthem," the man on the screen said, "I am Paul Samuelson, director of the State Department's Extreme Operations Group. The existence of the EOG is highly classified, so your security nondisclosure agreements are in effect regarding this discussion."

Alex nodded. "Of course, sir."

"You already know Trooper Ell Evander from your time in Turkey. She is with us on special assignment from the Washington State Patrol. And of course, you know Sam. Also with you in the room are Jessica Falcone, Leah McCarthy. I understand you've already met Allen Farrell. Together, they constitute the Home Team."

"I've heard rumors about a group like this. You all ran cartel interventions in Mexico a little while ago. Converted several cartels from growing and selling drugs to general agriculture?" Alex asked.

Paul nodded. "True. It's our Drugs to Ag program, which continues today. We recently relocated the Home Team to JBLM to expand its focus on the Pacific Rim, as well as the western U.S., Mexico, and Central America. Other teams are operating out of our Florida headquarters, covering other U.S. and world regions. You have been invited to meet with the Home Team to recruit operators for a second Home Team."

Alex held up his hands. "And which one of you tagged me back on the boat?"

Leah gave Alex a mischievous smile and wave. "Guilty. The nano-sized pellet that melts on contact and seeps through your clothes and onto your skin. Don't worry. It has a short half-life and no side effects."

"Should have known, but I am happy where I am with the rangers. I'm not looking for a new home," Alex said.

Paul nodded. "I understand. Just the same, I would like you to stay with us during the recruitment testing period on the off chance we stimulate some interest. That is what the U.S. Army Chief of Staff agreed to."

Alex sighed and nodded. "I am here on orders. I'll stick it out until you release me."

"Fair enough," Paul replied. "Now that the rest of you have returned from your travels and Alex has joined us, let's get to the business at hand."

Jessica picked up a small tablet computer. She tapped in a command, and a photo of Lee Chao appeared on the monitor to the right of the director's image. Dressed in a tailored three-piece suit, holding a bottle of champagne and smiling, Chao stood before a cargo ship, gleaming with new paint and brass fittings. Bold, gold lettering on the ship's bow identified it as the *Chao*.

"Humble guy," Leah said. "Named the ship after himself."

Jessica gave Leah a knowing look. "Let's not underestimate the man. Lee Chao is the president and owner of New Asian Imports and Exports, Incorporated. The champagne bottle was for christening his company's newest, largest cargo ship. It is the thirtieth ship in the company's fleet. Lee Chao is well-established in shipping, ground transportation, and commerce across the Atlantic; Pacific; North, South, and Central Americas; Europe; and Asia. His ships and subsidiary companies pick up and deliver merchandise on every major continent except Africa."

Jessica tapped the tablet's keys, and a spreadsheet appeared on the monitor to the left of the director's image.

"As you can see from these figures, Lee Chao currently holds the number five position in global commerce and the number two position in China—calculated in terms of influence, resources, annual tonnage shipped, and gross revenue.

"Recently, Lee Chao has made significant investments in acquiring at least a dozen large land-based transportation and logistics companies. At least twenty shell companies can be traced to him through U.S., Russian, Asian, Mexican, and Central American firms. His holdings in South America appear less clear, even though the money trail leads there. His financial interests may be linked to the drug cartels we've encountered in Central and South America. If we can confirm that, we could use our contacts there to gain some leverage over him.

"Lee Chao is the sole owner of the conglomerate. My calculation of his financial worth suggests he may be one of the ten richest people in China, if not the world. Moreover, his methods suggest plans to increase his standing in China and the world market, perhaps to solidify his position within China's government."

Paul appeared to key in command on the laptop on his end. Then, several paragraphs of narrative and a picture of an elderly Chinese man and a Caucasian woman with a fair complexion replaced his image.

"The NSA's files identify Lee Chao as half-Chinese and half-British," Paul said. "Our intelligence labels him as a man determined to prove himself to the Chinese government despite his mixed heritage. In addition, he appears to have a significant chip on his shoulder because of the discrimination he experienced in China during his childhood.

"Lee Chao did his graduate work at Oxford at his mother's request, which appears to have frustrated the man even more. He finished at the top of his class but returned to China the day after graduation and hasn't been seen near England since. Once back in China, he leveraged his father's connections to land an entry-level job at a small Chinese export agency. But for a man of his aspirations, that job proved to be a ticket to nowhere."

"His actions suggest he's out to prove himself to those in power in China and to eliminate doubts about his loyalties," Allen commented.

"I believe that's a good assumption," Paul said. "Without a doubt, he's a driven man."

Paul's image reappeared onscreen as he sipped from a stained white ceramic coffee mug. "It was shortly after he signed onto his first job when Lee Chao secured a post as a junior analyst with a more significant Chinese import/export firm. Through long hours and a willingness to do whatever it took to capture the notice of his employer, he rose rapidly through the company's ranks. After five years, Lee Chao's immediate supervisor died in an automobile crash. Through intimidation or persuasion, Lee Chao was promoted to the deceased manager's position as the number three executive in the company.

"Then the company's owner died in a similar auto crash, and the second in line for the top job disappeared without a trace. That left Lee Chao to pick up the reins. Anyone with second thoughts about Lee's ascension in the company either changed their minds, resigned from their positions, or disappeared. Two years after becoming president, Lee Chao purged the company's board of directors and became president and CEO. One year after that, he dissolved the board and assumed ownership through a majority acquisition of the company's stock."

"A real charmer," Leah said. "From our brief meeting with the man, I felt dirty being near him."

"How did he go about purging the board of directors?" Allen asked. "I thought most corporate board members have voting rights, even in China."

Jessica adjusted the right monitor to bring up an image of a burned-out building. "Everyone on the board died in a gas explosion that leveled their meeting building. Lee Chao called in sick at the last moment, so he missed the gathering and the explosion. The change in ownership occurred immediately afterward, reportedly backed by highly placed members of the Chinese hierarchy. That was also when the company was rebranded to its current name."

"The man is ruthless," Sam said in a flat tone.

"I'm afraid so," Paul said. "The only reason Lee Chao's remained off our watch list is because of his important friends in governments worldwide, including ours. No one has dared touch him for fear of the consequences."

"From what we found in the secret compartment in the shipping container in Turkey, a big piece of Lee Chao's business may include illicit drugs, technology piracy, and human trafficking," Allen said.

"The man's a pig," Leah added, "and he gets more piglike every time I hear about him."

"You're putting him on our radar now, I assume?" Sam asked.

Paul nodded. "Front and center. The Home Team is uniquely positioned to deal with this situation, and I have the Secretary of State's support to do so. Jessica has identified links between Lee Chao's subsidiary companies and the technology industry and relationships with high-level technology company executives worldwide. In addition, Jessica will gather evidence of Lee Chao's involvement with drug smuggling and technology piracy. The connection between Lee Chao and human trafficking, while obvious, will be handled by ICE, the FBI, and local authorities like the Washington State Patrol."

Ell came out of her chair, hands knotted in fists. "You're not going after him for the human trafficking? You have the evidence to convict Lee Chao now."

"I understand your passion for that part of Lee's business," Paul said, "but the lines have been drawn. Homeland Security, ICE, and the FBI have claimed exclusive jurisdiction over the human trafficking end of Lee's operations. We have all agreed to share information, but beyond that, our hands are tied."

Ell sank back into her chair, her face crimson with anger. "You can't be serious. Homeland and the FBI are so under-resourced they barely make a dent in the human trafficking situation. The only reason I followed the Boston lead and ended up in that shipping container was because no one else would or could move on it. No one had the bandwidth. With the resources you have at your disposal, something can finally be done to stem the tide of people sold into slavery."

"Ellen . . ." Paul started, but Ell stormed up to the screen to face his image directly.

"You need to do this, Director. You don't understand what those people go through. Some of them die in those shipping containers. The ones kept local are either worked to death on farms, hotels, or the streets as prostitutes. I lived with those people in that shipping container."

Alex felt his hand rise, almost involuntarily. "I'm with Ell on this one, sir. You may or may not know I was taken when I was ten, shipped to Thailand, and conscripted into the country's illegal Thai boxing network. During my four years there, I saw kids die for many reasons, never to be reunited with their families. I would have died there myself if it weren't for my faith and help from some kind strangers. This Lee needs to be taken down."

Paul frowned. "I hear both of you and sympathize, but the matter is settled. I have passed along the information Home Team gathered in Turkey and Shanghai to the Homeland Security Investigations office in Seattle. They will be looking into Lee Chao's involvement in human trafficking. So, from our end, the matter is closed."

Alex and Ell exchanged glances and what felt like a common commitment. Even if Alex returned to his unit, perhaps he and Ell could team up on their own time.

"I need you to develop a plan to get into the bowels of Lee's operations. Be ready to brief me in two days," Paul said, his on-screen expression focused on Sam.

"But, Director . . . " Ell started, but the screen had gone blank.

Alex watched as Ell faced Sam. "You have to do something about Lee Chao's human trafficking. You can't just hand it off to a bunch of desk jockeys in the other alphabet agencies. I know the people at the FBI, HSI, and state patrol. They're good people; but politics, red tape, and resource constraints tie their hands. With Lee Chao's drug-running and tech-pirating operation working in tandem with his human trafficking business, the opportunity to act is too obvious. Hurt one, and you hurt the others—and maybe bring him down."

"We all hear you, Ell, but we have our orders," Sam said.

"Then I'll do it alone," Ell said, her voice a deep growl as she turned and headed for the conference room door.

Alex felt an unexpected pang of jealousy as he watched Allen follow Ell toward the door and lay a calming hand on Ell's shoulder. "You're part of the Home Team now. You accepted the three-month assignment. As part of our team, you follow orders like the rest of us. Paul's only two steps from the president's office and reports directly to the secretary of state. If he says we must stay in our lane, we need to trust him."

Alex saw the anger drain from Ell's face. Finally, she brushed away Allen's hand and dropped into the nearest chair. "Mark my words. HSI won't do anything to ruffle the nation's political leadership's feathers, nor will the FBI. If Lee Chao is connected to those same people, nothing will happen."

Alex felt his heart grow cold as he realized he agreed with Ell's position. Maybe the Home Team was not the place for him.

Sam glanced at his watch. "It's 4 p.m. Let's meet back here in the morning and put a plan together. It's been a long couple of days, and we have candidates to test tomorrow."

"But—" Ell started, but Leah rose quietly from her chair and placed her hands on Ell's shoulders, cutting off whatever she might have said.

"I get it, sister," Alex heard Leah whisper. "As much as I still think you're a skunk for cheating at sniper school, I get what you're saying.

But trust me when I say we do a lot of good as the Home Team working our lane. We are successful because of the backing from the director and the secretary of state. So, we need to listen to their direction."

"But it's so horrible," Ell said, her voice hardly more than a whisper.

"I get it," Leah repeated. "You live in Bellevue, right? That's a two-hour drive this time of day, only to turn around and head back again tomorrow. So, what say you come home with me tonight? I've got a guest bed you can use while working with us. It'll save you a trip."

Ell nodded a mumbled thanks. Leah fished in her jeans pocket for a key, which she handed Ell, along with a scrap of paper.

"Here's the address and the key. Make yourself at home. I have a couple of errands to run, so I'll meet you there in a little while."

Alex had hoped to invite Ell for coffee or dinner to exchange their concerns and experiences with human trafficking. Instead, he felt his heart drop as he watched Ell follow Leah out of the room, tossing him a half-hearted wave as she left. *Was it just the human trafficking angle that had him wanting to spend time with her?*

Jessica turned to Sam, Allen, and Alex. "She took that hard."

"I get it, and I've been inside that system," Alex replied. "I was one of the lucky ones who got away."

"She's pretty passionate about human trafficking, and it's easy to understand why," Allen said. "The FBI has more than eighty-nine thousand open missing persons cases right now and insufficient agents to make a dent in the problem. Her niece is one of them, and Ell's had no news in five years."

"We have our orders," Sam replied.

"Whether or not she's going to follow those orders is the big question," Jessica said.

Allen found himself wondering the same thing about himself and whether he should reach out to Ell about their shared interest in shutting down Lee's human trafficking business. Then again, with the effect she had on him each time they were near, should he risk even that?

CHAPTER 17

Fan and her two minders sat in a dark blue SUV outside the visitor's gate to Joint Base Lewis-McChord. Facial recognition identified the woman at the port in Turkey as Ellen Maria Evander, a member of the Washington State Patrol. A call to the Patrol's Human Resource Management Department revealed Trooper Evander was temporarily reassigned to an organization located on Joint Base Lewis-McChord. With no better plan, Fan hoped their quarry would exit the base through the gate, and they could follow her.

The SUV's side window was fogged from two hours of waiting and watching. To kill time, Fan pulled out her laptop and accessed an application on the dark web. She'd used the app many times in the past to track known foreign agents. Now she hoped Trooper Evander and her home address—and perhaps her email address and phone number—might be listed. As she keyed in her query, the trooper appeared.

Fan glanced up from the laptop and saw a dark green Mazda Miata exiting the base. Behind the wheel was the person for whom they looked.

"Sometimes better to be lucky than skilled," Andy said from the back seat. "Heard that on an American movie."

"Follow her," Fan said, closing her laptop.

Devon backed the rented SUV out of the visitor parking spot and followed the Miata onto the southbound lane of Interstate 5.

"You have a plan in mind?" he asked.

"We plan to see where she's going. Then, if we're lucky, she'll lead us to the man she was with at the port, and we can take them both. If not, we observe her movements until we can fulfill my father's orders."

"Right," Devon said, stepping on the accelerator to ensure he didn't lose their target in traffic.

———————*////////*———————

When Leah opened the door to her apartment, a small two-bedroom ten miles south of the JBLM, Ell waited for her. Feet spread wide, hands on hips, Ell's red-gold highlights in her freshly washed hair glinted in the apartment's bright entry light.

"Why don't they see it? We need to shut Lee's operation down!" Ell said, the frustration carrying clearly in her pained expression.

Leah met Ell's flashing green eyes, turned, and locked the front door's security bolt. She shrugged off her thin jacket and gently shoved Ell toward the apartment's small living room.

"We've been through all that," Leah said.

"But this is an opportunity to strike a blow against human trafficking," Ell continued as she headed for a small side chair beside the living room's wide patio doors. "If we could shut Lee Chao down simultaneously as we cut off his drug and tech trade, we could make a real difference."

Leah pulled her pistol and holster from the small of her back and placed them on a small table to one side of the living area's entrance. She continued across the room to an overstuffed beige couch and plopped onto its thick cushions. Behind her, through large sliding glass patio doors, grew a long line of evergreen trees, backed by a view of the distant, snow-capped Olympic Mountains.

"The director always does the right thing," Leah said. "He said he's handed off the human trafficking information about Lee. We have to trust he knows what he's doing. I've worked with the man for more than five years."

"I don't trust anyone but myself," Ell replied. "I've been down that road too many times. When my niece disappeared, I tried everyone— the police, FBI, state patrol, and sheriff's office. But unfortunately, no one had the time or resources to help. Now, it's been five years and nothing."

Ell stood and marched across the room, slapping her holster and weapon on the table next to Leah's.

"I know the people at ICE, the FBI, state patrol, and Homeland Security Investigations. None of them will act until they've farmed the information they have to an endless number of analysts and assessed the political and economic implications of what they might do. Then, when they develop an action plan, they will have to have an additional round of endless reviews and approvals. In the meantime, another thirteen thousand people around the world will be taken each day. Who knows how many people could be saved during the time it takes the bureaucracy to grind its way to a decision?"

"I get it," Leah said after a protracted silence. "You want to make a difference. We all do. That's why I joined the Home Team when they recruited me out of the air force. How long have you been working human trafficking with the state patrol?"

"The past five years. I was recruited right out of the state patrol's academy. The patrol's Investigations Support Division is part of a human trafficking joint task force with Homeland Security Investigations and the FBI. I look young, and they needed people like me for sting operations. I've been involved in a half-dozen operations during that time. We took a lot of people off the streets and made several solid arrests. I'd hoped my involvement might lead to information about my niece."

"Any luck with that?" Leah asked.

"None at all, but I won't give up. I work her case whenever I have the time."

"Like when you ran off to Boston without backup?"

Ell let out a soft laugh, though without any humor in the tone. "Unfortunately, true."

Leah smiled as Ell continued. "For all I know, Maria is dead by now. Human trafficking victims last about four years before they die or escape, and she's been gone for five. But even as I say that, I know I'll never stop looking. She's my sister's only child."

"I hope you find her," Leah said. "When you do, I'd like to be there. Now, how about some food? I know a place that delivers."

"Thanks, but I think I'll pass. My stomach is churning. What I really need is a long walk, maybe a jog. Any ideas about where to go?"

Leah climbed to her feet. "I could go with you."

"Thanks, but if you don't mind, I need some alone time to process all this."

Leah nodded. "I get it. I've been there before. The Billy Frank Jr. Wildlife Refuge is not far from here. A nice four-mile trail with a boardwalk that winds through a beautiful delta leading out to Puget Sound. If the tide's in, you'll see seals, bald eagles, and seagulls."

"Sounds perfect," Ell replied, pulling her keys from her pocket. "I'll go now and see you when I see you."

"Be careful," Leah called out as Ell left.

CHAPTER 18

As the sun fell toward the horizon, Ell pulled her car into the parking lot at the wildlife refuge. Since the day was almost over, she wasn't surprised to find only one other vehicle in the parking lot. She glanced at the tactical watch the Home Team had issued her—an interesting device with the ability to send and receive emails, texts, and images on its small screen, as well as a built-in microphone for cell and radio service.

"Five p.m.," she muttered. "I've got a good couple hours before sunset and they close the park."

She climbed out of the car, instinctively feeling for the pistol holstered at her back.

"Oh man," she said when she found nothing there.

She'd left it at Leah's apartment on the little side table. Feeling naked without it, she considered abandoning her plans for a long walk. Then, looking around her and considering she was practically alone at the refuge, she thought better of it. The place was almost abandoned. What could happen?

Ell found a map on a wooden bulletin board displayed at the trailhead. It showed an easy half-mile improved trail through trees and open fields. This would, in turn, lead to a gravel road that linked the wooded path to the refuge's signature boardwalk. She memorized the map, noting how the trail and boardwalk spanned a good portion of the delta leading out to an estuary and the waters of Puget Sound. She hugged her light sweatshirt tighter around her body and set off.

The trail through the trees left her awed by its beauty. Tall maples and oaks, turned to gold by the early fall weather, flanked the gravel trail. Halfway along, two towering dairy barns, now maintenance sheds for the refuge's staff, stood side by side in memory of a time when the refuge was a working farm. Hundreds of brilliant white snow geese covered the broad wetlands beyond the barns like a churning snowfall as they paused in their winter migration south.

Ell emerged from the forest trail a few minutes later and onto a gravel road connecting the trail to the boardwalk. She noticed the tide was in. The area beyond that reached Puget Sound shimmered silver under the late afternoon sun. From where she paused, she could see the mile-long boardwalk—a winding wooden walkway suspended above the delta's waters on thick wooden posts. Viewing towers, like the watch towers for old west forts, stood at the entry, another quarter mile down the way, and, finally, at the end.

Hills covered with tall evergreen trees and occasional golden maples flanked the delta on the west. Mount Rainier dominated the view to the east—its brilliance illuminated by the lowering sun. The Olympic Mountains, with their line of tall snow-capped peaks, were visible to the north.

As Ell headed for the boardwalk, she heard harbor seals bark somewhere in the distance. A pair of bald eagles floated lazily above the waters beyond the boardwalk ahead of her, seeking an evening on the rising tide. So staggering was the view—and so distracted was Ell by the scenery—that she did not notice the man who stepped into her path until she had made a few strides along the way.

The stranger emerged from the boardwalk's first of three viewing towers as she approached it. She stopped when he appeared, then glanced back to the path she had just covered when she heard the crunch of shoes on the gravel behind her. A man and a woman approached from that direction, still ten yards back.

Ell faced the small, slender man standing spread-legged on the boardwalk ahead of him. She recognized him at once as the one with the rifle at the container yard in Turkey. The two behind her—an attractive Asian woman and a more muscular man—looked like the other two from the same encounter.

Ell raised her tactical watch and hit the transmit button on the side. "This is Ell. I'm at the wildlife refuge, and I need backup. The three from the Turkish port are here."

She wished she had her tactical headset to hear if anyone got her message. She calculated her odds and decided a one-on-one confrontation with the man before her was better odds than with the two behind her. If she could only get past him and put some distance between her and the others.

The man was of medium height, maybe 170 pounds, and had long, black bangs that hung over dark eyes. Wearing black jeans and a t-shirt, he looked gawky and angular. From her years of training from her father, her mother, the military, and the state patrol, Ell knew better than to take a person's outward appearance for granted.

She turned sideways to better assess the situation approaching from behind. The woman appeared athletic, even if strikingly beautiful in a form-fitting black jumpsuit. Her ready-position stance suggested a person with advanced hand-to-hand combat training. The man beside her looked more like a bodybuilder but stood lightly on the balls of his small feet—another person not to be taken for granted. The idea that muscular people couldn't be agile, quick, and deadly was a myth she'd refuted during her years of full-contact competition as a youth.

Ell lifted her hands to her sides, alternate palms facing the strangers. "I'm just here to see the sights. I am not looking for trouble."

Her eyes darted side-to-side as she spoke, running through her options. She had never used her martial arts skills for more than competing in tournaments until the fight with her captors in Turkey, but it looked as if she might have to now.

That thought brought back a mantra from her father, a private sector intelligence operator and master of numerous fighting disciplines. In her mind, she heard his words, "Attack. Attack. Always attack. Defense never won a fight."

Ell cleared her mind, slowed, and deepened her breathing as trained. The female attacker frowned, then said in perfect British English. "You stuck your nose where it didn't belong. You wandered where you shouldn't have gone."

Ell didn't take the bait by replying. The woman hoped Ell would drop her guard, engage in conversation, and let her defenses down. It was an old ploy she'd long ago been trained to ignore. Instead, Ell attacked.

Ell sprinted toward the man blocking her path to the boardwalk. Chin tucked to take a blow, Ell balled both fists and slammed them into the man's sternum and chin at full tilt. She felt a satisfying crunch as the man's sternum cracked and a puff of air left his lungs.

As the man staggered back, he lashed out with a roundhouse punch at her cheek. She ducked, and the man's fist passed harmlessly over her head. Then, after a deep breath, she exhaled sharply as she pushed left, swinging her left fist down in an arc and smashing into the man's thigh—leaning into him with her left shoulder and hip in a classic Tai Chi shoulder stroke. The contact between them felt electric.

Ell pulled away as the man staggered, then spun and prepared to snap his foot out in a roundhouse kick to her head. But instead of backing away, Ell moved inside the kick and spun a full circle on her fight foot with her right elbow high. As she came around, her elbow smashed into the side of the man's head, causing his eyes to bulge widely in pain and surprise.

As the man staggered, Ell ducked around him, then sprinted the few steps needed to gain the narrow choke point she had identified twenty yards ahead on the boardwalk, where the wooden path narrowed between thick pine railings.

Seeing what had happened to their compatriot, the male and female attackers closed on Ell with more cautious steps. The woman reached out a hand to steady the man Ell had knocked out of the way as they passed him, a gesture Ell found odd, considering the circumstances. A moment later, all three advanced on Ell. This time, she knew she was up against long odds. A sinking feeling settled into the pit of her stomach as she calculated those odds and came up feeling short.

The two men stepped forward. The slender man she'd attacked flipped open a curve-bladed knife, reversing the grip, so the blade pointed to the ground. She recognized the classic Kali position and recalled her mother's old joke: "What do you do if you meet a Kali master with one knife? Run. What do you do if you meet a Kali master with two knives? Pray."

As much as her parents had always been deeply religious, Ell was not sure she even knew how to pray. But even so, she whispered, "If

You're there, God, I could sure use a hand about now. Maybe even the guy with the baton?"

She felt an odd stirring following her words, the hairs on her arms rising as a calm chill began spreading throughout her body. As she searched around for a plan to take them on and live through the experience, she noticed the woman's eyes. They sized Ell up but also showed respect. Ell figured fighting at least offered better odds than surrender.

"Attack, attack, attack." The words echoed through her mind again as she flexed her knees and lowered her weight onto the balls of her feet, gripping the boardwalk's rough surface with her toes through the soles of her light running shoes.

The two men stepped forward. The man with the knife lined up to Ell's left, with the more muscular attacker extending his open palms forward. Ell registered the stance in a moment: Brazilian Jiu Jitsu. The man was a grappler. Not her strong suit. If they got her to the ground, she was done.

Ell prepared herself using Tai Chi compression breathing called Iron Shirt, forcing the air in through her nose and deep into her abdomen, holding the breath, then out through her mouth. In the first breath, her feet seemed to sink into the wood of the boardwalk, grounding her, stabilizing her stance. As she exhaled, she felt a surge of energy climb up her back and stream down her chest, her body feeling like it was made of steel. Movements around her seemed to slow, her vision clearing.

But in that last second, as she prepared to attack, a woman in torn jeans, a loose University of Washington sweatshirt, and wild, windblown red materialized behind her assailants.

As Ell watched in shock, the mystery woman came in low on silent feet, moving fast with powerful strides, hands extended, fingers spread wide. A thick ponytail of wild, curly brown hair flared out behind her head as she grabbed the woman in black from behind and jerked her backward, off balance, causing the woman to shriek.

Surprised by their boss's yell, the two men facing Ell paused and glanced back. Ell saw her opportunity and lunged forward, grabbing the knife hand of the slender attacker. She clamped down hard on the man's wrist with both hands and twisted hard right with her whole body behind the move, forcing the knife's point up and away from her. As the knife hit its highest point, Ell jerked the man's arm downward, twisting his hand so the blade pointed downward and driving the blade deep into his thigh.

The confrontation took only seconds. Then, with the first man down, clutching the knife dug into his leg, Ell spun to face her second attacker in time to feel a crushing blow smash into her right shoulder. She moved with the pain, bending forward at the waist, and lashed out with a powerful back kick that connected with her muscular attacker's groin, staggering him back a step.

Ell straightened, turned, and settled into her fighting position once more, her breathing deep, her shoulder throbbing. Remembering another element of her parent's training, Ell isolated the pain in her mind, put it into an imaginary box, and moved the box outside her body. A mind game for sure, but one that would hold the shock of the injury at bay for a time.

"I am toying with you, little one," the man said, crouching with his hands low and ready to grab her legs again. "You should just give up. I will make your death painless and quick."

Almost before Ell registered it, the man rushed in low. With no time to consider, Ell's response was pure instinct. As he dove for her legs, she stepped back, leaped straight into the air, tucking her knees to her chest, then crashing down and extending her legs as she crashed her left foot onto the top of the man's head—smashing him onto the boardwalk's wooden decking where the man remained, motionless and moaning.

Ell glanced back at the man with the knife in his leg and saw him wrap a belt around his upper thigh to stifle blood flow. On shaky legs, Ell backed away from the two downed men and took up a wobbly fighting position. She knew she didn't have much fight left and hoped she could endure. This differed from competition sparing without a doubt, where her life wasn't on the line. She relaxed as she looked up to see the closing acts of the mystery woman and the woman in black engaged in a violent dance of flying feet and fists.

They exchanged kick after kick, some landing with sickening thuds, some missing entirely as they danced around each other. In between kicks, fists flew forward toward a face, only to be blocked and countered by another punch or elbow aimed at a vulnerable part of the body. Finally, as the woman in black snapped a front kick toward the mystery woman's chest, she ducked right, brought both hands up, grabbed the woman in black's leg in both hands. Bracing herself, she drove the woman in black back to the boardwalk's rail. Then, still holding the woman's leg high, she lifted and shoved the woman over the boardwalk's railing.

The mystery woman paused a moment to examine the lady in black lying prone in the water below the boardwalk, then stepped over to where Ell was. "Let's get out of here before these clowns recover. When the park closes, I don't want to be here to explain what happened to these jokers."

"What you did back there . . . Thank you."

"Don't thank me. You did more than your share," the woman replied. "That hapkido move you put on the man with the knife was priceless. And the Tai Chi jump-stomp thing you did to knock the big one out was stellar."

Ell mumbled, "Only been in one fight like that before, and this was way more challenging. Just the same, thanks."

"We were both fortunate I took them by surprise. That may have helped a bit with those two guys, but you can bet God was looking out for both of us tonight. So, if you want to thank anyone, thank Him."

Ell laughed. "That's the second time I've heard that in the past week."

"Sounds like a trend. Maybe Someone's trying to tell you something."

They made it to the parking lot as three cars screeched to a halt on the pavement. The entire Home Team, including Alex, dashed from their respective vehicles with guns drawn.

"Looks like you've got friends," the woman said.

Ell turned to reply, but the woman was already gone. Ell spun about, trying to catch sight of her defender, but she was nowhere to be seen.

Alex was the first to reach her, taking her gently by the shoulders and looking deep into her eyes. "You okay?"

Ell shuddered under his gaze, feeling the hairs tingle on her arms and a chill streak down her spine. She sucked in a deep breath, then reached up and gently removed his hands from her shoulders.

"I'm fine, but you did miss the chance to rescue me a second time."

Alex felt his face redden as he stepped back. He forced out a quiet laugh. "Glad to hear it."

Leah approached, cast a quizzical glance between the two, then held up Ell's holstered Glock in her left hand. "You forgot something."

Ell took her gun and stuffed it at the small of her back.

"Message received," she said. "Did you all see the woman who was here a second ago?"

"Now you're just imagining things," Leah started, but Jessica laid a hand on her teammate's arm, cutting Leah off.

"I saw her," Jessica replied. "And I'd know her anywhere. Mary Magdalen O'Dell. Goes by Maggie. Last I heard, she was freelancing for the Drug Enforcement Administration. We worked a mission together before I joined the Extreme Operations Group years ago."

Sam whistled. "Maggie O'Dell? Now there's a legend and a name I haven't heard in a while. She worked with my team on a Special Forces mission to bring down the drug trade supporting a terrorist group in Afghanistan. That was years before I joined the Home Team. No one can outthink or outfight an opponent like that woman."

"Legend or not, she saved my bacon," Ell said. "I was ambushed by the same three people Allen and I ran into at the port in Turkey. Real pros, but nothing compared to Maggie. I wouldn't mind thanking her again when I see her."

"You won't find her unless she wants you to," Jessica said. "She's a ghost. That's how she's lasted so long in this business."

"Just the same—"

"It's time we get out of here," Sam interrupted. "The park will close any minute, and I expect we do not want to be here when the ranger finds those people you ran into."

"Maggie said the same thing," Ell said. "They were the same people Allen and I encountered in Turkey. At least those people are out of the game for now."

Sam chuckled. "Never be sure of that. Since this has happened so close to your escape from the shipping container and us finding the evidence we did, I am betting they work for Lee Chao. If that is true, we have not seen the last of them."

Ell nodded as they all turned toward the parking lot and their cars, noticing how Alex had moved to the back of the crowd. *Now, what is wrong with him. Just because it wasn't him who saved her this time . . . Then again, the look she had seen in his eyes when he saw she was all right . . .* She had to admit knowing someone worried about her like that did not feel totally bad.

———————

Fan surfaced in the water, her head aching from where it hit a pilon on the way down from the boardwalk. She felt a persistent bump against her side that focused her eyes. She spun toward the source and found the wide eyes of a harbor seal floating in the water a few feet away. The seal blinked at her once, barked softly, rolled over backward, and dove beneath the water's surface.

"Thank you, little one," Fan said.

If the seal hadn't brought her around, she might have drowned. Maybe that's what it meant when someone said to count one's blessings. Dripping wet and shivering from the cold and her injuries, Fan crawled painfully up the boardwalk's thick support post and back over the railing. She moved over to where Andy lay with his back against the railing—eyes closed and a tourniquet wrapped around his upper thigh. She nudged him with her toe.

He blinked his eyes and groaned. "We got our butts kicked by that girl," he said. "Who knew such a little thing could fight like that?"

Fan frowned. "You don't remember when I took you down the last time we sparred? Just because you're fighting a woman, you shouldn't underestimate . . ."

Andy raised a hand. "Don't worry. I won't make that mistake again."

Fan glared at them both. "I think you both were playing dead while I fought that female whirling devil who showed up from nowhere. Truth is, we were fairly beaten today, myself included. Tomorrow will be a different day. We'll track down the woman again, along with the man who was with her in Turkey. We now know they work out of the military base so that we won't fail next time. And once we've dealt with them, we'll find the woman who intervened today and deal with her. But for now, let's head to the hotel and regroup. If we fail to eliminate these threats as my father directed, the consequences for each of us will be harsh."

In her mind, Fan found herself admiring the two women she'd battled. Sure, she'd lost that battle, but what better way to improve oneself than face more skilled opponents and live to fight again?

CHAPTER 19

At nine that night, Ell pressed her thumb against the biometric lock at the Home Team's building on the Fort Lewis portion of JBLM. The lock clicked, and she tugged open the heavy steel door. She expected to find the place empty. Instead, the lights above the weight training and mat areas glowed brightly. She heard a grunt and clank as someone lowered weights onto a metal stand in the strength training area.

She limped over to a red and blue checkerboard mat area and saw Allen finishing a rapid set of bench presses in the free weight area. He sat up as her footsteps echoed across the building's concrete floor in his direction.

"This is a surprise. You're limping. Is that from the altercation at the wildlife refuge," he asked, lowering the weight bar to rest on the stand above his chest.

Ell shrugged and let her small duffle bag slip from her shoulder. "I didn't think anyone else would be here."

Allen nodded. "I work out here often in the evenings--alone time to work out my muscles and sort through my thoughts."

Ell wasn't sure what to say. Allen had been cold as ice during their trip to Turkey.

"I'll let you get back to your workout and stay out of your way. I plan to use the mats," she said.

"I'm headed there now," Allen said as he stood and wiped sweaty hands on his thin, gray sweatpants. "I planned to work on Tae Kwon Do forms we call poomse."

Ell smiled. "TKD is one of my martial arts."

"Maybe we could work out together?"

His offer confused and pleased her simultaneously—the smile on his face was the first she'd seen since she'd met him. Ell chewed on the thought. She had looked forward to some time alone—to work out how she felt about her forced transfer to the Home Team, what that meant to her career with the state patrol, and the unfamiliar feelings she had been developing toward Alex. More than all that, she needed to think through the EOG director's noninterference stand toward human trafficking.

Allen cocked his head slightly to one side. "If you need time alone, I understand."

Maybe some company would be nice, she thought. *Maybe they could spar a bit.* Perhaps they could spar. There was nothing like a good sporting fight against a skilled opponent to take her mind off her troubles, unlike the fight for her life she'd had earlier in the day.

"But it might be nice to spar a little if you're up to it."

"You're on," Allen replied. "I've already stretched and warmed up, so just give me a sign when you're ready."

Ell moved to the mat area as Allen returned to the bench press. She wore comfortable gray sweatpants and a thin compression shirt under a light gray sweatshirt. It would do for a friendly session of sparring. She pulled her hair back into a stubby ponytail and fixed it into place with a black band, then spent ten minutes moving through an abbreviated stretching routine that dated back thousands of years to the earliest Chinese martial arts. She figured if her body was still not warm after fighting for her life at the wildlife refuge, it was not likely to get any better.

Allen approached as she finished her warmup, removing his shoes and socks before stepping onto the mat.

"Qui Gung. Your warmup?" he asked. "I recognized the exercises and the sequence. I do the same routine every day first thing in the morning. It's amazing how on days when I follow that routine, I never seem to pull a muscle or twist a joint. If I skip a day, I generally regret it."

"My experience as well," Ell said. "Although it's hard to do locked in a shipping container with forty people for three weeks."

"True," Alex replied. "That must have been a tough ride, but you did free many people who'd be in much worse circumstances today if you hadn't been there."

"Also true, I suppose, although it did get me suspended from the state patrol. I worked hard to get into the patrol, but freeing those captives felt good. Then again, I'm coming around to the thought that my actions may have been a bit naïve and short-sighted."

"Was it about your niece?" Allen asked.

When she responded with a quizzical look, he replied, "This is a small group. Word gets around. "Her being kidnapped must have motivated your actions to some extent, and there are worse things than that. Your actions may have been poorly thought out, but your intentions were righteous. You freeing those people was a God job from where I stand."

Ell felt the need to shift the direction of the conversation before he began preaching to her about God, faith, and all the other things her mother had jammed into her as a child. Then again, she had prayed before the attack at the wildlife refuge, and here she was, still standing. Maybe she would give the God thing some thought—later.

"How about you?" she asked. "Why are you here in the dark of the evening, working out alone?"

Allen gave her a lopsided grin as he considered her question. He lifted his hands and shrugged. "Girl problems."

"No," Ell replied, her tone sarcastic. "A handsome surfer dude like you?"

"I get that a lot," Allen replied. "Even though I come from the New England area and couldn't surf if my life depended on it."

"I was just kidding," Ell said.

Allen nodded, then sat on the exercise bench he'd used for the bench press.

"Actually, a few months back, I asked my girlfriend to marry me. She accepted."

"That's great news," Ell said.

"It was and still is, kind of. She works for the Drug Enforcement Administration and was selected for a doctoral program in Texas. The DEA is covering all the costs, including her full salary while she is at school. It is a real opportunity for her, and I am glad she got the chance, but we haven't seen each other in months. With the Home Team deploying so much lately, we hardly have the chance to talk."

"Has she called off the engagement?"

"Not yet," Allen replied, "but I don't see how it is going to work with us so far apart for so long. A doctorate in anything takes two years of classes, then time for the dissertation. That can add another year or more."

"How long have you known her?"

"High school sweethearts," Allen replied, his gaze dropping to his feet. "Most of our lives, I guess."

"Before the Home Team, you were what? In the military somewhere and then special operations?"

Allen nodded. "Air force officer, and three years in special operations."

Ell laughed softly, then squatted so they were at eye level. "You made it through high school, years of military service, and special operations assignments, and she stayed with you through all that. Now, you're worried about a couple of years apart for something as important as her schooling?"

Allen ran a hand through his sweaty long blond hair. "I guess when you say it like that . . ."

"That's why you were so stony during our trip to Turkey. You were pouting?"

"Men don't pout. We sulk," Allen replied, the corners of his mouth turning up involuntarily.

Ell laughed. "Just for that, I will be extra tough on you when we spar."

Allen chuckled. "Bold words for a rookie," he said, standing and shoving her playfully back on her heels before heading for the center of the mats. "She did say her second year in the program could be done remotely. The third year is for her dissertation. Maybe she can do that anywhere."

"So, you may only be apart for a year. I assume you can use your vacation time to visit when you're not deployed. So, why exactly are you pouting?" Ell snorted. "Kind of wimpy if you ask me. Let's get to it. The evening's wasting."

Allen grinned. "You're certainly cocky for someone who weighs forty pounds less than me, has half my reach, and has had exactly two fights in her lifetime. Although, from what I heard, you held your own. And before you mop the floor with little, old me, thanks for the talk. Maybe you're not just a rash, hotheaded cop after all."

"I'll show you who's a hothead," Ell replied, moving onto the mat and taking up her standard left-foot-forward fighting stance.

"Fine. Then let's get at it," Allen replied with a wide grin. "Afterward, maybe I'll lecture you about not confronting the feelings you and Alex have for each other."

Ell shook her head. "You are way off on that one."

Allen chuckled, again. "Like I said earlier, it's a small team and word gets around. We all know what's going on, even if you won't admit it."

Ell let out a loud laugh that she found she did not quite feel. "No way. Prepare to be thrashed by someone half your size."

CHAPTER 20

E ll arrived at the Home Team's headquarters the following morning at seven sharp. Pastor Carson jogged over to meet her at the front door as she entered the building, towering over her five-feet-five frame by nearly a foot. He stuck out a giant hand that engulfed hers when they shook.

"Welcome, Trooper Evander," he said. "Evander is Scottish, right? Means bow-warrior or strong person."

"You're well-informed, Pastor, but it's just Ell," she replied.

"Got it." He glanced at a large, black watch on his left wrist. "You do realize you're late."

"Late?" she asked. "It's only seven."

A smile split the big man's face. "I'm the unofficial chaplain for the Home Team. I'm here most days to support them, except Sundays when I preach at my church. It's God's way of keeping me in shape."

Ell groaned. "Another religious reference? Will you guys ever stop? I'm not here to be converted. I'm just here to do my time and then return to my real job."

The pastor's grin disappeared. "My reference to God was not intended to put undue pressure on you. I'm a pastor in my day job. It comes naturally. Today, I'm one of your proctors for a day of skills testing that started over an hour ago for everyone else."

Sam jogged up, sweat beading his forehead. It was difficult not to notice the man's good looks, trim physique, and dark eyes.

"Good morning," he said. "You're late."

Ell nodded. "So I've been told."

"Good. I hope you got some rest after all the excitement yesterday."

"I may have been here working out last night," Ell replied.

"Good for you," Sam said. He pointed to the wall halfway down the building. "On the other side of the wall is an obstacle course. Take a few minutes to change into your sweats and warm-ups, then head in through the door on the left. It's fully equipped with a mud crawl, high wall, downed trees, climbing nets, and a dozen other obstacles. I think you'll find it challenging and interesting."

Sam glanced at his watch. "Today's Monday. That means we've cranked up the heat and the humidity as you'd find in Central and South America. Should give you a run for your money. The other recruits for H.T. Two are in there now with Leah, so jump in when you're ready."

"Whoa," Ell replied. "I'm no recruit." She lifted a hand to fend off any reaction from Sam or the pastor. "I'm just here to fill the time until I can return to my real job."

"No problem," Sam replied. "Just the same, if you're going to work with us for even a few months, we need to know what you can do. You will be observed and evaluated throughout the day and on several tests, just like the candidates for the Home Team. Based on our observations, we'll learn how you can best support the team while you're with us."

"I won't ride a desk," Ell protested, hands on hips and glaring. "I'll take my suspension without pay before I do that."

Sam cocked his head as a grin lifted one corner of his mouth. "There's no need for the attitude, Ell. All I'm asking is you show us what you can do. Obstacle course first. It will reveal much about you as an operator and team player. There's no real start or finish when you get in there. Just jump in anywhere handy. Spend thirty or forty minutes running through it as fast as possible. After that, I want you to meet Jessica in the strength-training area. She'll run you through your paces there. Then, you'll hit the firing range, sniper simulator, and then the mats to close the assessment."

Without another word, both Sam and Pastor Carson headed for the office side of the building.

Ell spent less than five minutes stretching and warming up for the obstacle course. Then, feeling both frustrated and anxious about the day ahead, she jogged to the door leading into the obstacle course area. She opened it, and the heat and humidity slammed into her. She found Leah pausing for breath at the base of a twenty-foot net like the ones used to board ships.

Leah offered her a grim smile. "Want to partner through the course?"

Her red-bronze hair and black sweatsuit were soaked, and a thick braid hung to the small of her back, dripping like a wet rag.

"If I won't slow you down," Ell muttered, her voice dripping with cynicism.

"Not at all," Leah replied, not rising to Ell's tone. "I remember you being fit from our time at the sniper course. We can work as a team through some of the obstacles."

Ell recalled how Sam had said the course tested teamwork and physical prowess.

"Lead on," she said, this time avoiding the cynicism.

Leah stepped up to the rope ladder, which was thirty feet to its peak and the same distance wide. The gaps between the horizontal and vertical strands of thick rope were at least two feet across. As Leah took hold of the thing, the ladder shifted and moved with a life of its own. She tugged at the ladder and launched herself vertically, grabbing a rope rung three feet above shoulder level. Surprised by how she'd jumped, Ell hesitated.

"Come on, little sister. Time's a wasting!" Leah called.

Ell jumped, only managing the rung below where Leah hung, then paused as the rope ladder twisted and stretched below her. She wrestled her feet into place two rungs down, then struggled to where Leah waited. Ell never imagined this sort of thing could be so challenging. She'd seen people climb rope cargo nets like this in old war movies, and it always looked so easy.

As Ell came to Leah's level, Leah climbed like a spider up a wall. Ell attempted the same, discovering the more she fought the rope ladder, the more difficult it became to climb. However, as she relaxed into it, her progress improved until she finally reached the top. She found Leah there, straddling the wooden beam at the top and reaching a hand down to her.

"I can do it," Ell said, waving off the hand.

"Give it a try," Leah replied.

Ell did and found herself thwarted at every attempt. The rope seemed to move, shift, and buckle even more at the top.

"I should be able to do this," Ell said, stopping to hang from the rope.

Sweat ran down her face in tiny rivulets. The air felt more oppressive from high atop the obstacle.

"That's not the point," Leah said. "On our team, we help each other. We all do some things better than others. When one is on top, we raise the others up with us, figuratively and literally."

Frowning, Ell took the offered hand, and Leah pulled her up the last two rungs with a single pull.

"I still think I could have finished it myself," Ell said as she swung her leg across the top beam.

"Perhaps," Leah replied. "But as I said, that's not the point. Let's head down the other side. That part's easier. Just use your hands as you go down. Keep your feet free and away from the net. If your arms can carry your weight, it's faster that way. Knowing how to get off anything quickly can help with what we do for a living."

"You've encountered rope ladders in the real world?" Ell's voice came out cynical again.

Leah frowned as she swung her legs over the edge of the beam and started downwards. "You'd be surprised. All too often."

They landed together at the base of the obstacle. Leah slapped Ell on the shoulder. "Nice start! You'll make it, yet."

"Oh, I'll make it," Ell growled.

They sprinted to the next obstacle, Leah leading the way. This one consisted of four rows of two-feet metal stakes arranged eight feet apart down a thirty-by eighty-foot area that created four lanes. The stakes held up a thick blanket of sharp, barbed wire. All that hung over a pool of wet, dark mud. Halfway down the obstacle sat a low wall.

Leah picked up a rubber rifle from a pile near the entrance to the obstacle and tossed another one to Ell. The rifles weighed about the same as a standard M16 rifle and were equipped with slings.

"Last one to finish the mud crawl buys coffee," Leah said as she slung the dummy rifle across her back. "Don't mind the mud. We keep it at forty degrees—cold enough to be uncomfortable."

"You're on," Ell said, stepping back as loud booms and screeches filled the air. "What in the . . . "

Leah cupped her hands to her mouth and yelled. "Audio stress. Loud sounds can sap you just as much as physical challenges. It can cloud your thinking, increasing the effort to do even simple tasks. It's part of this obstacle."

Ell nodded. "Then let's do it."

"You go, girl," Leah replied, dropping to a prone position and crawling under the first strand of barbed wire.

Ell dropped and headed down the next lane over. The freezing mud soaked through her sweats, submerging her halfway up her sides. Her rubber rifle snagged on the barbed wire as she moved forward. She rolled to untangle the sling, soaking her back as well. Soon, she found herself shivering.

Need to keep moving, she thought. *Movement equals warmth.*

Ell rolled back onto her front and noticed Leah already a body length in the lead.

Leah glanced over her shoulder and gave a little shrug. She mouthed, "It happens," as she saw Ell wrestling with the rifle's sling. Then, "Keep moving!"

Ell gritted her teeth, struggling to keep her rubber rifle free of the barbed wire and forcing herself to ignore the cold. Finally, she flattened her body further, shifted her rifle to her right side to keep it away from the barbed wire, and started forward—low-crawling and finally making headway.

Halfway through the obstacle, Ell caught up with Leah but then ran the top of her head into the wall halfway up the course. Then, a little to her right, she saw a small gap in the barrier, maybe a foot-and-a-half wide.

Ell saw Leah pass her rubber rifle through the gap in the wall, then follow the rifle through. Ell duplicated the move and left that element of the obstacle course behind. From then on, it was a race between the two women—crawling, slithering, dragging their rifles, and working through the remaining twenty feet of thick, soupy, freezing mud.

As one, Leah and Ell cleared the final strand of barbed wire and jumped to their feet. The loud noise stopped immediately. When the sound ended, a loud chorus of cheers rose from the edge of the course. Ell turned to see Sam, Jessica, Allen, and Pastor Carson clapping.

Sam stepped up to the two women. "Now that was a race! An amazing effort by both of you. I clocked your time on the low crawl. A personal best for Leah, and Ell matched it."

Leah turned to face Ell. "Nice going."

Ell nodded, determined not to be taken in by the group's cheerful attitude. She wanted no bonds of friendship with these people. She was temporarily here. She would do the work and leave when her time was done.

Leah smiled, then clamped a hand on Ell's shoulder. "Great work, but don't get cocky. There are ten more obstacles to go."

"And then you're mine on the weights," Jessica added. "And that's all before lunch."

An hour later, Ell dragged herself to the facility's front doors, where several vending machines stood. Her sweats were soaked and dripped with mud. Her feet felt like lead, and her mouth was parched. She'd lost count along the way, but by her reckoning, she'd worked through at least a dozen obstacles, including ten fully clothed trips up and down a twenty-five-yard lap pool carrying a forty-pound pack. She'd waded through a thirty-foot-long, chest-deep mud pit with submerged posts and boulders. According to Leah, she'd survived the test, but as she stood at the vending machines to get a power drink, she remembered Jessica saying this was only the start of the day. The state patrol's academy had been brutal, but it was nothing like this.

Ell dropped onto one of the worn couches near the building's entrance. Jessica showed up a second later.

"Tired?"

Ell let out a long breath. "Honestly, yes."

Jessica stepped over to one of the vending machines and dispensed a bottle of an energy drink. "Chug this, and let's get going. First, I need you to change your sweats, and then I get to run you through your paces in the strength area. We keep a change of sweats in the woman's locker room. Go change, and I'll meet you at the pullup bar."

"Marvelous," Ell said. She chugged the drink, climbed to her feet, and tossed the bottle into a nearby recycling bin. "Can't wait."

For the next hour, Jessica ran Ell through a gauntlet of pullups, pushups, standard sit-ups, inclined sit-ups, deadlifts, bench presses, and a half dozen other strength tests. She'd expected each test to be a single effort but was surprised when they turned into a marathon.

"Every test is based on a four-set best average, gauging your endurance and maximum strength," Jessica explained when they started at the pullup bar. "You'll do four sets of as many pullups as possible in two minutes. You get a thirty-second rest between sets, and then you will knock out as many as possible for another two minutes. You repeat that for a total of four sets for each of the test exercises. When you're done, I'll compare your results against statistical averages for people your size, age, and weight. That will tell us how strong you are relative to the general population."

Four sets of pull-ups left her arms burning. Another four sets of pullups, and she'd barely chinned the bar. Standard sit-ups followed, and then pushups, inclined sit-ups, bench presses, squats without weights, and squats with weights. They finished with bicep curls and triceps extensions with fifteen-pound weights. At the end of the hour, Ell's muscles felt like gelatin, spasming and cramping with a life of their own. She struggled to keep her feet under her as Jessica walked her back to the entrance and handed her another energy drink. Ell dropped onto one of the couches and chugged the drink.

"I'm guessing you're pretty tired," Jessica said, examining the tablet computer where she'd recorded Ell's results.

"I haven't had a workout like that in, well, never," Ell replied. Her hands tremored slightly as she held the empty can.

"You ready for the next test?"

"Do I have a choice?"

"We all have choices," Jessica replied. "You can quit and cool your heels somewhere else during your suspension from the state patrol, but I understand you'd be giving up pay and benefits. If you want to continue, rest for a few minutes, then head for the firing range and sniper simulator. I think you'll like that one."

Ell held up a shaking hand. "If I can get my hands to stop shaking."

Jessica laughed softly, the look in the tall woman's eyes kind as they met Ell's.

"Just breathe in through the nose and out through the mouth. You have a tai chi and chi gung background. Use that training. It'll settle you in no time. Bring the air into your lower abdomen first and then your lungs for a count of seven. Hold it for five, then release your breath from your lungs and stomach for another count of seven. Pause for a count of five, rinse, and repeat. Try it."

Ell did. After a few breaths, her hands stopped shaking, and her breathing slowed.

"After a lifetime of training, you'd think I'd remember," Ell groaned.

"You still want to give up?"

"Not a chance!" Ell replied.

"Glad to hear it," Jessica said, glancing at the tablet computer. "The strength tests have you doing pretty good for someone your size, weight, and age."

"Pretty good?" Ell asked.

Jessica sat beside Ell and showed her the tablet's screen. "You've got to understand your test today is what we do during every training session. For example, Leah has much less body mass than you but is fifty percent stronger. That's not because you're any less of an athlete. She's just benefited from this training regimen for more than five years. What we've recorded for you suggests you're in excellent shape for a person of your age and body type and that you can be trained to do better."

"What about you? You seem more like the intellectual type than all muscles," Ell said.

Jessica tapped a few keys and handed her the tablet. "Take a look."

Ell scanned the screen. Sam and Allen's scores were off the charts—almost fifty percent above average for a person their age and size. She looked at Jessica's numbers and gasped. She tapped the screen with a finger.

"You did this? Your strength-to-body mass ratio is twenty-five percent greater than anyone else on the team."

"Why so surprised? I may be taller and carry myself differently than the rest, but there's no reason anyone can't develop themselves to the same level given the right training, knowledge, and tools. I'm not stronger than Sam, for example, when moving large objects. But compared to other people of my gender, size, weight, and age, I do well."

"Can you help me reach that level?"

Jessica nodded. "I can—if that's what you want. We can meet here at the end of each day, four days a week while you're with us and not on a mission. If you follow my instructions and do maybe a little more on your own, there's no reason why you can't make a lot of progress over the next three months."

"Progress?" Ell asked.

"You'll make a start in that period, but you will pay the price. You won't like how you feel for the first couple of weeks, and it takes more than a few months to reach your optimum strength level. Remember, we need flexibility and speed, as well as muscle mass. It's a more delicate and complicated mix than you'd think. Even so, you'll see a big difference in three months."

Ell stood and stuck out her hand. "I'll take you up on it—and thanks."

Jessica shook the offered hand. "It's a deal, but if you start to crumble on me at any point, the deal's off. It's as much a mental game as physical, and not everyone is up to it."

"I am," Ell said, feeling as if she were standing taller than she had a few minutes before.

"Glad to hear it," Jessica replied. "Frankly, with all the missions we've had lately, I can use the extra workouts, too."

Jessica lifted a hand toward the door marked "Firing Range and Sniper Simulator." "That's your last stop for the morning. As a trained sniper, I expect it to feel like a break for you. However, if you need them, there are power bars, fruit, jerky, and other snacks in the conference room. So, feel free to pick up something on the way."

Walking into the firing range and chewing on a piece of beef jerky was like walking into a high-tech paradise for Ell. She'd grown up with guns, learning their roles as tools to be respected and handled with care. A skilled, knowledgeable gun handler was a safe gun handler. It was another point her parents had hammered into her head from a young age.

Just beyond the range's entrance, Ell found a wall-mounted rack with pistols, submachine guns, and short-barreled rifles. Below the weapons rack were neat stacks of metal boxes holding an assortment of ammunition. A paper sign hung above the weapons: "You fire it, you clean it."

Ell chuckled. "How many times have I heard that one?"

A few feet beyond where she stood were eight firing stations with loading tables and a space for prone, sitting, and standing firing positions. Movable silhouette targets hung down the distance of what looked to be a sixty-foot range.

Another door on the opposite side of the room from the entry had "Sniper Simulator" stenciled on its glazed window. Ell felt her heart skip a beat. This would be fun.

Ell chose a .9mm Sig Sauer P365, noting it was the longer barreled XL version built for everyday carry. She quickly located two empty clips and the needed ammunition and went to one of the firing positions. This was her preferred handgun, although her bosses at the state patrol preferred the same caliber Beretta. It'd taken a lot of pleading for them to allow her to carry her Sig.

Ell donned a set of earmuffs and eye protection and moved to the first firing line. She took a forward shooting stance—left foot forward and right slightly back with her weight balanced on both feet. She snugged the Sig's checkered polymer grip into her right hand and racked a round into its chamber with her left, then cupped the butt of the pistol's grip in her left palm. As quickly as she could pull the trigger, she sent ten rounds into the target halfway down the range. The bullet holes formed a small cluster directly over the target's heart.

With her right thumb, Ell pressed the button on the pistol's grip and dropped the empty clip. She slapped the loaded clip into place with her left hand in a single, smooth motion. She rattled off another ten shots. All ten landed on the upper portion of the silhouette's right shoulder.

Behind her, Ell felt, more than heard, soft clapping. She ejected the second clip, removed her ear protection, and turned to find Sam standing there.

"Nice shooting," he said. He pulled a Sig Sauer P229 pistol from the holster at his hip, ejected the clip, and locked back the slide. After visually confirming no round in the pistol's chamber, he handed it to Ell. "Try this. It's the—"

Ell whistled. "It's the .40mm Sig. Never shot one, but always wanted to. Do you mind?"

Sam tossed her a loaded clip. She grabbed it with one hand.

"It rises a bit more with each shot than the .9mm, but once you get used to it, it's a smooth pull."

Ell shoved the clip into place, faced the target once more, and hefted the pistol. "It's heavier, for sure, and the weight's more forward in the barrel. But I like it."

Sam chuckled. "Go for it."

Ell pulled off a single shot, hitting the center of mass on the silhouette target. She grinned, pulled off the remaining nine bullets, sighed, and turned back to Sam, grinning.

"You weren't kidding. That is a nice pull," she said. "I love this weapon. The larger bullet must have additional stopping power."

Sam nodded. "I've never liked the thought of shooting another person, but if I must, I prefer to get the job done as quickly and humanely as possible. A .9mm is a good gun, but I was trained to fire at least three times to stop an adversary with the .9mm round. With the .40mm, you only need one. Stretches the useful life of a ten-round magazine, too."

Ell handed the pistol back. Sam slipped another loaded clip into the butt, racked a round into the chamber, and re-holstered the Sig.

"I can see why you like it," Ell said. "I was told I'd be tested here."

"Yep," he said. "I'm here to do that. And we just got the pistol firing part out of the way. From your state patrol and army file, I know you've trained on carbines like the M4A7 we use. After how you handled the pistols, I think you can probably handle a carbine just as well."

"I can," she replied, not bragging but simply stating a fact.

"I believe you." Sam made a note on the small tablet computer in his hand. "Then, let's move into the sniper simulator. I'll watch from the sidelines while you work through the sniper simulation."

Ell followed Sam into the sniper simulator room. It was set up with four firing stations facing what looked like a massive movie screen.

Two stations were equipped with an M21 Special manufactured by the Rock Island Arsenal. The rifle always reminded her of the gun her father carried when hunting deer. The M21 was an older model rifle, but these two looked as if they'd been updated and modified. The traditional wooden stock had been replaced by matt black polymer with a telescoping butt plate. However, the rifle's twenty-six-inch blued barrel and bolt action looked the same. Based on the army's national match grade M14 rifle, the M21 proved itself over and over through the years as one of the military's most reliable rifles.

The other two stations were fitted out with Remington M24 Model 700 sniper rifles. The M24 was another variation on the army's reliable M14, also with a twenty-seven-inch barrel but with a semi-automatic action. These two rifles had tan, green, and black camouflage composite stocks and twenty-round magazines.

The M24s were state-of-the-art. She'd spent a lot of time with that rifle at sniper school, although she'd fired the M21 as well. All four rifles had long scopes attached, with an unusual array of switches on the viewing end. She recognized the design of the scopes—the same scopes she'd snuck into the sniper school test and used to beat Leah in the final exam.

The sound of the simulation room's door banging closed behind her cut off what Ell was about to say about the scopes. Instead, she turned to find Leah removing a tactical vest and setting it beside the door.

"You ready to give this a try?" Leah asked.

Ell frowned and turned to Sam, who nodded. "You're going to be shooting with Leah."

Ell shrugged. "A rematch from sniper school?"

Leah picked up the M21 from the first firing position and held it to Ell to examine.

"You notice the scopes, right?"

Ell picked up the first rifle, an M21, and rubbed a finger down the scope's length.

"The same one made by my father's friend's company. It's the same design I used to beat you at sniper school."

Leah walked over to the second firing position. "Almost the same. Improved even more over the past five years. Line-of-sight lasers calculate the range to target. Peripheral lasers scan out to thirty-five degrees around the projected path of the bullet, assessing the movement of objects in the air as small as dust motes that indicate windspeed and the effects of heat on the bullet's trajectory. Calculations are carried out by a microcomputer in the scope, with a heads-up display for the shooter that recommends adjustments for windage, drop, and the effects of ambient temperatures. It's a great scope, even better than the one you used five years ago."

Leah flashed Ell a smile, her eyes bright with anticipation. "No unfair advantage today. You ready?"

"Always ready, always on target," Ell replied, quoting the motto of the sniper school she and Leah had attended so long ago.

"You take the first firing position with the M24. I'll take the one next to you. You'll hear the same sound from the rifle as if you'd really sent a round down range. The rifle will buck in your hands when a round goes down range. We'll be pulling off standard 7.62 rounds, although the simulated gunpowder has been upped to give the weapon more punch at a longer distance. The scope's been modified to record hits and misses to within a few inches and report them to

Sam's tablet computer. We'll be shooting at five hundred yards for the first ten shots and a thousand for the second ten rounds."

"When you're both ready to go, I'll key the simulation," Sam added. "The targets will appear in a heavily wooded area, as you'd find in Central America. You'll each have ten shots. The M24 is semi-automatic, so there's no need to reload. I'll move you to a thousand meters for the second ten rounds. I'll vary the windspeed throughout the test, although I'll keep it reasonable."

Leah snorted. "No hurricanes like last time?"

"I admit that was fun, but not today," Sam said. "We need to get a good idea of how Ell can handle a realistic situation under pressure. You'll both be firing from an elevated position. You'll have two-and-a-half minutes to identify your targets and pull off the first ten rounds. Another two-and-a-half minutes for the second ten rounds."

"How will I identify my targets?" Ell asked.

"Each tango will have a red X somewhere on its body. There will be innocent bystanders, so you'll want to confirm the mark before you shoot. You both ready?" Sam asked.

"Ready," Leah replied.

Ell had a flashback to the heated time she'd had with Leah after she'd won the competition at sniper school. As much as she thought she'd been smart at the time, what it had done to their relationship was not pretty. She felt her gut clench at the thought.

"Ell?" Sam repeated.

"Why not?" Ell said.

Sam frowned at Ell's response. "If you don't want—"

Ell waved off his next words. "I'm sorry. I'm ready."

"Take your firing position."

Ell tucked her right leg under her and sat atop it, her left leg bent at the knee and extended forward in a classic kneeling position. She hefted the M24 rifle, noting its average weight, and telescoped the rifle's stock to fit snugly at her shoulder. A detailed image of a wooded landscape appeared on the screen before her. Nestled in a small clearing was a cluster of houses and narrow streets. A half dozen buildings were small warehouses, as you'd find at a cartel compound. The other buildings looked like tiny adobe houses and cottages, some with thatched roofs. Through each setting, people milled, walked, and sat on benches.

"Leah will target the warehouses for the first ten shots. Ell, you take the houses to the right. After I move you to a thousand yards for the second ten rounds, you can target the entire scene. Remember to find the red marks on your tangos before firing. Ready, begin."

Ell scanned the scope's heads-up display and the initial assessment of the firing conditions in the upper left corner of the scope's field of view. Distance: five hundred meters. Windspeed: zero. Drop fifteen feet. Heat factor at 15 percent.

She scanned the houses. She heard the sharp smack of Leah's weapon firing as she did. Leah had already found her first target.

Ell forced her breathing and heart rate to slow and located a red X on the hip of a man dressed in a business suit near a house. The branches of a small tree obscured his head, but his body was in full view. She lined up her shot and pulled the trigger. The rifle bucked in her hands, precisely as she would expect the actual weapon to do. Her target dropped. A hit!

To her right, she heard two more shots from Leah's position. Leah had taken three shots to Ell's one. She needed to pick up the pace. She scanned the other targets around the houses and located a woman walking from one building to another with a red mark on her shoulder.

But when she was about to squeeze the trigger, she noticed a new number on the screen: lateral motion. It read two miles per hour, left to right, as the scope tracked her target's movement. Ell adjusted her lead to match the woman's stride and squeezed the trigger. Splinters of wood flew from the building as the simulated bullet struck a house as the woman passed behind it.

"Rats!" Ell whispered, but she was already scanning for another target.

She found the remaining eight targets in the village location and settled into a smooth rhythm. First, she identified the target, confirmed the scope's numbers, adjusted her line, and squeezed the trigger. She scored hits on all eight remaining targets, finishing her first ten-round session a full minute after Leah.

When they were done, Sam approached with his tablet computer. "Nice shooting," he said. "Leah scored ten for ten. Ell, you took down nine of your ten targets and finished within the two-and-a-half minutes. So, you'll both have the same amount of time for the open shooting at one thousand meters. Not bad shooting, Ell, but you'll have to do better before we can use you as a sniper in the field. We need you to fire with certainty when you're called on."

"She just needs to become familiar with the simulation," Leah offered, surprising Ell with her support. "She's a dead-straight shot."

"Even so," Sam replied. He keyed in a command on the tablet computer, and Ell watched as the scene pulled back to a thousand yards, the village moving to the center of the screen. "You'll both be targeting the village. You have ten rounds and will be shooting at the same ten targets. Your goal is speed and accuracy. The one who knocks down the most tangos wins. You can use as many of your ten rounds as you like to make your shots."

"We're shooting the same ten targets?" Ell asked.

Sam nodded. "All ten will be visible all the time. You need to find them and take them out. Many people will be around those targets who could be innocent bystanders, so your shots will not be easy. You must be careful and accurate. We often experience this situation in the field, so we need to know what you can do."

"Understood," Ell said, moving to a prone position and resting the stock of her rifle on a sandbag at the front of the shooting position.

Ell examined the village on the screen. Several targets would likely be obvious, with the other seven or eight more challenging. With Leah's experience, she would probably go for the easy targets first, leveraging her familiarity with the exercise to knock them down quickly and gain the advantage.

Ell could not match Leah's greater experience with the simulation, so she'd use a different tactic. She would search for the more challenging targets Leah would likely pass by on her first round of shots, like the woman Ell experienced moving between buildings in the earlier test. If Ell could focus on those more difficult shorts and let Leah take the obvious ones, she might be able to get a jump on Leah without having to compete with her directly.

"Ready," Sam called. "Begin."

Ell scanned the village as she heard Leah take her first shot. Sure enough, she spotted a man moving from one building to another at a rapid walk. She checked the scope's numbers and shot. A hit!

In front of that man was another person who appeared as an elderly woman. Ell did a double take and spotted the designated mark on the woman's shoulder. She took the shot just as the sound of Leah's rifle went off again.

Ell scanned the sides of the village and found two men standing together within a crowd of women. One of the women and the two men had red X's on their shoulders. Ell waited until the numbers on her scope's display settled on the nearest tango before taking a shot that took out one of the men. As she did, Leah pulled off two more shots in rapid succession.

Ell regulated her breathing, calmed her heart rate, and lined up on the other man, who had ducked behind a woman, exposing only his head. She eased the scope's crosshairs onto the man's face and pulled the trigger. He dropped as Ell shifted her sights to the woman, who had now dropped to a crouch and scurried toward the back of a nearby building. With only seconds before the woman disappeared from view, Ell led the woman's progress and squeezed the trigger. The woman dropped just as Ell heard Leah pull off two more shots.

"Cease fire," Sam called. "All tangos are down."

"How'd we do?" Leah asked.

"It's a tie," Sam said. "I've never seen a more exciting contest. I may have to rethink your readiness for the field, Ell. You choose the more difficult targets. Five shots, five tangos down. That was great shooting."

"Beginner's luck," Ell heard Leah say, but when she jerked her head around, she saw the smile on Leah's face. "It really was nice shooting, sister. Then again, let's see how you do in the hand-to-hand combat coming up next."

They repeated a similar simulation using the M21. They tied each time.

When they finished the final round, Ell exclaimed, "That has got to be the best video game of all time!"

Ell noticed the sudden shift in Leah's mood and glanced over to Sam, whose eyes, while still fixed on Ell, mirrored Leah's.

"What? What did I say?" Ell asked.

"It's complicated, but there's something you need to understand," Sam said. "This is an engaging simulation. But when we engage in real situations like the ones you went through on the simulator, each target represents a life we may have to take. Weapons are part of what we do, and taking a life is a real potential for us; but we don't have to like it. We'll applaud our achievements with weapons and other fighting skills, but we never celebrate anything akin to taking a life. It's why we spend so much time practicing on simulators like this and in the field. Any person can shoot well with enough practice. What we need on this team is *more* than that. We need snipers who can shoot so well, they can deliberately wound or drive off a tango rather than kill them. It's not always possible, but it's something we always keep in mind."

"We take responsibility for each person who falls in our crosshairs," Leah said. "Our work is exciting, stimulating, and challenging; but taking a life is something we take seriously."

"But they're just animations," Ell said, feeling her previous exhilaration wane.

"True," Sam said, lifting a hand toward the simulator's projection screen. "In here, each animation reminds us of our responsibility to protect and preserve life while completing our missions. The simulation is never just a video game to us."

Ell felt a knot forming in her stomach. "I've never had to take a life."

"I hope you never do," Leah replied, "but it is common in our work."

Ell met Leah's gaze and found both sincerity and concern there. She followed as Sam and Leah headed for the door out of the simulation room and then the firing range. Leah paused at the door leading from the firing range to the weight training and mat areas and glanced at her. Ell noticed Leah's customary, mischievous grin was back in place. Leah pointed at the sign next to the weapons rack, then at the pistol Ell had left at the shooting position earlier.

"'You shoot it, you clean it,'" Leah said. "See you at the mat test."

"Your next stop is the mats," Sam confirmed as he held the door for Leah. "Once you finish cleaning your pistol and get some lunch, we'll meet there. That testing will likely take a while, so be sure you get something to eat in the conference room. After the mat test, we'll gather in the conference room and review the results of today's testing."

Ell touched Leah's sleeve as she turned to leave. "What's the mat test?"

"Hand-to-hand combat. Full contact. You'll spar against a member of the Home Team. Have you ever trained at that level?"

Ell nodded. "I have in tournaments."

"Then think of this as a tournament. Just don't hold back," Leah added, then frowned. "If it concerns you, you can pull out. The last thing we want is for you to get hurt."

Ell squared her shoulders. "No, I'm in. I'll be there in fifteen." But she wondered what she had gotten herself into.

CHAPTER 21

Ell toed up to the edge of the mats, estimating the space at least eighty feet across and equally wide with two-inch deep mats in a wide four-foot blue and red checkerboard pattern. Near where she stood, a line of eight folding chairs ran down the side of the mats, each with a name on the back. Four men and three women occupied the chairs. Near the end of the line, the eighth chair had her name on it.

Everyone in the chairs looked incredibly fit. Aria was petite with the near-perfect posture and trim of a runner. A third woman named Bon-Hwa, who went by the name Bono, had long, dark hair and copper-colored skin and was slightly taller than Ell. She appeared to be of Korean descent. The third woman, Carla, was tall and ebony-skinned with black hair, dark eyes, and a bright smile. When she moved, the muscles in her arms, torso, and legs rippled beneath her thin sweats.

The men ranged from an angular athlete of her height named Marcus to a giant of a man named Walter, who she guessed stood well over six four and had the physique of a bodybuilder. Sitting next to Walter was Barry, a scrawny guy who looked as if he had spent too much time in front of a computer. Barry and Walter chatted like long-lost friends. The man in the chair beside hers looked more like a male model. He had a slender physique; chiseled facial features; an overly square chin; and perfectly quaffed, long, brown hair. He ensured she knew his name was Steve when she took her seat.

The final man of the group, occupying the last chair in the lineup, stood out from the rest like a shiny coin among older ones. A bit shorter and leaner than the rest, he sat in his chair with a calm smile and eyes that seemed to miss nothing. His look gave her the impression of curiosity, humor, and interest when he glanced her way. It was like he knew the punchline to some joke no one else got.

Ell's thoughts drifted back to the times she'd encountered him before and found herself intrigued by the guy but initially couldn't figure out why. She was curious about how a face-to-face encounter would be, but Sam stepped onto the mats before she could get to him and drew everyone's attention.

"Each of you will face one of us in full-contact sparring. We'll be using all four corners of the mats to expedite the testing, so be wary of someone fighting their way into your corner of the mats when you're up. We won't stop the session if that happens. You'll just have to deal with it. We go until there are three falls or a major submission. You have five minutes to warm up on your own."

Someone in the line of chairs groaned, and Sam laughed. "I'd apologize for what Jessica and the obstacle course did to you before you came to this point in the testing, but that's life for you. I've never been on a mission when I was totally fresh. We want to see what you can do after giving your all. So, good luck. You're going to need it."

Sam's words drew several laughs from the group.

Steve leaned toward her and extended his hand.

"Excuse me? You must be Ellen."

Ell shook his hand but dropped it quickly. He was obviously interested in her, but she was not into him.

"It's Ell," she replied.

Before he could say more, she stood, moved behind her chair, and started a short stretching routine.

"Was it something I said?" Steve asked, followed by a chorus of laughter from the male candidates sitting closest to him.

Ell felt her face redden. As she spun around to give Steve a piece of her mind, she felt a tap on her shoulder.

Leah stood there, wearing the same gray sweatpants and dark t-shirt as the rest of the Home Team. Her golden-bronze hair was pulled into a thick braid, and her dark eyes showed intensity.

"I'm not sure if you noticed, but the guys you're here with today have at least thirty pounds on you, and they're all experienced military operators."

Ell raised a hand to cut her off. "Allen said as much when we worked out together last night. I realize I can't compete with them, but I will still give it my best. Besides, I'll be fighting one of you. So, I don't have to worry about the others."

Leah laid a gentle hand on Ell's shoulder. "A person never knows what they're capable of until they're put up against it. I've seen your figures from testing. You've done a passable job, and believe it or not, I would like to see you do well here, too. We could use another strong woman on the team."

Ell's eyes widened, which brought a smile to Leah's face. "Is that so surprising?"

"Well, yes. But I appreciate that," Ell replied, feeling an unexpected sense of sisterhood with Leah—one she'd never expected after the stunt Leah had pulled at sniper school.

"Then let me give you some advice," Leah said, "from a person who stands at least three inches shorter than you and who people generally mistake for small and frail."

Ell laughed. "I'd never take you for that."

Leah chuckled. "Exactly. Small doesn't mean lacking in determination or power. Watch as I spar with the first guy on my list today. Watch Jessica, too, and see how we deal with people who outweigh, outreach, and outmuscle us. Watch how we avoid their hands and move away and around them rather than confront them directly. They can't take us down if they can't get their hands on us. But on the other hand, if their reach and leg kicks are that much longer than yours, move inside their punches and kicks.

"You've got more than two decades of fight training behind you from the military, state patrol, and your parents. You'll be facing Allen when you're up. Since you worked out with him last night, you know he's an incredible athlete and fighter. But I've bested him as many times as he's beaten me. My strategy is never to let him get his hands on me. Instead, I fight from his weak spot—inside his reach. Spend your energy that way, and you'll hold your own."

"I will," Ell replied, then patted the hand Leah still held on her shoulder. "And thanks."

Leah smiled as she turned away, then tossed a final word over her shoulder. "You're just lucky you don't have to face me."

Once Leah was gone, Ell reached as high as she could with both hands, rose on her toes, dropped forward with a straight back, and laid her hands flat on the floor. When she rose, Steve had stepped beside her.

"Heard what the tiny Home Team member said. It sounds like good advice. I'm going to use it myself. I must face Sam. He's reportedly one of the best empty-hand fighters in the world. That's why his call sign is Mike Tango, M-T, or Empty for short. I understand Jessica is the only one who has beaten him."

"We women can be surprising that way," Ell replied with a sidelong glance.

"True that," Steve said, reaching out his hand again. "Luck," he offered.

"Right back at you," Ell said, shaking the hand and meeting his eyes. Then, she snapped her gaze away from Steve's eager eyes. "Get back into the game, girl," she whispered to herself after he headed back to his chair.

Ell turned as Jessica called out from the edge of the mats.

"Candidate Walter Drake, you'll face Leah in the far corner of the mats. Marcus faces me in the corner to the right. Aria will face Sam in the next square. Steve Madigan will face Allen in the remaining corner. Please take your places."

Sitting out the first round, Ell watched as Marcus Wilbur, a stiff-backed man with a trim, athletic physique and the light hair and weathered skin of a person too long in the sun, jogged over to meet Jessica in the far corner of the mats. He stood several inches above Jessica and smiled a look that came off more as a sneer than a greeting. Jessica laid her tablet computer on the mat's edge and faced Wilbur from about six feet. She bowed and smiled at the man.

"Candidate Wilbur, you are an expert in judo, jujitsu, and Okinawan karate. You've been with Special Forces for three years and applied for Delta Force but didn't make the cut. Why not?"

"That's old history," Wilbur replied with a growl.

"Just the same, answer the question," Jessica said, her tanned face a calm mask.

"I was injured. Besides, what would any woman know about Delta?"

Leah paused as she approached her candidate in another section of the mat, then turned to face Wilbur from across the mats.

"Can I tell him, Jess?"

Jessica nodded. Ell wondered how much effort it took for the woman to remain so calm in front of so much arrogance.

"Jessica was a member of the Special Forces and Delta Force before joining us. She was one of the first women to qualify for the unit," Leah said, her grin wide. "Saying that never gets old."

"Give the word when you're ready, Wilbur," Jessica said, her face calm and eyes intense.

"The word is given," Wilbur growled.

Wilbur lowered into a crouch, hands spread and reaching forward. He side-stepped a tight circle to the right with Jessica at its center. Jessica remained in the center of that circle, arms loose at her side, moving slightly so she continued to face him. Wilbur feinted sharply left with a shoulder, then rushed in low, diving for Jessica's legs. Jessica turned at the hips, one hand sweeping down and taking Wilbur's shoulder, using his forward momentum to carry him past her as she stepped aside.

Wilbur slid to a stop, then spun left. As he came out of the turn, he met the flat of Jessica's left foot as it arched high in the air and crashed into the side of his head. Wilbur crashed to the mat, stunned.

"That was half speed, Candidate Wilbur," Jessica said as she reached down to help him up. "Next time, I won't hold back."

Wilbur grabbed the offered hand with both of his and jerked Jessica forward. Unsurprised by the move, Jessica moved with Wilbur's motion, bending her knees and lifting her captive's right hand high. She rotated Wilbur's wrist with her right hand, grasped his elbow with her left, lifted them both high, and pivoted his arm. She came out behind him, the tips of her right hand's fingers digging into his palm while the thumb pinched down on the back of his hand, spreading the small bones painfully.

Ell recognized the move in a moment: a hapkido full lock. With his wrist locked and elbow captive, Wilbur had to go wherever Jessica led him. Still behind him, Jessica snapped out a low sidekick to the back of his knee. The joint buckled, and Wilbur crumpled to the ground face first.

Jessica retained her grip on his hand and elbow and twisted both further, working against his shoulder joint. She held him there for less than a minute before he tapped the mat three times with his free hand, submitting. Jessica immediately released her grip and stepped back.

"Lucky fall," Wilbur growled as he climbed to his feet.

"When I tried to help you up, you tried to turn my goodwill against me. It shows a definite flaw in your character. I suspect that's why Delta rejected you. I will give you one more try to prove yourself."

"I'll take it," he growled.

Without waiting for Jessica to get set, Wilbur lunged forward and feinted left as though diving for her legs again. He grinned as Jessica leaned away from the feint, appearing to fall for the ruse. As she did, Wilbur snapped a vicious front kick to her chin.

As the kick was about to land, Jessica turned at the hips. The kick slid by her face, missing cleanly. In the same motion, she dropped into a crouch, slid under the kick, and reached up with both hands to create a "V" between her fingers and thumbs. She caught his leg and clamped down with both hands, twisting his leg left and pulling it down toward the floor. Caught by his momentum once again, Wilbur fell with her.

Jess squatted on one knee as they went down, chambered her right foot to her hip, and shot her foot straight into Wilbur's side. The kick sent the cocky candidate onto his toes as Jessica released his leg. Coming down, he crashed full length on the mats.

Jessica rose slowly and stepped over to the downed man. Crouching over him, she placed one hand on his sternum with the other balled into a fist and cocked inches above his face.

Wilbur met her eyes, shook his head slowly, and tapped the mat in submission.

"Good choice," Jessica said. She offered him her hand yet again.

"You'd help me up after what I did?" Wilbur asked, taking her hand and rising to his feet.

Jessica dropped his hand and wiped her palm on her sweatpants as if ridding herself of something vile. "A wise man once told me never to fight fair when fighting for your life. He was probably right in a real situation. But on the other hand, knowing when to fight and offer a hand are equally important. We call it the ethics of combat. Unfortunately, I believe you lack those ethics."

Jessica paused. Leah, Allen, and Sam took a break from their own matches and lined up beside Jessica. "Pack your bags and leave. You're done here," Jessica said.

Wilbur turned away without a word. Then, a moment later, Ell heard the bang of the facility's front doors slamming shut behind him. She then glanced at the other three squares of mats, where the other matches picked up where they'd left off.

Of all people, Leah faced Walter. She stood two paces away from where the man lay on the ground.

"Come on, Master Sergeant Walter Drake. Get up," Leah said. "We're just starting to have fun."

Drake climbed slowly to his feet. "It's not fair. You're so small. I'm afraid I'll hurt you. Then you take advantage and throw me around like a rag doll."

"Likely excuse, Master Sergeant," Leah said, a broad smile illuminating her face. "Think of me as a fly, buzzing around your head and annoying you. You'd swat that fly, wouldn't you? This time, try not to let all those muscles get in the way. I certainly won't let them get in my way. Why did you agree to come here if you don't give this your all?"

"I've found few things worth my time in this world that could challenge me. So, I thought this might be different."

"I think you spent too much time getting all those degrees in school. You got soft, Mr. Ph.D. in Engineering."

Ell heard the other candidates in the chairs chuckle, but not too loudly after seeing what had happened to Wilbur. But of course, that could have been any of them under the right circumstances.

"Fine," Drake said.

Drake took a fighting stance, fisted hands before his face. Leah remained where she was—hands at her sides, knees flexed, arms relaxed. Then, with a speed that surprised everyone, Drake stepped forward and lashed out with a left perfect snap front kick. Leah leaned right, and the kick sailed past her face. But Drake kept his left foot in the air, turned sideways at the hips, and snapped a short roundhouse kick to her head. Leah turned her head to the right, and the kick glanced off.

"Impressive for a big man," she said as he lashed out with another front kick, this time with his right foot.

Leah shuffled sideways to avoid the blow.

"The big man can move after all," Leah said, the smile never leaving her face.

"Thank you," Drake muttered, driving Leah to the edge of the mats as he lashed out with another front kick-roundhouse combination, then leaned in with a flurry of punches and jabs.

Leah ducked under the kick, crouched, and slid inside the reach of Drake's punches. Then, coming in low to within a few inches of the man's chest, she slammed both fists on both sides of the big man's chin. Drake staggered back, shocked and shaken. Leah followed him as he did, staying so close he couldn't land a punch or chamber his leg for a kick.

Drake tried to wrap Leah in a bear hug, but Leah ducked below his arms again and slithered from his grasp. Then, Leah landed three lightning-fast knuckle punches to the outer side of the big man's thigh. Drake's expression registered the shock as Leah's strikes crushed the dense nerve bundle running down the outside of his upper leg. He wobbled backward, attempting to regain his balance.

Leah then leaped into the air, her left leg bent at the knee like a high jumper. At the last second, she drove her left leg downward and scissored her right foot up to crash into Drake's chest. He sat down hard.

"I surrender," he croaked.

Leah reached down with both hands to help him to his feet. Walter bowed, then wobbled again. Leah rushed forward, wrapping both arms around the big man's waist to steady him.

Just as with Jessica's actions, Ell found herself amazed by the graciousness of the Home Team, even in full contact competition.

"Thank you, Agent McCarthy," Drake said as he sucked deeply. "Thank you for the lesson."

"You only tapped out once, big man," Leah replied. "You still have two more attempts to take me down."

Drake nodded. "I know, but I also know I cannot best you. You have my admiration and respect."

Leah smiled, stepped forward, and rose on her toes to slap the big man on the shoulder. "You have humility and character, big man. I'd serve with you any day. And if I can ever help you progress with your fighting skills, please know I'll be happy to help."

Drake nodded without another word, then quietly returned to his seat at the side of the mat.

Ell watched all this with an open mouth, wondering what she saw. She thought these would be full-contact matches, fighters continuing until one couldn't fight any longer. But instead, the members of the Home Team appeared to instruct more than test.

Ell watched as Alex stood at the center of the mat facing Allen, sweat streaming down both men's faces. They'd been going at it for several minutes, neither one getting the better of the other. They looked like two windmills whirling with fists and feet flying. A red blotch appeared on one side of Alex's face, but he grinned. She wished she could have seen more of the action between them instead of watching Jessica and Leah's matches.

"You ready to give up yet, Alex?" she heard Allen ask.

Ell felt a little thrill as Alex waved away Allen's suggestion. "Why, when I'm winning?"

Allen laughed between heaving breaths. "I don't think so."

Alex was the man who had rescued her in Turkey. She might not be here today if not for him. She found watching him spar with Allen, showing so much skill and responding with such good humor to be more exciting and touching, all at once. She began to root for the man.

As she watched, Allen lashed out with a sudden left jab. Alex swatted it away with an open palm, then stepped forward with a left jab, then a right to Allen's face. Allen deflected each blow with a forearm.

Twenty minutes passed with Allen and Alex exchanging punches and kicks with matching blocks, twists, and turns until Allen finally stepped back and smiled.

"Well done. That was the most fun that I've had in days.

"Thanks, just the same, but it was just a bit of basic tae kwon do defense," Alex replied, wiping a stream of sweat from his forehead with his sleeve.

"Not likely," Allen replied. "I saw Karate, Kung Fu, Krav Maga, and even a little Tai Chi in there."

"I bow to your greater knowledge," Alex replied.

"Want to go again?" Allen asked.

Alex bowed deeply at the waist toward Allen. "I think I'll follow my large friend and concede. However, if I need to best you again to be a member of your team, I may not be up to it. You are more skilled than I am, for sure."

Allen returned the bow. "I appreciate your humility, honesty, and character, even if I might not agree with you about our relative skills. You can return to your seat."

As Alex returned to his seat, Ell approached him, her smile wide. "That was amazing."

"I don't know about that, but it was fun. And speaking of skills, I will never forget watching you take on all those men in Turkey to save those people. You have my sincere admiration."

Ell smiled again, awkwardly, and felt herself suddenly go shy. What was the effect he seemed to have on her? Minutes ago, she was her usual confident self. Then, in a minute . . . She shook her head at the confusion she felt in her mind, her heart as she headed back to her chair.

Soon, she heard her name called to face Sam in the next round.

"I thought I'd be facing Allen," she said.

"Surprise," Sam said, grinning.

Ell felt her stomach tense. This man was one of the best.

Sam sensed her uneasiness. "I understand the confrontation at the wildlife refuge was your first actual fight. I don't want you to worry about that. I just want you to do the best you can, so we know how we can leverage your skills while you're with us. Can you do that?"

"I can try," she replied.

"And you know you can tap out or withdraw at any time," Sam said.

"If you know about me, then you also know I'm not likely to do that."

Ell saw his eyes sparkle as he laughed. "I figured as much. Let's see what you've got."

Ell squared her shoulders just as a loud bell chimed from the direction of the conference room. Sam's expression changed immediately. "This will have to wait. That's an emergency call from our headquarters in Florida. They don't happen often."

CHAPTER 22

Ell heard her cell phone vibrate in her duffle bag as she returned to her chair by the mats. When she retrieved the phone, the name on the screen read Special Agent Williams. She moved a few yards off from the rest of the group to take the call.

"Trooper Evander," Williams said when she connected the call. "I hope you remember me from Turkey."

Ell wasn't sure what to say, so she said, "Yes."

"I'm just calling to check on you . . . to make sure you made it to your new assignment. You went through a lot while in the shipping container and during the rescue in Turkey."

This was the man who had accused her of being precipitous when she fought back against the human traffickers and when she had had no other choice but to act or be victimized along with the others in the shipping container.

Ell pushed down the anger rising in her gut and replied. "I appreciate your concern, but I'm fine. What can I do for you?"

"Glad to hear it," Williams continued. "Were you able to recall or learn anything new after your experience in Turkey that might help us?"

"No, sir," she replied.

Her wariness of the man increased by the second. Where was he headed with this?

"No problem," he replied. His tone sounded positive and supportive, which was odd considering the last time they met and how the conversation went. "I'm glad you're doing well. Have a great day."

What an odd call. He must have known she wouldn't want to hear from him after he warned her off from any future work with Homeland Security Investigations. So, why in the world would he call now?

Jessica interrupted Ell's thoughts as she stepped over to face the candidates. Ell found it difficult not to be intimidated by the woman, regardless of how friendly she seemed each time they met. But she'd seen Jessica in action in Turkey. Now, having seen her handle Wilbur on the mats, all Ell could see was a tall, dark-haired warrior to be treated with caution. Ell wondered if she could ever be as calm, collected, and professional as this woman.

Jessica smiled as her gaze lingered on each candidate in turn. "Thank you all for being here today. This testing is about expanding our Home Team. While we only tested half of you in full-contact sparing, we now face an urgent matter that requires us to delay the rest of the testing."

A collective groan arose from the candidates.

Jessica raised her hands to calm the group. "I know you're disappointed. We enjoy the sparring, as well. However, with what's come up and what we know about each of you, we can determine whether you qualify for our team. So please gather your belongings and meet in the conference room. We'll announce who we invite to join the Home Team then."

Ell and the other seven candidates stood as one. It was a unique moment, being there with the rest of the candidates, being considered their peers, and being considered for membership in a team of top-tier operators. Ell found herself standing a little taller, even if she had no intention of staying beyond her suspension period from the Washington State Patrol.

Or did she? Her attitude toward the Home Team and the candidates had changed over the past few days. She'd seen the Home Team's strength, confidence, and grace as they ran everyone through their paces. She recalled how they rallied to her rescue at the wildlife refuge, even though she wasn't an official member of their team. Ell wondered what it would be like to be a member.

And then there was Alex. What if he became a member of the team? The answer came to her as soon as the question formed in her mind: she'd loved once before, until that mission in Afghanistan, when she had lost so much . . . when she'd sworn not to get close to anyone ever again.

Either way, I'll know in an hour, she thought.

The candidates gathered in the conference room—settling into chairs and leaving the far end open for Sam, Jessica, Allen, and Leah. When the Home Team filed into the room a few moments later, Sam stood, lifting a hand to draw the candidates' attention.

"You were all invited here as potential members of our team. That much, you know. You may not know that the Home Team is part of a larger covert organization called the Extreme Operations Group. The EOG is chartered under the State Department and reports directly to the Secretary of State. Our purpose is to confront any security threat to the United States. Many groups have similar missions, but most are constrained by the turf on which they're allowed to operate. We have no such limitations. The Home Team and the EOG's many other teams operate within and outside the United States borders as need dictates."

Sam paused, gathered his thoughts, and continued. "As the name of our organization suggests, the EOG specializes in unconventional approaches to solving our nation's problems. In the last six months, we supported a drugs-to-agriculture initiative in partnership with the Mexican government to encourage drug cartels to convert from illegal to more legitimate operations. Those ops involved everything from attacking cartel strongholds with high-tech paintball guns and rubber bullets to reasoning with cartel bosses about the disadvantages of not signing on for the program."

Some in the room laughed and said, "Reasoning? I bet that's exactly what it was."

Sam grinned. "We may have twisted a few arms along the way."

Alex raised his hand. "You scared them into converting their enterprises?"

Sam shrugged. "I'll say we set the stage for the State Department and the Mexican government to follow up with incentives and lucrative contracts for the cartels that agreed to change."

Sam glanced around the room to emphasize the seriousness of his following words. "Assignment to the EOG is voluntary, although our existence is highly classified. Please keep that in mind. We are an off-the-books group, without a doubt."

Ell noticed several nods from around the table before Sam continued. "The bottom line is we anticipated inviting four of you to join us today. However, based on the outcome of the testing, we've changed those plans."

Jessica stood. "Barry Whitman, please stand."

The thin, pale candidate that Ell had pegged as a computer geek struggled to his feet.

"Barry," Jessica said. "You are uniquely qualified in signal and information technology and crypto and electronic counterintelligence. We need those skills on our team. So, we would like you to join the Home Team. Of course, you can decline our invitation and return to your home unit without prejudice, but we'll need your answer today."

Whitman's cheeks blushed bright red, drawing a chuckle from the other candidates.

"You bet," Barry replied. "I mean, I'd be honored."

"Thank you. You are currently a first lieutenant in the army. While you will retain your military rank and pay in your official records, you, and anyone else who accepts our invitation today, will function as an equal partner with the rest of us."

Jessica smiled. "Welcome to the team, Barry."

Leah spoke next. "Master Sergeant Walter Drake, please stand."

The giant of a man scooted his chair back and towered over the conference room table.

"Yes, ma'am," he replied with a grave expression.

"Master Sergeant Drake, I have never met a more honorable man than you. What you may lack in fighting skills, you make up with desire and character. We need a logistics and overwatch specialist to run this headquarters and support our operations. We believe you are the person for the job. You have a background in ordinance, logistics, and transportation and a doctorate in international politics. You have two tours of combat under your belt and appreciate what it means to provide overwatch for a team in the field. We want to invite you to join the Home Team, understanding the conditions just explained to Barry."

Drake nodded. "Absolutely. But you did promise to help me with my fighting skills."

Leah laughed. "I did, and I will. Welcome to the team."

Sam rose again. "Will the rest of you please rise?"

Five chairs scooted back as Alex, Aria, Bono, Steve, and Carla stood. Sam lifted a hand in Ell's direction. "You, too, Trooper Evander."

Surprised, Ell complied.

"The six of you possess the character and qualities we need on the Home Team. Trooper Evander is destined to return to the Washington State Patrol, but we'd like to invite all of you, including Ell, while she's with us, to join the Home Team. You are an exceptionally skilled, experienced group of people. Please indicate your agreement if you accept our invitation."

Alex raised his hand. "I'm a ranger commander. I love my unit. I'm not in the market for a new job."

Sam nodded. "We anticipated your response, as did your battalion commander. It's why you were placed on orders to report here, rather than simply invited for the day. Your battalion commander felt you might relate to our mission and be a valuable addition to our team. He suggested we retain your services for at least two weeks, knowing and appreciating your loyalty to the rangers. You bring a great deal of experience and skill to the table, and we'd like to have a chance to convince you."

Alex shrugged, then sat down. "My orders say I'm here with you until relieved, so I'm in for now."

"And the rest of you?" Sam asked.

Carla, Aria, Bono, and Steve all nodded in turn.

Sam turned to Ell. "When it gets right down to it, you also have a choice. The work we do can be dangerous. You can leave at any time without prejudice."

"I'm in!" Ell said, surprising herself with enthusiasm in her response. Once the words were out, she cut a quick glance to where Alex sat. He returned her gaze with a nod and an expression in his eyes she found hard to interpret. Was it simple acknowledgement or was it something else?

Sam drew her attention away from those thoughts with his next words. "Then we have our team. Welcome to the Home Team."

"Praise God," she heard Leah whisper to Allen. "We've tested so many up until now."

"We got lucky with this group," Ell heard Allen reply.

CHAPTER 23

Sam, Leah, Jessica, and Allen remained in the conference room after everyone else left, their mood somber.

The tablet computer on the table in front of Sam chirped. "Video call coming in," he said. "Must be the director with the details of what's happening."

He tapped a command on the tablet, and Paul Samuelson's face lit up the room's central screen. The sixty-four-year-old EOG director and retired CIA operative looked even more tired than usual.

Paul wiped a hand over his head, ruffling his typically crisp, close-cropped gray hair into a spiky mess. "It's later here in Florida, so I won't keep you. However, we've got an immediate situation that needs handling. To that point, you will have another caller connecting in a few seconds. Please allow her to access your system."

As if on cue, the tablet computer chirped again. Sam tapped another command, and the screen to the right of Paul's face lit up. The woman whose face filled the screen was young, freckled, and deeply tanned. Her long, heavily curled brown hair accented her tired green eyes.

Sam recognized her at once. "Maggie," he said. "Sorry I missed you at the wildlife refuge, but thanks for giving Trooper Evander a hand."

"Yo, Mags," Leah said.

She'd worked with Maggie while still a part of the mainstream military. The memory of how Maggie had charged a tango hideout single-handedly while Leah provided sniper support remained in her mind like it happened yesterday.

"Hello, Sam. And you, too, Little Shooter. I still owe you for covering me in Iraq that time," Maggie said, nodding to Leah. "I would have stayed for a meet and greet the other day, but I had somewhere to be. How's the woman I met at the refuge doing?"

Jessica gave Maggie a solemn nod. "Ell's fine but thinks you're some sort of superhero."

"I was briefed earlier today by the director about Ellen's presence on your team, but you should have seen her out there. She held her own in that fight, taking on two skilled operators while I tackled their boss. As for the superhero thing, I'm too human for that call sign," Maggie replied.

"Amen to that for all of us," Sam replied.

Paul cleared his throat to draw everyone's attention. "Agent O'Dell has been on staff at Drug Enforcement Administration for the past five years, working drug smuggling cases carried out by large international shipping companies. Maggie will fill you in on the details of what's come up. But before she does, know that I've confirmed what she's about to tell you through both the DEA and Homeland Security."

Maggie ran a deeply tanned hand through the mess of thick brown curls. While decidedly feminine, as she spoke, Maggie's face was lined with the effects of sun, weather, and the leanness of an active life in the field.

"I've worked the Interstate Five corridor from Los Angeles to the Canadian border for six months. That strip of asphalt is a major thoroughfare for all things illicit—from drugs to human trafficking to anything a criminal could want. We've recently identified a major foreign transport firm with a large presence there. But until now, our efforts to identify that company have hit a dead end. I got my first break when I encountered Trooper Evander at the wildlife refuge. The leader of the people who attacked her is a woman linked to drugs and stolen computer and aircraft technology smuggled through the port of Seattle, Port of Tacoma, Port of Kalama, and other ports up and down the western coastline."

"Ell feels the woman who led the group at the wildlife refuge is the same one we encountered in Turkey," Allen said.

Maggie nodded again. "She's the daughter of Lee Chao, the head of New Asian Imports and Exports out of Shanghai. We've suspected his involvement for some time but, until now, lacked a direct connection. We feel his daughter's presence here may provide that link."

"Sam and I visited with Mister Lee Chao a few days ago," Leah added. "He's a real trip."

"Perhaps we can exchange information about this group."

"Of course," Jessica replied. "I'll ship you what we have on your secure line."

"Sending you my secure number now," Maggie said.

The tablet in front of Sam chirped again. He tapped a command, and an aerial view of a field surrounded by trees appeared on the screen to the left of Paul's image.

"What you're seeing is an area just south of Tumwater, Washington, a few miles off Interstate Five," Maggie explained. "It's a small farm owned by a man away on vacation. Fifty acres of open pasture are surrounded by tall trees and the Deschutes River on three sides. A house, several outbuildings, a barn, and a narrow farm road flanks the east side of the property."

"I know that place," Sam said. "It's not far from a tourist farm and bakery that I patronize."

Maggie grinned. "Best apple fritters in the area. We have solid intel that an exchange will occur at this location this evening. We believe Lee's group will use the area to unload shipping containers into smaller trucks to move the illegal goods to their final destinations. According to my source, the containers include heroin, methamphetamine, and barbiturates. We know from experience when they stage their merchandise like this, they normally take on other items for the return trip. It can be anything from pirated technology to weapons, drugs, or people. This group is known for its human trafficking and tends to move their victims in large numbers instead of the ones and twos we often see."

"What do you expect in terms of firepower?" Leah asked.

"Lee Chao's operations tend toward many men with numerous guns. So, I expect they'll have a dozen or more shooters in place when this goes down."

Jessica let out a low whistle.

"That's why I'm calling you," Maggie replied. "It's too short of a notice to get help from our usual sources. The FBI and Homeland Security are fully committed elsewhere, and a VIP in Seattle from the White House has the state patrol in a low hover. We may be able to get their support, but it'll be iffy at best."

"How many people have you got?" Allen asked.

"You're looking at her. But we could make a real dent in their operations if you can lend a hand."

"We'll be there," Sam replied. "We'll plan to rendezvous south of here near the Olympia airport. There's a small road west of the airport where some state warehouses are located. It's private and empty of prying eyes at night and not far from where the operation will go down."

"I know the place," Maggie replied.

"What about overwatch?" Maggie asked. "We could use some aerial backup and comms."

"I'll bring my sniper rifle and get there early," Leah replied. "Judging by the tree line in the picture, I should be able to find a sniper-hide within easy range. Ell's a crack shot, even if she doesn't have much experience. She might be helpful."

"With the number of tangos expected on site, we're going to need her," Sam replied. "We have a new team on board, Maggie. We'll bring them online for this. With you and the rest of us, we can do this."

"We can put the big man, Walter Drake, on comms," Allen said. "Barry Whitman can handle the drones and provide the aerial view."

"I don't see we have any other option," Paul added. "We don't want to lose the opportunity to make a dent in the drugs flowing up the western corridor."

He paused, then directed his following comment to Sam. "Make it happen, Sam. Get Home Team Two into the action."

"Roger that, sir," Sam replied. "Roger that."

CHAPTER 24

Ell found everyone gathered in the conference room later that evening. Walter gave her a thumbs up as she entered. Steve Madigan waved her to a chair beside him on the far side of the room. She saw a chair open next to Alex and avoided it. This was her first mission with the Home Team. She did not need the distraction.

"Big crowd," Steve whispered as she took the offered chair.

She nodded as Sam stood to address the crowd, kitted out in full tactical gear: skull helmet, black tactical cargo pants and shirt, webbed carry vest with an assortment of magazines and smoke/flash grenades, and pistol in a thigh holster. Underneath the vest was what looked like body armor, although much thinner than she'd worn on the job with the state patrol. Leaning against his chair was one of the M4 carbines she'd seen in Turkey. Leah, Allen, and Jessica were decked out with the same gear, although each with a slightly different assortment of grenades and magazine pouches.

"Loaded for bear," Ell whispered.

"Sure enough," Steve started, but Sam cut off anything else he might have said.

"We'd hoped to give you some time to train and adjust to working with us before deploying, but as I mentioned earlier, something's come up. Call it on-the-job training."

Carla was slumped in the chair beyond Steve, booted feet crossed on the arm. "Situation normal for the Special Forces'" she called out. "No reason to change things now."

Everyone laughed, including Sam. "All too true. And if history proves out, it'll be the case here more times than naught."

Jessica tapped a command on the tablet computer that always seemed to be with her. A picture of the Tumwater exchange site appeared on the left screen at the front of the room.

"We will be deploying to this location, about an hour's drive south of here. Each of you will be kitted out as we are. Once issued, the equipment will be yours to keep and maintain. Walter will assign you each a cage in a locker room where you can store your gear when not deployed," Jessica said.

Jessica laid her M4A7 on the table in front of her.

"You'll each get one of the new M4A7 carbines. Ell and Leah will be the exceptions. They'll be issued an M4A7 and an M24 or M21 sniper rifle. They'll be using those rifles on the operation this evening."

Ell felt her heart skip. She has trained as a sniper but never had to fill the role. Would she be up to it?

Jessica glanced at Leah and then Ell. "We'll expect you both to hit the road in the next thirty minutes to set up sniper-hides in the trees around the site before the tangos arrive. Leah will be point until the main body arrives. We realize we're throwing you into the pool's deep end, Ell, but we really need your help with this."

Ell nodded. "I won't let you down."

"Walter will run comms from this end," Jessica continued. "Those of us on the Home Team have cochlear implants for receiving secure communications. You'll receive those implants, but until then, you'll be issued tactical headsets. We haven't had time to assign call signs, so we'll use first names over our secure channel. You'll each be issued a forearm tablet computer and holster to strap to your non-dominant arm for additional communications and data display. Your tactical watches contain embedded microphones."

Sam picked up the briefing. "Barry will be our tactical geek or TEEK."

"Familiar with the name. Proud to own it," Barry replied.

Ell decided it would be hard to dislike the gangly geek. He was always such a positive guy.

"Good to hear," Sam said. "Much of our success will depend on what you see and transmit to us in the field. You and Walter draw a drone from the storeroom to provide overwatch. They're a new technology, but nothing you can't handle; and they can easily cover the distance from here to the site. You'll fly and operate them from here. Jessica can answer any questions you might have about the technology."

Barry's face brightened. "Drones are always a good time. Will do," he replied.

"We don't have much time to prepare," Sam continued, "but each of you is an experienced field operator. Jessica will lead the Home Team element for this operation. An agent from the DEA will be on site to lead H.T. Two. I will provide on-site command and coordination from the farmhouse you see in this image. Leah and Ell, our snipers, will report to me."

Steve raised his hand. "Exactly what are we getting into?"

"Our assignment is to support the DEA and interdict what may be one of the largest shipments of illicit cargo to hit the area in a long time," Sam replied. "There may be two forty-foot shipping containers and additional trucks. The opposing force could be as many as two dozen experienced operators. This is no training exercise. I need you all on your toes. Any more questions?"

No one raised a hand, so Sam continued. "Walter and Allen will help you draw your gear. I realize this is a trial-by-fire for you; but you are all experienced operators, and I have complete confidence in you."

Bono rose from her chair. "We've got this, right?"

"Hooah," the team roared.

CHAPTER 25

F an stood at the edge of a farm road near the Tumwater exchange
site. She'd researched the place thoroughly. The owner was away
on vacation for a month. The pipe gate on the gravel road leading
from the main road down to the open pasture was flanked by trees
and a river and secured by a new Master padlock. But the lock was no
match for her long-handled bolt cutters.

Fan rubbed her hands together in anticipation, wiping a thin
veneer of sweat from her palms. *Perhaps this operation will prove my
potential to my father,* she thought—my adopted father. She rolled
the words around in her mind: *adopted father.* Did he see her as his
legitimate daughter or just another pawn he moved on the chessboard
of power he navigated with obsession?

Twenty-seven years ago, Lee Chao had found Fan wrapped in a dirty
cloth on the side of the road outside Shanghai. She had been abandoned
at less than a month old—just another female child born to a family
that wanted a son in a country that limited families to one child.

As her father often reminded her, his mercy and grace saved her
life. Cold, hypothermic, and half-starved, she would have died had
it not been for him. He'd taken her to a private hospital for the rich,
claiming she belonged to him. Given his power and position, no one
questioned his suddenly having a baby.

A series of wet nurses, nannies, and tutors had raised her while her father traveled the world, making business deals and searching for ever-greater wealth and power. Every day of her childhood was spent in a long line of schools and with the best martial arts coaches money could buy. By age twenty, she'd built the knowledge and skills her father felt needed to fulfill her eventual role in his company.

On her twenty-first birthday, he'd gifted her a vice presidency, overseeing the legitimate operations of his large and growing shipping empire. This evening, she found herself on one of her father's less legitimate operations—another of his desperate acts to gather the money he needed to secure the power a man born half-Chinese and half-English needed to prove himself to a government distrustful of anyone not of pure blood.

The thought of what she was to do tonight soured her stomach. So much training. So much schooling. And for what? To be a common criminal? To traffic the things that ruined people's lives . . . to take those lives away from them?

Fan sucked in a breath to clear her head as Andy and Devon approached. They'd driven two of the four large rental trucks they'd use for the cargo transfer and distribution tonight. Both parked their trucks on the side of the road leading to the gate.

"Mistress Fan." Andy bowed slightly. "The other two trucks should be here any minute."

"What of the men?" she asked.

"Twenty men in the back of these two trucks, each armed with MP5s and pistols," Devon replied. "Once we move the trucks into the field, they will deploy to provide cover and supervise the unloading of the vans. Each has been given their assigned task."

Fan pointed to the trees lining the pasture below. "I want someone in those trees."

Devon winced. "You did not request a sniper. Our men have only MP5s and pistols."

"Regardless, identify your best two men and have them scale two trees. Position one close to this gate and another fifty meters down the tree line. I want them up high and well-concealed in case this operation is compromised. Anyone interested in what we are doing is to be eliminated. No exceptions. Am I clear?"

"Yes, ma'am," Devon replied. "It will be done."

"Are the men prepared to assist with unloading the shipping containers and loading the trucks?" she asked.

"We have the labor we need," Andy said.

"Good," she replied. "Follow our plan to the letter. We must succeed today. Get back to your trucks and get ready."

As they turned away, Fan scuffed at the gravel of the road with the toe of her black military-style boot, then ran her right hand down the side of her form-fitting, black tactical coverall. Her hand came to rest on the grip of the Walther .9mm pistol holstered at her hip.

Ten years ago, all she'd wanted was to serve her father. The excitement, the challenge of the tasks assigned to her as a teen and later as an officer in his business, seemed so enthralling back then. It didn't matter that he flirted with the law, even to the extent that the Chinese government sent emissaries to meet with her periodically to express their concern about the embarrassment his non-legitimate business ventures might bring to the country. Each time, they requested she talk with her father and advise caution. Each time they did so, her father dismissed their concerns.

"When I have enough power and enough money, they won't worry about such things," he'd replied more than once. "That is the key. Money will give us the power we need."

She continued to support him, working feverishly to support his goals. But as the years passed, the gloss wore off the adventure to be replaced by the worry of discovery, arrest, and life in jail in some distant country. Thoughts of how she'd been discarded as a child entered her mind more often, but this time paired with a growing empathy for the people her father trafficked to make his millions. She wondered how many people had biological families they loved and cared for and how her father ripped those lives away.

And then there were the Closet Christians she'd met at Starbucks. At first, she'd found it hard to buy into what they said. She considered reporting them to the local state police. That would make her a hero of the state. Her father would have been so proud. Perhaps that last thought and her growing reservations about her adopted father kept her from doing exactly that.

Fan nudged another rock with the toe of her boot, her hand still resting on the pistol at her side. During a rare moment alone, while Devon and Andy were out renting the trucks, she had called the man who led the Closet Christians. While still not sure why, she'd hinted at her involvement in what she termed questionable activities. Instead of shunning her, the man had prayed for her over the phone that God, in His mercy, would forgive her sins. When the prayer ended, the man said, "God has a plan for you. Your life is the way it is for a reason. What you must do will become clear in His time and way." She wondered what would become clear—and how.

The roaring engines of the two trucks returned her to the moment. She walked to the gate, picked up the bolt cutters, and removed the padlock. She swung the gate wide and waved the first truck through.

The four large rental trucks pulled into a line facing the trees with their tailgates facing the open field. Minutes later, the first of two five-ton trucks pulling forty-foot shipping vans stopped next to her at the gate. She waved them through and watched as the trucks eased the shipping containers down the gravel road and positioned them side-by-side with their tailgates facing the four other trucks. As they moved into place, twenty black-clad men with guns piled out of the nearest two rental trucks and took position around the perimeter.

Fan stopped mid-stride as the back of the other two rental trucks opened to discharge fifty men, boys, women, and girls. Half the men with guns moved the people into a line between the shipping containers and the trucks, kicking and shoving them as the people meekly moved into place. One boy, not more than twelve, protested. One of the black-clad men butt-stroked the boy with his MP5, knocking him to the ground. She watched as the boy was kicked repeatedly as an example to others who might protest.

Like automatons, the people unloaded the shipping containers— passing large boxes of raw heroin, methamphetamine, and other drugs from person to person and then into the backs of the four rental trucks.

As Fan watched, she calculated. In addition to the tens of millions of dollars her father made off this shipment of drugs from a cartel in Mexico, he stood to make at least twenty thousand a head for the crowd of workers on the sex trafficking and human bondage market. That meant another 1.2 million dollars toward his plan for dominating the world's shipping industry and proving to the Chinese government he was worthy of acceptance into their ranks.

The drugs were terrible enough, but the people . . . She found it difficult not to think again of herself as a baby—tossed away by her family, sent off to die—and the plight of these people.

———————————

Lee Chao's private cell phone chimed in his opulent Old Shanghai office. He gave that number to no one except a small circle of close friends and associates in the Chinese government. He thumbed the button to accept the call.

"This is your friend in the president's office," the voice said.

Lee Chao recognized the man's voice at once as the assistant to the president's primary advisor on trade.

"I am always grateful for your call," he replied.

"Perhaps not so grateful when I relay my message for you," the man said.

"You have always guided me well. I am happy to hear any advice you might offer."

"Very well," the man said, his voice hushed, obviously speaking from an insecure location. "Word has reached the highest levels of government about your company's suspected involvement in activities that could prove embarrassing to the Chinese government. We have approached your daughter with our concerns several times, but to no avail. As a result, I have been requested by my superior to contact you directly."

"My daughter so informed me," Lee Chao replied, controlling his tone while anger seethed inside him.

They'd taken his donations to each official without protest and accepted the stolen technology they used to pirate designs for the market. So now, he was a potential embarrassment?

After a second's hesitation, the man continued. "The specific concerns deal with the trafficking of illegal drugs and human beings. Many people within our government feel your company should remove itself from those lines of business."

"I have heard no protest in the past when the rewards of my ventures were shared with those people," Lee Chao said.

"Not an attitude I would recommend," the man replied. "The international climate is a fickle directorate, and the politics always complex. So, what was acceptable in the past may become intolerable in the present, and less so in the future."

"I understand," Lee Chao said, although he had no intention of stopping any of his business's ventures, illegal or legal. He was too close to the position he wanted.

"I am glad you appreciate the situation," the man said. "I wish you and your adopted daughter a bright future."

Lee Chao heard the click of the disconnection, then wondered why the man had brought up his daughter. The thought left him uneasy.

CHAPTER 26

Ell sat thirty feet up in a tree stand in a hundred-foot pine one hundred yards west of the target location. In green-mottled camouflage coveralls and a hood of pine branches, she had a perfect view of the lowland valley. Two meters north of her position, where the tree line ran north-south with the river's flow, Leah sat in another tree stand nestled in a two-hundred-foot cedar.

"Ell, status check," Leah whispered over comms.

Ell tapped the surface of her tactical watch's display with the tip of a black-gloved finger, activating the watch's microphone. "Status three," she replied. The number indicated she was positioned to engage.

"Roger, Ell," Leah replied. "Overwatch, this is Leah. Sniper team is status three. Two forty-foot shipping containers and four moving vans have entered the field. A large number of people are moving cargo from the van to the trucks, supervised by at least two dozen armed tangos."

"Roger. Team One is staged north of your location in the farmyard. The other is south of you and across the river. When Sam gives the word, the teams will move in from both sides."

"This is Team Two," Maggie said. "Roger, Overwatch. We are status three, as well, and have a good fording location to cross the river. The sound of the river and the trees should cover our approach."

"All teams prepare to launch," Sam started.

"Hold," Ell said. "The people moving the cargo are not volunteers."

Sam's voice came over the air, his tone abrupt and commanding. "You're your comms, Ell. You do not have operational control."

"I confirm Ell's report. I count at least fifty innocents being used to move the merchandise from two shipping containers to four trucks," Leah interjected. "I also see the woman Ell described from her encounter at the wildlife refuge. She appears to be supervising on the ground. The innocents are scattered throughout the loading site. If we attack now, in force, there could be casualties."

"Those civilians will be used as human shields," Ell added.

There was a long pause before anyone spoke again. Then, finally, Sam came over the air again.

"What do you suggest, Ell?"

"I believe the tangos will load the civilians in the shipping containers once they've finished transferring the cargo to the trucks. We should hold our positions until the innocents are in the containers, in one place and out of harm's way. The tangos arrived in the back of the trucks. I expect they will depart the same way. Once the armed tangos are in the trucks and off the site, I suggest we take the trucks as they head north or south up the farm road. Secure the trucks, the drugs, and the bad guys without peripheral losses of life."

After another long pause, Sam spoke again. "We're going with Ell's plan. Jessica and her team will cover the trucks heading north from the site on the farm road. Maggie and her team will move to the road and cover the south route. Take those trucks with the tangos inside to minimize the opposition, if possible. Alex, Allen, and I will join Ell to take the shipping containers before they leave the field. Teams acknowledge."

Maggie replied first. "Roger. Team two relocating to the south road."

Jessica replied next. "Team one moving to block the road north."

Ell replied next. "Leaving my hide and heading to the valley floor. Sniper overwatch is on Leah."

"This is Leah. Status three for overwatch. Let's do this, folks. Quietly, quickly. No one gets hurt."

"Overwatch, put a call out to the state patrol and sheriff's office. See if they can get a few cars out here to support us," Sam said.

"Overwatch, roger," Walter said. "God's speed."

We can use all the help He can offer us, Ell thought.

A fine drizzle descended on the area as Fan reached the trucks positioned in the lower field. Her long, ebony ponytail wicked the moisture from the edges of her face but left her dark eyes stinging. She wiped a thinly gloved hand across her face, the other hand still on the butt of the .9mm pistol holstered at her hip. She glanced at the matt-black chronometer on her left wrist.

The group needed to finish loading the trucks in the next few minutes before some passerby noticed the suspicious late-night activity on the vacated farm pasture. They'd been lucky so far.

The rental trucks were almost loaded as she approached the two massive green steel shipping containers. All fifty captives appeared to work like the slaves they were to avoid beatings or worse. She grimaced at the thought, then glanced to the farthest rental truck in time to see one of her men drag a young girl behind the truck.

Fan made it there in seconds, slapping the man's hands from the girl and delivering two rapid crushing punches to the man's face and solar plexus. The girl screamed and fell to the ground as the man lost his grip. The man staggered, then took a lunging step toward Fan.

"You may be the paymaster, but you can't . . ." he started.

Fan drove a fist into his sternum with all the force she could muster, turning her hips and shoulders into the strike. She felt a satisfying crunch as her fist crashed into the cartilage of the man's sternum. He stretched out on the ground, retching and clutching at his chest.

Fan stood over the man. Then, while he watched with wide eyes, she drew her pistol with its short suppressor. The man reached for the gun with both hands.

"You can't," the man protested.

Fan kicked his hands away, recalling how her father had slapped her for some grievous error when she was young and beaten her with a belt over some failed task or chore. She realized now just how much the fear of those beatings drove her life—how this man's victim no doubt felt the same sort of fear when the man dragged her behind the truck. No one should have to be afraid like that.

Fan did what she had to do, then helped the young girl to her feet and pushed her toward the line of other captives, who still moved cases of drugs from the shipping containers to the trucks.

"Not a word to anyone," Fan whispered when the girl met her gaze with hopeful eyes. Fan shook her head, then said, "I cannot help you beyond what I just did. You are who you are and where you are. I suggest you make the best of it."

Fan turned back to view the loading area. The captives moved cargo silently as her guards watched. *Her* guards. She felt something twist in the pit of her stomach and examined the feeling—the same one she had felt when she and her two minders visited the port in Turkey. Something was wrong. Something was about to happen.

She kept her pistol drawn as she keyed her earbuds' microphone. "Andy."

"Yes, mistress," Andy replied. He did not sound happy. She knew he hated human trafficking as much as she did.

"Something's wrong," she said. "There's been no traffic on the road above us since we've been here. Even at this hour, I anticipated someone coming along who you'd have to deal with."

"It could just be our good luck," he replied.

"You know I trust nothing to luck. Check the snipers," she repeated.

"I will do so," Andy replied.

She called out for Devon, who responded immediately. "Yes, mistress."

"How long until we are loaded?"

"A few minutes at most," he replied.

"I have a bad feeling. Finish up now. Get the moving trucks rolling and the captives loaded in the vans. I want us out of here in the next five minutes."

"It will be done," Devon replied.

Fan hiked up the gravel road to the pipe gate. Stopping, she turned back in time to see her men closing the doors of the shipping containers and piling into the backs of the four rental trucks. And then she saw something else.

CHAPTER 27

Ell climbed down from her perch in time to see Fan stand straddle-leg over one of her men and then execute him and walk away without a second glance.

"She's a cold one," she mumbled into her mike.

"Say again?" Walter asked from overwatch.

"The woman in charge just executed one of her men," Ell whispered. "She's headed back up the road to the gate. The tangos are piling into the backs of the trucks and closing up. I count seven tangos remaining at the exchange site. Two are in the process of pushing the people into the shipping containers and closing them. I'm moving to the shipping container closest to the trees now."

Her radio clicked. "This is Alex. Moving to the second shipping container."

Another click over comms. "This is Allen. I am status three at the farmhouse and closing fast on the site. I'll take position in the field north of the shipping containers to provide backup as the rest of you take the field."

Leah chimed in then. "Leah: status three. I have you all on visual."

"This is Overwatch," Walter added. "The drone is overhead. I confirm seven tangos on the ground, including the boss lady headed to the gate."

Ell made it to the side of the shipping container without being noticed, just as the last two moving trucks climbed up the gravel road to the gate leading out of the farm. She pounded softly on the shipping container's metal side.

"You inside the shipping container. I'm a friend."

"Please get us out of here," a soft voice cried from inside.

"Working on it," Ell replied. "Everyone, lie on the floor. We're going to attempt a rescue. There may be shooting."

"Please help us," the voice repeated.

The pops of rifle shots split the air and two bullets smacked the side of the shipping container inches to the left of Ell's head. She dropped, rolled, and sighted her sniper rifle's long barrel in the direction of the sound. She immediately spotted the sniper fifty feet up in a tall cedar.

"I've got a sniper in the trees," she said into her tactical watch.

"Hold your fire, everyone," Sam replied. "I want those trucks with the tangos on the road before we engage the tangos still with the shipping containers."

"Roger," Ell replied, removing her finger from the trigger of her rifle.

Ell rose to a crouch and scooted around the end of the shipping container, her M24 sniper rifle hanging from her left hand. Once under cover, she shifted her rifle's scope to infrared, snugged the rifle's stock against her shoulder, and took a bead on the sniper she had identified. Next, she ran her scope down the tree line. *Where there's one sniper, there's usually two.*

Sure enough, she found another sniper in a slender pine tree, eighty feet to the left of the first one, closer to the road leading into the area.

"Leah," Ell whispered.

"Go ahead," Leah replied.

"I've located the sniper who took a shot at me, but there's one more, too." Ell gave Leah the snipers' locations. There was a pause as Leah processed the information.

"The one nearest to the road is a clear shot for me, but I have no shot at the one closest to you. You take that one, and I'll get the other once Sam gives the word."

"Roger," Ell replied. "When Sam gives the word."

With a roar of heavy diesel engines, the four rental trucks passed through the gate at the top of the gravel road. Engines revving, two trucks turned left, heading north, and the other two went in the opposite direction.

"The drone confirms all trucks are out of the field as anticipated. Only the shipping containers and the rigs pulling them remain," Walter said over comms. "I see a driver in each of the two rigs pulling the shipping containers and two others acting as ground guides. Three more are hanging back like they're supervising, in addition to the boss woman at the top of the road leading from the field."

"Those must be the big man's daughter and her sidekicks," Ell whispered.

Ell felt the cold, rusted steel shipping container rock when she said the words. A second later, the truck pulling it fired its massive diesel engine. She pounded on the side of the shipping container.

"Get down." She hoped they heard her.

Just then, Alex came over comms. "This is Alex. I am in position at the second shipping container. I see the driver and ground guide preparing to depart. Status three."

"This is Sam. Snipers, you are clear to engage."

Ell swung her rifle around the corner of the shipping container, drew a bead on the first sniper, and took the shot. She watched the silhouetted figure on her infrared scope lurch back, then tumble from his perch. Then, she shifted her scope's field of view in time to see the other sniper fall from his taller perch as Leah took her shot.

"Enemy snipers are down," Ell said into her watch's microphone.

"Nice shooting, ladies," Jessica replied over the comms. "We have the two northbound trucks locked down. Not a shot was fired. The armed tangos are locked in the back. The driver is secured."

"This is Overwatch," Walter replied. "The sheriff's office has dispatched two cars to your site. ETA is ten minutes."

"We'll hold the trucks and tangos here until they arrive," Jessica replied.

"This is Maggie. We have the two southbound trucks secured. State patrol and their SWAT team just arrived. We've handed the trucks, cargo, and tangos to them."

"Nice job, everyone," Ell heard Sam reply. "Allen, close in on the shipping containers and support Alex. I'll move in and back up Ell. Has anyone got a line on the woman and the other three tangos?"

"This is Walter," he said from overwatch. "No trace of the men and the woman. The field is clear besides the drivers and ground guides with the containers."

"This is Alex. Allen is with me. We're good to take the truck and shipping container. You good to go, Ell?"

"This is Leah. I've got the ground guides covered. I'll keep an eye out for the missing tangos."

"Ready on your word, Ell," Alex said, as Sam moved beside him at the end of the second shipping container.

Ell pulled back the bolt on her sniper rifle and seated a fresh round from the rifle's magazine.

"Let's do this," Ell said as she rammed the bolt back into place.

Ell charged around the left side of the shipping container and up to the truck's cab. She found the ground guide approaching the driver-side door of the cab. Without breaking stride, she fired her rifle from the hip. The round took the ground guide in the chest. He dropped but not before Ell heard Leah protest, "I had that shot lined up."

Ignoring Leah's words, Ell twisted right and raised her rifle in time to see the truck's driver raise his hands—fear on his face. She stepped back as Sam jogged up, slapped her on the shoulder, and moved to the truck's passenger side door. He pulled it open, pointing the barrel of his M4A7 carbine at the driver.

"If you've got a gun, pull it out slowly, and drop it outside the truck. Then show me your hands."

Whether or not the man understood English didn't matter. An M5 machine gun materialized in his hands, slid out the driver-side window, and clattered to the ground at Ell's feet.

Ell glanced at the other truck, where Alex drew down on the driver. From her position, she could see the driver draw a weapon and twist in the seat toward Alex. A rifle cracked, and the driver went down sideways on his seat.

"Bingo," Leah said over comms.

Another rifle cracked, with a lighter tone than the first shot. Ell glanced over to see Allen standing over the truck's ground guide.

"Thanks so much," Alex said into his mike as he rolled the driver over and then zip-tied the man's hands. "Looks like the driver's only winged. I'm glad Allen was there when he was. That man had the drop on me."

"We've got four tangos unaccounted for," Sam said. "Three men and the woman, Lee Fan. Anyone have eyes on them yet?"

A full minute passed before Overwatch came over the air. It was Barry this time. "We've run the entire area with the drone. The field is clear. Those tangos are gone."

"I'm not seeing anything from my position," Leah said.

"Good enough. They must have headed for the hills when things went south. Nice work, all," Sam said over comms. "Let's wrap this up and head home."

"This is Walter. The sheriff has a van on the way to take custody of the human trafficking victims. And the state patrol's human trafficking response team will also be on-site within the hour."

Ell felt a wave of pride wash through her. They'd interdicted a huge shipment of drugs and freed many people who could have ended up anywhere in the world as slaves or worse. This is why she got into law enforcement. This mattered.

On the other side of the low-flowing Deschutes River, beyond the trees from where the Home Team cleaned up the attack site, Fan crouched with her two minders. The thick stand of shrubs hiding their position smelled of dried grass and the pines that hung overhead. Their hiding spot also afforded a clear view of the activities in the field beyond the river's rushing waters.

"This is the second time these people have beaten me in as many weeks," she mumbled.

"Your father will be furious," Andy said.

"No doubt, but there's not much we can do now," she replied. "We fall back, regroup, and report in. Perhaps he will allow us to live for another day if we tell him the truth."

She turned at the sound of soft-soled shoes padding behind them. One of the hired gunmen from her team approached, not attempting to hide the sound of his steps. She didn't know the man, only that her father had hired him along with many others to support the mission. She wondered how the man remained alive and free, given that she, Andy, and Devon were the only one's not taken or killed by the Americans.

The man crouched beside her. "My respects, Mistress Fan," he said in Mandarin. "You have been squarely defeated again."

Fan swallowed hard and replied in the same language. "Where were you during the fight?" she asked.

"I found cover near the river," the man replied.

"Coward," Andy muttered.

Fan cut him off with a raised hand. "He is correct in what he says. And I'm glad someone besides the three of us survived that debacle."

The man nodded, then in a motion too quick to follow, drew a pistol and shot Fan's two minders between their eyes. Fan watched, speechless, as the men drop silently to the ground.

Fan's pistol appeared in her hand, her draw nearly as fast. "You had no authority, no right . . ."

"Your father felt someone inside his organization must be revealing plans to our adversaries. The Americans were well-informed about this operation. Who else knew your plan besides these two? Your father ordered me to eliminate anything suspicious at the source."

"And if you decided it was me?"

212 HOME TEAM 2

The man had lowered his pistol to his side but seemed to think better of it and raised it again. Fan shot from the hip, taking the man beneath his chin. He dropped to lay next to her two men, who had guided her growth and development since she was a child. She would mourn them later, she decided, then laid her pistol at her feet. She unzipped her tactical overalls and stepped out of them. Underneath, she wore jeans, stylishly frayed at the knees and a blue flannel shirt.

She retrieved a faded jean jacket and baseball hat from a backpack she'd secreted a few yards off the day before. She donned those and stuffed the tactical coveralls and her weapons into the backpack. *Never work without an exit plan,* Andy had always said. She felt her heart sag as she glanced down at the body of her lifelong friends and minders but pushed the thought aside as the need to escape became paramount.

After an easy thirty-minute hike across pastures and down a long, dusty road, Fan located the Ducati motorcycle she'd left near an abandoned doublewide trailer near a dilapidated barn. She powered up the motorcycle, navigated the short distance to the interstate, and sailed up Interstate Five toward Seattle a few minutes later. As she drove, she found some solace in the wind rushing past her helmet, until she remembered what she must do next.

She keyed her helmet's embedded cellular phone. "Call Lee Chao," she said.

The voice-activated satellite phone connected the call. Her father answered on the second ring.

"How did it go?"

"We were set up. Everything is lost. Our men were all captured or killed. The same people we encountered in Turkey were there—I'm sure of it—along with a host of others. They called in local law enforcement, so I had to leave."

"I thought our man on the ground had the locals and the feds tied up," Lee Chao protested. "He's very well positioned."

"I'd ask for your money back," Fan replied, regretting her sarcastic tone as soon as she said the words. "They knew everything we did before we did it."

She squeezed the clutch and dropped a gear with her left foot, picking up speed as she passed a semi-truck and trailer in the center lane. Reckless driving, she knew. It could attract the attention of the state patrol. Then again, her most recent failures and the fact her father was prepared to end her life today left her without regard for safety or sanity on the road. Both left a burning feeling in the pit of her stomach.

"We need to end this," her father roared. "We need to send a message to the people in our government that we are strong and capable. These failures cannot be tolerated."

"Yes, Father," Fan calmly replied, slowing her motorcycle to five miles above the speed limit as she approached the city limits of Olympia, Washington.

"What about the two men with you?" he asked.

"They are dead," she replied. "Your man suspected them of duplicity and executed them."

"What of that man?"

"He is no longer with us," Fan replied. "He mistook me for a traitor. So, I corrected his judgment."

Silence filled the air as they both considered their following words.

"That's probably for the best," Lee Chao said after a full minute passed. "No loose ends. Too much has gone wrong. We had another shipment intercepted by the authorities at the Toronto airport today."

"I was not aware of the Toronto operation," Fan said, uncertain exactly how she felt about its failure. It was a strange feeling. She'd always supported her father, even though his involvement in criminal activities bothered her.

"That is no matter. You were fully occupied elsewhere. But it is not the end of things," Lee Chao said. "Find a place to stay. We will talk then."

But should I actually call you and let you know where I am? Fan wondered. *Who can I trust—really?*

She recalled Devon's words one day during tactical operations training. "Criminals don't live by rules. You can't expect them to live by your rules any more than anyone else's."

At the time, he'd been talking about the people her father often hired for his less-than-legitimate work. Now, she wondered if he had also been talking about her father.

———— *////////* ————

Night blanketed the thick brush and trees across the river as Leah and Sam examined three male bodies under the glare of Maggie's flashlight. Maggie towed the body of the heavier of the three men.

"My informant. I worked for years to turn him."

"Sad to hear that," Leah replied. "Can you confirm he worked for Lee Chao?"

Maggie nodded. "Yep, now he's dead. And from this man, we learned that Lee's deep into everything from illegal drugs to technology, weapons, and human trafficking."

"If you knew he was behind all this, why haven't you taken him down?" Leah asked.

Maggie ran a hand through her thick curls and removed several small twigs. She examined one in the glare of her flashlight, then tossed it away.

"Politics. We have captured this one and several others, including one just yesterday in Canada. But his organization is so layered with subsidiaries, it's been impossible to tie anything directly to him. It's even more difficult because of his political connections. Where influence can be purchased, the man's bought them wholesale."

Sam frowned. "I'll get the sheriff's office to process these bodies. But on the good side, we freed fifty human trafficking victims today and took a lot of illegal drugs off the street. So, your informant's death wasn't totally in vain."

They turned as Ell crunched through the waist-deep brush to join them, a flashlight illuminating her way. She ran the light over the three bodies.

"I assume one of these is how you knew about his op," she said, her eyes on Maggie.

Maggie nodded. "Yep, and I hope you don't mind if I pray briefly over him before we go. This man sacrificed his life to help save those people today and to help shut down the flow of illegal drugs."

The comment confused Ell, given Maggie's reputation as a kick-butt operator. But, then again, she saw a lot of spirituality among this unique group's operators. And yet, they all seemed so grounded. Maybe her mother was right when she taught Ell about the Bible and God when she was little—and the good that came with faith.

Ell bowed her head with the as Maggie prayed in silence, then softly said, "Amen."

Everyone joined in with an amen, even Ell, who repeated the word awkwardly a beat later than the rest. While it seemed a strange thing to do after a firefight, praying like that also brought an unfamiliar warmth to her soul. She reached out a hand and touched Maggie on the arm as they started back for the road. Maggie paused and turned back to her.

"You prayed for these men, but what about the others who died today?" Ell asked.

"I pray for all of them, Ell, every night. I never forget any of them. But we did good work today. We saved all those people from captivity and worse, and there's no way to count how many lives we saved getting those drugs off the streets. But even with all the good we did, I never forget those who died on my missions, on our side, or on the opposition's. I pray for them all."

Maggie's words stirred something inside Ell, but Sam called out before she could respond with another question. "We need to get back to headquarters. We just received some good news about a new technology that can help us prevent shipments of weapons, drugs, and captives of human traffickers. But unfortunately, there's a change in the wind, and the director wants us to work on it in the morning. I know it's late, and we're all tired; but it would be great if you could join us, too, Maggie. I'll even have Walter and Barry supply fresh doughnuts and coffee."

Maggie glanced at her watch and yawned. "For the doughnuts, I'll do it."

CHAPTER 28

After a quick shower in the headquarters' locker room, Alex found Sam, Ell, and the rest of the team in the conference room. The place was starting to feel like a second home. Sam leaned back in a chair, cradling a steaming cup of coffee in one hand and a doughnut in the other. He raised the doughnut in salute.

"Nice work today."

Alex nodded and headed for the small table containing the food and drinks. He retrieved a chocolate doughnut nearly as big as his hand and a cup of coffee, then slid into a chair at the far end of the table as Sam exchanged his coffee for the tablet controller for the room's video.

Paul Samuelson's image appeared onscreen to the far left while the Defense Advanced Research Projects Agency logo, or DARPA, popped up on the center screen. A man wearing a tan, green, and black battle dress uniform appeared on the remaining screen to the far right. The rank on his uniform identified him as an army colonel. The DARPA man looked fresh and alert, despite it being three hours later at his location in Virginia and near midnight for the Home Team in Washington state.

Paul hefted a chipped ceramic mug and took a long swallow before saying, "Good evening, or should I say morning? I know it's been a long time since any of us has slept. First and foremost, nice job out there in Washington this evening. I've already heard from the DEA, and they're over the moon about the haul you made. It's a ten-year record for the number of pounds of drugs recovered during a single operation. It's even bigger than what the Home Team recovered a few months back when they discovered a subsurface vehicle loaded with drugs that had been towed into the Port of Olympia by a freighter."

Leah groaned. "There goes our record."

"If I may continue," Paul said, giving Leah a knowing look. "I will direct my next words to Ell."

Ell raised a hand. "I'm here, Paul."

"Last time we met, we discussed human trafficking not being in the charter for the Extreme Operations Group. I'm happy to inform you that it has changed. With the volume of human trafficking in the United States and elsewhere around the globe, it has been deemed in the national interest for us to get involved. The secretary of state issued the order this evening after I woke her to brief her on your operation today. I believe your recent successes sealed the deal."

Alex watched Ell's expression brighten, feeling a smile creep across his own face.

"Thank you," Ell said, glancing toward Alex and returning his smile. "That's great news."

"It gets better," Paul continued. "Sam has been briefed on what you're about to see, but I'll let Colonel Adams from DARPA explain it. It is a very exciting tool to add to your arsenal, particularly given our new mission."

The colonel on the right-hand screen smiled. "As Paul indicated, I work for DARPA. My specialty is drone technology and how we can fit them with lasers and then use them to track drugs, technology, weapons, etc. In 2014, a prominent research paper reported that lasers were successfully deployed in aircraft to remotely detect leaks over oil and gas pipelines in wilderness areas. The equipment identified methane and hydrogen sulfide leaks with as little as six parts per million in the ambient air. We've successfully migrated the technology to drones for use in identifying a variety of airborne elements."

"I've heard about this," Barry said. "The lasers shoot a beam at a target and then record changes in the laser's reflected light based on the stuff hanging in the air the laser's beam passes through. Archeologists always use this technology to map the ground beneath thick jungle canopy when searching for archeological sites. They call it Light Detection and Ranging, or LiDAR."

The colonel nodded. "Exactly. We've taken that to a level where we can identify methane and hydrogen sulfide particles when they appear in the ambient air beyond normal levels. If those levels deviate enough, the laser's reflected light is infinitesimally altered. So, we can record the departure of the laser's reflected light from normal and then use further investigations to determine the cause.

"We applied the technology to identify potential radiation sources in vehicles and buildings we suspected held nuclear devices or dangerous radioactive materials. Our results were unremarkable, but as a byproduct of our research, we discovered when those lasers passed through the air next to a container holding organic matter such as food, humans, drugs, or oils associated with weapons, the lasers could detect their presence. The law of entropy says organic material decomposes rapidly, even when applied to humans. We found the lasers detected airborne particles sluffed off and exhaled by humans. Once tuned, our lasers detected those products with near-perfect accuracy."

A low murmur traveled around the conference table. Alex appreciated the team's excitement. If the lasers mounted on drones could detect the degradation of oils used to preserve weapons and the chemicals used to produce ammunition, the benefit would be huge in the battle against illegal arms dealers.

A black drone that looked like an eighteen-inch-long rectangular box with rounded corners and what looked like two oversized claws extending forward replaced the logo on the center screen.

"We call this the crab," the colonel said. "Its official name is Remote Laser Detection Device, or RLD2. When we use four of these in synchronous flight, we can program them to quickly scan an amazing amount of ground. The lasers work fast and provide their data in near-real-time. We've successfully used a flight of four crabs for a search and rescue mission for a pilot lost in a thick jungle in Panama."

"Thank you, Colonel Adams," Paul said as the colonel concluded his presentation.

Alex's imagination swam with the thought of what the new drone could do in the battle against drugs, weapons, human trafficking, and who knew what else?

Sam picked up the presentation from the director. "The director has authorized Home Team to test the crab drones in the field. We'll receive several of them in the next two days. Walter and Barry will lead on receiving, setting up, and testing. I would like them operational within the next two days. Once they're ready to go, I want Ell and Walter to take them out for a spin. You will hit the ports of Tacoma and Seattle, along with any locations of opportunity you may identify along the way. Your objective is to check out the crab drones and identify leads on the potential movement of drugs, technology, weapons, and human trafficking victims."

"Finally," Ell said from across the room.

Ell's enthusiasm was contagious, and Alex felt a smile creep across his face. Once again, he wondered at the feelings the woman raised inside him.

"Now, there's hope," he heard her say.

"To hope," Alex replied, raising a hand.

As he said the words, Alex wondered precisely what he hoped for. The mission or something else?

CHAPTER 29

F an spent the next day locked in a room at the Hilton in downtown Seattle. She had failed again and had no idea what her father had planned for her now. Additionally, the two people she trusted most in the world were gone.

Her planning for the Tumwater operation had been so thorough, the path to success so clear. It had to have been someone inside the operation who'd alerted the authorities. She wondered if one of her two minders, the closest she'd ever had to friends, were at the core of it. She cast the thought aside. There's no way they'd betray her father.

Sleep evaded her as the evening crept into the night and the night into morning. So instead, she spent the hours running through a series of body-weight exercises and stretches on the hotel room's rough carpeting. She ran through complex patterns of martial arts moves, kicks, punches, and feints until she'd worked herself to a full sweat several times. But despite all the exercises, she found little relief from the concerns that plagued her. Training had always worked in the past. Why not now?

At six in the morning, the familiar chime from her cell phone interrupted the last vestiges of her workout routine. She punched the button on the screen to receive the call.

"Good morning, Father."

"I saw the news when I woke up. The American authorities call it a record-breaking drug and human trafficking interdiction."

"Yes, Father," she replied tonelessly. "As I said yesterday, they were waiting for us."

"Between your operation and the one in Toronto, we've lost one hundred million U.S. dollars in drugs headed for the North American market."

"And the human captives," she added.

Lee Chao snorted. "Those people mean nothing compared to the drugs in those shipping containers. I'm not interested in one million dollars in human bondage revenue when we lost a hundred times as much with the drugs. Clients were waiting for the merchandise. Now, I must spend valuable time mending fences with our buyers instead of moving our plans forward."

She wanted to say, "Your plans," but held her tongue. So instead, she said, "Yes, Father."

"Tell me what you have done to avoid another horrible failure like this one in the future," Lee Chao demanded.

"The American authorities must have had people inside our organization feeding them information," Fan said. "I worked through it in my mind after everything was done. The only possible informants must have been our own people. If it was them, my two minders are no longer a threat. You saw to that."

"Take it as a lesson," Lee Chao replied. A long pause followed before he continued. "Your two assistants were with you since childhood. They were your playmates when you were young and your trusted advisors when you assumed a role in our organization. Your sacrifice is noted. Perhaps losing them is adequate atonement for your failures."

"Atonement?" Fan growled. "There can be no atonement for what we do, Father. The drugs we move around the world ruin peoples' lives. The technology we steal from others feeds your ambitions with our government. Our human trafficking is immoral at its core, ruining countless lives."

"Stop!" Lee Chao yelled. "We have been through this before. We are doing what we must to secure our place in our homeland. Once we have climbed to a superior position in the shipping world and secured our position within China's government, we may have the luxury to pick and choose what we do. Until then, we will sacrifice whomever and whatever we need to achieve our goals."

"But I cannot—" Fan started.

"You will do as I say, daughter," Lee Chao growled. "Rest assured; I know you're changing attitudes since you met those people in the Christian underground."

Fan sucked in a breath. How could he know? She'd been so cautious.

"It is my business to know everything you do. You are my family; you will inherit this company when I join my ancestors. If I hear one more word from you about the so-called morality of what our company does or does not do—if I even think you are judging me for how I've taken this company forward in the past ten years—I will reveal the identities of your Christian friends to the authorities."

If he knew the names of the Closet Christians, he could turn them over to the government, and they would all disappear. She could not let that happen. It was checkmate, and she was the loser.

"I will do as you say," she said after a long pause.

"Good. I have another opportunity for you. I have some shipping containers headed for the Port of Seattle. They should arrive in the next few days. I expect you to receive them, get the merchandise trans-shipped onto trucks, and then deliver them to our customers in the western United States. I will send a crew of hand-picked men and women to assist you. It is all arranged. All you must do is ensure it goes smoothly. Watch your encrypted email for the details in the next few hours."

"I will do as you say," Fan repeated.

"That's my girl," Lee Chao replied. "Make me proud. The consequences of failure are too horrible to consider."

Fan started to reply, but the call was already disconnected. She had to succeed in this last operation to ensure the safety of her friends back in Shanghai—and perhaps her own safety. But once the mission was over, she would have to figure a way out from under her father's thumb. If she did not, how could she ever atone for what *he'd* done—and all that *she'd* done over the past years?

She'd been reading her Bible in secret for several days. What was it her friend had said was in the book of James? Something like whoever knows the right thing to do and fails to do it has sinned.2

She thought of the Closet Christians. What would they think if they knew all her father had done? And what did they think of her— one guilty by association?

---

2   James 4:17

CHAPTER 30

Dark clouds crowded the sky as Ell pulled into the parking lot at the Billy Frank Wildlife Refuge, hoping for another attempt at a relaxing walk through the refuge's beautiful setting. Instead, the weather promised nothing but rain; but she needed a walk, a jog, or something to blow out the cobwebs from a week crowded with events and changes she wasn't prepared to process.

Tall pines surrounded the refuge's parking lot, rustled, and sang their quiet songs in the light breeze. The air felt moist and tasted of salt from the incoming tide off Puget Sound.

She let out a long breath as she stepped from her car and locked it. On her last visit, a crowd of operatives had determined to capture or kill her. She hoped that threat was past. Today, she needed rest. And what better way to do that than a four-mile walk surrounded by water, trees, bald eagles, and other wildlife?

She stretched briefly at the rear of her car, smoothed her blue cotton sweat suit, and tightened the strings of her running shoes. She slung a fanny pack around her waist—the hiding place for her snubnose .38. At least she didn't forget that this time.

Ell scanned the trees surrounding the parking lot one last time, then jogged down the access trail that wound through a mixture of tall oaks, maples, and other trees. She was headed for the Nisqually Delta and its long boardwalk. Moving easily, she passed two tall cattle barns that once held a large herd of cows but now stored park equipment. To her left were several hundred acres of wetlands, flush with singing birds and marshes crowded with Canadian geese. A few minutes later, she emerged from the wooded path onto the short gravel road leading to the boardwalk.

The delta's expansive mud flats were flush with water. A riot of small gulls hovered above the silver expanse along the boardwalk as they hunted for small fish carried in by the tide. Ell paused at the gravel road, scanning the trail behind and ahead of her for threats. Scattered couples and singles, some with long-lensed cameras, occupied most of the trail ahead and the boardwalk in the distance. She perceived no threat from any of them. Nor were there any black-cloaked ninjas in sight. Definitely good news.

Ell leaned into her jog but had gone only ten yards when she heard a call from behind. She slid to a stop and spun around to find Mary Magdalen O'Dell jogging up behind her.

"Didn't get enough of this place last time?" Maggie asked, panting hard.

Maggie wore a light gray, form-fitting training suit with white stripes down the arms and legs. Her curly hair was pulled back in an impossibly thick ponytail that extended out the back of a Seattle Mariners baseball cap.

Ell forced a smile, unsure of how to respond to the woman who'd effectively saved her life, then led the Home Team in a complex, record-breaking drug and human trafficking interdiction operation.

"I didn't get the breather I'd hoped for last time," Ell said.

"I'd say not!" Maggie replied. "As long as foreign operatives are not assaulting you, this is the place to come. I come here for the same reason whenever I'm in the area. Want some company?"

Ell shrugged. "Sure."

Maggie lifted an eyebrow. "I'll take that as a less-than-enthusiastic yes. Walk or jog?"

"I'm sorry," Ell replied. "It's been a long couple of days. Your company would be welcome."

Ell kept her stride even, her rhythm smooth, and her arms loose at her sides. They made it down the quarter-mile stretch to the boardwalk's entrance before Maggie broke the silence.

"Not much of a conversationalist, are you?"

Ell smiled, keeping her eyes forward. "Even though you saved my bacon last time we were here, I don't know much about you. The people on the Home Team like you and say you're some undercover legend, but that's all I know. I'm sorry, but I'm not a trusting person."

"Fair enough," Maggie said. "What would you like to know?"

As they reached the wooden boardwalk, they moved easily together, their footfalls pounding the wooden deck in unison.

"You work for the DEA?" Ell asked.

Maggie nodded. "Yes. So far, so good."

"As I said, the Home Team thinks you're some sort of legend in the covert world."

Maggie laughed. "That's stretching it a bit. I'm not old enough to be a legend."

"Are you willing to add to the story?"

By this time, they had passed the first observation tower, where a pile of harbor seals lay on a small island twenty feet west of the boardwalk. The elevated wooden trail continued for over a mile on wooden decking supported by thick pylons and lined with high wooden railings. The observation tower looked much like an old fort's corner buttress, watching over the entrance to the boardwalk where Maggie and Ell had earlier faced her attackers.

"Sure, where I can," Maggie replied. "You appreciate the nature of my work, much like the necessary secrecy of the human trafficking sting operations you were involved in with the state patrol."

"You do your homework," Ell said.

"It's how you stay alive in my business," Maggie replied. "But first, let's take it down to a walk. The boardwalk can get slick when the tide comes in and the humidity is up like today."

Ell dropped her pace to a fast walk, again matching Maggie's casual stride as they moved along the rough wooden surface of the boardwalk.

"Your fighting skills suggest you've been involved in altercations like we faced many times before," Ell said.

Maggie nodded. "True enough. I spend most of my time undercover and working solo. You must be able to take care of yourself to work in that situation."

Ell paused and placed her arms on the boardwalk's thick wooden railing as two bald eagles glided over the delta's silver waters.

"I've worked with several agencies as an employee and contractor," Maggie continued.

"Including the Home Team, I assume."

"I've worked with several of them as individuals, including Sam and Jessica, but never with the team as a whole. But I know the people on the Home Team well enough to respect them as talented operators.

Some of the best, in fact. They are definitely on the side of God and good, and I appreciate that," Maggie said.

"God?" Ell said. "What's He got to do with it? I can hardly imagine Him being anywhere near what any of us are involved in. The Home Team fights drug runners and cartels. In the state patrol, I face street criminals and those who would sell you and your kids into slavery. Look what happened to the evacuees in Ukraine when Russia invaded. So many children and women taken by human traffickers and sold like cattle." Ell felt her anger rise and her tone stiffen. "There's no God in that. Only evil."

Maggie lingered next to Ell, her arms folded atop the rail. She gestured down to the base of the boardwalk's thick pylons. Several harbor seals stared up at them with wide, dark eyes.

"I'll admit the evil we fight is everywhere and sometimes overwhelming," Maggie said. "But God doesn't make that happen. People make that happen. I believe the work you and I do is an extension of God's hand, and He's right there with us in the battle. We're his agents for good. Satan's no more than a fallen angel who can't stand against God's overwhelming power. It's up to us to carry His fight forward and know He is always with us."

"Like when I was in the shipping container for three weeks," Ell said, returning to the boardwalk's long trail into the estuary. "That was horrible. Then I had to face our captors."

"Exactly. From what I understand, you received the help you needed to do that. First Alex and then the Home Team. If that wasn't a God job, I don't know what was. The report quoted a woman who claimed you were her angel of hope. That was God, again, working through you."

Ell felt her cheeks redden at the comment. "I just did what needed to be done."

They turned and resumed their walk up the boardwalk.

"That's what we all do. Nothing less. Nothing more," Maggie said.

After several long seconds of silence as they walked, Maggie continued. "I've worked for the CIA, NSA, FBI, ATF, and many other lettered agencies over the last ten years. I've traveled the world and nearly given up so many times against the odds I faced. The death, the depravity, the lost lives, and the innocence of those who shouldn't have had to deal with such things. I felt as you did until I looked into the eyes of a young mother and her child on a mission in the Middle East. Three local men had taken them, using the war as an excuse to exercise their moral depravity."

Having served overseas herself, Ell appreciated how hard it might be for Maggie to talk about the experience.

Maggie continued. "Our job that day was a simple canvassing mission—to look in on the woman and her daughter and people like that and distribute food and medical supplies. I entered their house and found them both naked and bound. The men were laughing. Two were stripping off their clothes. As I entered the building, a third man drew down on me with an ancient AK47. His gun jammed. My Beretta didn't. I dropped him and then took out the other two men as they scrambled for their rifles. When the smoke cleared, I remember my pistol slipping from my hands as I fell to my knees and vomited. All I could think of is what the mother and daughter might have suffered had I arrived a second later."

Maggie sucked in a deep breath.

"Why are you telling me this?" Ell asked as they approached the observation tower at the far end of the boardwalk.

"I'm getting to that. Then, another soldier from my team showed up and cut the woman and her daughter free. The next thing I knew, the mother and child hugged me. I remember their words so clearly. 'You are our angel,' they said. 'God sent you.'

"I got angry and tried to shove them away. I wanted to strike out at someone, anyone, but as much as I tried, that mother and daughter clung to me. The soldier who'd happened on us gently separated the mother and child from me and said, 'They're right, you know. Today, you were their angel from God. Who else could have known they needed you here on this day and sent you to save them? As much as we are trained to do what we do, never forget we are on God's mission to help these people.'"

"That's pretty bold, making a religious statement like that on a government mission. Couldn't he have been punished for it?" Ell asked.

Ell heard Maggie chuckle under her breath. "Do you think I'd tell our superiors he'd comforted me as he did? Right then, he was *my* angel."

Ell looked at the wooden planks of the boardwalk as they continued toward the far end. "He was there for you when you needed him, just as you were for the woman and her daughter."

"Put a capital H on the 'He,' and you have it right," Maggie replied. "The mother confirmed it as she stepped between me and my backup, cupped my face in her hands, and said, 'No matter how much evil you have seen, never forget the good you did today because God directed you to our house.'"

"You believe that?" Ell asked.

Maggie nodded. "I do. We had a list of houses to check that day and choices we could make. So, what led me to look in that specific house at that specific time? I could have skipped that house like so many other abandoned places in that war-torn region, but I didn't. So, as a result, that mother and daughter are alive."

"Was it all worthwhile?"

Maggie nodded. "Without a doubt. The mother and her little girl now live in a different region and are both very much alive and doing well. The little girl is in school, and the woman has a good job. I connect with them occasionally to remind myself of the good we do."

Ell snorted, then wished she hadn't. "And you think God had something to do with all that?"

"I do. When I returned to my house, I knelt and prayed for the first time in my life. I didn't know how to pray, but when I reached out to God, I felt the presence of a higher power. The more I prayed, the more my sadness, grief, and frustration eased. The next day, I found the man who'd been my backup on the mission. He told me how to accept Jesus as my Savior. Every day since, I feel His presence."

They resumed their walk, pausing at the observation tower to look over Puget Sound and the snow-capped Olympic Mountains.

"And that made *everything* better?" Ell asked.

"Not by a long shot," Maggie said. "But knowing God's there to guide me gives me the peace of mind and confidence that someone always has my back, no matter what or when. I know I do what I do to serve Him in the battle against evil. It keeps me going, and it keeps me hopeful."

They walked silently back down the boardwalk, Ell considering Maggie's words. Several bald eagles coasted on thermals in the distance.

A large fish jumped into the waters to their left. In hot pursuit, a seagull dove into the water. A flock of small, gull-like birds hovered a few feet above the water's surface, then plunged face-first into the water—sometimes emerging with a small fish, sometimes with empty beaks.

Ell waved toward the small gulls who beat their heads against the water.

"I feel like those birds, beating my head against a wall of water and coming up empty so many times, especially concerning my niece."

"That sounds a bit pathetic," Maggie replied, slapping a friendly hand on Ell's shoulder. "When you accept God, you know you're not alone. But, then again, the more I get into my faith, the more I realize none of this was ever my battle in the first place. It's God's. And if God is the one doing the fighting, and we're His instruments of battle, how can we possibly lose?"

Ell turned to find Maggie's tired gray eyes staring back.

"I wish I shared your faith."

Maggie smiled, the lines in her face disappearing as if by magic and her eyes brightening.

"It's not that hard." Maggie followed with a soft chuckle. "Do you realize you're talking to a woman named after one of the most underappreciated and most important women in the Bible? As a kid, I used to hate that."

"What person?"

"Mary and Magdalene are my first and middle names."

"Ah," Ell replied. "You were named after the prostitute in the Bible?"

Maggie nodded. "I was. And it bothered me until I accepted Christ. After that, I learned there was no proof Mary Magdalene was a prostitute. But on the other hand, she was one of Christ's most devoted disciples. She supported Him and the other apostles during their travels. She and the apostle John were the only ones with Jesus when He died on the cross. And she was among the first to discover Him when He was resurrected."

"She wasn't a prostitute?" Ell protested.

Again, Maggie waved off the question. "One of the Catholic popes started that rumor. There's actually no evidence. I spent a lot of time reading about her. She was brave and stood up when many didn't believe Jesus had been resurrected."

"A strong woman," Ell said.

Maggie nodded. "Once I learned all that, I figured my namesake was a good role model. I now feel my name and what I do is a gift from God."

"I have a niece who was taken." Ell wasn't sure why she said it, and, in the next instant, she felt tears welling in her eyes. "I've looked and looked for her and . . . nothing."

Maggie slung an arm around Ell's shoulders. "Don't give up on your niece. Believe you're involved in what we're doing for a reason. If you trust in God, He'll see to your niece's safety, and you may well play a part in that."

"It's hard to swallow after so many years with no progress. She's probably dead by now."

"I get it," Maggie replied. "Sometimes, the progress in our fight against evil comes slowly. It looks like this boardwalk that seems to wander into the distance without end. But I do believe things happen for a reason, for God's reasons. Realizing He has a plan for all I do helps me get through the toughest times. We can discuss it more if you feel the walls are pushing in on you. I'll give you my secure number."

It was Ell's time to take a big breath. "Oddly enough, I have been thinking about the whole God thing for some time now. I know Alex and the Home Team go to church. Maybe I could try it out."

Maggie smiled, her eyes sparkling. "Maybe with Alex?"

Ell felt her cheeks grow hot. "Maybe . . . A long time ago, I let myself care about a man—another soldier in my unit. A sergeant like me. On our last mission in Afghanistan, we lost him. We carried a lot of people out after a firefight I thought would never end, but he didn't make it. I swore then I would never let myself care about another person like that. It's just not worth the pain."

"And now?"

It felt like Ell's cheeks warmed even further as she replied, "Let's just say I'm reconsidering."

They both laughed.

"I saw how you looked at him in the conference room. So maybe we could all go to church together. I want to visit Pastor Carson's church, where many of the Home Team go. I've heard about the church; the man's a legend in the covert operations world."

"Thanks," Ell muttered. "I think I'd like that."

"Any time, sister, any time," Maggie replied.

CHAPTER 31

A t six in the morning on Monday, Sam stood at the edge of the Home Team's mat area, sweat-soaked and feeling better after a good workout.

"Good morning."

Sam looked up to find Jessica sitting in one of the folding chairs at the mat's edge. How long she had been sitting there, he couldn't know. The woman moved more quietly than anyone he had ever known.

"Tough morning?" she asked. "I've noticed how you often log in early when we're up against a tough situation."

"It's that human trafficking thing . . . Ell's message came through loud and clear, and she's right. It's a problem that doesn't get enough press, and we are now in the middle of it."

"I did some digging over the weekend," Jess replied. "Washington is part of a human trafficking network that includes California, Hawaii, Canada, and many ports up and down the West Coast. The latest report indicates eleven hundred new cases of human trafficking happen each year just in this state."

"That doesn't include the cases not reported."

They turned to find Ell standing nearby.

"That number is probably much larger," Ell continued. "My niece and many other kids under eighteen were taken in King County. Now, five years later, she could be anywhere within that network or around the globe. She was a troubled kid, always running off, but that didn't mean she deserved to be thrown into the sex trade or become slave labor on some farm or dive restaurant."

Jessica nodded. "Most of the cases in Washington State involve sex trafficking, but a surprisingly large number involve people taken for slave labor. According to some reports, King County tops the list in the state, probably because it has the state's largest port. Surprisingly, several smaller counties are responsible for the lion's share of sex trafficking. They border the Columbia River, which provides many locations for offloading and loading victims. Unfortunately, small law enforcement groups serve those counties."

"What amazes me is how many people in the U.S. don't think human trafficking is an issue," Ell said. "In one year, eleven thousand cases of human trafficking were reported in the United States. California tops the list almost yearly—followed by Texas, Ohio, and other states. It's a problem kept well under the radar, although not for lack of effort by many law enforcement agencies."

Sam ran a hand through his close-cut black hair, then wiped the sweat on his workout shorts. "We are going to get involved in this."

"Glad to hear it."

The group turned to find Alex approaching the workout space, his duffle bag in hand.

"I've read your file, Alex," Sam said. "And I can understand why."

"What's that mean?" Ell said.

"Alex was taken when he was ten," Sam said.

Alex set his bag down and dropped into a chair next to Jessica. "I came from a Christian family and spent a lot of time attending youth groups and events associated with our church. We didn't know that in that quiet Pennsylvania town where no one locked their doors at night, a human trafficking ring was active and growing."

"They got you?" Ell asked.

Alex nodded. "Right out of my parent's front yard. And I wasn't kept local. I spent four years in the jungles of Thailand as a punching bag at an illicit Thai boxing school. Kids like me were imported for an illegal kids' fight syndicate. Most of the boys died during those fights or from disease or malnutrition. I was a lucky one. Turned out I had a penchant for martial arts. I survived by learning from my experiences. I studied the Thai kids' moves, practiced in the night when I wasn't fighting or doing endless chores, and eventually became pretty good.

"I had won several fights by the time I was fourteen, which caused the head trainer to notice me. He set up a big fight between his son and me, never thinking I'd survive the experience. I won the fight and seriously injured the boy. I received word later that they would take me into the jungle and kill me that night because of what I'd done. So, I made a run for it when everyone was at dinner. I followed logging trails left by the elephants. I made it to Bangkok and then to the U.S. embassy four days later."

"It's amazing you made it all that way alone," Jessica said.

"I ran into missionaries on my second day out. By that time, I'd been praying my brains out. They showed up just when I needed them most and fed me and gave me water. Those people and my faith kept me going through those four years and the days in the jungle."

"Were you reunited with your family?" Jessica asked.

Alex met her eyes, then shook his head slowly. "They died before I got home. My father, Sam's uncle, was a senior noncommissioned officer with the military police. He retired early to take up the search for me. My mother was a soft-spoken woman, an accountant, and a devout Christian. I think the situation killed both of them. My sister was two years older than me. The state put her into foster care when my parents died; but she ran away, and I haven't seen her since I was taken."

Alex held up his hands. "But I'm past that. When I got home, I encountered some great people who were great role models. My foster father was a retired army sergeant major. His wife was a saint, if ever I've met one. They're why I went into the service after graduating high school."

"That's why you were watching the shipping container in Turkey?" Ell asked. "Your own crusade?"

Alex held his hands wide. "Guilty, but it's not been much of a crusade. When I'm not on deployment with my ranger company, I spend my time tracking down opportunities to help human trafficking victims. So, when I met you in Turkey, it was the first time I'd gotten a decent lead through the government's crime assessment network in two years."

Sam reached out and clapped a hand on Alex's shoulder. "You made a real difference on the Tumwater op."

"We all did," Alex replied.

Ell smiled and gazed around the group. "Anyone want to spar? I'm feeling strong and in the mood."

Alex let out a low laugh. "You're on."

As Alex and Ell moved to the mats for their workout, Jessica looked at Sam and asked in quiet words, "I wonder if they're fighting or if it's something else?"

Sam smiled. "Those two seem connected in a lot of ways. I'm not sure it'll be much of a fight."

CHAPTER 32

That evening found Ell fidgeting in Olympia's Ram Restaurant and still chewing over her conversation with Maggie. Here she was on her first date in she didn't know how many years. In the army, the training occupied her time. In the state patrol, the academy had. Now came her work with the task force.

"What am I doing here?" she muttered to herself.

She'd surprised herself when she accepted Steve Madigan's invitation to meet for dinner, even though she'd made him agree not to call it an official date. A non-date, she'd said. He'd not attempted to hide his interest in her over the past week. Sitting here waiting for him to arrive, she wondered how a person who'd just worked through dangerous missions could be so intimated by an evening out with a nice, good-looking guy.

She felt awkward, decked out in new skinny jeans and a loose-fitting green sweater she hoped would set off her eyes and cover the pistol holstered at the small of her back.

At five foot five, Steve was not the tallest man on the team by far; but with his deep tan, a black buzz cut, and startling aqua eyes, the thirty-year-old ranger cleaned up well. Slim and muscular, he seemed comfortable with his stature, and she liked that they stood eye-to-eye.

She had researched the U.S. Army Rangers after that long look Alex threw at her across the conference room table. It had shaken her to her bones, but not in a bad way. But it did make her wonder about the type of people Alex and Steve might be.

She discovered that only 40 percent of those who applied to the ranger school were selected. A person had to be both tough and intelligent to make the cut. Then to be chosen for the Home Team . . . well, that said a lot.

And then there was Alex. She got the impression that as good a guy and as competent an operator as Steve might be, Alex might be twice the person with his quiet competence, upbeat attitude, and faith. So, why was she here instead of out on a date with Alex? Simple. Alex hadn't asked her. This is why dating was so complicated and probably why she'd avoided it for so long. But Steve's broad smile drew her away from those thoughts.

"You clean up nice," she said as he slid onto the stool beside hers.

Steve wore casual chinos, a polo shirt open at the neck, and brown suede loafers. His eyes sparkled in the restaurant's dim overhead lights.

"You look amazing," he said. "I'm glad you agreed to come, even if you demanded we call it a 'non-date.'"

They both laughed as the pert, blonde waitress with an infectious grin showed up. She balanced four plates on a tray with one hand and held an order pad in the other.

"Something to drink?" the waitress asked.

Steve seemed to catch Ell's thoughts and said, "We'll both pass on that, but I would like one of your famous burgers."

The waitress grinned. "Of course. Let me take these dishes to the kitchen. I'll be right back to get your orders."

As they waited for the waitress to return, their conversation flowed easily. Steve told a few stories about when he had been assigned to the Drug Enforcement Agency for a training exchange between the DEA and his ranger battalion. He'd taught tactical skills to the DEA's action teams while they exposed him to their approach to seeking out and preventing illegal drug shipments within cartel distribution networks.

"Much of the work was done here in Washington state," he concluded. "I grew up not far from here."

Ell shared her story about life as a child and how her parents trained her early in all martial arts. She also told how their stories about fighting crime led her to serve as a sergeant in the military police and how she had seen action in Afghanistan.

"Wait," Steve said as she wrapped up her story. "I think I heard about you. You dragged your teammates out of a serious firefight and killed a dozen or more enemy troops who'd ambushed your detachment. You got the Silver Star for that, with a 'V' device for courage, right? Some said you should have gotten the Medal of Honor."

Ell dropped her eyes and felt the joy of the evening slipping away. She seldom talked about what happened that day in Afghanistan. It was in the past, but the story seemed to follow her wherever she went.

"Can we talk about something else? I lost some good friends that day."

Steve nodded and changed the conversation's direction. "I heard about your niece from one of the other team members. I understand Alex was a human trafficking victim. For all the man's bluster, I don't see how he can be any good at what he does after all that."

Ell's hackles rose. "I think Alex is driven by his experience in the same way as I am by having my niece taken. And I haven't seen any bluster. Just the opposite."

Steve glanced at his menu. "You came to his defense pretty quickly. Something there I should be aware of?"

Ell's cellphone vibrating in her pants pocket cut him off. She pulled it out as Steve's phone went off, too. She glanced at the screen. Emergency deployment. Report immediately. It was probably for the best. She had no interest in continuing the evening with Steve after what he'd said about Alex.

"We're going to have to take a raincheck," she said as the waitress returned to take their orders.

"Military?" the waitress asked.

Steve nodded, and the waitress shrugged. "No problem. Happens all the time. Thanks for your service and have a safe evening."

"Short date," Steve said as he stood from his stool.

"Short non-date," Ell corrected him, forcing her tone light. "I bet this happens a lot to members of the Home Team."

"For rangers as well," Steve replied. "This would have been a rare night off for me. Too bad we had to end it so early."

"Yeah," Ell said as they stepped through the restaurant's doors into the brisk evening air.

Suddenly, a petite woman with long, black hair stepped into their path a few yards away. Ell dropped a hand to Steve's arm.

"It's that woman from Tumwater and the wildlife refuge," she whispered. "I'm sure of it."

She felt, rather than saw, Steve move his hand to the grip of the Beretta at his side.

"She must be here for me," Ell said, sliding her hand under the hem of her sweater and gripping the handle of her Sig Luger. "She's tried twice to take me down. She's here to finish it."

"She has a lot of gall showing up here alone, or she's got back-up somewhere," Steve replied. He nodded toward a line of shadowed storefronts across the parking lot. "I'll move off like we're ending our date. I'll take position across the lot in the shadows. I'll be only a few seconds and an easy shot away."

Ell nodded, then flinched as Steve leaned in to kiss her on the cheek.

"Thanks for meeting me for dinner, dear," he shouted. "I'll see you next week."

Ell took a breath. She hadn't been kissed in years in any fashion or form. It felt awkward when Steve did it.

"Yes, of course," she stammered. "See you at work."

Steve strolled across the parking lot as the woman continued her approach. Whatever else Steve might be, he was a ranger. His presence in the shadows comforted her.

Ell drew her pistol and let it hang at her side as the woman stopped two steps away, then sat on a bench beside the restaurant's front doors.

She glanced at Ell, then patted the seat next to her. "I'm not here to do you harm—especially not out here in the open with your friend across the street. Come. Sit."

The woman hardly looked like a hardened criminal—let alone a drug runner, technology smuggler, or human trafficker. Instead, she wore stylish white slacks and a delicate blouse decorated with tiny purple, green, and yellow flowers. A long tan vest covered the blouse and draped over her lap. Her dark almond eyes reached up to Ell from a small oval face and flawless tanned complexion. A thin, red-brown highlight ran through her hair on the left, running down from her temple and ending in a thick cascade of ebony. She lifted a hand to tuck the strand of lighter hair behind an ear and used her short, manicured nails to tap the seat next to her again.

"Seriously. Really. There's something I'd like to talk about. You will not need your pistol."

Ell thumbed the checkered grip of her Sig but kept it to hand as she took the offered seat.

"Why are you here? You failed to take me out at least once, perhaps twice if you count the Tumwater operation."

The woman offered Ell a wan smile, then glanced at the parking lot stretching before them.

"My name is Lee Fan," the woman said. "As you already know, I'm sure, my father is the man your organization is hunting."

Ell nodded. "Again, why have you come here when you know I could easily call my associates and have you picked up?"

Fan reached into a pocket of her long vest and pulled out a passport written in Chinese. Ell examined the cover. The word DIPLOMAT was embossed in gold letters across the top.

"I don't fear you or your law enforcement agencies."

Ell handed the passport back. "Diplomatic immunity. Must be nice to know people in high places."

Fan pocketed the passport. "It has its benefits, but that is not why I am here. I have eluded my father's people for the moment but may not have much time. My father's business is a complex and involved enterprise. I disapprove of a great deal of what he does, but I am his daughter."

"I am aware of that, but I'm not sure what that has to do with anything," Ell said.

Fan raised a hand to cut off Ell's next words. "I believe, given time, I can convince my father to reconsider several of his criminal enterprises; but it will take time, and my success is not guaranteed."

"You're saying you will stop the human trafficking, drug running, and technology smuggling?" Ell said. "Why would you do that?"

"Let's just say I have recently found reason to reconsider my involvement in those lines of business. Call it a new moral imperative. But as I say, I know what I hope to do cannot happen overnight. My father is ruthless and well-connected. His personal goals require money and providing unique goods and services to powerful people in my country and elsewhere."

"Why, in heaven's name, should I believe a word you're saying?" Ell demanded.

"Why, in heaven's name, indeed. Do you believe in God, Ms. Evander?" Fan asked.

"What has God got to do with this?"

How often had she heard God's name in the past week—and now from a hardened criminal?

Fan let out a soft, almost silent chuckle. "I'm just finding out what He has to do with all this, but it seems He may have invested quite a lot in the things we do."

"Excuse me if I have doubts about that, given your history," Ell said. "But again, why should I believe what you say?"

"For one, should my father discover I've talked with you at all, I am sure he would not let me live," Fan replied.

"I agree you took a risk coming here to meet me. But again, to what end?"

Fan stood and smoothed the front of her blouse under her vest. "Until I successfully change the direction of my father's business, I suppose I want someone on your side to know not all of us agree with what my father does. Perhaps I'm even asking for forgiveness in advance for what he may have me do in the future."

Ell stood and turned to face the woman. "That sounds like empty hope and so much garbage. You want us to believe in you, but you're still going to move ahead with human trafficking, drug running, and technology theft? If you want our support, you need to do better than that."

Fan reached for her vest pocket. Ell braced herself and gripped her pistol tighter. But Fan didn't draw a pistol. Instead, she handed Ell a small envelope.

"Perhaps you will accept this as a good faith offering. I hope you will consider it when we next meet."

With that, Fan turned away and headed into the depths of the restaurant's dark parking lot. Ell followed her with her eyes but soon lost her in the gloom. She listened for the start of a vehicle but heard nothing.

After a time, Steve stepped out of the shadows. "What did she want?"

"I'm not sure," Ell replied. "She seemed intent on apologizing for what she and her father do for a living, as though that would make a difference." Ell held up the envelope. "And she gave me this."

"Open it."

Ell lifted the flap on the envelope and removed two pieces of paper. She gasped as she examined a photo of a young girl.

"It's my niece," Ell whispered. "This photo must have been taken when she was abducted five years ago."

Steve gestured to the other piece of paper. "And that?"

Ell held the paper to the light leaking from the restaurant's window behind her. "It's a note. It says they take pictures of every person taken by their organization. The note says my niece is on a farm near Kennewick, Washington. The grid coordinates are provided."

Ell turned to Steve and hugged him tightly, tears flowing down her cheeks. "She's alive!"

Steve wrapped his arms around her and whispered, "Let's go get her. Kennewick's only a four-hour drive, and I know the area."

Ell stepped back, wiping her face with the sleeve of her sweater. "There may be others at that location. If so, we'll need to free them all. That means we need a plan and additional resources."

Steve raised his cell phone, and the urgent message from the Home Team headquarters still glowed across its screen. "And we've got this."

Ell nodded. "Let's head back to headquarters. I hope Maria can make it long enough for us to do whatever the Home Team needs now. After that, nothing will keep me from getting her back."

CHAPTER 33

Ell and Steve arrived at the Home Team headquarters forty minutes later. Walter Drake and Barry Whitman met them at the door. At six foot four, Walter looked intimidating in his black tactical overalls; mocha skin; wavy, black hair; and muscles that strained the seams of his uniform. By contrast, Barry stood half a foot shorter, and his tactical overalls hung on him like an ill-fitting suit. Both wore grim expressions.

"The director is waiting on the conference room video screen," Barry said.

Alex, Carla Caruso, Aria Akamai, and Bono were already there. Ell pulled up a chair next to Steve at the far end of the table. The director's face appeared on-screen at that moment.

"Barry and Walter have the details and can brief you later. I'll give you the *Readers' Digest* condensed version of what's happened. I sent the Home Team to Germany yesterday to intercept a weapons shipment. Unfortunately, the order came down on short notice. Jess, Allen, and Sam traveled together on the group jet. They confirmed their arrival in Nurnberg but went dark immediately after. Leah traveled separately for personal reasons, and now she's in the wind. I have no idea if she even made it to Germany.

"If I were to guess, there's a leak somewhere, and the opposition was waiting for Jess, Allen, and Sam. Leah may have noticed that and moved into the shadows. She likely doesn't trust our communications or contacts in Germany."

Paul paused, as if collecting his thoughts, then continued, his eyes boring into everyone in the room.

"I need H.T. Two to find the Home Team and bring them back. The German government is unaware of our presence in Nurnberg, and we must keep it that way. The details of the weapons shipment suggest traitors inside the German government and ours. If you can recover the weapons, fine, but rescuing the members of the Home Team is your primary mission."

Paul frowned. "I know you are all on a rare evening off, but I need your help. I want you geared up and in the air within the hour. Walter will handle the logistics. He and Barry will provide overwatch from Joint Base Lewis-McChord. Given his tactical background, I'm delegating operational command of this mission to Alex. A lot is at stake, so please follow Alex's directions to the letter."

Paul looked at Ell. She'd left him a voicemail summary of her meeting with Fan while they drove to the headquarters.

"Thanks for informing me about your niece. You are not obligated to function as a de facto Home Team Two member because of your situation with the state patrol. I will not begrudge you if you decide not to participate in this rescue mission and instead follow up on the lead to free your niece."

Ell faced Paul. "There's nothing to decide, sir. The Home Team accepted me as one of their own from the beginning. They came to my rescue at the wildlife refuge, even though they hardly knew me. I've grown to like and respect them too much not to help bring them home. No one has confirmed that my niece is being held captive on the farm in Kennewick for the past five years. If that proves to be true, I doubt her situation will change much over the next forty-eight hours. But I would ask the team's help freeing her once we return."

Paul offered a rare smile. "I'm glad to hear your decision. We need all the help we can get with this one. Once you're back from Germany with the Home Team in tow, your niece will be our next priority."

Ell glanced around the room. Bono and Aria gave her raised fists and smiles. Alex met her eyes with that unsettling gaze and easy smile of his, the one that twisted her gut each time.

"We'll get them back," Alex said, "and then we'll round up your niece."

CHAPTER 34

The members of H.T. Two allied at the Extreme Operations Group's hanger on the McChord AFB an hour later. With darkness closing in, the air on the tarmac felt chilly and damp and lingered with the scent of jet fuel. Under the watchful eye of Sybil, their pilot, they loaded four large duffels of weapons, equipment, and ammunition into the jet's hold.

"Sam, Jessica, and Allen were taken prisoner or worse?" Ell whispered. "How did that happen? Security is so tight around here."

Alex tossed his bag into the storage compartment, then laid a compassionate hand on her shoulder. "If they're alive, we'll find my cousin and the rest of the team."

"And if not?"

"We'll do what we need to do to keep those weapons out of enemy hands and bring those responsible to justice," Alex replied.

Ell laid her hand atop his and felt an electric charge run through her. She shoved the confusing, pleasant sensation aside and gave Alex her best strong smile.

"Yes, we will."

"Wheels up in ten," Sybil called from the boarding stairs. A retired air force pilot and criminal investigator, Sybil Carmen had flown for the Extreme Operations Group for ten years. Tall, blond, and beautiful;

proficient with most handguns; certified as an emergency medical technician level four paramedic; and licensed to fly anything with a rotor, prop, or jet up to and including a Boeing 737, she projected an easy confidence Ell found comforting.

"Belt in and get some rest," she said. "It's a nine-hour flight and a nine-hour time difference. We'll arrive at four in the afternoon tomorrow, German time."

The jet's cabin offered two long couches to the rear of the passenger compartment, which could be configured as medical treatment beds. Six executive lounge chairs swiveled 360 degrees along the forward walls. At the far rear of the plane was a small galley and restroom. Below the restroom's door was a drop-hatch used for high altitude low opening or HALO parachute insertions. But, of course, they wouldn't use the HALO chute today.

Alex took the most central of the lounge chairs, unsnapping his tactical harness and setting it and his pistol on the floor beside his chair. Bono and Aria each took one of the couches. Ell marveled how Aria appeared to fall asleep as soon as she stretched out on the couch. Carla, Steve, and Ell dropped into three of the remaining lounge chairs. Carla offered a continuous stream of questions and comments for Alex to consider as he formulated their plan for arrival in Germany.

The jet's twin engines roared, and the plane lifted smoothly into the air after a short roll down the runway. Beyond the windows, Ell saw the tree-studded grounds of Joint Base Lewis-McChord drop rapidly from sight beneath them. As Sybil banked the jet east, Ell caught the outline of Mount Rainier's rounded form in the distance, its broad white snow fields and glaciers shadowed in darkness.

Two weeks ago, I was a simple state trooper. Now, I'm on a mission to Europe to save a team of tier-one operators.

The words sounded only in her thoughts as she considered her situation. Should she be happy, intimidated, or confused by all that had happened to her in the last few weeks? Oddly, as many times as she had been placed in danger, this thing they were doing, the people with her on this adventure—all felt right. As if she were exactly where she belonged.

As Ell glanced around the jet's small passenger compartment, she marveled at the diversity of H.T. Two's membership. Carla, the ex-navy SEAL, had midnight skin, bright eyes, a wide smile, and an infectious positive attitude and was wearing baggy jeans and a floppy University of Washington sweatshirt. Steve, the U.S. Army Ranger, had a deep suntan and was wearing skinny jeans and a Sea Hawks football jersey. Diminutive Aria, a surprisingly robust navy special operations officer, was in black jeans and a Hawaiian blouse that hung loosely at her sides. Bono, with her exotic good looks of Korean descent, was a human intelligence sergeant with the army special forces and had on smooth-fitting slacks and an elegant blouse in dark green and gold that emphasized her dark eyes and black hair.

Back at Lewis-McChord were Walter, the intellectual giant with a knack for logistics, and gangly Barry, with his fantastic grasp on anything involving technology.

And then there was Alex—the calm one. The one who managed a smile no matter the circumstances but also projected a level of competency that set everyone around him at ease. No one objected when Paul gave Alex operational control of this mission. Well, maybe Steve chafed a little. She'd seen it in his expression. But even Steve backed off once Alex got Walter rolling on the logistics, Barry on setting up comms, and the team en route to the jet.

And just how do I fit in with this group? Ell wondered. Not the tallest or the smallest. Not the most athletic or the most skilled. Given her youthful appearance and bright green eyes, the state patrol recognized her value as a competent, skilled law enforcement officer who could pass for someone much younger. That didn't seem to matter here. Capable in martial arts and weapons of all kinds and compared to the other members of H.T. Two, Ell wondered if she brought anything at all to the table.

Alex reached over to tap a finger against her forearm as if reading her thoughts. Their eyes met, and his message was clear. She was in good company and would do fine. How did the man do that? It was as if he could read her thoughts.

When Sybil announced the plane had leveled off at twenty-five thousand feet, Alex swiveled his chair to face the rest of the team. Sybil stepped out of the cockpit to listen as he briefed the team.

"Here's the situation, folks," Alex said. "We don't know much except Jessica, Sam, and Allen made it to Nurnberg. Somewhere near there, the arms transaction was scheduled to go down. Their communications went off-line thirty minutes after they landed at the airport. It could be a simple comms failure, or they may have been captured or worse. Leah is somewhere in the city, probably hiding until help arrives."

"Leah's comms could still be online," Carla said.

Alex nodded. "Good point. She may be staying dark until she hears from the right person. The Home Team members receive comms through an embedded device, much like a cochlear implant used to aid the deaf. So, they may all hear us without their captors knowing. It's something we should consider."

"If their cochlear implants haven't been removed," Steve said, tapping his left ear, where the tactical earbud rested. "Even if they haven't, they still won't be able to talk to us without their captors knowing."

"Another good point," Alex replied. "We'll assume they can hear us and that Leah may be reluctant to transmit until we prove who we are."

"What's the plan, boss?" Aria asked, slouched against the back of the jet's couch with one leg dangling over the edge of the couch's armrest.

"We'll land at a small airfield on the outskirts of Nuremberg," Alex said. "We'll split into teams of two. Bono will remain with Sybil and the aircraft to secure our way out of there once we're done. The other teams will search the airfield's perimeter and another area not far from where the arms deal was reported to happen. It was the site of the old Nuremberg Army Hospital that closed in the early 2000s. We'll hunt through those areas first, then adjust our plan as needed. Walter has identified several special operations command units training with the German military. They can provide backup if needed." Alex rubbed a hand across his close-cropped black hair, his dark eyes intense. "I wish we had more."

"I've worked with less," Steve said.

"Haven't we all," Aria added. "I'm for some shut-eye while we can. Tomorrow's going to be a busy day."

"Smart woman," Carla said.

Ell was about to pitch in when she noticed Steve tapping a message into his tactical watch.

Now, that's something I need to learn how to do before we land, Ell thought.

The Tumwater operation was so sudden, and she'd received the watch just before then and didn't have time to investigate its operation. Messages, embedded microphones, time of day that shifted automatically for each time zone, and the ability to sync with any number of applications on the satellite cell phone and forearm tablet computer she'd been issued. This watch could be her lifeline if things got dicey, which seemed to happen every time she went out with the Home Team.

They touched down at Nuremberg Airport, a short drive of four-and-a-half kilometers from the city. What little information they had suggested, Leah made her way to Frankfurt by commercial plane, then took an overnight train to Nuremberg. From that point, it was anyone's guess.

Three black SUVs awaited them at a private terminal on the east side of the airport. Alex gathered the team together, and they moved their weapons and duffels from the plane to the backs of the vehicles.

"From this point on, earbuds should be in and turned on," Alex said. "They're preprogrammed to group operational channel number one, the same one used by Home Team when they arrived in Germany. You all have a tactical watch, forearm tablet computer, and holster. Even though we're all wearing civilian clothing, do your best to obscure the forearm tablets and your weapons. Once we're in the vehicles, everyone touches base with Barry to ensure comms are up and clear through all three devices. Underground tunnels litter this place. We'll need to be careful if we need to enter any of those tunnels. In those cases, we may have limited comms, although the crab drone can act as a signal repeater when we're underground. Regular check-ins are every hour on the hour.

Whoever got the drop on the Home Team's must be good at their jobs, so be on your toes."

Steve raised a hand. "What about the crab?"

Alex nodded. "Right. Who here feels the most comfortable with operating a drone?"

Steve raised his hand. "I've had a lot of practice with drones. I can find a location on the airfield's perimeter and set up there. If anyone notices me, I'll look like any other geek having a little fun tracking airplane takeoffs and landings."

Alex nodded. Their earbuds clicked once.

"I resemble that geek reference," Barry said from his location back at Lewis-McChord. "Comms are up and active, guys. And I do love my drones, so don't mess it up, Steve. I want it back in one piece."

"Will do, your geekiness," Steve replied.

Everyone laughed, something they all needed about then.

"It's settled, then. The plan was for Home Team to approach the southwest corner of Nuremberg's old town buttress' walls, then fan out through a series of tunnels that converge there. They were to move underground to the old Nuremberg Army Hospital site, where the lead suggested the arms exchange would occur. I want one person to start there. Can you do that, Aria?"

Aria nodded and tapped in the coordinates for the Nuremberg Army Hospital but paused before heading out as Steve spoke up. "I don't think that's a likely location for any large weapons cache."

"Go on," Alex said.

"I was stationed in Germany for several years, not far away in Wurzburg. Unfortunately, those tunnels under the old hospital site are narrow, confined, and difficult to navigate with anything larger than a wheelbarrow. A better location might be right where we're standing. In addition, several large, abandoned underground storage warehouses are in this area. To store and move a large cache of weapons, you'd need a place like one of those, along with easy transport in and out."

"Okay," Alex said. "How do you suggest we handle this, then?"

Again, Ell wondered at Alex's patience as he considered Steve's input.

"I'd suggest a team check out the southwest area of the airport between us and the city. Another team could search the downtown train station if Leah went there and is hiding. A third team could search the airport's west, north, and east perimeter. I can use the drone's lasers to identify access doors to the underground tunnels that show evidence of recent use and that might be wide enough to move a large cache of weapons."

Barry clicked his mike to draw their attention. "I can program the drone's lasers from here to identify disturbed earthworks."

"And just what will I do with my time if you're doing all the cool stuff from your end?" Steve asked.

"Don't worry. You'll be driving," Barry replied. "Believe me when I say I'm sacrificing a lot by letting anyone else pilot the drone."

Alex clapped his hands together softly, drawing the team's attention. "We have a plan. Ell, you're with me. First, we'll do the airport's north, east, and west perimeters."

Ell felt her heart skip, then forced the feeling aside. *So, he chose me as a partner. What's the big deal? I'm a competent operator. He sees that.*

Alex continued speaking into his tactical watch so Barry and Walt could hear. "Steve and Carla will work the drone around the airport's perimeter. Aria can check out the Nuremberg Bohnhoff to see if Leah's still in the area. Bono and Sybil will be our reserves back here with the aircraft."

During the brief pause that followed, Alex and the team heard three distinct clicks over their earbuds—the universal signal for help.

Alex tried but failed to suppress a grin. When the second series of three taps sounded, Ell heard him say, "That's got to be Leah."

Alex spoke into his tactical watch again. "Overwatch, I'm shifting to my satellite phone."

"What's going on?" Steve whispered.

"Hang on a minute," Alex replied, then felt his satellite phone buzz as an incoming text arrived. He glanced at the phone's screen. It was from Leah.

"Safe and secure. In hiding. Send a ride. Bohnhoff."

"Leah was monitoring her sat phone," Alex explained. "When I spoke to Barry over my phone, it was a Trojan call to him but intended for her."

This time Ell's satellite phone buzzed. "I've got a text. She must be roaming from number to number to avoid being traced."

Ell examined the text. "She'll be at the train station's east side, near the maintenance yard gate. Honk once, pause, and then honk twice to identify yourself."

"On my way," Aria said. "I'll pick her up and return as soon as possible."

"Good," Alex replied. "The rest of you head out. I'll message you over your tablet computers, so ensure they're strapped on and powered on."

"On it," Carla said as she and Steve retrieved the drone from the back of an SUV.

Alex turned to Ell. "Now, we wait for Leah to see what she's learned. Until she arrives, you and I can walk around the airport's perimeter to see if we can find anything. Then, we'll stay together and work our way north."

"Let's do it," Ell said, feeling the excitement of the mission rising in her.

This was H.T. Two's first official mission, and the team had accepted her as one of their own. This went far beyond what she'd signed up for when she agreed to spend her three-month suspension with the Home Team.

Now, she just had to perform. Still new to the world of covert operations, she wondered how she would stand up with the rest of her seasoned team.

CHAPTER 35

A twenty-foot span of brush-covered ground separated the airport's perimeter fence from a surrounding forest of young pine trees. The ground beneath the trees was littered with patches of low scrub but still looked more like a tended park than a wilderness space. Germany was known for its tended woodlands, swept clean by forest service labor. The land around the airport appeared to be no exception.

The sun peeked through the trees as Ell moved north along the west side of the perimeter fence, ten feet from the barbed-wire-topped chain link fence. Alex moved parallel to her path, five yards deeper into the trees. The air smelled of pine needles and dry brush. Lost in the moment, Ell kicked a loose patch of brush aside as she walked northward, then chastised herself for the noise she'd made. If she wanted to be an operator at the level of the Home Team, she needed to do better.

She knew Alex was doing the same thing a few yards away. She tried to imagine how he'd move through the trees, walking like a cat on tinder. She recalled her tracker training at the state patrol's academy: place the toes of the lead foot down first, feeling for something that might move or make a noise, then shift the full weight of her body onto the forward foot. Repeat with the next foot. It was not long before the sequence of toe, foot, move forward became routine, and she moved through the sparse tree line in relative silence.

Ell felt her tactical watch vibrate. She glanced at its face. Aria was on her way back with Leah, whom she'd found at the gate to the train station's maintenance yard and extracted without difficulty. No additional details were available. However, knowing Leah, she'd keep her thoughts to herself until she could meet Alex in person.

Ell found it curious that the Home Team, which supported the western United States, Mexico, and the Pacific Rim, was tagged for a mission in Germany. She had to assume the Extreme Operations Group's European teams were fully deployed on other priority missions when the order came down for the Home Team to move out. Otherwise, why would the director send one of his best teams into an area they knew so little about on such short notice?

There are too many layers to this thing, Ell thought, as she moved silently through the brush and saplings. There must be a traitor inside the Extreme Operations Group or another agency for things to have gone so wrong.

She felt her cell phone vibrate this time and pulled it from her pocket to examine the screen. It was a text from Special Agent Williams from Homeland Security Investigations: *Need your help with an urgent mission of special interest. It may be related to your case from Turkey. Available?*

Ell thought the message odd since he knew she was on assignment from the state patrol. Why would he contact her directly?

She tapped in a quick response. *Fully engaged. Not available.*

The response came back instantly. *Understood. Our loss.*

At least he didn't try to pull rank on her.

Ell returned to her search. She examined the tablet computer strapped to her left arm and the tiny map Barry provided on-screen. They were near the northeast corner of the airport. She heard a rustling in the trees ahead of her, drew her pistol, and moved behind a clump of trees. She relaxed as Alex stepped from the trees ahead of her. Several sprigs of fir hung from the arm of the football jersey he wore.

A nice look, she thought. Less operator, more vulnerable. Unconsciously, she reached up and patted her brown hair into place, then realized what she had done and let out a soft huff. *Get a grip, girl! This is definitely not the time.*

Ell stepped from behind the trees and met Alex in an open space carpeted with damp, ankle-tall grass.

"Anything?" Alex asked, brushing the sprig of fir from his shirt.

Ell shook her head. "Nothing more than nervous birds."

Alex lifted his tactical watch to his lips. "Anything to report from your end, Steve?"

"Not a thing," came the reply. "Nothing on the drone's screen but treetops and clear air."

"Wrap it up at your end as soon as you've covered the entire area. Then you and Carla move to the northwest corner of the fence. Stop by the vehicles on the way and grab the duffels with the M4A7s. We haven't found anything either, but I have a feeling about this. After that, we'll meet and work together to cover the space north of the airport."

Alex turned back to Ell. "I think it's a good bet Jess, Sam, and Allen were taken at the airport. Normally, they would have checked in with Overwatch when they moved into position, but I don't think they got the chance. Instead, I think they were taken as they stepped off their plane."

"But where's the jet?" Ell asked.

"A good point," Alex replied. "One we'll need to check out."

Ell pointed toward the fence. "Let's continue, so we can complete our search and meet up with Steve and Carla."

Alex nodded and headed back into the trees to parallel Ell's path along the perimeter fence. Ell hadn't moved a step before her cell phone vibrated again. She glanced at the screen and saw Alex do the same.

"It's Aria and Leah," Alex whispered. "I'm going to have them meet us right where we are. Steve and Carla can wait for us at the northwest corner."

Alex tapped in his instructions to Aria. A team-wide reply came immediately. *On our way.*

Alex and Ell silently squatted on their heels at the edge of the clearing. The only sounds were the breeze wafting through the treetops, the occasional bird chirping, and a honeybee that seemed inordinately fond of Ell's left shoulder. Then even that noise stopped. Ell and Alex drew their pistols and eased deeper into the trees.

A text from Leah popped up on Ell's tactical watch. *Arrived. Entering the clearing.*

Ell tapped her watch with the barrel of her pistol. Alex glanced at his watch, stood, and entered the clearing he and Ell had previously occupied. He gave Ell a palm-down signal, telling her to remain undercover. Ell watched as Leah entered the small clearing, followed a moment later by Aria, Steve, and Carla.

"The gang's all here," Carla said, her tone dry as she dumped two duffels into the center of the clearing. She unzipped them, handing an M4A7 carbine to each person, along with two extra magazines. "I know you told us to wait at the northwest corner of the fence, but we saw Aria and Leah and figured we'd tag along."

Alex waved them into a tight circle, calling Ell forward. Everyone except Carla squatted on their heels in a semi-circle. Carla faced outward, watching their backs.

"Glad to see you all," Leah said. Her long, auburn hair was matted, twisted into a messy braid, and slung over one shoulder. Her face was scuffed by grease and dirt. "I just wish I had more to report."

"Nothing at all?" Alex asked.

Leah shook her head. "I don't think the rest of my team made it far before they were taken. I couldn't do much of a search over the past day, but I can tell you I didn't see any signs of major air or truck traffic entering or leaving the airport. So, they have to be near."

"I'm the least experienced person here, but it feels to me like the Home Team was drawn to this unfamiliar terrain so they could be taken," Ell said. "Everything's too pat. The Home Team doesn't work in this area. All the other group teams are fully occupied."

"I was met by an armed committee as soon as I stepped off the train," Leah added. "I was fortunate to get away. I think Ell's got it right."

"But that means our operations must have been compromised inside the group," Carla said. "I heard the EOG encountered the same situation a few months ago during their last set of missions to Mexico. That's why security is so tight now."

"It's impossible to keep things tight enough in a situation like this," Steve said. "This operation was a joint effort with the DEA, ATF, HSI, and FBI. So, the leak could be in any one of those groups."

Alex's eyes narrowed. "We can deal with the leak later. What matters now is we locate Sam, Jessica, and Allen. Leah, you come with

Ell and me as we search the north end of the airport. We're looking for any obvious entry point for underground tunnels or storage spaces big enough to handle a large weapons exchange."

Alex turned to Steve. "You said there was nothing from the crab drone at all?"

Steve glanced at Carla, who remained stoic and unreadable. "Not a thing."

Alex continued. "I think Ell and I have covered the east side of the airport pretty well. I want to take a deep look at the north end. It's farthest from the terminal and away from direct observation from the aircraft hangers and tower. Carla, you take a position at the northwest corner of the fence. You'll be our flanking guard. I want Aria to range northeast through the trees and do the same. You both can check for tire tracks or other signs of vehicle activity that might offer a clue. If you find anything, alert Steve, who'll fly the drone over the area and transmit pictures to our tablet computers. Steve will continue to fly the crab drone along the perimeter fence and keep an eye on the airport's runways. Use some of those fancy lasers to scan below the treetops and see where dirt may have been disturbed or where we might find an entrance to the tunnel network that runs under this place."

"Got it," Steve replied.

"Call out if you find anything or see anyone. But be careful," Alex concluded.

Everyone headed off on their assignments, disappearing quietly through the trees. Ell, Leah, and Alex spread out and walked the airport's northern fence line, with Ell closest to the fence, Leah ten yards deeper into the woods, and Alex ten yards farther in.

Ell had walked only a few minutes when she encountered a large, unnaturally flat space between several stands of trees. The terrain around it was lumpy and irregular. Tree roots protruded from the ground, but the land between the trees looked perfectly flat.

Ell tapped a message into the tablet computer strapped to her left arm. *I've got something. Triggering my GPS locator.*

Alex replied with his own text. *Aria and Carla, continue your search and move to your positions. Leah and I will check out what Ell found.*

Once Alex and Leah joined her, Ell and Alex positioned themselves on opposite sides of the open flat space, a few yards into the trees. Leah approached it directly, squatted, and ran a finger along the odd space's edge until she located a thick metal edge. She tapped it lightly with her knuckles, and it rang hollow like an empty drum.

"A metal hatch," Leah whispered.

"Pull back. I want everyone here before we tackle this thing," Alex replied.

As Alex spoke, the six-by-ten-foot metal hatch lifted a foot into the air and slid silently to the right, shoving forest debris from its top as it moved. Leah backed away and crouched. All three of their M4A7 carbines aimed at the hatch as it opened and revealed a dark underground space.

"I've got the drone overhead," Steve said over comms. "I see heat signatures inside the opening."

"Carla and Aria, converge on our location," Alex said. "Overwatch?"

"I've got you," Barry said from his overwatch position. "I have got a U.S. Air Force Jaguar drone circling your location. She has raptor missiles and a good visual of your location."

"Roger, Overwatch. Aria, when you get here, hang back. You're the cavalry in case we need you."

"Roger," Aria replied.

"Bono, status?" Alex called.

"All's good at the aircraft. Sybil found out the Home Team's jet took off before the team was taken. It's headed back after refueling and should arrive shortly."

"Roger," Alex replied. "Remain in location and protect our ride."

A double click signaled her understanding.

Alex, Ell, and Leah dropped to prone positions, carbines targeting the hatch. Six gray helmets rose with AKs at eye level as the hatched approached fully open. As soon as the AKs cleared the edge of the opening, they erupted in fire, bullets flying in all directions.

"Hold your fire," Alex whispered over his watch's mike. "They know we're here, but not where we are."

"Roger. Status three," Leah replied, indicating she was tactical and ready to move on the shooters.

"Ell. Status three," Ell said into her watch's mike.

"Carla?" Alex asked.

Nothing.

"Aria?"

"I have eyes on you from fifteen yards back," she replied. "I can be there in a second if you need me."

"Steve?"

"The drone is holding above your location. I have an idea," Steve replied. "Overwatch, configure the lasers to max hot."

"Lasers are hot," Barry confirmed.

"Everyone, hold position," Steve said. "I have a lock on the AKs. Firing lasers now."

The men from the tunnel's hatch were now at shoulder-level and rising, still pumping rounds in every direction as they continued upward on some lift inside the tunnel opening.

As Ell watched, the attackers' weapons began to glow and then smoke as the crab drone's lasers heated the metal in their weapons. The tangos dropped their AKs to avoid the scorching heat and drew their sidearms. Pistols extended in all directions as the men from the tunnel leaped from the underground entrance and crouched at the edge of the opening. Behind them, Ell saw another group of attackers peer over the entrance's edge.

"Engage," Alex said over comms, his voice level and calm as the bullets flew over their heads. "Defend yourselves and clear the way. We need to get into that tunnel. Overwatch, prepare the Jaguar drone for launch on this location on my word."

"Roger. Standing by," Barry replied.

Ell took sight of an attacker facing her. She snugged the stock of the M4A7 to her shoulder, sighted on the attacker's left knee, and pulled the trigger. Blood spat from the man's knee as his leg crumbled underneath him. He fell to one side with the barrel of his pistol aimed at Ell's face. Fire blossomed from the pistol and dug a furrow in the dirt beside her shoulder. Ell sighted again and ended the encounter.

For the next few minutes, bullets flew, and rifles barked. Ell quickly emptied her carbine magazine and took out two more attackers. She swapped magazines only to find the battle was over as soon as it had begun.

Despite the noise and the adrenaline coursing through Ell's veins, the battle lasted less than two minutes. Alex called for a report as a bright flame erupted in the sky northwest of their position, followed by a loud boom. The flames quickly dissipated into a puff of smoke and descending metal and plastic fragments.

Barry came over the line. "Someone just took out the drone. You've got someone on your eastern flank with a surface-to-air missile."

"Roger, Oversight," Alex replied. "Aria, you're on it. Find and neutralize the shooter."

"Roger," Aria replied. "Before I do, I've located five trucks positioned a click due north of your position. Also, one SUV and four large vans. I'm marking the GPS coordinates on my tablet's area map."

"Carla, you there?" Alex said, again.

When no response came, Alex said, "Aria, watch for any sign of Carla. Unfortunately, we've lost contact with her."

"Roger. On it," Aria replied.

Ell glanced back to the open hatch cover as it started to slide back to the closed position.

"The hatch!" Ell screamed.

"On it," Leah replied, scrambling to her feet and charging forward.

Ell grabbed a thick chunk of branches beside her and joined Leah at the hatch.

"Great minds and all," Leah whispered as they arrived at the hatch in unison. They both jammed their thick pieces of wood under the edge of the hatch cover. It ground to a halt, leaving the opening accessible.

Alex stepped up as the hatch stopped moving. "Nice job."

"Think they're down there?" Ell asked.

Alex nodded. "It's the only thing that makes any sense. Otherwise, why would anyone send a reception committee to meet us?"

"There's only one way to find out," Leah said.

"Yep," Ell said. "But I'm not anxious to dive through that hatch without knowing what's down there."

"Good point," Alex said, then raised his tactical watch to his lips. "Steve, report to our location and bring the crab drone."

"On my way," Steve said.

Steve arrived a few minutes later.

"How good is the crab drone at flying in tight spaces?" Alex asked.

Before Steve could respond, Barry came over the air. "I can configure it for closed space flight. It can show lights or fly dark using infrared or night vision. Its lasers can guide the way like a form of sonar. Cameras can display what it sees on tablet computers. Don't forget the hot lasers that can be fired to open locks and cut metal. I also have an extremely bright flood light that can blind attackers working in a dark space—even take out their night vision devices."

"Where were these things on our last mission to Mexico?" Leah asked.

"Technology advances at its own pace," Barry said.

Steve set the drone on the ground at his feet. "You want to drive, Barry?"

"Thought you'd never ask," Barry replied. "Lighting her up now." The drone's four props spun. "I'll take her down the access point. You all can follow, depending on what she finds."

"She?" Ell asked.

"I call her Gretel," Barry replied. "Because you all are in Germany. You know, the Hansel and Gretel story and all that?" The crab drone lifted off the ground and hovered, its four small propellers humming nearly without sound. "Heading down now."

The drone swung above the hatch and dropped gently out of sight. Then, a light flashed so bright that Ell, Leah, and Alex stepped back from the entrance to avoid being blinded. A series of yelps and heavy boots thudding followed the burst of light.

Ell checked the screen of the tablet computer. The image showed a half dozen men high sprinting down a tunnel perhaps twelve feet tall and equally wide. A string of dim lights lined the right wall, connected to their power source by wires coated with frayed cloth. The floor of the tunnel glistened with moisture.

"The entrance is clear," Barry said.

Alex nodded to Steve. "You're with us. I'll take point with Leah and you trailing me. Ell will pull up the rear."

One at a time, they dropped through the tunnel's entrance. Moving at a crouch with M4 at eye level and scanning side to side, Alex led the way. Steve and Leah followed with weapons pointed high. Ell felt oddly calm as they advanced, pacing behind the other three with sideways steps. She felt no fear or apprehension, just a sense of competency from working with an equally competent team of professional operators. That they trusted her to guard their backs lifted her spirits. She felt like one of them, like she belonged.

Ell's tablet computer vibrated on her arm as Alex raised a fist and signaled palm-down. Everyone dropped to a knee. An image appeared on Ell's tablet that showed the tunnel ahead. It opened into a large cavern. Six men faced their direction in a defensive line, with every other man either standing or kneeling and holding their rifles in a firing position. Behind the men loomed a sizable flat space cut from the rock with stacks of green metal crates arranged in neat rows. Above that, more ancient lights flickered in the darkness on the far wall. On a ledge against the back wall, Ell saw three people bound hand and foot to three chairs.

"I count three members of the Home Team to the left of the stacks of crates," Barry said over comms.

Ell watched onscreen as the drone's camera zoomed in, clearly identifying Sam, Allen, and Jessica.

"Our people are maybe forty yards ahead of where you'll enter the cavern. I count four tangos guarding our team members and the six blocking your path. Three tangos are in static position on a ledge ten feet above the Home Team. The fourth is squatting on the floor in front of our people. He appears to be in some conversation with them."

"Good intel, Overwatch," Alex whispered. "Can you light up the six tangos ahead of us as we hit the opening to the cavern? Blind them as you did before?"

"Roger that. I can also heat their weapons."

"Please do so," Alex replied. "Leah, Steve, and Ell, be ready to move on my mark."

The screen on Ell's forearm tablet lit up as Barry blasted the cavern ahead with light, but it darkened just as quickly. Alex pumped his fist in the air twice and waved them forward.

"The drone is tracking you. You should hit the opening to the cavern in five seconds at your speed. This update as you go: Carla is down," Barry said.

"Down?" Alex replied as he slowed and swung his M4's sights to eye level.

"Aria found Carla with the ground-to-air missile launcher. Carla drew down on her, but Aria put her down. Two unknown armed operatives were with Carla. They're down, as well."

"Good work, Aria," Leah muttered.

"You will approach the opening to the cavern in three, two, one. Cover your eyes. I will flash the cavern one more time," Barry said.

The drone's floodlight flashed a third time as Ell and the others shielded their eyes.

"I show all six tangos struggling with their vision. Suggest you move on them now," Barry said.

"Roger that," Alex said. "Advise Aria to cover the hatch leading into this place and guard our exit."

"Roger," Barry replied.

Ell, Alex, Leah, and Steve came online, side by side at the cavern's entrance. All cut loose with the M4s, each aiming low to avoid ricochets or stray bullets hitting the Home Team on the shelf above.

Ell flinched as pain seared her left thigh. She wobbled but forced herself to remain upright. Another second and the six men guarding the entrance to the cavern were down.

On the ledge above, Ell saw the three men who guarded Jessica, Sam, and Allen draw pistols and aim at the Home Team members. In unison, Leah and Ell both dropped to a knee. Leah aimed left and dropped the guard, as Ell took down the one on the right. From what Ell could see over her M4's sights, they both took down the middle guard with simultaneous shots.

"Now that's teamwork," Leah muttered.

"You got that right, sister," Ell replied as she climbed to her feet.

"Steve, go find the missing tango," Alex yelled through the smoke from the weapons fire.

Steve sprinted toward the ledge as Ell and Leah scanned the cavern for the final tango.

Steve returned minutes later. "That last person is nowhere to be found," he reported. "There must be another way out of here."

"Good enough," Alex replied. "Steve, stay on overwatch inside the cavern while I go free the Home Team. Ell and Leah, check the tangos, gather weapons, triage the wounded, and administer first aid where it makes sense. Barry, keep the drone airborne and watch for the escaped tango."

"I've got one breathing," Ell said a few seconds later. "Looks like a broken shoulder. He's lost a lot of blood but may be treatable."

"The rest are dead," Leah added. "Overwatch, alert the locals we have at least one tango for first aid and medevac once we clear the area."

"Roger. On it," Barry replied.

Alex appeared at Ell's side with Jessica, Sam, and Allen trailing behind.

"Amazing work today, Ell," Alex said. "Think you can bind that guy's wound to keep him alive until the authorities arrive? Then, we can use any intel he might provide."

Ell nodded as that odd feeling rushed through her again—the look he'd given her. But as quickly as the thought came to mind, she shoved it aside. "Get a grip, girl. Now is not the time."

"What?" Alex asked. "I can have Steve . . ."

"Sorry. No," Ell muttered, feeling foolish. "I can wrap the shoulder and stop the bleeding. I'll get the zip ties on him, too."

"The one that got away," Sam said. "Tall guy, dressed differently from the rest of the guards . . . maybe in a business suit. He spoke like an American."

"He wore a mask and moved and spoke like a trained operator," Jessica added. "He appeared to be in charge."

"We need to get out of here," Alex said.

"Of course," Sam replied, "but it deserves saying that you folks did amazing today. It was an exceptional op. I think H.T. Two has found its legs."

"What about me? I drove the drone," Barry said over comms.

Sam raised his tactical watch to his lips. "You, too, Barry. Nice job. Once we're clear, alert the locals. Tell them there's at least . . ."

"Fifty crates of weapons and ammunition along with the wounded tango," Barry completed Sam's thought. "I counted them using the drone."

"They knew we were coming," Ell said. "When we opened the hatch leading into the tunnel, they were waiting for us."

"You're right," Leah said. "They also must have had details about when Sam, Jessica, and Allen arrived in the country. We have a real problem with our security."

"I thought we had enough of this during our last mission when we found two traitors within the group and two more at the state department," Allen said. "At one point, even I was a suspect."

"Pretty sure it's not you this time," Leah said, elbowing Allen in the ribs.

"Hey, you're bleeding," Leah said to Ell.

Alex was immediately at her side. "There's a lot of blood," he said, stooping down to examine the wound on her leg.

"It's just a graze," Ell said, although she felt woozy as she spoke.

"Just the same, I'll wrap some gauze around it," Alex said. "Sybil can treat it once we're headed home."

"Out of the way, rookie," Leah said, gently moving Alex aside. "I'll take care of the bandage. She needs a sister's care, not ranger medicine."

Alex bristled, then relaxed and smiled. "Fair enough," he said. "She's all yours."

They double-checked Ell's work bandaging the wounded tango, then made their way to the hatch leading out of the tunnel. Ell limped as she pulled up the rear once again. They reached the tunnel's access point a few minutes later and found Aria standing guard with Carla's body beside her. Next to Carla was the firing tube and case for the surface-to-air missile Carla had used.

"She was working with someone here on the ground," Aria said. "We didn't bring any weapons like that with us."

"Well, that may explain how they knew so much about what we were doing today," Sam said, "but it still doesn't explain how they knew about us arriving a day ago. We didn't know anything about the interdiction mission until minutes before we were tasked to leave Lewis-McChord."

Sam's cell phone chirped. He sent Steve and Aria into the trees to guard the perimeter as he put the call on speaker and gathered everyone else together.

Paul Samuelson's voice came over the line. "Report."

Sam waved to Alex. "It's your mission. Brief the man."

"The Home Team's safe. We had one casualty: Carla. She turned on us and knocked down an Air Force drone, then attacked Aria when she tracked her down. She had three accomplices, but Aria took care of business. I have to own that one. I should have been watching for the signs she had turned."

"We all missed that one," Paul replied. "And we will be doing a deeper dive into her background. The two jets are on the runway, gassed up and ready to bring you home. Great work, all!" The call disconnected on the next beat.

"Let's go home," Alex said.

"Amen to that," everyone replied—except Steve.

CHAPTER 36

Sleep evaded Alex as the jet made its way home from Germany. Images of Carla lying on the ground, Ell's niece held captive on a farm for five years, and his conflicted need to tell Ell he was developing feelings for her rattled through his mind.

Everything about Ell seemed so perfect. She was bold and opinionated but also brave, solid, and skilled beyond what she recognized about herself. Like him, she was dedicated to justice, but it wasn't just that. It was her smile. No, it was her eyes or how she looked at him when she saw him admiring her from a distance.

Then again, they were both operators working for the same agency. In his experience, those romances never worked out. He'd tried it once with a female ranger. It was not a good memory.

Alex sighed, which drew a questioning glance from Aria. She slumped in the chair next to his—her eyes groggy and her dark hair scattered around her face in a messy veil.

Alex shook his head and waved off Aria's concern, but the thoughts about Ell lingered. He could well imagine how Ell felt, hoping beyond hope her niece would be rescued—as he'd hoped for rescue during those four years in Thailand. Ell had enough on her mind. He'd just have to cage his feelings and lock them away so they wouldn't get in the way of whatever they needed to do. Then again, he'd soon be headed back to the ranger battalion and she to the state patrol.

Or would he?

Second thoughts about leaving the Home Team and the EOG confused him about his goals. The Home Team and Home Team Two were special groups, staffed by operators who were way above his expectations.

His cell phone chirped. He glanced at the screen. The message was brief: *Subject remains on the grounds. No change in status.*

Ell didn't know he'd called Director Samuelson just before H.T. Two lifted off for their mission to Germany. The director, in turn, arranged for the local tri-cities FBI office to stake out the location where Ell's niece was being held. This latest text meant the girl was seen at the farm earlier in the day and was still there.

Alex smiled at the thought. It felt good knowing in a day, maybe less, Ell would have a chance to rescue her niece. If nothing else, at least he'd know he'd helped.

Alex felt the cell phone vibrate again as another message came through on his phone. As he watched, the screen lit up with a picture of the young girl the FBI team identified as potentially being Ell's niece. The image matched the girl's description exactly as Ell had described her.

Alex glanced around the plane's cabin. Most of Team Two were sleeping, except for Ell. She looked directly at him, but her gaze was distant and a little unsettling. He beckoned her over. Ell's eyes narrowed, but she unbuckled her seatbelt and walked down the aisle to squat beside Alex's chair.

He raised the screen of his cell phone for her to see. "I thought you might want to see this."

Ell gave him a quizzical look, then focused on the cell phone's screen. It took a second, but then her lips formed a silent "oh," followed by the wide grin he'd grown to like so much.

"You found her," she whispered, a tear streaking down her cheek.

Alex nodded. "I had some help."

The next thing he knew, Ell was in his arms, holding him tightly and shaking with silent sobs.

"You found her," she repeated.

The warmth of her against him felt natural. When she finally pulled back, he said, "There's an FBI detachment watching the place. She's there, and she's alive."

Ell leaned forward and gave him another bone-crunching hug. "I won't forget you did this for me."

As Ell returned to her seat, Bono cracked an eye and winked at Alex. "Nice job, boss," she whispered before shifting position and returning to soft snores.

———— ////////// ————

Home Team Two's jet stopped in Virginia to refuel. As they all stretched their legs outside, Alex's cell phone rang. It was the director again.

"Are all the members of the team with you?"

"They're close," Alex answered.

"Gather them. I have some news."

Alex brought the team together and put the call on speaker.

"I think it's time Ell's niece gets her freedom. If the other members of H.T. Two are willing, I suggest we divert you all to the airport in

Pasco, Washington, close to where she is being held. Go get the girl out of there and anyone with her."

Ell felt her heart race. She glanced around at the other members of the team, who all gave an approving nod.

"I can't imagine anything better," Ell said.

"Good," Paul replied. "I'll give Sybil the okay for the change en route." He paused a moment as the sound of computer keys being pounded came over the line. A few seconds later, he said, "And I'll have transportation for you at the airport. Go non-lethal on this one. None of you have used high-tech rubber rounds before, but you can figure it out. They're ceramic-coated rubber, formulated for high-velocity firing. They can break bones and even kill if you strike someone in the head or another vital organ. We keep a stock in the hold of every plane. I'll have Barry and Walter get you the latest satellite pictures of the airport, the farm, and the route to her location while you're in the air."

"I can't tell you how much—" Ell started.

Paul cut her off. "As I told you before, combatting human trafficking is now officially a part of the Extreme Operations Group's mission. So, you all go do what you must to rescue Ell's niece. Ell, I'll coordinate with the Washington State Patrol and local sheriff, so they know what we're up to."

"We'll develop a plan en route," Alex said. "We'll text you with the details as soon as we have something."

"No offense, Alex, but I want Ell to take the lead on this one," the director replied. "She has the most at stake."

"Roger that, sir," Alex replied, but Paul had already disconnected the call as usual.

Alex glanced at Ell. "It's your mission. Let's get back on board and build a plan. We're all here to support you."

She nodded to Alex, then glanced at each of the operators. "Let's do this as a team—as Home Team Two."

CHAPTER 37

Fan dialed her father's number from her hotel room that overlooked Puget Sound at the north end of Seattle. The place was famous for hosting the Beatles rock group in the 1960s, although that was the furthest thing from her mind as she connected the call.

Her father answered the call with a growl. "What?"

"I am checking in, as you requested," she replied.

Her father paused, then asked, "How are the preparations for the Seattle operation? This one must succeed."

She'd made contact earlier in the evening with the leader of the six-person mercenary team her father sent to Seattle to staff the mission. They'd met in her room to develop their plan. It would be her father's most extensive operation by far. With all he'd lost over the past weeks, including the latest loss in Germany, her father needed to raise the money for his plans in China.

Four shipping containers of human cargo would be in the shipment leaving the Port of Seattle. They had been gathered from across western North America, from Texas to Los Angeles, and from Seattle and Vancouver, British Columbia. In addition, there would be another two shipping containers of drugs and another with expensive prototype computer equipment. Seven shipping containers in all. The complexity of the operation and the ugly nature of the drugs and human trafficking roiled Fan's stomach.

"The man you sent to lead the mission seems competent and well-versed in tactics. I believe he and his team are well qualified to support your needs," Fan said.

"He may be well-qualified, but never doubt the success or failure of this operation rests squarely on your shoulders. Much is at stake. Success will place me well above the target funding I need to expand operations and gain the notice of the powerbrokers in our government. We will both reap the benefits of the success. Fail, and the consequences will be grave."

Fan considered his words. Aware of the failure of the Turkey and Washington operations, the German operation was a new topic for her.

"I was not aware of an operation in Germany."

"I used resources from inside the U.S. government—people I've paid a lot of money over the past years. They almost pulled it off, capturing several U.S. operatives we faced previously, but another American team intervened."

"Why didn't I know any of this?" Fan demanded.

"No need. In fact, I wasn't sure how much I could trust you."

"I have always supported you," Fan said. "And until these last few weeks, I have always succeeded."

"You've changed. I think it's your new friends, those Christians you met. They are responsible for your recent lack of commitment."

Fan started to protest. She had only met with them once, but then she paused. The more she thought about them and how the group felt, about God and all . . .

Her father seemed to interpret her silence as an admission of guilt. "Of course, I know about them. I explained that earlier. I believe it was Devon who told me, not that it matters any longer."

"But father, those people present no . . ."

"Like your deceased minder, the Christians no longer matter. I reported them to a friend in the People's Armed Police Force. All are now in custody. So, you need not concern yourself with their silly beliefs any longer," her father said.

Fan felt her chest constrict, or was it her heart? The Chinese People's Armed Police Force, or PAP, was a powerful group. That China was officially an atheist country suggested that her new friends were in dire straits if the PAP held them.

Fan placed her forehead against the cool back of a tall leather chair and let her ebony hair spill around her in a sad cascade. A single tear slid from the corner of her eye. She didn't know what to say. There was nothing she could say.

"By your silence, I see my actions have had the desired effect. Now, I expect you to focus your intellect and training on the success of the Port of Seattle operation two days from now. Whatever you need, I will provide. Simply ask. Make me proud, daughter."

Fan tried to respond, but her father disconnected the call before she could formulate her thoughts. She had just begun to consider the Christian way—so gentle, kind, and faithful—and now they were gone, lost in the bowels of some prison.

Fan dropped into a chair and gazed through the room's wide windows to the waters of Puget Sound and the islands beyond. As she did, she retrieved the business card of the man who'd led the Closet Christian group. She dialed the number, expecting no answer, but desperate to reach someone.

"Hello?"

The answer came in a whisper and on the first ring.

"This is Fan," she said.

"What do you want? Haven't you done enough? I'm the only one left, and I'm in hiding. How could you do this to us?"

Fan swallowed hard. "I . . . I didn't know until just now. I didn't realize my father knew I'd spent time with you."

The man paused before responding, then said, "I should have assumed you were unaware of your father's actions. You and he are so different. Please forgive me for judging you harshly."

"You ask me to forgive you after all that's happened? He is my father."

"I believe you when you say you had no hand in our friend's capture by the police. Forgiveness is an important message taught by our Savior," he said.

Fan wiped at the tears streaking down both sides of her face.

"My soul aches," Fan said between sobs.

"Pray to Him, Fan. Reach out to Him, and He will be there for you. You don't need me or anyone else to do that. Wherever you are, He will be there with you. Surrender yourself to Him, and He will provide what you need."

Fan let out a long breath. "I will pray. Thank you for speaking with me."

"Of course, but do not call this number again. I will dispose of this phone in case they monitor your calls. I wish you all the best and hope our paths cross again under better circumstances."

Fan lowered her eyes to pray, but a knock on the door startled her. She moved to the door and checked the security hole. It was the leader of the mercenaries. Behind him stood six other men—tall, strong, and competent. She swallowed hard and opened the door. Her prayer would have to wait until later.

CHAPTER 38

Home Team Two's jet touched down at the Pasco airport five hours after the director's call. During their time in the air, Ell, Alex, Aria, Bono, and Steve reviewed the satellite images Wayne and Barry provided. They revealed a farm of approximately one hundred acres, consisting of a large alfalfa field, several small apple orchards, and a large tract of land at the back of the property covered by a healthy stand of marijuana plants. A quick check of Washington State's Liquor and Cannabis Board files by Barry revealed the marijuana grow was off the books and illegal.

A sprawling single-story house rested at the front of the property, abutting a narrow farm road. A hundred feet behind the house was a tall dairy barn, standing at least thirty feet to its rounded peak. To the east of the house and barn, forming the third side of a rough rectangle, was a low, long shed at least thirty feet long.

Steve suggested the longer building might once have been a chicken coup. The open space between the buildings looked like bare, packed dirt and weeds.

Barry provided an infrared image of the buildings from an army satellite diverted from its coverage of an army training base near Yakima, Washington. It revealed four heat signatures inside the house, another twenty in the chicken coop, and several dozen animals in the barn.

The team agreed the chicken coop was the likely location for Ell's niece and any other human trafficking victims. Ell suggested two members of the team go there to free the captives. Ell and the rest would take the house to eliminate any threat from that direction. They'd approach the farm during the evening meal when the place was likely quieter. The local authorities would be brought into the plan once the site was secure and Ell's niece was in hand.

Another farm abutted the target property to the south. It appeared to be a horse ranch with numerous outbuildings, paddocks, and animals lazing in the afternoon sun. Beyond the farm and its irrigated property, the surrounding land appeared to have short brown bushes.

"Simple and direct," Alex had said when Ell laid the plan out. But then again, Ell knew most plans endured until the first contact with the opposition. Fortunately, she had her team. After Germany, she held them in high regard and knew if anyone could pull off the rescue, it was them.

When their jet stopped for refueling, each member had changed from the civilian garb they wore in Germany into black tactical cargo pants, shirts, and baseball hats provided by the group's logistics team. Each wore a webbed tactical harness over thin bulletproof vests and M4 magazines loaded with ceramic-coated rubber bullets. They carried their pistol in thigh holsters, loaded with standard hollow point bullets. KA-BAR knives hung at their hips. Aria called it full-beast mode once they were all kitted out, and Ell had to admit the group looked impressive.

As the jet pulled to a stop on the tarmac near a private hanger, the light outside showed that evening was quickly approaching. Intense heat—much hotter than usual for September—assailed the team as they stepped off the plane. Ell felt sweat run down her sides beneath her tactical gear as she descended the narrow boarding ramp. Or was that just her nerves causing it? A lot was at stake. In a few hours, her niece would be free if everything went according to plan.

They made their way a short distance to two large SUVs parked at the southeast corner of the hanger. A man and a woman in slacks and windbreakers with DEA in yellow letters across the back walked off, waving over their shoulders as they headed for the street beyond the airport's perimeter fence.

In her left hand, Ell lugged a heavy weapons duffle containing her M4A7, more loaded magazines, and clips for her Glock. Each of the other team members carried the same load, except for Steve. He carried the crab drone.

"The Drug Enforcement Administration works out of this airport," Steve explained, as he stashed his gear and the crab drone in the back of one of the SUVs. "I traveled here several times when assigned for joint training with their Yakima office."

Ell nodded. His knowledge of the area could be a real plus for the operation.

Alex stepped up beside her. It felt good to be near him. Steve was a great guy and, from all accounts, an excellent operator; but there was just something about Alex, something solid and level, that set him apart.

"Daylight's fading," Alex said. "We'd best get moving."

Ell called up the directions to the Kennewick farm on her cellphone. "It's a two-and-a-half-hour trip from here. We'll get there well after dark and should be able to move on them when we arrive."

"If they actually eat dinner when we think they do," Steve countered. "For all we know, they may be away from the farm by the time we arrive. So, maybe we should consider waiting until morning to do this."

"We won't be doing that," Ell replied, her voice low and hard. "My niece has already spent far too much time away from her family. She's not spending another night at that place if I have anything to say about it."

Steve stepped back as Ell pounded home each word. "I was just saying . . ."

Aria moved up beside Ell. "I'm with Ell on this one. You have no idea what it's like for someone to think they own you. I've spent time with a fair number of jerks and know something about the attitude, if not this specific situation. I vote we go get the girl now."

Steve turned to Alex. "Alex?"

Alex stepped up, putting himself between Steve, Ell, and Aria as Bono watched from a pace away. "You're talking to the wrong guy. You already know I was held for four years by people like the ones holding her. As far as I'm concerned, if you don't like our plan, you can stay here with the jet or catch a bus home."

Steve let out a harsh laugh. "I never believed that story about you being a human trafficking victim. Not for a second."

Alex took another measured step forward, coming nose-to-nose with Steve, his voice low as he spoke. "I don't care if you believe it or not. You're just fortunate my God tells me to love my neighbor, even people like you. Now, are you in for this operation or not?"

Steve let out a long sigh. "I'm in. Besides, I'm the best drone pilot you've got without Barry here."

Alex pulled open the driver's side door of the first SUV and waved Ell inside. "You want to drive? She's your niece."

Ell noticed how Bono raised a single eyebrow and smiled at Alex's offer.

"No, thanks," Ell replied. "I'd rather spend the trip thinking through the plan."

"Fair enough," Alex said, climbing behind the wheel. Bono took the back seat as Ell slid to the shotgun position next to Alex. Aria drove the other SUV with Steve in the front seat beside her. As the two SUVs left the airport, the last bit of sun faded against a fire-red horizon.

"After five years, it'll all be over soon," Ell said as Alex headed for the highway.

"Yes, it will," Alex replied. "Yes, it will."

CHAPTER 39

Two-and-a-half hours later, H.T. Two pulled off a paved two-lane and bumped their way along a dirt trail that paralleled an irrigation ditch running between the horse ranch and the farm where the captors held Maria. The team unloaded near a shack the Washington Department of Natural Resources used to monitor water flow. Barry provided the latest image of the property.

"The latest shot, taken fifteen minutes ago, shows no lights burning anywhere except the main house," Ell said. "The chicken coop and barn are dark. Alex and I will approach the house through the back door. Steve and Aria can take the front. Bono will watch our backs from near the chicken coop and keep people inside quiet if necessary. We aim to take whomever's in the house without raising a ruckus, then clear the outbuildings. Make sure your suppressors are secure on your M4s. We don't want to wake up the neighbors."

Steve and Aria launched the drone as Alex and Ell moved into the darkness, their path lit only by a full moon. The hard ground along the irrigation ditch was covered in brittle scrub that crunched under their boots and smelled of overcooked, un-watered grass. Minutes later, they were at the back of the barn, watching the house from across an open yard of packed dirt and fading dandelions.

Ell gave Alex a thumbs up, and they raced across the yard to the back of the house. Ell lifted the tablet computer strapped to her forearm and tapped in a message: *Status two at the back of the house. Steve? Bono?*

Steve's response appeared an instant later: *The drone is up. No movement anywhere. Redeploying the drone and packing it away. Will move into place with Aria at the front of the house.*

Barry provided an additional message. *The heat signatures at the front of the house in a single room. Four souls. Twenty or more in the chicken coop, motionless. May be asleep.*

Finally, Bono responded. *Status two at the chicken coop. All quiet.*

Ell responded with *Status Three. Entering the house now.*

Ell eased the back door open. She said a little prayer of thanks as it swung on silent hinges. Alex led the way, moving forward in a crouch, M4A7 at eye level, Ell following on his heels. They cleared the back entry, a small mud room, and finally, the kitchen before encountering anyone.

"In position. Status two," Aria whispered over comms.

Good call on the comms, Ell thought. *There's no way to check the tablet computer now, and it was good to know Steve and Aria were in place.*

"All teams, status three. Go, go," Ell said into her tactical watch's mike as she and Alex crashed into the home's tiny dining room.

The sound of wood shattering followed them as Aria burst through the front door. They surrounded a small dining room table on three sides, where they discovered a man, a woman, a teenage girl, and a teenage boy in dirty coveralls. All four raised their hands.

"Don't shoot," the man said. "Take what you want. Just don't hurt us."

"Hands on the table," Alex barked.

They responded immediately, the boy knocking over a glass of water. The woman appeared to be in her mid-fifties and the man slightly younger. Both looked like they'd had a tough day, although Ell found no sympathy in her heart for them as she examined the boy and girl.

Ell recognized Maria in an instant. She looked much older than her pre-capture pictures, but she still had the lean appearance of her mother, along with her striking green eyes and dark, wavy hair.

The man almost imperceptibly crept his left hand toward the table's edge. Aria closed on him and snugged the barrel of her M4A7 against the back of his neck. He froze. Aria reached down and retrieved a .38 special from behind the man's belt.

She gestured toward Ell. "No more tricks. You listen to that woman, and you may live to see tomorrow."

Ell slung her carbine onto her back and moved around the table, squatting on her heels to meet Maria eye-to-eye. When Ell removed her black baseball hat, the girl's eyes widened.

"Aunt Ellen!" she cried, knocking her chair over as she lunged to wrap her arms around Ell's neck.

"It's me, Maria," Ell said, pulling the girl into a long hug. "And thank God it's you."

As she held Maria closely, Alex and Aria zip-tied the man and woman's feet and wrists, leaving them in their chairs.

When they were done, Alex glanced at the young girl in Ell's arms and nodded to Aria. "Makes it all worthwhile, doesn't it?"

"Roger that," Aria replied. "This is why we do what we do."

Ell moved Maria to arm's length and nodded toward the young boy sitting at the table. "Who's the young man with you?"

"That's Darryl," Maria replied. "He's like me. He doesn't have a family. We were the best behaved today, so we got to eat with our owners, just as if we had a real family."

"Well, you do have a real family. They're in Seattle, waiting for you to come home," Aria said from behind Ell. "Can you tell us who's in the chicken coop?"

"But they told us . . ." Maria started.

"These are not good people, Maria," Ell said. "They took you from your family and lied about them being dead. You know me, and I would never tell you a lie."

"I . . . I guess," Maria replied. "Are you going to take me home?"

Ell nodded, and Maria threw her arms around Ell once more. "I want to go home more than anything."

"What's in the chicken coop, Daryl?" Alex asked, beckoning to the boy.

"That's the dormitory where we sleep. There are a lot of kids in there. Some of them have been here a long time."

The man smiled at Maria and said, "You're already home, girl." Then, he turned his eyes to Ell. "We're family to these kids. We gave them a home. Before us, they were runaways or worse."

"Some of them came off the streets. They had no homes," the woman said, blowing a strand of matted hair from her forehead's dirty, oily pale skin. "As he said, we gave them a place to live."

"And made money off them," Ell said.

The man nodded. "We made a little money loaning them out to our neighbors. Nothing wrong with that. Parents have been doing that with their kids forever."

"These kids are your prisoners," Alex said. "There's no remedy for that."

"Do you see any guards?" the man asked. "We don't need no guards. The kids love it here."

"Are there any guards, Maria?" Aria asked, moving to the girl's side.

Maria shook her head. "No. We work hard, but they explained how lucky we were to have a roof over our heads and food to eat when no one else wants us."

Ell felt her anger rising, then the touch of Alex's hand on her arm. That touch centered her, warned her, calmed her. She gathered her wits and glanced down to meet Maria's eyes.

"Well, it's over now, Sunshine. By tomorrow, you'll be home with your mom and dad."

Maria's tears flowed anew. "No one's called me Sunshine in a long time."

Ell lifted her tactical watch to her lips. "Overwatch?" she said.

"This is Overwatch," Barry replied.

"Alert Homeland Security Investigations, the FBI, and the Benton County sheriff's office. Tell them we have at least twenty kids for pickup."

"On it," Barry replied.

"Sincere thanks, Overwatch," Ell said. "We'll be on station until the locals or the FBI arrives. Alert our pilot we'll be ready for exfil immediately after, with one additional passenger."

"Roger," Barry said as Ell terminated the connection. "And congratulations on finding your niece."

Alex lifted his watch and keyed its mike. "Steve, we need you in the main house to guard the tangos while we check the chicken coop."

Steve's response was immediate. "I'd better stay out front, in case there are any unexpected visitors."

"No need for that," Ell replied into her mike. "We need you in here now."

"Roger," Steve replied.

Ell's cell phone rang a second later. It was Director Samuelson.

"Barry's kept me up on the action. Nice work, yet again, H.T. Two," Paul said.

"It's an answer to many prayers," Ell replied.

"I've done my own share of praying since I learned about your niece. As you said, prayers answered."

As they spoke, Ell saw Steve pass by the window on his way to the house's back door.

The man zip-tied at the table also saw Steve, thrashed in his chair, and yelled, "I want a deal. I want a deal."

Aria approached the man from behind, again snugging the barrel of her M4 against the back of his neck. "What deal could you ever want?"

"I want a deal!" the man repeated, spit flying from his lips.

Ell released Maria and approached the man. She held her cell phone in one hand, the connection still open to Director Samuelson. "What deal?"

The man nodded toward the window. "That man. I know him. He's in this. I have proof."

Ell placed her watch to her lips. "Steve, get in here now."

"But . . ." Steve started.

"It's important," Ell said.

A few seconds later, Steve entered the dining room through the kitchen, his carbine slung across his back. In his right hand, he held his pistol, barrel pointed forward.

"This man claims to know you," Ell said.

Aria disappeared as Steve entered the room, then came up behind him and placed her hand on Steve's gun hand. She removed the pistol from his grip in a smooth motion that left him cradling his wrist.

"That's the man," the human trafficker said. "He worked this area with the people who delivered the kids at the port on the Columbia River, not far from here. He also provided the drugs we use to keep the kids under control when they first arrive."

Ell met Steve's gaze as he struggled anew against Aria's grip, but she had him in a full lock, levering his hand painfully against his wrist joint with her thumb on his palm and her fingers pinching the back of his hand. Aria twisted Steve's hand up and away, increasing the pressure and the pain, and moved against the man's shoulder, taking him to the ground face first. Alex then moved in, placing the muzzle of his M4 against the back of Steve's head.

"This is ludicrous. I've never seen this man before," Steve groaned.

"You were paired with Carla in Germany," Aria said. "You were with her when she brought down the air force drone. So, you were a part of that, too, weren't you?"

Steve's voice cracked as he spoke. "I don't know anything about that!"

The man at the table smiled, his thin lips baring yellow, cracked teeth. "I've got proof in my office—pictures from when the kids arrived each time they were delivered. He's in those pictures. Said he worked for the DEA."

Alex covered Aria as she snapped zip ties around Steve's wrists and cinched them tightly. Steve yelped as the plastic dug into his sore wrist.

"You hear all that, Director Samuelson?" Ell said.

"I did," Paul replied. "When the FBI arrives, turn Steve over to them. I'll alert them. I look forward to hearing what he says once the FBI is done with him. First Carla, now Steve. A bad day."

"We got the Home Team out and freed a lot of kids," Ell said.

"Good point," the director replied. "Maybe not totally a bad couple of days."

"I'm not telling you anything," Steve yelled.

"Finish up and head home as soon as possible," Paul continued. "In the meantime, I'll have Jessica and Barry dig into Steve and Carla's financial records. I bet we'll find what we need there to convince Steve to cooperate."

The director disconnected the call, and Ell pocketed her phone.

Alex walked over and laid a hand on Steve's shoulder. "You should reconsider. Tell us who you've been working with. You can still find redemption and gain support from those who matter. It's never too late for that."

"Leave me alone," Steve groaned.

"I'll be praying for you," Alex whispered at a level only Ell could hear, then turned away.

Aria used her knife to cut away Steve's tactical vest as he lay on the ground. "You won't be needing this any longer," she said. "You don't deserve to wear it."

"Roger that," Ell said. "Let's go home."

CHAPTER 40

The Home Team and H.T. Two gathered in the headquarters conference room early the following day. Paul Samuelson stood at the front of the conference room. He must have traveled all night to get here. Ell wondered if the man ever slept.

Having seen him in person only once, Ell thought the director looked different than she imagined. Because of his reputation as a past member of a CIA tactical team, she expected a tall, broad-shouldered man. Instead, he was short and stocky and projected a sense of intellectual, rather than physical, strength. He was dressed in rumpled brown slacks and a worn camel sports jacket. The grip of a large pistol protruded from under his coat.

Paul paced back and forth but stopped when Maggie entered the conference room. Contrary to the last time Ell saw Maggie, the tall, brown-haired DEA agent now wore stylish slacks and a white, sleeveless blouse. Her curly hair was pulled back in a thick braid. She nodded a silent greeting to the room and slid into a chair at the head of the table between Sam and Jessica.

"Glad you could make it, Agent O'Dell," Paul said.

Maggie nodded but held her peace.

"First and foremost, nice work over the past several weeks by both teams," Paul said. "H.T. Two proved itself under fire. I could not have asked for more."

"Here, here," Sam said.

"You bunch of rookies saved our bacon," Leah added.

A round of applause followed from around the room.

"About those traitors . . ." Paul continued. "Each candidate for H.T. Two was sent invitations based on their military records and experience. Carla and Steve both worked for the military and had experience with joint operations between federal law enforcement agencies and the military. Carla turning traitor surprised us and the unit she previously worked with. Same for Steve. He'd worked with DEA before and made connections during that time. We searched his call history, online presence, and emails and found messages from another person who works for the federal government. We're tracking that person's identity now. Unfortunately, Steve and his fellow traitor used an internet provider address we cannot trace. We're guessing the other person may be in Lee Chao's employ."

Ell's heart sank. She'd hoped Fan was serious about changing things in her father's business. Now this.

Samuelson continued. "Steve was offered a lot of money to thwart the operation in Germany through his contact with the U.S. government. We know that much. He appears to have bribed Carla, and she took the bait. We saw a money transfer into her account just after she destroyed the air force drone."

Bono raised a hand. "How could Steve get past the background checks for the rangers if he was taking money from outside?"

Jessica took the question. "We think there are people on Lee Chao's payroll in numerous agencies, including the army's human resources group. There's a deep network in place to support Lee's operations. Several federal agencies will work to uncover the network and put it down."

Paul raised his hand to draw back their attention. "I know you're all due some time off, but before you go, I'd like to hear from Agent O'Dell."

Maggie stood. "Since your last mission, my team at the DEA tested one of the new crab drones. The results were exceptional. The drone's reflective lasers tested accurately for detecting drugs at one thousand feet when stored in shipping containers. The drones also identified humans we placed in test containers with one hundred percent accuracy."

Walter snapped his fingers. "I knew it had potential."

"And you were correct," Maggie said. "We want to try the crab drones over a larger area. Paul has agreed we can take one of the drones and use it to inspect a port for signs of drug smuggling and human trafficking. We'd like two of you to do that for us at the Port of Seattle. We've heard rumblings about another smuggling operation going down there soon but have been unable to gather enough evidence for a search warrant."

Ell was quick to raise her hand. "I'll volunteer."

Maggie chuckled. "Thought you might."

"Me, too," Walter added.

Maggie glanced at Paul. "Looks like we have our team."

Paul looked at Ell and Walter. "I'd like you to get going tomorrow. The rest of you clean up your gear and stand down for a few days."

Everyone cheered.

"Now, get out of here, but don't go too far in case Ell and Walter find something and require backup," Paul yelled.

As Ell left the conference room, she noticed Sam standing near the door with his fiancée, Consuelo. He beckoned Ell over.

"You remember Connie?" Sam asked.

"Of course," Ell replied, holding out a hand.

Consuelo ignored the hand and pulled Ell into a warm hug. "I came to talk with you, Ellen," Connie said. "If it's not an imposition."

"Of course not," Ell replied as the woman released her and gestured to two chairs at the conference table, surprised by Connie's use of her proper name. "What can I do for you?"

"It's about your niece," Consuelo replied, her large, dark eyes narrowed in concern. "I run a public health clinic in Olympia for the poor and homeless. We have many human trafficking victims in the groups we serve. As a result, we offer services to human trafficking victims and their families. I want to invite your niece and her parents to attend one of our sessions."

Ell felt her emotions swell at the thought of her niece, so strong a presence before her kidnapping and so changed over her absence. She'd received a call from her sister, saying her niece had refused to leave her bedroom since they'd picked her up at the base last night. Ell knew from her work with the state patrol's human trafficking task force that the transition from victim to family environment could be difficult for the returnee and the family members.

"I'll call my sister right away. I'm sure they'll want to take you up on your offer," Ell replied.

Consuelo handed her a business card. "Have your sister call me as soon as possible. We've made much progress with the people enrolled in our program."

"Thank you," Ell said. "My sister has lived with guilt because of Maria's disappearance. Although she did nothing wrong, she and her husband felt they'd somehow caused the situation rather than the criminals."

"It's a common feeling for the parents of trafficked children," Connie replied. "But we can help. We'll assign a victim advocate to help them through the process, and they will see results. I promise. The Washington State Department of Social and Health Services has funding to help with expenses. We'll help them access those funds so Maria can return to her family, school, and society."

"Thank you, Consuelo," Ell said.

This time, it was Ell who pulled Consuelo into a long, warm embrace.

As Ell left Sam and Consuelo, she remembered she had no place to stay for the night before working with the drone the following day. She spun around and located Leah next to the sniper simulator. Leah had changed into her workout gear, and her long brown hair hung freely down her back and sides.

"Leah?" Ell called.

"Yes, you can stay at my place tonight," Leah replied, as though reading Ell's thoughts. "We'll find your own digs after you finish the drone project."

Ell gave Leah a thumbs up. *Wait a minute*, she thought. *Why would I need my place here when I might be returning to the state patrol in a few months? Being part of this has never been a part of my long-term plan.*

Then again . . .

CHAPTER 41

F an sat in her rented Ford Expedition at a fast-food restaurant a few blocks south of the Seattle-Tacoma International Airport. She stared at a soggy egg English muffin sandwich and fried potato wedges. *How Americans survive on this food defeats the imagination,* she thought.

The day was clear and sunny. The sound of the traffic on International Boulevard hummed through her vehicle's closed windows. Tall hotels, restaurants, and long-term parking lots lined the boulevard as far as the eye could see.

Fan glanced at her watch. Another two hours, and she would meet the team at the Port of Seattle's cargo entry point. To that end, she wore stained overalls with the logo of a local equipment maintenance company, stolen by her team from a uniform laundry two days before. Her phone chirped. She pressed the call receive button and raised the cell phone to her ear.

"You are ready, my daughter?" her father asked.

"I am," she replied, knowing the operation's plans were in place and well thought through. Even so, she had to force down the sick feeling in her stomach that had plagued her lately, and it wasn't just the food.

"I am glad to hear it," Lee Chao replied. The connection was so clear, it sounded like he sat next to her in the vehicle. "And your team?"

"Briefed, rehearsed, and ready," she replied.

"Do I hear a note of skepticism in your voice?"

"Hard not to after you had my two lifelong friends killed by one of your own people after the last mission, then advised me of the dire consequences should this operation fail."

"I was simply protecting our interests when I had your friends eliminated. You know that's true in your heart," Lee Chao said.

"Our interests?" Fan repeated. She slowly shook her head, glad her adopted father could not see her expression. "I expect your new man has orders to do the same to me should I fail you today."

Lee Chao paused before responding. "I have always treated you well, daughter. Haven't I given you a rich life—one you would never have seen if I'd left you lying in the street when you were just a baby?"

She'd heard the story too many times to be impacted. She rolled down her car window and dropped the bag of uneaten fast food on the asphalt beside the vehicle. She'd littered and hoped someone would arrest her for it. Then again, she might be the next bag of soiled leftovers deposited on the street if today's mission went badly.

"Of course, Father," she said. "I am eternally grateful for your generosity. Now, I need to go and meet up with my team. We're converging at a small container staging yard a few miles south of the port. We've paid the owner a fortune to take the day off. From there, we will send all seven containers to the Port of Seattle for loading on the *Sea Maiden*."

She envisioned her father grinning widely.

"My newest vessel was a nice touch," he said. "And I am glad you took the extra precautions to coordinate off-site. I paid a lot of money to gain influence with the business alliance that runs the port, but I am wary of leaks like those that thwarted our last operations. I can't have those carefully nurtured relationships at the ports threatened for any reason."

Too late, she thought, as she recalled the mess made at the port in Turkey and during the exchange in Tumwater. "I thought you plugged those leaks when you killed my friends," Fan said, then wished she could take her words back. Her father could be a dangerous man.

"Don't be insolent." The anger in Lee Chao's voice was apparent.

"Please accept my apology, Father. I know you were looking out for my interests."

"That's better," he replied. "Now, go meet your team and get the job done. No failures this time. This is the largest shipment of technology we've ever made from the United States. We will make a fortune. Fortunately, the company that makes so many of America's computer chips has lax security."

"And the humans?" she asked.

"More than one hundred of them will be in the four containers. They will bring us over two million dollars. It is not a lot of money compared to the other cargo, but we need all the revenue we can gather at this point," her father said.

After a pause, Lee Chao continued, "Our country's leaders are hungry for the technology, and the cartels we support need the drugs. So, that's where we will make our real money. When this operation is successful, I can finally assume my rightful place in our government. I will expand our company so that no one will doubt my power and authority."

Fan felt her stomach churn, forcing down the acid flavor yet again as she replied, "Yes, Father."

"And when you are successful, perhaps I will use my considerable influence to have your Christian friends released from prison," Lee Chao added.

Fan felt the anger rise at his words. She knew he would do no such thing. Freeing Christians would be a slap in the face of the men he wanted to impress. Her thoughts drifted to the conversations she'd had with the Closet Christians and then to the Bible she'd acquired. Something in their character—how they talked, acted, and accepted her despite her father's role in China—told her they were good people and that their faith was powerful. She smiled at the thought and then at the words she'd read about perseverance against worldly evil. The words spoke to her, and she felt a strength rising inside her that felt clear, good, and true. She reached for the vehicle's ignition and started the engine, knowing her days with her father were numbered. After this one job, things would change one way or another.

CHAPTER 42

The following day, Walter and Ell pulled their SUV into the parking lot adjacent to the Port of Seattle's seaport cargo terminal. Over three million shipping containers flowed through the port yearly, totaling over 280,000 metric tons of cargo. Seventeen shipping lines used the port resources, making it a gateway for regional, national, and international trade and North America's fourth-largest shipping container port.

Ell scanned the port with binoculars as Walter pulled the crab drone from the back of the SUV and set it up. She was helping with the laptop used to monitor the results of the drone's survey just as a dented Chevy Focus pulled up alongside. Maggie O'Dell stepped out a second later.

"Yo, Mags," Walter called as he positioned the drone's props.

"Yo, yourself, big man," she replied.

Ell couldn't help but notice the soft flush of pink creep across the tough female agent's cheeks as Walter greeted her.

Maggie stepped up beside Ell, gesturing to five tall cranes towering over the port in the distance. "Those are the Seattle port's newest loading cranes. They stand more than three hundred feet tall—North America's largest and most capable cranes."

Ell glanced from the cranes and around the rest of the port. "This place is massive."

"You should see some others, like the one in Los Angeles. It's even bigger and a city in its own right," Maggie said.

"We're ready," Walter called from the back of the SUV.

Maggie and Ell returned to the rear of the SUV. Walter pointed at the open laptop sitting on the vehicle's tailgate. You can monitor what we find as the drone covers its search grid. On the left side of the laptop's screen is a port map. The red triangle is the drone's position. The right side of the screen will show a visual from the drone's belly cameras. The letters DRG, HMN, AMO, and EXP are in the top right corner. Those stand for drugs, humans, ammunition, and explosives. When the crab's lasers take their measures, figures ranging from zero to ten will display next to each label. The higher the number, the more likely we find something."

He handed Maggie and Ell tactical headsets. "Overwatch," he said, "we're ready at this end."

"Status two here," Barry replied. "Launch the crab, and I'll fire up the lasers. They should already be configured for your search. I've programmed a grid search from a thousand feet, starting with the ships currently loading containers or that have most recently been loaded. From there, the drone will move to the shipping container staging and holding yards and finally to the truck routes leading in and out of the port."

"Roger that," Walter said. "Lifting off."

Walter toggled its controls. The crab drone lifted six feet in the air, then hovered as Walter checked the laptop's screen to ensure everything was working. Once he confirmed it was, he flipped a switch that moved the drone onto autopilot, which would take it through its preprogrammed search routine.

"That was quick," Maggie said. "From what I heard, my team at the DEA took much longer to carry out their tests."

Walter rolled his eyes. "If you can play a video game, you can fly this thing, and Barry programmed it to fly on its own. So, all we have to do now is wait and see what it shows us."

They watched the image on the laptop's screen as the drone hovered above a huge ship under the super-cranes Ell had noticed earlier. Numbers immediately started flashing at the edge of the screen.

"I'm seeing significant numbers for explosives on that ship," Walter said.

Barry responded a moment later. "I have the ship's manifest in front of me. It lists a large, legit shipment of chemical fertilizers. That probably accounts for the readings. I think we can discount those numbers. Anything else?"

Maggie examined the numbers as Walter pointed them out on the laptop's screen. "No significant numbers for drugs or ammunition. And the numbers associated with human beings are pretty small."

"That's about right for the crew required for a ship like that. Sounds like the drone is working as it should," Barry said.

"Roger that," Walter said. "I'm hungry."

Maggie slapped Walter on the back, jarring the big man a step forward. He twisted around to meet her with a surprised smile. "Probably takes a lot to feed a man of your proportions," she said. "I brought PBJs for the three of us. They're in the back seat of my car."

Walter smiled, his even white teeth gleaming against his mocha skin and dark eyes. "Yes, ma'am," he replied. "Thank you, ma'am."

"I've programmed it to skip administrative and fueling areas. That should cut down on the search time," Barry said over comms.

While Ell listened to Maggie and Walter pass good-natured jokes and flirt, Ell occupied herself with the laptop's screen and the image of the ground as the drone rapidly flew and scanned the ships in port. No significant data resulted, beyond what they should expect from a normal distribution of cargo types headed out or coming in from the ocean. But when the drone moved to a shipping container yard near the super-cranes, the numbers popped.

"Hold on, boys and girls," Ell said. "We've had a spike in numbers across the board for drugs and human beings. They're in the high nines."

Walter and Maggie joined her at the back of the Suburban as Ell pointed to the laptop's screen.

"I can direct the drone to repeat the search of that grid," Walter said, then tapped a command on the laptop's keyboard. "It could have been a glitch. A repeat search, conducted at a lower speed, should verify it one way or another."

"This is Overwatch," Barrie said over comms. "All systems are nominal with the crab drone. All indications are the numbers you've seen are valid findings."

"Let's see what we come up with when we repeat that grid," Walter said. "If there's a problem with the drone, now's the time to find it."

Ell felt her heart sink. If Walter thought the crab drone was throwing false data, her hopes for using it to track human trafficking victims might be out the window.

"I'm programming the drone to repeat the last grid," Barry said.

On the computer's screen, Ell saw the drone slowly hover about each stack of forty-foot steel shipping containers in the staging area.

"Find it. Find it," she whispered.

As Maggie, Walter, and Ell crowded around the laptop's screen, the drone slowed to a crawl above several stacks of shipping containers.

"Dropping to five hundred feet," Barry said.

As he spoke, the numbers for drugs and humans jumped again.

"Bingo!" Ell said. "Hold the drone in position there."

The numbers onscreen hovered at a 9.2 for drugs and a 9.1 for humans.

"That's a valid measure," Barry said from Overwatch. "I'd say we've found what Maggie was looking for."

"Can you zoom in on the cargo containers in that yard with the crab's belly camera?" Maggie asked, touching the real-time visual display with the tip of her finger.

Walter laughed. "You just did. This computer has touch screen commands."

"Are you seeing this, Barry?" Ell asked.

"I am. I have a duplicate screen on my desktop at headquarters. I see at least a hundred containers there, staged for loading."

"Is there any way you can finetune your sensors to isolate the numbers to a few containers in that area?" Maggie asked.

"I can do that," Barry said, "but it depends on the shape of those shipping containers. If they're relatively new, there will be fewer leaks for particulate matter to escape from inside. Older containers tend to have more holes from rust and wear and offer better access to airborne particulate matter."

"Or tiny fans that human traffickers put in their containers to keep the air barely flowing for the victims inside," Ell replied, feeling the anger inside her rising as she recalled her three weeks of captivity and how the ship's crew provided barely enough water and food to keep her and her fellow captives alive.

"Calibrating the lasers now," Barry replied. "Start your scan at the west side of the container yard. It's a roughly rectangular area, and the containers don't appear to be stacked more than two high. Walter, you drive using the manual controls and hold the drone in position over each stack. I'll work the lasers container by container. Warning. This will take a little time."

"Take the time," Maggie replied, her expression intent on the screen. "If there are people and illegal drugs in those metal coffins, we must find them."

Ell stepped to the side of the Suburban's tailgate and retrieved her bulletproof vest, tactical harness, and M4A7 carbine. She tugged the vest over her head, tightened the Velcro straps, and slung the harness around her shoulders. Next, she clipped the harness at her waist and across her chest. Then, she pulled a magazine of hollow point bullets from her vest and slapped it into the carbine with the palm of her hand.

"You getting ready for a war?" Maggie asked.

"Something like that," Ell said. "I'm not standing by when people may be in those containers. I know too well what that's like.'"

"I'm with you," Maggie replied and retrieved her gear from the trunk of her car.

"Bingo!" Walter called. "I've got a fix on the containers with the high numbers. We got lucky. They're all on the far west side of the staging area, where I started the manual search."

"That's good news," Ell said, "but continue your search in case there's more."

"But there's bad news," Barry added. "We do have a nominal ammunition measure. It's coming from a group of people who appear to guard those containers."

"Can you get a clear picture of them?" Maggie asked.

"Zooming in," Walter replied, finding a cluster of four people standing at the north end of a stack of containers. He pointed to the tops of four heads shown on the laptop's screen. "Those are guards, positioned as they are."

"I count three stacks of two containers and another by itself in the group," Barry said over comms. "From the numbers, it looks as if four of the containers have human beings in them—and a large number at that. Those containers are blowing human particles into the air. Must be the fans Ell mentioned. Another two containers appear to be loaded with drugs."

"Can you get a better shot of the people guarding those containers?" Maggie asked. "There must be more than the four we see."

As Walter adjusted the picture, Maggie called out, "Wait! Zoom in on the group at the front of the container stacks."

When Walter did, the tops of four heads again came into view.

"Could one of those heads be the oriental woman you ran into at the restaurant and the wildlife refuge?" Maggie asked, turning to Ell.

As they watched in real-time, the second person on the right rubbed the back of her neck, rolled her head from side to side, then turned her face to the sky as if shaking out a kink in her neck.

Ell swallowed hard. "It's her. That's Fan, the daughter of Lee Chao. The same person who tried to kill me but then gave me my niece's location. Alert Sam and the rest of the team. We need to move on this."

"Tell him we're going operational," Maggie added.

"On it," Barry replied, "but I've got more bad news."

"Go ahead," Ell said.

"I've scanned the port's logs," Barry said. "The cargo containers in the holding area are scheduled for loading on the *Sea Maiden* in the next forty-five minutes. The teams from Lewis-McChord can't get there that quickly. On another note, the *Sea Maiden* is one of Lee Chao's flagships."

Another voice came over the air. "This is Sam. I've been monitoring your communications. I've got Jessica, Leah, and Allen here with me. Alex, Aria, and Bono are in the shooting range with the sniper simulator."

"I thought they had the day off," Ell said.

Sam laughed. "Super troopers apparently never take days off. So, we'll gear up, and I'll call in a favor with the special force's Blackhawk jocks at Fort Lewis. I'll have them beeline us to your site. We can be there within the hour, but you will need to hold up loading those containers until we arrive. If those containers get on Lee's ship, things will be more complicated considering who owns the ship, the law of the seas, and so on."

"Ell and Walter can approach the shipping containers and Fan's guards. I'll head for the cranes and see if I can tell the crane operators to shut down. That won't get us much time since time is money for these people, but it may help somewhat," Maggie said.

"I'll alert the state patrol," Jessica added. "They have a detachment near the port. They may be able to provide backup if they have people available. There is also the Port of Seattle police."

"When they come, have the state troopers hold off on the sirens and lights," Maggie said. "We need to catch these people off guard.

Too much drama could spoil this for us. There's no telling what Lee's people might do to those held in the shipping containers if they see us coming."

"I'll pass the information to the state patrol and the Port of Seattle police. They'll hold back until you give the word," Jessica replied.

"There's only three of you, but you're going to have to do the job until we can get there," Sam said. "See you in an hour."

"God's speed," Maggie said in reply. Walter followed with an amen of his own.

The EOD director's voice came over the air next. *Is there any limit to the communications capabilities of the Extreme Operations Group?* Ell wondered.

"I've been monitoring, like Sam," Paul said.

"I've already contacted the Port of Seattle police and the state patrol. They're rolling on a bomb threat at the airport. Odd coincidence. Given all that, I think the Home Teams will be your calvary."

"We'll handle it, sir," Ell said, then turned to Walter and Maggie. "Gear up, Walter. Put the crab into a hover above the container yard to give us visuals on our forearm tablets. See if you can tag the suspicious containers on the image and earmark our locations as we move."

"I can do that from here while Walter kits up," Barry said. "Taking control of the drone now. You are free to go. I've got this."

"Thanks, little buddy," Walter said, setting the drone control in the back of the SUV, grabbing his bulletproof vest, tactical harness, and carbine. "Let's do this," he said as he slammed the SUV's hatch closed and slipped into his gear.

CHAPTER 43

Fan stood at the front of one of the shipping containers with Quan, the leader of the mercenaries her father provided for the operation. The rest of the men scattered around the edge of the stack of containers, providing cover and roaming the site. Did she refer to the human trafficking victims as merchandise in her earlier conversation with her father?

"God, forgive me, please," she whispered.

At least the people were finally quiet. Quan had his squad spray a potent sleeping gas into each shipping container. The effects of the gas would last until well after the containers were loaded and the ship was out to sea.

"It feels too quiet," Quan said.

The man carried an M5 submachine gun like a natural extension of his body and moved with surprising grace for a man of his size and girth. Even on the gravel surface of the container yard, his steps made no sound. A man to be watched, Fan decided. No doubt he had specific instructions regarding her fate if the operation failed.

"Take another walk around the yard," Fan said, in a tone not to be argued. "I've got a call to make."

She dialed a number her father had texted just before her team moved the containers into the port's staging area. *Call this number as a last resort,* his message had said.

"Yes," came the male voice at the other end. The man spoke with a decidedly American accent.

"I was provided your number. You have a team at the Port of Seattle."

"I do," the man answered. "Three men ready to move in on your signal. The authorities will not challenge us."

"I have a bad feeling," Fan replied. "Position yourself as closely as possible to the container staging area without being obvious."

"That won't be a problem. My team and I patrol the area routinely. No one will question our presence."

"Make it so—" Fan started, but the line was already dead.

Fan frowned at her phone. She felt that sense again, like in Tumwater, that her father had his hands directly in this operation and was positioned to act rashly should things go sideways. Then again, her situation was not nearly as dire as the situations of those her father had taken from their homes or off the streets for his human trafficking market. So many people crammed into the containers. Those people were nothing more than merchandise for her father. It was so wrong.

Quan returned to her side. "Everything's clear in the immediate vicinity. I will remain with you from now on. I've got orders from your father to ensure your safety."

I just bet, Fan thought.

She gripped the pistol holstered at her side. Now, she had to worry about two groups coming after her if the mission failed: the Americans and her own team.

Fan looked from the container yard to the tall cranes, several hundred meters away. Active a few minutes ago, the cranes now appeared to be at full stop. Several containers hung from their long cables above the ship below, swinging slightly in the morning breeze.

"I wonder why they're stopped," Quan asked.

Fan glanced at her watch. "Probably the afternoon break. I understand the laborers here work for unions and have strict agreements about such things."

Quan laughed, although the sound carried no humor. "That is why our government will one day rule the world. Everyone is so lazy everywhere else."

"Lazy. Right," Fan repeated, wondering again about the sudden work stoppage. "Just the same, pull your men together. Put two men on top of the container stack and position others to the rear of the containers. Ensure they keep their eyes open for anything unusual. I have a feeling . . ."

CHAPTER 44

Ell and Walter cut through a chain link fence leading from the parking lot into the port's expansive facility. The container yard was only a mile distant, but between them and the container yard appeared endless rows of low buildings, fenced areas, and parking lots. They also needed to work their way there without being seen by the port authority staff or Fan's people.

They jogged a winding path around vehicles, buildings, and container storage areas as they closed in on the staging yard where Lee's people had their containers. While Walter and Ell made their approach, Maggie took the SUV and headed for the port's headquarters building. Once there, she planned to use her DEA credentials to stop *Sea Maiden* from being loaded. She hoped it would give them enough time to execute their plan and for the rest of H.T. Two and the Home Team to arrive and back them up.

This was an act of desperation. They had no idea how many tangos guarded the shipping containers. And for all they knew, Fan and her men already knew she and Walter were headed their way and waiting in ambush. Fan might well have her own drones in the sky above the port, watching their every step. But then there were people stuffed in the shipping containers like cattle. She had to free them. She could not allow another person to be trafficked like her niece.

Walter and Ell reached the container staging area twenty minutes later, crouching behind a five-ton truck parked near its back entrance. Ell lifted their forearm tablet computer to examine the layout displayed by the crab drone's view from overhead. Without asking, Barry zoomed the picture in on six people congregating at the containers' front. As they watched, three of the six dispersed and patrolled the container stacks. Two others climbed atop the stacks, taking up prone sniper positions. As they did, the fifth gunman and the woman leading the group disappeared between the stacks.

"They're deploying as if they know we're here. How can they know that?" Ell whispered.

A voice over their comms answered the question. "This is Maggie. I got the port to shut down the loading operation but only for thirty minutes. After that, they must resume operations to meet their contractual obligations."

Sam's voice came over the line. "We're loading the Blackhawks. We'll be there in forty-five minutes."

"Roger," Ell replied. She turned to Walter. "Looks like the rest of the gang won't make it here in time. We must make a move with as little gunplay as possible. The steel walls of those shipping containers are strong, but a standard hollow-point round could punch through and injure someone inside."

"Then we need to do this quietly," Walter replied. "Perhaps Agent O'Dell can provide some cover as we move about our business."

"So formal, Walter?" Ell replied. Then she said to Maggie over comms, "Can you get to the top of a nearby crane and be our sniper?"

"I'm sure I can. There's a small crane about one hundred yards from where you are. It would be the perfect spot. On my way now."

"Thanks, Mary Mags. No bad guys get out of this yard before the cavalry arrives," Ell said.

"Roger that," Maggie replied.

"Call when you're in position."

"ETA five minutes or less," Maggie replied.

With one minute to spare, Maggie came over comms again, breathing hard from her run. "With help from the port administrator, I've relieved the crane operator and am now in position. It's a long climb up and not for the faint of heart, but I've got you covered. I have visual on both you and three of the opposition: the man and woman out front and one of the men patrolling the north side of the containers."

"Now, we move," Ell said.

"We should take the two on top of the containers first," Walter said.

Ell nodded. "Agreed, but quietly."

Walter hefted a large rock he'd found near the base of the truck they'd hidden behind and handed her a tire iron he found in the truck's cab. They each strapped their M4s across their backs. They waited until Lee's three men, who patrolled the perimeter of the container stacks, passed by the rear of the containers, and resumed their walks to the front. When the men were out of sight, Ell and Walter climbed the sides of the two container stacks using the metal rungs built into the side of the forty-foot metal boxes.

Ell and Walter crested the top of the two shipping containers simultaneously. Ell removed her boots, set them aside, and then eased her way across the top in her stocking feet. She noticed Walter do the same and then parallel her at a crouch on the next container over.

Ell closed within a few yards of the man, who appeared to listen to music on his earbuds. Then in her peripheral vision, she saw Walter in line with her on the other shipping container. He leaped forward and crashed down astride his target. He raised his rock and crashed it down on the man's head. She did the same with her target, using her tire iron. Her man jerked once, then went limp. She bound the man's wrists and legs with thick zip ties, then stuffed a rag into the man's mouth.

She glanced at Walter, who gave her a thumbs-up. No need to report their progress and risk being seen or heard. The view from the drone would say it all to anyone watching.

"Nice job," came Barry's soft voice over her tactical headset.

Ell moved quickly off the shipping container and pulled on her boots. She met Walter in the space behind the containers, noticing on the screen of her forearm tablet computer that Lee's guards had begun their return trip. Walter made a chopping motion with his hand, then waved it left, telling her he'd go in that direction and for her to go right to take out the two patrolling guards.

She nodded, and Walter dropped to all fours, carbine still strapped across his back and pistol in his hand. He crept to the left side of the container stacks, peered around the corner, gathered his feet under him, rose, and sprinted out of sight.

Ell followed suit, heading for the opposite side of the container stacks. She consulted her tablet computer and the image from the drone. She saw two men positioned just around the corner of the container nearest her. She took a deep breath. Two at once would be a challenge. She'd only had her first real altercations with adversaries less than a week ago.

Maggie's voice came over the headset, as if reading her mind. "I've got your back, girl. I can't see Walter, but I can see the two you're headed for. I've got a suppressed M4 with a laser sight targeting both of them."

"Can you take them both?" Ell whispered into her tactical watch's microphone, remembering her conversation with Sam and Leah in the sniper simulator.

"Are you kidding me?" Maggie replied. "The distance is too far to be that accurate. I figure I can knock one down with no problem, but no guarantees on the second man. You're going to have to take him."

"This is Sam. If you can capture one of those men, we may be able to interrogate him and get what we need to take down Lee Chao. On the other hand, your safety comes first. Do what you need to do."

"You can do it, Ell," she heard Alex say over comms.

A month ago, Ell would have laughed at the idea she could do what Sam suggested. Then again, this wasn't back then, when she'd been a relatively untried state trooper with a good deal of training but little hands-on experience. This was an extreme operation of the highest order.

"God, everyone says You're out there. Please guide and keep me safe so I can help the people in those shipping containers."

Her prayer surprised her, sounding like something her mother might say. But then again, her mother had been one of the most successful intelligence agents of her time. Alex and the Home Team members all relied on their faith. Even tough-as-nails Maggie called on the Lord. Maybe it was time to make the same commitment. It would be nice not to carry the burden alone all the time.

"I've got the second man you'll see when you come around that corner. You've got the other," Maggie said, snapping Ell's thoughts back to the moment.

Ell peered around the container stack in time to hear the angry buzz of a suppressed bullet sizzle in. One of the men jerked back, then crumpled. A second bullet sizzled in, and the second tango dodged right and turned from where Ell stood to avoid the shot.

"My tango's down," Maggie said. "You're on, Ell."

Ell sucked in another breath, then sprinted for the operator still standing. With her M4A7 still strapped across her back, she came in low and hard. The man heard her coming, spun, and raised his MP5 just as another shot from Maggie sizzled in. He ducked the bullet but was caught off guard enough for Ell to bowl him over and take him to the ground.

As the two collided, Ell grabbed the man's MP5 by its barrel with one hand. With her other hand, she grabbed the MP5 by its firing mechanism and twisted the weapon, trapping his trigger finger in the guard. His finger snapped with a loud crack.

The man groaned and jerked back. Ell moved with his motion, slammed his MP5 hard against his chest, and shoved him back farther. Ell reached out with her right foot and hooked the man's ankle, trying to sweep his leg. The man didn't fall for it but lifted his foot over hers and kept his feet.

Ell continued to push the man backward, but his greater weight stole her advantage. The man shoved her away, spun, and lifted a near-perfect roundhouse kick toward her head with his right foot.

Ell ducked under the kick, grabbed the man's leg, and jerked him toward her. As he leaned toward her, she locked the extended fingers of her right hand into the tip of a spear and thrust them hard into his stomach. The guard's eyes rolled in pain, but he spun right and crashed his elbow into the back of her bruised shoulder.

Ell's whole body shuddered, but she forced the pain aside and punched the man in his chest. The impact made him lean back while she twisted left at the waist like coiling a spring. At full coil, she reversed direction and spun hard to the right, her right elbow high. The point of her elbow connected with the man's temple. She felt the man gasp and then wobble. Taking no chances, she rotated at the waist again, raising her left fist high and crashing it against the side of the man's head. This time, he dropped.

Ell sagged and dropped beside the unconscious man. "My guy's down," she said over comms. "I'll zip tie and gag him. I need to catch my breath."

"That's my girl," Maggie replied. "Proud of you."

"This is Walter. I'll need a couple of stitches when we get home, but my two are down. That's six guards accounted for."

"Only two to go," Ell whispered, climbing back to her feet. "Fan and one other."

"Twenty minutes out," Sam said over comms.

"The port's going to start loading containers again any minute. We can't wait," Maggie said over comms.

"I'm going back up top," Ell said. "I bet Fan and the other man are hiding between the stacks, out of the drone's view."

"Changing to infrared," Barry said.

Two red dots appeared on Ell's tablet computer as Barry reconfigured the drone to detect heat signatures. The image showed a person crouched near Walter's position on the opposite

side of the containers with the other at the front of the container
Ell stood beside.

Ell jerked as a shot cracked through the silence. Then, she heard a
grunt from Walter over comms.

"I'm hit," he whispered. "And the man's closing on me."

Ell marked Walter's position and sprinted around the back of the
container stacks. As she ran, she shifted her carbine to her left hand,
holding it like a pistol while holding her pistol in her other hand.

When she rounded the corner of the last shipping container, she
saw a man standing over Walter, gun drawn for the insurance shot to
guarantee Walter's death.

"Not on my watch," Ell growled and snapped off a shot from her
pistol and carbine instantly.

One .9mm bullet from her pistol took the man through his left
leg. The shot from her carbine went high, striking the man on his
right arm. The tango staggered and shifted his M5 to his left hand but
didn't fall. Ell stopped, sighted her pistol on the man's left shoulder,
and pulled the trigger again. She saw the man's shirt jerk and red mist
burst from the opposite side. The man staggered but somehow stayed
up, still looming over Walter and still gripping his MP5, which he
now pointed toward Ell.

Another shot cracked at close range. The shot came from Walter's
.32 caliber hideout. The bullet took Lee's man at an upward angle
under his chin. The man dropped, landing across Walter's legs.

Ell ran to Walter, shoved the dead guard off his legs, and pulled
Walter against the side of the shipping container. In the distance, she
heard the whop-whop-whop of the Home Team's Blackhawks closing
on their location.

"I'll be all right, but you better do something about the leader of this group. She fled from us in Tumwater and nearly killed you at the wildlife refuge. We can't let either happen again," Walter said through the pain.

"Do you have eyes on the woman, Maggie?" Ell asked into her tactical mike.

"I do. She's—" Maggie started.

"I can help you with that," a soft voice said behind Ell. "Now, please lower your weapons."

Walter tossed his .32 aside as Ell rose and them turned to see Fan less than ten feet away. "Do you have a target?" Ell whispered over comms.

"Not this time," Maggie replied. "But I'm getting off this crane and heading your way. The Blackhawks are down and unloading, but the team will take time getting to you. If you can hold her for a minute or three . . ."

"Okay," Ell said, her words directed to Fan as she lowered her pistol to her side and let her carbine clatter to the ground.

"Both your weapons," Fan repeated.

"I don't think so," Ell said. "You're either going to kill me, or I'm going to kill you; but I have no chance without a gun in my hand."

Fan frowned, the sights of her pistol pointed squarely at Ell's face. "This is a quandary then, isn't it? Let's assume you can't raise your pistol and kill me before I shoot you. It's easy odds, given my position and the range of the shot. In that case, your death is likely."

"We will have to wait to find out," Ell replied, her right hand sweating against the pistol's grip.

"Humor me," Fan said. "I think you'll find it interesting. So, given our situation, I figure I have two options. First, I kill you and escape. If I do that, my father will likely kill me for having failed on this mission. Option two is letting you live and escape, in which case he will probably kill me for not disposing of you and failing on this operation. Either way, I experience the same fate. Then again, in option one, both of us die. In option two, only I die."

"The answer seems clear," Ell said, boldly raising her gun to point at Fan's chest. "You surrender."

"To you, that is obvious perhaps, but not to me," Fan replied. "In that case, I would probably be put to death for my father's crimes. That hardly seems like a good outcome."

"You haven't shot me yet," Ell said, "so I'm thinking your conscious has gotten the best of you. But on the other hand, even as much as you helped me free my niece, I see no evidence you will stop trafficking humans and smuggling drugs."

Ell held her aim squarely on Fan's forehead. "And I don't plan on letting you continue."

Both women paused—Ell's expression intense, Fan's somewhat sad. Then, at that moment, a voice called from beyond the nearest shipping van. Ell recognized it immediately.

"I'm coming out, and I'm unarmed," Alex called. "My hands will be empty. Don't shoot."

Fan shifted her pistol's sights to cover Alex as he stepped into the open, dressed in full tactical gear, except for his empty holster and missing M4 carbine. Ell kept her pistol aimed at Fan, although her shoulder injury and the bullet wound in her leg were beginning to tell. The pistol's sights wavered slightly off target as she covered the woman.

"You will both receive a message from your superiors in the next minute. So, you need to listen closely to those messages," Alex said. "It's for everyone's good."

Fan's cell phone rang. She frowned. "I should have put it on silent."

"Go figure," Ell said.

She slightly increased the pressure on her pistol's trigger as Director Paul Samuelson's voice came over comms.

"Do not harm Lee Fan, Ell. I am ordering you to stand down and let her go. And tell her to answer the call on her cell phone."

Ell kept her eyes on Fan as she let out a long breath. "You have got to be kidding," Ell muttered. Then, to Fan, "I just received a message over comms," she told Fan. "My boss says I'm to let you go and that you should answer your cell phone. He's ordered me not to harm you, despite all you and your father have done."

Fan holstered her gun and tapped the receive button on her phone. "It seems we both have people who want to talk with us."

Ell slipped her satellite phone from its holster on her tactical vest with her left hand while she kept her sights on Fan's forehead. The phone chimed, the screen announcing a call from Director Samuelson.

"As I said over comms, stand down. I can see you onscreen from the drone, and you are not to kill that woman. An associate in China and I have agreed, meaning Fan will be going home. The secretary of state has endorsed the agreement."

"But—" Ell started.

"I know what I'm asking, especially after all you've been through, but I want you to stand down."

Ell disconnected the call without replying and slipped the phone back into its holster. She aimed her pistol at Fan as the woman completed her call and turned around to face Ell. Fan made no effort to draw her pistol.

Fan lifted her eyes to Ell. "It seems there is a third option, after all—one where my father disappears, and I assume control of his company."

Ell didn't reply, so Fan continued. "That was a call from a highly placed person in my government. My father has disappeared or, should I say, been made to disappear. The Chinese government wants me to assume control of his business. They believe I will provide a more positive image for the company and our country. I have agreed to do so."

"And the human trafficking?" Ell asked, the pistol not wavering in her hand.

"That is ended as of now," Fan replied. "I will provide a complete file of the people taken by my father's company for as many years as possible. After that, you should be able to rescue many of the human trafficking victims and arrest many people complicit in those crimes."

Ell nodded. "That's something, at least."

"Ask her about the drug trafficking," Ell heard Maggie say over comms.

"And the drugs?"

"Also ended," Fan said. "It will be halted immediately. I have sufficient resources to convince the cartels my father worked with to look elsewhere for their shipments."

"And the technology theft?" Ell added.

Fan replied with a wry smile. "Two out of three isn't bad, right?"

Ell chuckled. She holstered her pistol. As she faced Fan, she recalled the faces of the people her team freed in Tumwater and

Rosa's face when they'd been released from the shipping container. Was that only a few weeks ago? And how could she forget Maria's face when she recognized her aunt at the Kennewick rescue?

Anything Ell might have said next was stifled by four sharp cracks of weapon fire. Her pistol flashed in her hand as she turned to face the sound, noticing Fan also held her gun.

The two sprinted toward the source of the sound, side by side. As they rounded the stack of shipping containers, they found three men in tactical uniforms face down on the gravel lot. Behind the bodies stood Special Agent Williams from Homeland Security Investigations and three other men in blazers and ties. Each had a pistol in their hand, barrels smoking.

"Well, well," Special Agent Williams said as he holstered his weapon. "Stand down, boys. This is the famous Washington State Trooper Ellen Evander, and . . . I don't believe I've made your acquaintance," he said to Fan.

Ell interrupted before Fan could reply. "This is an associate. She's backing me up on an operation."

Williams glanced at where Alex stood a short distance away, his M4A7 carbine covering all four men. "And that menacing figure?" he asked.

Ell considered her response, then said, "My partner. I never leave home without him."

Williams nodded, then gestured to the men lying dead at his feet. "Three of mine. As good as we are at HSI—and I do mean we are the best—we do encounter the occasional bad seed. I suspected we'd been compromised when we were delayed rescuing your group in Turkey. That happened more than once and may be associated with an unknown group of American operators being ambushed in Germany. Of course, you wouldn't know anything about that, would you, Trooper Evander?"

"Nothing I can think of," Ell replied, working hard to suppress a grin.

"No matter," Williams said, catching the nuance in Ell's response. "I did my own internal investigation at HSI and discovered a secret secure line in our systems used by several of our people to communicate with one Lee Chao, a shipping magnate from China. After that, it was simple to follow our traitors here and dispose of them before they could get the drop on you and your friends."

Ell nodded. "Thank you, I'm sure. That pulls together several loose ends for us."

Williams gave Ell a crooked smile. "I'm glad, I'm sure. You're not working for the state patrol, are you? And this woman isn't really your associate, is she? It's that Home Team group we discussed in Turkey, isn't it?"

Ell smiled. "I have no idea what you're talking about."

Williams huffed. "Your response says it all, but I'll count on that back-brief someday soon."

Sam jogged up as Williams turned to leave. The HSI agent turned back as Sam slung his M4A7 across his back and stuck out a hand. "Secret Service Agent Collins. Pleased to meet you."

"And I'm Santa Clause," Williams replied, shaking the offered hand. "But I am pleased to meet you, whoever you are."

Sam gestured to the bodies. "Those yours?"

Williams nodded. "Our cleanup crew will take care of them."

"Of course," Sam said. "We have our cleanup to do at our end."

Williams smiled. "Heard the shooting. Saw some of the action from a distance. Trooper Evander says I might get briefed eventually."

Sam nodded. "That's a definite maybe."

Williams shrugged, gestured to his agents, and walked away.

Ell and Fan headed back toward the shipping containers. "You know anything about all that?" Ell asked.

"My father may have arranged for some men on his payroll to be here and protect his interests. I believe that may have included eliminating me if my mission failed. However, I doubt they were aware of my father's change in status, so it seems your people have done me a service."

"Well, thank God for that, anyway," Ell said finally.

Fan gave Ell a wan smile, then repeated, "Thank God. I'm finding He does have a way of making things happen."

"You, too?" Ell asked.

Fan's smile warmed. "I expect so."

Ell glanced down and then said something she never thought she would have said a month ago. "God bless you, Fan, as you walk a different path in the future."

"And you," Fan replied. "I'm still learning about God and faith, but I do pray that His face shines down upon you as you go forward in your life. And I hope we meet another day on better terms."

Minutes later, Ell was surrounded by the members of both Home Team and H.T. Two, slapping her on the back and checking to see if she was okay. Her bruised shoulder pulsated by the time they were done, but her heart glowed. They'd done important work today, and she was a part of the team who made it happen.

CHAPTER 45

E ll watched as Allen and Bono retrieved a stretcher from one of
the Blackhawks and hauled Walter to the aircraft. Several of the
tangos survived the fight, were patched up, and then held by Aria and
Leah for interrogation by the FBI.

Sam approached Ell as she watched her team members open the
shipping containers containing the human trafficking victims. "The
people in the containers are out cold," he said. "The FBI will have a
team here in a few minutes to take charge and help them recover
and investigate another container where we found stolen technology.
Turns out two others held drugs. The DEA is on its way to retrieve the
drugs. All in all, quite a haul."

"What about Fan?" Leah asked.

"She's gone," Sam replied.

Ell glanced back to where she'd last seen the woman. Fan was
nowhere in sight. Ell smiled. "I'm happy about that."

She explained what Fan had said about providing a list of people
taken by her father's human trafficking operation and shutting down
the drug smuggling.

Sam walked toward the Blackhawks, leaving Alex and Ell alone
at the edge of the cleanup operation. Alex placed a hand on Ell's
wounded shoulder, causing her to flinch.

"You okay?" he asked, jerking his hand back

Ell nodded. "I'll live."

"I was worried about you back there," he said.

He held out a hand as Ell's anger rose. Another man who thought she needed to be protected, that she needed rescuing.

"Don't get me wrong," he said. "I knew you'd do what was needed and had the skill to carry it out. But I was still worried about you."

When she saw the look in his eyes, her anger dissipated. Maybe having a guy who respected what she could do on her own but still cared enough to worry about her might not be such a bad thing.

"I'm sure you'll be headed back to the state patrol soon," Alex said, "but I would like to stay in touch, if that's okay. I know I'm not the most expressive person and that you may not be looking for any kind of relationship . . . "

Ell rose on her tiptoes and kissed Alex's sweat-stained cheek. Alex pulled her into a warm embrace.

"Sunday is only a day away," Ell whispered as she released him and flashed a bright smile. "I'm thinking of going to church for the first time in a very long while. I wonder if you might go with me and maybe go out for lunch afterward."

"Church and a date?" Alex asked.

"Well, yeah, pretty much," Ell replied.

"You bet. It doesn't get much better than that!" Alex replied.

Sam called over comms. "Time to head out. The FBI and DEA are almost here. We need to be gone when they arrive. Maggie will stay and fill in the blanks for them. Leave the SUV for Maggie. We'll all ride back in the Blackhawks. Load up now."

Alex smiled as he and Ell jogged side by side to the helicopters. Then, through the loud noise of the copter's props, Alex yelled, "A date, really?"

Ell smiled and nodded. Silly man. What did she have to do to make him understand how she felt?

As Ell reached the chopper, she saw Bono, Aria, Sam, Jessica, and Leah—all jogging with footfalls in common rhythm toward the two Blackhawks. It was quite a sight, all of them moving in unison. Such a team. As a group, they got results but never left their humanity behind. The thought of leaving them and returning to the state patrol left an unexpected hollow in the pit of her stomach.

She glanced over to where Maggie stood at the doors to one of the open shipping containers. Maggie caught Ell's eye. She waved and smiled as Ell climbed aboard the Blackhawk with her teammates, friends, and Alex.

EPILOGUE

The chill air behind the breeze off the delta at the Billy Frank Jr. Wildlife Refuge brushed Ell's cheeks, freshening her skin as she looked out over the silver waters of the estuary leading into the Nisqually Delta. Standing under the cover provided by the boardwalk's farthest observation deck, she watched tall white clouds roll in from the west, converging between where she stood and the snow-clad Olympic Mountain Range in the distance. *It'll rain tomorrow,* she thought, *but it'll be a cleansing rain.*

She heard footsteps behind her and turned to see Alex approaching. In a second, they were in each other's arms.

"How do you feel?" he asked a long, warm few minutes later. "You surprised me when we went to church together and you accepted Christ as your Savior. With everyone there except Aria and Allen, it turned into a full-scale celebration. And I've been so busy, I haven't seen you since."

"I guess we've both been pretty busy. That's one of the reasons I asked you to meet me here," Ell replied. "I feel different now—lighter, better, positive. I don't have the words to express it. I owe you and Maggie for helping me see how good it can be to accept Christ into my life."

Alex pulled her toward him again. "I am so happy for you."

When they finally released each other, they looked out over the shining waters of the estuary, leaning close against each other's sides. Ell slipped her arm around Alex's waist, and he returned the gesture. Then, as they settled into a comfortable silence, Ell heard a familiar voice call.

"Hey, you love birds."

They turned to see Maggie approaching hand-in-hand with Walter. They made quite a pair—Walter, the muscle-bound intellectual gentle giant, and Maggie, the wild-haired freckled woman whose head came up to Walter's shoulder at best.

Aria and Barry followed behind them. They weren't exactly holding hands, but the expression on Barry's face suggested he might like to. *Another odd couple,* Ell thought—Aria, with her petite form, spine of steel, and Polynesian beauty and Barry, pale, gangly, and with shoulder-length hair he never combed.

"Great minds think alike?" Ell offered.

"Guess so," Walter replied, wiggling his eyebrows. Maggie punched him in the shoulder.

"This is my place, too, and Aria and Barry were in the room when I suggested to Walter we come here. But I also heard some interesting news," Maggie said as the four stepped under the observation tower's roof.

"I was just about to tell Alex," Ell replied. She turned back to him and took both of his hands in hers. "You didn't hear from me yesterday because I spent the day with the chief of the state patrol and the patrol's director of investigative services. It took all day, but the bottom line is that I am leaving the state patrol."

"You're kidding, right?" Alex exclaimed. "You love law enforcement."

"I'm not leaving law enforcement. I'm just changing teams. I'm joining H.T. Two."

Alex's smile widened. "You're not alone. I never thought this would happen in the beginning, but I'm resigning my ranger command and joining H.T. Two, as well."

"Then, let's make it one big, happy family," Maggie added. "Bono isn't staying. I was at headquarters when she told Sam. She's been recruited by army military intelligence to work out of South Korea. Her background, physical appearance, and command of the language make her prime for the job. She has a lot of experience in that theater and can do so much good."

"I did not see that coming," Ell said. "Bono worked so well with everyone."

"I think that's just the kind of person she is," Maggie said. "In any event, that left an opening in H.T. Two, so I'm leaving the DEA and joining the rest of you."

"One big, happy family," Alex said.

"Happy is right," Walter said, "but Director Samuelson is going to have a fit when he learns half of his team is dating each other."

"If I know the man at all, he will adapt," Maggie said. "He'll be thankful he has people he can trust working for him."

"I can't imagine a better group of people to work with than you folks," Ell said.

"Amen to that," Alex replied.

Halfway around the world, Fan walked the familiar concrete paths of Binjiang Park, the waters flowing slowly in the distance. People littered the grassy lawns with picnics. She glanced briefly at a group of forty or fifty people practicing the tai chi form's elegant, slow movements in an area overlooking the river.

As she neared the coffee shop, six pairs of hands waved in her direction from the patio—the Closet Christians. Their release from jail was one of the conditions for Fan to take over her father's company. She smiled at her friends' warm greeting. A calm peace spread over her body as she entered, ordered a coffee mocha, and joined them at their table.

God really is good, she thought, *and this is going to be a very good day.*

THE END

COMING SOON...

FINDING HOME

The rain poured down in sheets, soaking through Allen's thin black tactical shirt and cargo pants as he hunkered down on the cold gravel, his back against a low, crumbling concrete retaining wall. The barrier was hardly tall enough to conceal his head and shoulders from the six gunmen in the squat, white stucco building ten yards behind his position. The red tile-roofed house sat in a tiny enclave of similar buildings surrounding a small, cobbled plaza in the tiny town of Tuxpan, Mexico, a few hours east of Puerta Vallarta, a popular tourist destination. Normally occupied by a husband and wife working for a Christian non-governmental organization, or NGO, today, the little house held five hostages and the cartel thugs.

And another bomb.

There is always another bomb, Allen thought.

With knees pulled close to his chest, Allen cradled his short-barreled M4A7B carbine rifle across his lap, his mind a mixture of frustration at being stuck in this rain while the higher-ups in his chain of command debated his team's next move and his bleak thoughts about his own life. Rivulets of cold rain ran down the back of his neck, soaking his undershirt and sinking his mood further into the conflict between doing nothing when so much was at stake and his own need to be away, to create distance from this perilous situation and his own crumbling future. He reached down and wiped the wet gloss off soft-soled desert boots that felt like soggy sponges kept too long under a kitchen faucet.

Are You there, God?

While he knew the answer to the question from a lifetime of faith, current circumstances had led him to wonder. Everything today seemed so wrong.

"Would someone please turn off the faucet?" Allen finally mumbled, trying vainly to raise his own mood with the weak humor. "Enough is enough."

Leah McCarthy sat two feet to his right, crouched down in a similar position, and glanced his way as she wiped the water off her own rifle with a soggy scrap of cloth. The diminutive special operator, team sniper, and tough-as-nails jiu-jitsu master flashed startlingly blue eyes his way as he met her glance. "When the four of us signed onto the Home Team, the EOG never promised sunny weather," she said.

The acronym Leah used referred to their parent organization, the Extreme Operations Group. As part of that organization, Allen, Leah, and their other two teammates constituted the Home Team, a forward operational element that reported to the U.S. Secretary of State. Their role as an elite covert operations team found them deployed around the world and across the U.S. to combat those who threatened their country or its allies.

"Besides, I love this stuff, and so do you. So quit the moaning and groaning I keep hearing from you," Leah added.

Allen let out a long sigh.

As if reading his dark thoughts, Leah wiped a dripping strand of red-bronze hair from her deeply tanned face and tucked it under a black baseball hat worn backward. "Then, again, it would be a bit more convenient if the bad guys hadn't chosen such horrible weather for this operation."

The other two members of the Home Team, Jessica Falcone and Sam Anthem, were ranged further to Leah's right, both sitting in similar positions with their backs to the low plaza wall.

"No one said criminals were smart, Romeo," Sam replied.

Leah's formal call sign was Romeo Alpha. She hated the informal moniker. Allen smiled as Leah growled her usual response to Sam's use of her call sign's abbreviated form. "It is not an appropriate call name for a female operator. I really need to change it."

Sam Anthem, call sign Mike Tango—or Empty for short—chuckled but kept his gaze forward. Allen's virtual twin at five ten, with a finely-tuned athletic stature and highly trained physical abilities, Sam served as the Home Team's unofficial leader and empty hand-fighting expert. Unlike Allen, with his paler complexion and shoulder-length blond hair pulled into a short ponytail at his back, Sam was darker-skinned with short-cropped black hair covered by his own dripping tactical baseball hat, bill forward.

Allen grumbled deep in his throat. He and his teammates were like a family in so many ways—siblings who comforted, teased, cajoled, and relied on each other often for their very lives. Normally, their presence and sarcastic humor comforted him, calmed his thoughts. On most days, he found a form of solace in the challenging, often dangerous missions he and his team were assigned. With so much on the line with each deployment and their success rate as a group, he normally found a deep sense of pride and affiliation with the elite membership of the Home Team. But today? Not so much.

In this instance, their mission was to rescue the U.S. Ambassador to Mexico's daughter and son, along with two other children and their nanny. All five were held in the tiny, red-roofed, stucco building not thirty feet away, with a bomb and a ransom demand due to expire within the hour.

Allen leaned forward, glancing around Leah to where Sam sat, just as Sam raised a large-faced black tactical watch to his lips and spoke into the device's embedded microphone. The words came out clearly across the communications implant each team member had behind their left ear.

"I just received an encrypted text from Director Samuelson," Sam whispered, wiping the water from his face with the back of a dripping gloved hand. "Paul says we need to wait a while more before we take the building. The ambassador wants more time to negotiate with the captors."

"You've got to be kidding," Jessica replied.

Call sign Charlier Papa, or Cap for short, Jessica crouched between Leah and Sam. Tall, angular, and beautiful, Jessica Falcone served as the team's political and technological resource. As the talented, accomplished, mixed martial artist turned to face Sam, water poured down the thick ebony braid that hung down her slender back from beneath her tactical baseball hat.

"During her recon of the house, Leah confirmed the table with the bomb under it, the four kids sitting on the table and the nanny standing close by. She also ID'd the six cartel thugs. She did that hours ago, with the bomb's timer clearly visible and time running out. We don't have long before this situation goes from bad to worse and the hostages die. We need to move on the place now."

Allen felt his tactical watch vibrate on his right wrist. He frowned as he raised it to eye level and wiped the water from its screen. It was a text from Mallory, his fiancée and Drug Enforcement Administration agent, currently completing a DEA-sponsored doctorate at Baylor University in Waco, Texas. He was supposed to be with her there right now. He let out a long breath as the words and his worst fears materialized across the watch's tiny screen.

"Where are you? Of course, you can't tell me. That is three times in two months you have let me down. I carved time out of my research just for us and now this...again. When you were headquartered out of Florida and I worked in D.C., before your team's move to Washington State, we at least had our weekends together. Now, it's like we don't exist for each other at all. Your work is important, I know, but this isn't working. Don't bother calling me when you get done with whatever you are doing. We need a break, and I need to think all this—and us—over."

Leah glanced over at him, searching his face with her eyes. "What's that all about? You look like you just lost your best friend," she said.

Allen swallowed as a sharp pain cut through his heart. "We need to finish this, and I need to get out of here, now."

How many times had his life been turned upside down by one priority mission after another somewhere in the world? He never complained, always leaned into the greater need of the team. And now he had just lost the woman he planned to spend the rest of his life with, whom he had known and loved since they were kids.

Allen leaned forward and poked an angry finger in Sam's direction. "We need to finish this. Jessica said it: we should have moved on the house hours ago. If the bosses in D.C. and Florida can't make up their minds, I'll do it for them."

Leah clutched at Allen's arm with small, strong fingers. "Don't do it, man. The bosses have spoken, and the director has never let us down. We need to follow his lead."

"Not this time," Allen replied. "He doesn't have any idea what's on the line for those people in that building—or me—while the talking heads fiddle with their politics."

Sam's voice came over Allen's cochlear implant. "We need to wait, Fox," Sam said, using the familiar form of Allen's own call sign: Foxtrot Tango. "Paul knows what he's doing."

"Nuts to that," Allen growled. "You all stay here, while those kids are put at risk and my life falls apart. I am going in. Then I am gone."

"Hold, Fox," Sam replied, leaning across Jessica as he spoke. "Stay with the plan."

"I'm tired, Empty," Allen replied. "I have had enough of politicians trying to figure out whether they want those kids to live. No kid's dying today if I can prevent it. I'm going in there with or without you all. I am the team's explosive expert. I'm going to take out the thugs in that building, then defuse that bomb and save those kids. And then I'm going home."

Allen saw how Sam drew back against the wall as Allen let the words fly and almost regretted saying them. On a mission years ago, a little girl had died when Sam's mission went sideways. Sam had not been to blame, but Allen knew his teammate carried the pain of her death with him wherever he went.

Even so, Allen's frustration with the politicians was so high, his own anxiety so burning inside his heart, he figured he had little to lose. And those kids had everything to lose. If the EOG director dropped him from the team for saving those kids, he could live with that.

Allen met Sam's glare directly, his expression intense, fierce. Finally, Sam shrugged ever so slightly and raised his watch to his lips. When he spoke into its microphone, he directed the call to the EOG headquarters, where the mission was being monitored by Director Samuelson and his overwatch team. "Overwatch, this is Mike Tango. We are status three and engaging now."

In Home Team parlance, a status of one meant the team was in position. Two meant the team was ready to move. Three meant they were engaging the target. Apparently, they were about to engage as a team. Not just Allen on his own.

Allen nodded grimly as Paul's voice came over his communications implant, his words clipped, to the point. "This is Overwatch. Hold your position as directed."

Allen rubbed at his leg muscles, then gathered his feet beneath him. He smiled again as her heard Sam's reply. "We have a situation on the ground that demands we act now. I repeat, we are status three and moving on the target."

"You have been ordered to hold your position by the ambassador," Paul replied once again.

"We can't do that," Sam replied, gathering his feet beneath him as Leah and Jessica did the same.

Allen would later recall hearing the director's deep sigh as he realized that the Home Team was going to move on the target regardless of anything he might say. After a short pause, Paul replied, "Godspeed."

"Roger that," Sam replied. "Empty, out."

Allen said a soft prayer under his breath. *God, please guide me and my team. I may not be able to do much about my future with the woman I love—I may have doubted Your presence—but those kids need us.*

Allen turned, staying low, then placed one hand atop the low plaza wall and vaulted over. He hit the ground, carbine barrel forward, feet churning the broken concrete and gravel of the weathered plaza floor. He didn't need to glance to either side to know that Sam, Leah, and Jessica were on his heels.

ABOUT THE AUTHOR

David Pratt is a native of most of the U.S. west coast, from Bakersfield, California to Anchorage, Alaska. A retired U.S. Army officer and private sector project manager consultant, he is based in Olympia, Washington, and spends the majority of his time living and wandering the Pacific Northwest with his wife and family. Mr. Pratt has wide and varied publication credits, including magazine articles and short stories in a variety of regional and national magazines and journals, and six fiction and nonfiction books. His guiding light in life is Our Lord Jesus Christ, and his focus is glorifying God in all he does. He considers his wife, family, and friends as some of God's greatest blessings in his life.

For more information about
Dave Pratt
and
Home Team 2
please visit:

www.daveprattbooks.com
www.facebook.com/DavidPrattBooks

Five years ago, Braelyn's daughter died. Her marriage imploded, and Forest Hill became her sanctuary. Five years ago, Drake became lost in overwhelming grief, and he lost his heart to divorce. After serving in the army, Drake is looking for a new life, and he stumbles upon Forest Hill. During a chance meeting, Braelyn and Drake discover a poaching scheme that throws them into a spiral of overwhelming emotions and danger.

Charlotte Hallaway needs to come to terms with her father's death. He had been her only family, and she wasn't handling her grief well. It was just supposed to be a few weeks of peace and quiet to process it all, but then she saw them—a drug deal and a murder within seconds of each other. And they saw her. Now running for her life, Charlotte boards a bus to escape her pursuers and wakes up the next morning in the woods without a memory of how she got there or of who she is.

The world looks up to the sky in anticipation as the Pennychuck Atmospheric Carbon Reduction System comes online. Finally the chance to eliminate global warming will be obtainable. Within moments, something goes terribly wrong. Dr. Pennychuck races to find the underlying problem that caused so much destruction and when he has to rely on a surprising ally, they delve into a conspiracy deeper than they can fathom.

www.ingramcontent.com/pod-product-compliance
Lightning Source LLC
Chambersburg PA
CBHW051132030726
47504CB00004B/825